x^0

a novel

by

Sherrie Cronin

DEDICATION

To my father, who loved and encouraged his
two daughters with all his heart. Driving with him
across Western Kansas talking about science fiction
is my best childhood memory and was
my first inspiration to write a novel

&

To my Nigerian coworkers and friends,
with thanks for reminding me every day how
the ways we are all alike are so much bigger
than the ways we are different

**This novel is volume
one of six
in the collection
46. Ascending**

Copyright 2011 by Sherrie Cronin
All rights reserved. First Edition. Published 2012
by Cinnabar Press, Montgomery, Texas 77316

ISBN-13: 978-0-9851561-0-7

No part of this book may be reproduced in any form by any electronic or mechanical means, including information storage and retrieval systems, without permission in writing from the publisher, except for review.

Cover design and illustration by Jennifer FitzGerald of www.MotherSpider.com
Images and maps used under license from shooarts/Shutterstock.com, Vartanov Anatoly/ Shutterstock.com, skvoor/ Shutterstock.com, and Daniel M. Nagy/Shutterstock.com

This book is work of fiction and, with the exception of news items, public figures, and cultural information, the events and characters in it are imaginary, as is the organization x0 and all contents from its website. No character, company, or group of people included as part of the fictional narrative is intended to represent any real person or group. The author is not responsible for the content of third party websites.

Why are some words underlined?
(A note to my paperback readers)

This book was originally designed to be read on an electronic reader and it included up to five links per chapter that led to photographs, music, news reports and opinion pieces designed to enhance a reader's enjoyment of this novel. Obviously no such links are possible in a paperback book.

Please be assured that these links were always supplementary material and the book itself stands alone and requires none of them. However, I have left the original links underlined in this print version so that a curious reader knows that further information is available on certain subjects. The complete URLs are listed at the end of this book and they are also available as live links on the book's website at http://www.tothepowerofzero.org.

Interested readers who do seek these out are encouraged to support the referenced artists, news outlets and web sites, and to give some consideration to the charities to which a couple of the links take them. However, if you paid for this book you have contributed already, because ten per cent of the proceeds from this book are being donated to Doctor's Without Borders.

You may contact the author at lola.zeitman@gmail.com and seek out Lola Zeitman on facebook for more information about her skills and adventures. If you enjoyed reading this, please look for y^1, a second novel about another member of the Zeitman family. Also watch for z^2, which will be available in early 2013.

Also, for those whose love of math is meager or memory of high school algebra is weak, allow me to remind you that any number (twelve, two hundred and sixty-eight, or four billion) raised to the power of zero equals one.

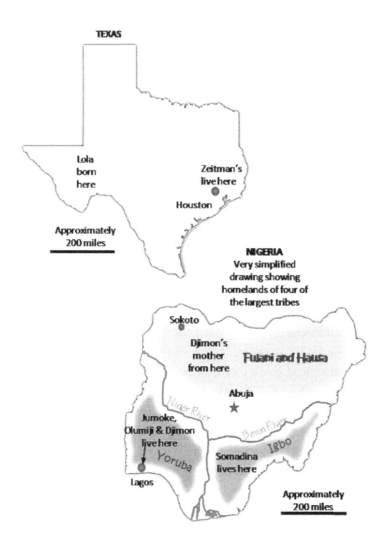

Before
Chapter 1. A Start: February 1986

Who was making those noises? Gurgling … loud … intermittent … they had woken her just as she was finally falling asleep. And yet, instead of finding the sounds annoying she found them intriguing. She repeated the latest one in her head. Not quite right. She tried again. A little higher in pitch, a little faster in pace. Yes, that was better. She started to try to match it again, but was interrupted with delight by a new sound. Oh good. Another one. A little softer and lower. And shorter in duration. She tried duplicating that one. Oh, that was not even close. Try again.

What the hell am I doing? She awkwardly pushed herself up into a semi-sitting position against the pillows and looked down at her giant belly. As her mind cleared, she realized that in fact she herself was making those noises, keeping a gentle syncopated rhythm with her husband's soft snoring by producing a series of mildly unhappy gurgling sounds. They were coming from a stomach that was clearly and understandably tired of trying to digest food while being crammed into an increasingly smaller corner of her body. She gave her belly a gentle rub through the sheet. Just a few days more, she promised it. Then came the realization that she had asked the wrong question.

Who had been listening to the noises? She eyed her belly curiously as she took slow breaths, willing herself to calm back down. And after awhile, the rhythm of the revolving blades on the ceiling fan combined with her sheer fatigue to finally let her doze back into a restless sleep.

Lola Zeitman woke up early the next morning, eager to get the day done. Her teacher husband was already out the door, as was his habit, with a note left behind saying he would check in by phone later, maybe several times, and to call him if anything, anything at all, started to happen. She smiled. It would have been nice to linger over his stark handwriting, savoring that sense that it was all going to be all right which he somehow managed to convey. However, being late to work today was not an option.

Lola considered herself mature at twenty-six, good at meeting life's responsibilities like showing up to work on time, and dressing better than usual when she was making a presentation. She knew the rules. But unfortunately, dressing better had become increasingly more difficult as the pregnancy had advanced. Today's other presenters would be all male of course, most of them also hired over the last few years fresh out of school with their shiny new master's degrees, brought here to fill the oil industry's sudden burgeoning need for geoscientists.

Reagan's Secretary of the Interior James Watt had made many a bad decision, in Lola's opinion, including <u>banning the Beach Boys</u> from performing in the D.C. mall. But even though his social conservatism and apparent disregard for the environment made him one of Lola's least favorite cabinet members ever, his decision three years ago to open up virtually all offshore federal waters to drilling had personally affected Lola in ways that politics seldom did.

Lola had originally seen herself researching earthquakes, or maybe in the best of all worlds becoming an expert on the geophysics of other planets. Then the oil companies had come to campus, dangling riches as they scrambled for new hires who could interpret the massive amounts of seismic data they were acquiring to compete for the "billion acres" James Watt bragged that he had just made available to them. She and Alex were newly married, very broke, and wanted children before too long. Just a few years could get the debts paid off. The other planets could wait.

And thanks to the Watts decree, in 1983 the number of offshore tracts leased by oil companies jumped from over a hundred to over a thousand, and in 1984 Lola and Alex joined the mass of young professionals who over the years quadrupled the size of the sleepy little Cajun town of Lafayette, Louisiana. Even the 1986 dip in oil prices had not significantly slowed the offshore machine, and Lola and her colleagues were about to recommend more leasing and more drilling. The guys would be clad in their inexpensive suits, selling their scientific interpretations and their ideas to a sea of older men in more expensive suits whose career advancement would have granted them a slight bit more freedom in tie color choices.

x^0

Only Lola would stand out in her giant wine-colored jumper, carefully laid out last night before the hours of tossing uncomfortably had begun. She had bought it to wear just for occasions like this because she loved the deep intense red of it, and she thought it maybe, kind of, brought out the reddish highlights in her dark brown hair, which frankly was just about the only part of her which still looked good right now. And she had paired it with a very conservative white blouse. But she sighed as she picked it up. No. It really was too intense. She stood out enough. Lola turned to the meager supply of "big enough" clothes left in her closet and with resignation she reached for the navy pinstripe jumper that she had almost worn the stripes off these past few months. It was still her best shot at blending in. One more time, she promised the well-worn material. If there is ever a baby number two I promise I will buy you reinforcements.

As she brushed on just a touch of blush, she caught her own eye in the makeup mirror. She had been avoiding thinking about last night's odd disruption. "Weird night, huh?" she asked the eye in the mirror. The magnified iris seemed to widen slightly at the question.

"Yeah. Right. No time to deal with metaphysical mysteries this morning. We have an offshore oil prospect to sell to upper management today. We are going to be responsible for our first federal lease. We are going to show that we are just one fine geophysicist no matter how pregnant we are. I am. Why do I always talk to myself like there are more of me? ... Get a grip Lola. Go act like a scientist." She pulled on the now barely adequate maternity pantyhose with a brusque efficiency, stuck her swollen feet and ankles into her lowest navy heels and achieved something that was a cross between an uncomfortable waddle and a confident stride as she headed out the door.

The office was lively with the expectation of the arrival of upper management from Houston. Upper. Like they would drift in on clouds. Lola chuckled at the image. People often told her that she didn't have much of a sense of humor, but that was because they were generally people who told jokes that Lola did not find funny.

She had no trouble coming up with jokes of her own that made her laugh.

She smelled fresh pastries in the conference room mixed with printing fluids from the rolls of meticulously drafted maps. The walls were covered with poster-sized displays which had been carefully colored by two overworked techs who had been overly supervised by all the eager young geologists and geophysicists anxious for the brief chance to show just how smart and savvy they were. Nervous middle management types were double-checking the displays, the pastries, the ties of the presenters. And the pastries again. Lola thought that her boss Chuck was on his third donut. His bulging waistline attested to his habit of eating when nervous. It also attested to the fact that being geophysical manager for the Offshore Gulf of Mexico Western Exploration Division made him nervous a lot.

"Zeitman, you're not gonna pop that baby out in the middle of our big presentation are you?"

Chuck called all the guys by their last names, all the secretaries by their first. He had been a little confused about what exactly to do with her when she had started there a year and a half ago fresh out of school, but after a few awkward months of almost never referring to her by name at all, he had settled on considering her an honorary guy—called by last name only. And even though after fewer than two years of marriage "Zeitman" still seemed to Lola to be her husband, not her, Chuck's decision had still suited her well. She knew she was a fairly pretty young woman, and it set a genderless tone with her coworkers that she liked. In fact, after she became Zeitman to Chuck, almost everybody had been relieved simply to consider her a short and slightly misshapen guy who could interpret symbols produced by sound waves bouncing off rocks as well as the next guy. Maybe even better than some. And until she had the poor taste to shatter that illusion by becoming increasingly more pregnant, Chuck had actually gotten fairly comfortable with her. Now it seemed that he was back to the awkward jokes.

"Oh God. Not the blue pinstripe jumper again Zeitman. We're gonna take up a collection and buy you some new clothes. Wait. You don't need new clothes. Or maybe you do. You gonna be pregnant forever?" And so on.

She picked up her roll of maps, smiled nervously, and headed to her office to run through her presentation one last time in her mind.

Chuck watched Lola walk to her office with a small sense of amazement. He honestly admired the hell out of her, though he would never have considered saying so. His own wife had spent most of her ninth month of pregnancy on their couch, generally complaining, while he fetched ice cream and anything containing bacon bits which she had inexplicably started to love. But Lola, to Chuck's pleasant surprise, had shown up to work every single day. Smiling. True, her thick, normally unruly dark hair had gotten noticeably wilder over the last few months and her wardrobe had diminished, but otherwise she had looked professional, worked hard, and asked for nothing special. Hell, she had even expected to take her rotation going offshore to oversee data acquisition from a wellbore, before the health and safety guys had informed him that there was no way he was to send a pregnant woman offshore. And then the legal folks had shown up in person in his office to make sure he had gotten the message.

Which was fine. He had been content to watch Lola's quick little bird-like movements and ever-present goofy smile as she approached her due date. Chuck knew it probably wasn't obvious from the way he acted, but he always liked meeting people who exceeded his own expectations. It was he who had originally gone to bat for this petite female geek with a certain fearlessness about her, agreeing to add her to his team by recommending not only that the company make her a job offer, but that they even offer her the same salary they offered to the guys. He'd been warned against the latter, told that she'd probably get pregnant, and he would lose productivity from her. No, Chuck thought, he did not regret his decision a bit. Hell, she even smiled at his dumb jokes, which was more than she did for a lot of the other guys.

Lola knew that she smiled too much. She smiled when she was happy, or amused, or even just content, and now she was smiling as she sat in her office reviewing her materials and munching on the apple slices she had brought for breakfast. People thought she was always happy, but they did not understand that she unfortunately also smiled when she was nervous, sometimes when she was sad—she didn't know why—and she certainly smiled when she was embarrassed or felt awkward or just plain didn't know what to say. Which, being on the shy side, happened a lot. She'd smiled often in college, especially in all the math and physics classes when the professors looked at her funny on the first day of class. She'd smiled her way through every doctor's exam she'd had to have since she got pregnant, and she smiled her way through the most awkward moments at work. She'd smiled like crazy the three times they'd sent her out to offshore drilling platforms before she got pregnant, with the ironic effect that the guys offshore seemed to like her because, as one bluntly pointed out to her, she seemed so much friendlier than the other stuck-up women (okay, he had not actually used the term "women") who occasionally showed up out there in one professional capacity or another. "We like you because you smile at us," he'd explained. And with that, she had smiled again.

And the last couple of months … well, she'd smiled through spontaneously offered child-rearing advice, uninvited labor horror stories, and two male coworkers asking if they could please put their hands on her belly. She'd said yes, she really wasn't sure why, and then stood and smiled uncomfortably while they marveled at how firm and taut a pregnant stomach actually was.

Now she was smiling, and eating her apple slices, which she did enjoy. Alex kept buying other alternatives for their grab-and-go breakfasts, but she kept choosing the simple apple, over and over. She looked over the agenda and noted that she was fourth on the list of presenters. As was customary, she would be called by the secretary after the first presentation ended and allowed to enter and sit quietly in the back of the room after the second presenter finished. Normally she would be expected to return to her office and work after her own presentation was over, but given that she was three days away from her due date and everyone was glad that she had made it as far as today, she had already received permission to go home and put her feet up when done. Maternity leave would officially start tomorrow.

When her turn came, Lola walked to the front of the room and smiled. The president of the company, an older attractive man with a great deal of charisma, sat in the center seat and, upon seeing a young female, smiled and raised one eyebrow out of habit in a more than friendly greeting back. He was flanked by the two most important senior executive vice presidents, both seated close enough to lean in and whisper sage advice as required. Other assorted VPs, directors and managers had established themselves in approximate order of importance on either side of the trio, with the occasional overly aggressive or politically naive manager seated above or below his station. Lola's boss and his two counterparts, the reservoir engineering and geology managers, sat at one extreme end. Chuck looked like he needed another donut. Chuck's boss cleared his throat.

"Our fourth prospect today will be presented by, uh, Lola. Zeitman. Lola got her master's degree just eighteen months ago from UT and started with us straight out of school and she has done a great job mapping in the West Cameron area. That is despite a little, uh, inconvenient medical situation which we hear can be remedied."

There was assorted laughter.

"Please gentlemen, do not say anything to upset her. The last thing any of us wants to do is to deliver a baby here in this room today!"

Slightly louder and more boisterous laughter followed.

"No, no, no," the president surprised his entourage by throwing up his beautifully manicured hands in mock agitation. He was in a good mood today.

"Say anything you want, gentlemen. Talking is not the activity that sets off labor with a very pregnant woman," he chuckled knowingly. "Trust me, I know what really sets labor off".

The chuckle spread to others and took on an even more

knowing tone, first from those who really knew what he meant and somewhat more slowly but no less knowingly from those who didn't. Lola, knowing damn well what activity he was referring to, was aware that any response from her at all would be unwelcome. So she waited quietly for the noise to die down before she began to speak. She pursed her lips to forcibly reduce her nervous smile.

"I am here today to recommend that this company make a substantial bid on a block in southern West Cameron," she began quietly. "The map behind me shows a faulted four-way structural trap with sizable potential."

Her delivery was professional, courteous, calm. She knew that her ability to read a room and deliver recommendations accordingly was one of her more unique assets, and this was no time not to rely on it. Most anyone trained in her profession could analyze data and make a decent map. Most could study those maps and assess the best places for oil to likely be trapped. But few scientists seem to possess that ability to take the numerous points of a recommendation and sense how to best present all that data. Few could read a room so well, knowing instinctively when and what to push and when to step back, how hard to sell various aspects, or not, and how jovial or serious or humble or confident to be.

When Lola finished, she knew she had done her job well. The block would receive a good-sized bid from her company and the company might well win the lease from the Mineral Management Service. Then they might drill a well. They might find oil. And if they did, more cars and planes would run and more homes would be lit and heated. In 1986, to Lola and those trained in her profession, the discovery of oil in the Gulf of Mexico seemed like only a fine and beneficial thing.

She left the presentation feeling proud of her own part in it, although slightly bothered by its boisterous preamble. She could not quite put her finger on why. She knew well enough that no offense had been meant and she would hardly have expected Chuck, or his boss or his boss's boss, to ever interfere with whatever good cheer they were fortunate enough to have upper management exhibit while visiting them. But somehow, it seemed smarmy. Like she was the butt of a mildly dirty joke that she had been forced to listen to without being permitted to respond. Wait, there was no "like". Actually, she thought, that is exactly what had happened.

When she got back to her office, she saw that the secretaries had carefully taped three pink phone message forms to her door. The first one said, "Alex called to wish you luck." It was the careful cursive handwriting of the secretary that liked Lola and went out of her way to be helpful to her. It had a little smiley face added for effect. A different cursive script advised that "Your sister called to make sure everything was okay." Oh dear. Lola's younger sister Summer had been very emotionally involved in this upcoming first arrival in the family and Lola had not called her in days. Worse, this personal piece of information was from the secretary who had made it fairly clear that she was not pleased at having a professional woman in the group, and, near as Lola could tell, even less pleased that said professional woman had the audacity to defy stereotypes by finding a perfectly fine man to marry her. The second cursive script informed her curtly on note three that "Alex called. Again."

The geoscientists who had already made their presentations were gathering in the break room, laughing, kidding each other, giddy with the relief of being done and no longer needing to be nervous that they would inadvertently make that one stupid remark or observation which everyone laughingly referred to as the CLM. Career limiting move. You want to promote whom? Isn't he the idiot who once said …?"

In a corporate culture in which almost everyone was smart and good at what they did, it was the little memories of "farting in church" as one coworker called it, that would stall a rise upward. Apparently, no one had "farted". The relief was so thick Lola felt as if she could smell and taste it.

"Hey. Lola," a friendly young geophysicist greeted her as she joined them, welcoming her into the circle of laughter. "What do you call it when a school bus in New Orleans filled with little black kids drives off a bridge into Lake Ponchartrain?"

Lola was confused by the question. What? Was this a tragedy off the news? Surely not a joke. "I don't know. What do you call it?"

"It's a start," the young man chortled. At Lola's blank face, he tried harder. "Get it? Lola, it's a start."

Lola was so surprised she honestly didn't know what to say. The first thing that came out of her mouth was a response she had given no thought to at all. "So what do you call it if a bus full of white kids goes off a bridge into Lake Ponchartrain?"

The whole break room looked at Lola. Unspoken office rules were that if someone made a joke, you laughed. If it was a bad joke or it offended you, you only laughed politely and then you were free to complain to them or, more likely, to others about it later in private. Folks worked long hours together and public confrontations were as unacceptable as, well, public farting. Lola could sense that she was inching across a line. She tried to soften it without backing off.

"So what do you think a group of black people call it if a bus full of white kids goes off a bridge into Lake Ponchartrain?" she rephrased her question carefully.

And he looked back at her as if she had just grown three turquoise heads. "I guess they'd call it a start too," he said lamely.

And because neither one of them knew what else to say after that, pretty much everyone in the room started saying something about anything else. Once no one was looking directly at her, Lola quietly went back to her office. She felt annoyed with herself for not having confronted the man more directly. What was wrong with her? She in no way supported this kind of racism toward any group, and she'd been frankly shocked to hear it from one of her educated coworkers. On the other hand, she knew that even with her meekly offended response, she'd pay the price for "not having a sense of humor" by now being excluded from the office banter even more than she had been. Great.

She sat at her desk for a minute. You know, she really did not feel like saying goodbye to anyone now that she thought about it. Time to go home, even if the only home they'd been able to find in the middle of this housing boom was a rental without central air or heat, sitting above ground on cinderblock stilts allowing who-knew-what to live underneath. She picked up her purse, and left without saying a word.

Alex was waiting for her at the small house they were renting, stretched out on the well-worn hand-me-down couch, his soft blue eyes checking her carefully for damage of any type, his long arms outstretched to hug her. He was a tall man, and stocky at twenty-eight years old. He was always trying to lose weight, to drop down to the level of those wonderful college athlete days he had had before she had known him, but the truth was that she liked him the way he was now. He felt solid, like no matter how hard the winds of her own emotions blew she could hang on tight to him and it would all be okay. She let herself be engulfed by his arms, enjoying his freckled skin, the soft sandy hair on his arms that matched the unkempt dirty blond hair on his head.

"So how is my favorite geophysicist doing?" His hug pushed away much of the strange feelings swimming inside. She let herself be held for a minute. Then she had a very odd idea, one she could not begin to justify to herself, much less to him.

"I am really ready to have this baby," she began.

"Hey, me too," he answered. "My back has been killing me since you got pregnant, remember?"

"Do you recall learning about oxytocin and how it sets off labor?" she persisted. "You know, a woman releases it when she breastfeeds and when, well, you know …"

"Yes, I was listening during Lamaze classes," he laughed. "Okay, at least during any part that actually used the word 'orgasm.'"

"So," she began. And let her hand continue the thought.

"Hey, wait a minute Lola. Easy girl. Not that I want to ever discourage this sort of behavior, but I am not sure this is a terribly good idea right now. I am not even sure it is a terribly possible idea. It has been at least three weeks since we have … and geez dear, no offense, but you have gotten huge in the—"

Alex stopped. It did not take a genius to see that this was not going in the loving, concerned direction he had intended. She was tired. Uncomfortable. Probably overwrought from the presentation, certainly on a hormonal trapeze, and he was willing to bet the house that she was about to cry. So he did the only sensible thing he could think of. Which of course led to the next thing and the next and of course it was possible … What was he thinking? It was always possible. And four hours later after a pleasant afterglow nap during which Lola seemed particularly pleased with herself, they left for the hospital just as the contractions were approaching ten minutes apart with consistency.

And the hospital sent them back home. With instructions to go walking. Thus it would be twenty more long hours before they were actually in the birthing room, by then both of them sleep-deprived, scared, and crabby. It would have been nice if the birth had been the joyous and easy experience they had imagined, but the fact was that this was a first pregnancy and the baby, although in the correct position, was big, with a large head. The end of labor was particularly slow and difficult, and another, less understanding doctor would have given up and done a C-section. As it was, Lola ended up on oxygen with an IV, neither of which she wanted, and at the very end she gave in further and accepted an analgesic as well. Alex curtly informed the nurse that he personally was ready for any drugs WHATSOEVER which they were willing to give him.

And so it was that Zane Alphonse Zeitman was born at 6:48 p.m. CST on February 20, 1986, to tired but happy parents. He was a pretty baby, with his father's long lashes, and his mother and father eyed him with the wonder that most first time parents do their child. He exhibited an easy-going cooperative nature from the very start. As Lola tentatively held his face close to her breast for the first time, she could not help thinking, "Ye gads. What the hell do I think I am doing? I have no idea." Then Zane latched on with an instinct possessed by virtually every newborn mammal on earth, and Lola muttered to herself, "okay … that's it. We are going to show them that we are just one fine mother child team here no matter how good a scientist we are. I am. Good grief. Get a grip Lola. Relax and act like a mama." And she did.

Because giving birth is followed by the mind-numbing

exhaustion that comes with raising a newborn, it is understandable that for the next several weeks Lola gave no thought to the odd little experience with the noises in her belly. In fact, by the time she finally remembered it, she wasn't even sure it had really happened.

Raising a child is hard work too, and it does get harder when there are more children, no matter what anyone says. And over time, there were more. Holding a job where a boss tries to milk all the energy he can from one does not exactly create a situation conducive to much reflective thought. Ask almost anyone with a job about that situation. And let's face it, being a decent and caring spouse takes time and energy, particularly when time and energy are in short supply. Hell, sometimes just getting out of bed in the morning and managing a bit of occasional compassion along with basic hygiene and on-time bill paying can pretty much fill up one's time and one's head. So, clearly Lola did not spend time thinking or wondering about hearing anyone else's thoughts in her brain. She was busy. In fact, for the next two decades she was usually very, very busy and often very tired as well. And, there was never a real reason for it to come up. Not, that is, until twenty-three years later, when the memory would come storming back and demand to be recognized.

Chapter 2. A Beginning: February 1993

The noises were the worst part for five-year-old Somadina only because she knew who was making them.

As the women came and went from her mother's tiny house amid her very own mama's cries and moans, Somadina could sense their worry in the way she could sense so many things that the grown-ups thought she could not, and she knew in her vague child's way that something was terribly wrong.

"This time next month you will have a little brother," her father Ikenna had proudly told her a few weeks ago.

"Yes papa." She knew that her father loved her dearly, as she loved him, but she also knew that for some reason this second child, this son, meant the world to him.

"Remember what your name means, Somadina."

"I know papa. May I never be alone. And starting soon I will not be. I will have a little brother to help mama take care of always."

He smiled at her sharp mind. This little girl was bright and would be a source of great pride to him. And it was only an extra blessing that she was pretty already. With her mother's very large eyes and direct clear gaze, she sometimes seemed like a little carbon copy of his dear Amaka. With all of her gifts, Somadina would do well in life, possibly a run a little business or be a leader in the women's community, and she would likely bring a high bride price as well. For all the great hardship in his childhood and youth, Ikenna recognized that today he was, beyond a doubt, a very lucky man.

But that had been fourteen days ago and Ikenna knew that during just this short amount of time his luck had changed. True, the depth of his love for Amaka was unusual. Wives with his people were often taken as more of a matter of practical arrangement, and Ikenna had defied convention by passing on taking a second wife even though there was adequate money to support one, and it was of course an expected thing to do when Amaka produced a girl child for him as his first born and then failed to get pregnant again for such a long while. But no, he had ignored his own father's vehement wishes and instead further professed his love for only Amaka, cherishing and embracing their fine daughter, and assuring all that a fine son would be produced as well in due time.

And then the second pregnancy had begun and gone so nicely. Amaka had glowed with a health and joy which had fortified his belief that not only was a son on the way, as it should be to reward him for his love and loyalty, but that it was also a son who would be strong and smart and capable, to make up for the sad loss of Ikenna's only two brothers those many years ago. And then Ikenna's father, the great and proud man that he was, would no longer have to watch his lineage wither on the vine. He would no longer be frustrated with his only surviving son, this immature younger child who had been too slow to grow and marry for the aging old man's impatient nature and who had then compounded the situation by falling so deeply in love with one woman that he would not even try to make sons with others.

But now his son was having a problem being born. In his haste to come into the world and greet his father and grandfather, the midwife had said, the son had entered the birth canal wrong and now beautiful Amaka had been in labor much too long. Ikenna spit in disgust. It was hard for him to ignore completely the old Igbo discomfort with any unusual problems involved in giving birth. He told himself that it was not Amaka's fault. The midwife in this village was not as good as in many others, it was plain to see. It was a skill to bring life into this world, and she had little modern training. He should have taken Amaka back to her own hometown, where her village had lifted itself up by building an up-to-date maternity center and where the women who handled such things were Amaka's own relations and were well known for their abilities.

Amaka had asked this of him, just fourteen days ago. But no, he had to listen to his own stupid pride, his own stupid desire to have his son born here on his father's compound, to see his father's face himself when the old man was given the news. He had put his wife and unborn son at risk for a personal moment of satisfaction. He no longer deserved his good fortune. Ikenna sat on the ground in despair.

Meanwhile, the women attending to Amaka were beside themselves. They also knew that the midwife was relatively untrained and inexperienced, having taken the business over from her own recently and prematurely deceased mother. She had struggled with every difficult birth she had attended to since she had been on her own, and this baby was butt first, once considered an abomination by the older and more superstitious. The problem was worsened by the fact that this baby's knees were bent, with one foot stuck alongside the butt. Amaka was fully dilated and had been pushing now for hours without success. Gentle attempts to move the baby or even the baby's one stuck foot by hand had yielded nothing but more intense screams, and the midwife knew that eventually neither mother nor child would survive. What to do? What to do?

One of her youngest assistants came back with more hot water. "You know the Hausa woman nobody likes?" she whispered. The midwife nodded. Everyone knew the Hausa woman, who kept to her home and almost never came out. "She actually left her house to call to me because she feels sorry for Amaka. She has heard the screaming. She guessed what is happening. Her sister is a midwife! With the Hausa. And she says that they have remedy for a case like this and she wants to talk to you."

"Will she come here?"

"I do not think so. But go to her quick and I will watch Amaka." And so the midwife ran.

Ikenna looked up from his grief. The stupid inexperienced midwife was standing in front of him and she looked happy. Ikenna jumped up. "My son?!"

"Not yet," she said. "But I may have a solution. It is something the Hausa do, called a gishiri cut. If we do it the boy should be born just fine. But there is some risk to Amaka, and to her ability to bear more children later."

Ikenna said nothing.

"We will certainly lose them both if we do not try this," she added. "With your permission?"

Ikenna sighed. Really, what choice did he have?

Any well-trained midwife the world over would understand

that cutting the vaginal wall cannot solve a problem caused by a baby stuck inside pelvic bones. But this midwife was not particularly well taught, inexperienced, and was desperately open to suggestion. To make matters worse, in her fear and ignorance, she made the cuts large and deep. As a result, Amaka's shock and trauma stopped the contractions long enough for the desperate midwife to force the baby's body upward to dislodge the foot, and for a rapid breech birth to then occur. In that sense the midwife was very lucky. The baby lived. But the exhausted and nearly unconscious Amaka <u>bled out before the midwife was even aware</u> of how serious the situation was.

    Ikenna watched the midwife come toward him with fear in her eyes. She held a bundled crying child. This was most unusual.
    "Amaka?" he asked.
    She only stared at him, dazed, and Ikenna knew. He stood motionless for a few seconds. Though he was a modern man who made every effort to put superstitions aside, it was hard for him to suppress the sense of dishonor and shame which the Igbo had long associated with death in childbirth. He swallowed with a very dry mouth and focused on his affection for Amaka. That is what mattered. How would she want him to greet his son?
    Softly he turned to the baby and said the best he could come up with. "You must be a very special son," he whispered, "to have cost me so much." Then he saw the look in the midwife's eyes and he knew the rest of the story.
    As deep disappointment sank in, the pity in the woman's eyes began to offend him in a way he could not explain. His anger towards her started as only small ripples of irritation, but before he could stop them the little undulations had grown into larger and larger waves of rage. He yelled to the midwife.
    "Get. Out. Of. Here."
    The young woman stood horrified.
    "Do you understand me?"
    The midwife opened her mouth to speak but Ikenna cut her short.
    "No, you do not speak to me. Not now. Not at any time in the

future. Do not ever even look at me. Do not even breathe in my presence."

The woman froze. Ikenna knew that his fury was reaching unreasonable proportions but he was unable to stop it. If he were not careful he knew that he would hurt the midwife and he also knew that that would accomplish nothing. He took a few ragged breaths and turned away so he could think. His breathing became more normal. His mouth once again had saliva.

Indeed, the midwife was only stupid. She couldn't be blamed for that. He must try to be rationale. His first problem was that he now had this tiny baby girl who had taken from him what he had loved most. He could ask that this child go live with her mother's kin, which was tempting and would be acceptable under the circumstances. But, wait. There was little Somadina, pulling on his shirt.

"Papa?" Her wide eyes were full of questions.

And Ikenna thought to himself that she was the only piece of joy he had left in life. If the baby girl went, then Somadina too might go to live with her maternal aunts in another town, and then he would see her only on occasion. But if he insisted on keeping both girls close, Somadina would still bring him comfort. Meanwhile he'd just have to find someone to watch the infant and to see to it that she brought him a minimum of trouble.

That meant, of course, that now he would need a new wife. Make that two. And quickly. Any fertile women would do. He knew his father well enough to know that neither condolences nor congratulations would be forthcoming from the old man for today's events, and if he set something matrimonial in motion quickly, he could share that news with his father the next time they spoke. It would make the encounter so much easier.

Somadina gently let go of her father's sleeve and waited. She knew from everything she picked up that her mother was gone, even if she had no idea of where. Though Somadina was both saddened and scared by that knowledge, at the moment she was focused on her father, who was right there but seemed in a very real sense to be gone as well. She could not think of words to describe his lack of presence, even to herself. But she knew that in her mind she usually saw a door when she approached her papa and that the door was usually open wide. And when that happened, she knew that he would be happy to see her and play with her. Every once in awhile when she approached him she would instead see that the door was only open a crack, and then she would know that he was busy or bothered, and she should leave him alone. She had heard him say often how she was such a wonderful child because she never asked for his attention when he had other matters to attend to. That comment baffled her. She wasn't doing anything unusual, she just checked his door before she spoke to him. But now she saw his door, and it was shut tight like she had never seen it before, with locks and bolts and huge scary vines with giant thorns growing over it at a frightening speed. Baffled, she backed away carefully.

In spite of the most unfortunate circumstances of Amaka's death, Amaka's family was not happy to leave the girls in the father's village. But others intervened to explain that given how very much the father loved Somadina, her presence might help him heal in his grief. It was a reasonable hope, and so Amaka's family acquiesced. However, the family had concerns.

To begin with, Ikenna showed no interest in selecting a name for the new daughter and there was a good bit of consternation in both families as the naming ceremony approached. Finally, one of his sisters suggested Nwanyibuife. Ikenna snorted a mirthless laugh, and agreed. For although the name translates literally as "a female is worth something too", it was often used in an ironic sense by a disappointed father.

Causing even more consternation was Ikenna's total lack of involvement in the well-being of the child. He showed no desire to play with or display any affection to the little girl. His youngest sister was making milk for both her own infant and her one-year-old, and she was willing to suckle Nwanyi while she was at it. Although Nwanyi received quick feedings from her tired and busy aunt, and was given cursory care by Ikenna's two new wives, the fact was that she received remarkably little genuine affection during her first months of life.

    Except for her time with Somadina. For when Somadina listened to her little sister's cries, she cried herself. She understood that little Nwanyi was supposed to be a brother and was now in trouble because she had not been one. And she understood that the coming of the baby had made her mother very sick and that was why her mother was gone. But Nwanyi was cute in a scrawny way and so helpless and sometimes so very unhappy. Somadina, who felt the baby's hunger and loneliness every day in ways she could not explain, just wanted to hold and comfort her little sister and make it all better for her. So Somadina did what she could.

    As for her father, she mostly avoided him after Nwanyi's birth. Ikenna, when he was not engulfed in his grief, was generally preoccupied with his new wives, neither of whom seemed to have all that much use for Somadina. And then after the almost simultaneous arrival of not one but two baby half-brothers a little over a year after Nwanyi was born, Somadina barely saw her father at all, losing touch with the one living person with whom she once had the closest of emotional ties.

    So Somadina changed too. She began to withdraw, and the ability to sense what others were thinking that she had simply taken for granted, began to fade. Others noticed that she seemed to have lost much of her almost eerie perceptiveness. By her seventh birthday, she was an unusually independent little girl, willingly doing the chores assigned to her and excelling in the local grade school to which Ikenna had decided to send her for at least a few years, but otherwise most content to just be alone.

    One day when seven-year-old Somadina was watching Nwanyi while she was napping, her sister began whimpering in her sleep. She brushed her cheek gently to wake her from the bad dream, but Nwanyi just curled up tighter and whimpered more. So Somadina made a solemn promise to her two-year-old sister that when she, Somadina, was bigger and had more power, she would look out for Nwanyi and would keep her safe. In fact, Somadina swore to become as powerful and influential as a woman could become, just so she could do a good job of keeping her promise.

And after the "promise ceremony," as she thought of it in her own head, Somadina felt much better, even if the sleeping Nwanyi had not understood just how serious Somadina had been.

Part I. Face Painting for World Peace
Chapter 3. January 2009

Who wouldn't be nervous? Lola eyed herself carefully in the full-length mirror, hoping her best floral print skirt and matching jacket weren't too colorful. She felt like a child headed off to her first day of school. It had been more than twenty-four years since she had started a new job, and she still wasn't sure how the time had flown by. Today's uncertainty was both disconcerting and a little exhilarating.

"So how do I look?" she asked 13-year-old Teddie, her resident fashion expert and her only child still living at home.

"Mmmmm … not bad mom. It is a little '90s. And try to calm the hair down if you can. Here. Use my straightener. It's already hot."

"You know I really cannot believe that these things are safe for one's hair," Lola said as she reluctantly pulled Teddie's gizmo around her thick auburn brown hair. She sighed. It was a fact that most of her better clothes were from the '90s, back when standard office fashion had still been more formal. They had been bought as Lola's company had consolidated in Houston, and as she had flirted briefly with being in middle management before returning, with some relief, to the role of rank-and-file worker. She smiled ruefully, realizing that decision was pretty much what had doomed her to an eventual lay off in a world where you rose into management, segued into a related specialty, or worked your way into becoming "overpaid" compared to the youngsters with whom you could be replaced. With whom, in fact, she had been replaced.

So, the usually brightly dressed woman with congenitally unkempt hair, a too frequent smile, and a knack for finding oil, had found herself back in the job market, "severed" from her allegedly deeply appreciative former employer of almost two and a half decades, and about to start work as the sole geophysicist for a small start-up company in Houston whose best opportunity to date was acquiring shallow drilling rights on a land deal in the Niger Delta. Offshore Nigeria.

Well, Lola thought, oil was oil. And though the stuff had

turned out to be incredibly nastier for planet earth than she'd known it was when she started to look for it way back when, the fact remained that the world still needed it for now, and she was still good at finding it. And people were still willing to pay her well for doing so. Which was particularly good given the mortgage on their beautiful home and all the expenses they had somehow managed to amass over the last twenty-four years.

"So how is my favorite geophysicist?" At the end of day one, Alex met her with a hug as she entered the kitchen. The smells of sautéed onions and garlic added to their friendly hello. As a teacher, he had always gotten home before her, and it was the family's good fortune that he liked to cook. He hadn't said much about what she'd gone through the last few months—the surprise layoff last fall, her reluctant job search at forty-nine years old, the contacts at the old company too nervous to return her calls lest she be contagious, and finally, the interviews, the waiting, the getting hired. But she knew that he knew, and both his culinary efforts and his giant engulfing hug tonight said it all.

"Well, I'm in a little room with no windows for the first time in twenty years," she laughed, "and I'm on lousy loaner computer 'til mine comes in, and these guys have a drilling obligation and need me to work up a location on this lease by the end of March."

"Sounds like fun."

"The more interesting news is that this company actually employs two Nigerian geologists. Right here in Houston. They have more Nigerians in the office here too, and they have a little office in Lagos because they believe in being involved in the country where they do business. I think that they are trying to be the good guys compared to big multinationals that just come in and take what they can."

"It's got to be nice to be working for the good guys? Relatively speaking, anyway?"

"Yeah," she mused. "It is. And the folks I met today were great. At least with this particular group it seems like office politics isn't their main activity."

"No one tried to get you to put forty million dollars of theirs in our bank account, did they?"

Lola rolled her eyes. "You know, I bet the average Nigerian is pretty damn embarrassed by that. Don't you dare make that joke near my office."

And Alex thought to himself, *That's interesting. She likes these folks already.*

Ikenna was genuinely undecided, and it was an uncomfortable feeling which he did not enjoy. For the past fifteen years his life had been predictable and pleasant, more so than he had thought possible. There were still times, of course, when he thought of his one great young love Amaka with sadness, but his two new wives had been fertile and friendly and had brought him no cause for grief. He could not say he shared that much of his heart or mind with either, but socially and physically each of them met all his needs, and the fact that they had become friends with each other was certainly an added bonus. And the nine children they produced between them were, well, more than he deserved. He thanked God every day for the mercy of a second chance.

And now that he was older and more sensible, he regretted his emotional withdrawal in that dark time after Amaka's death. Heaven knows he had tried hard over the years since to regain the understanding and affection of his oldest daughter Somadina. But Somadina seemed to still blame him for his lack of affection for Nwany and his neglect of both girls as he wallowed in his own grief. She had never warmed to his new wives or to her half-siblings, or for that matter to much of anyone in the years after her mother died. In fact, she had become something of a rarity for an Igbo girl—a person who preferred solitude.

Which was why the acceptance of a marriage offer for her had been such an easy decision. True, Somadina had expressed no desire to be married, and so Ikenna had waited patiently until she was well past eighteen. When Azuka and his parents had asked for her hand, Ikenna knew that although the family lived in the same village, they had moved there only a generation ago and luckily bore no relationship to Somadina, making the union acceptable. Better yet, Ikenna knew Azuka to be a reasonable young man, of a good traditional family, with skills he was learning from his own father on how to repair small devices and machinery, and Ikenna knew that those skills would one day help provide for Somadina and her children in a changing world.

It was true that the boy was only Somadina's age and rather young for marriage, but he seemed genuinely to like Somadina, and she seemed to at least not object to him, and she clearly had no particular attraction to another that would interfere. At eighteen it had been time, and so Ikenna had readily agreed, believing that whatever affection he had not been able to give Somadina himself while she was growing up could now somehow be made up for by providing her with a good husband. And once her first child, a grandson, had arrived to the joy of all, he had felt that he had at last done right by her and some of his guilt was eased. But not all.

Which is why this second decision was so difficult. He had barely managed over the years to demonstrate a forced warmth to his second daughter Nwanyi, but he had genuinely tried, after the combination of time, his new wives, and the arrival of more children had helped heal the throbbing gash in his heart. And God himself must know that Nwanyi had not been easy to love. She had not had the good fortune to inherit her mother's warm nature nor her beauty, but had grown instead into a short, scrawny girl who tended to be silent and secretive. She did not have Somadina's intelligence or confidence, but tended to hang back nervously, all too obviously craving encouragement and approval. Ikenna had tried to find something he liked about the child, but it had been hard.

Nonetheless, the guilt for his poor behavior persisted, as did the feeling that he would never be whole in Somadina's wide and penetrating eyes until Nwanyi somehow found some happiness. So the plan seemed simple enough. Secure an equally reasonable young man from an equally respected family to marry Nwanyi. It was of course understood and accepted by Ikenna that this would require a significant reduction in the normal bride price, a sacrifice that, under the circumstances, he was more than willing to make because once

Nwanyi was a happy wife and mother herself, then certainly all would be forgiven and Ikenna's self-respect could be fully restored.

Then several weeks ago had come the unexpected but very generous offer from the Yoruba man named Djimon. He was a very serious man, a bit thinner and shorter than most, but well muscled, and his stature paired nicely with Nwanyi's own. His age, perhaps mid-thirties, had its benefits and disadvantages. He was obviously well off, which was a plus, and well educated with an advanced degree in some fancy field Ikenna knew little about. However, there was prestige in the fact that he taught university classes in the subject.

Nwanyi would be a second wife, <u>which could be good or bad</u>. It certainly would put less pressure on Nwanyi to perform household chores and to reproduce often, which might be better for Nwanyi's reticent nature. She would of course move to Lagos, to her husband's home in Western Nigeria, which would not sit well with Somadina, but would probably be a relief to everyone else. Including, he had to admit, to himself.

Nwanyi, safely married, well cared for, and out of sight. And a huge bride price, as Djimon had insisted, given entirely to the father. Why was he hesitating?

For starters, the entire process was far too rushed for Igbo tradition. Furthermore, Ikenna was not a stupid man. He knew when a situation might be too good to be true. Things about this unusual arrangement bothered him. What was the hurry? Why not take the time for a proper courtship? Furthermore, these days some of the bride price often went directly to the bride, to give her a little independence, perhaps a means for education. Ikenna was well aware that he had done poorly by not sending Nwanyi to any formal schooling, leaving it to Somadina to educate her younger sister. She could remedy this as an adult, but Djimon had insisted that in his household such would not be necessary.

Perhaps that was a cultural difference. Ikenna thought to himself that he knew too little of this household. A typical Igbo father and mother would investigate the background of a suitor thoroughly if it was not already known, and would turn down an offer in which the family exhibited qualities that caused them concern. But Ikenna had no real means with which to investigate this older stranger from a distance. And he had to admit that the man's choice of Nwanyi was strange.

Ikenna decided, for the time being at least, on not deciding. Rather, he would arrange a second meeting with Djimon to discuss his concerns. It was only right, for both Nwanyi and to honor Amaka's memory.

The first couple of weeks in the new office left Lola with the realization that she actually knew almost nothing about Nigeria. She could only name one town (Lagos, which it turned out wasn't even the capital anymore). She wasn't sure who had colonized it (though she was willing to bet on England) or when it had become an independent state. In fact she had to face the sad fact that she knew almost nothing about Africa in general, and now that she thought about it her knowledge of anything outside of North American and Western Europe was pretty damn limited. Time for a little work on the internet.

In 1994 Lola's father had been diagnosed with cancer. He was fifty-nine years young at the time, and she, her mother, and her sister had been determined to help him fight the disease with all the love, medicine, and technology they could collectively muster. Lola—as the scientist—had investigated the newfangled thing known as the world wide web. It was a scarier place then, with few safe pathways, harder to avoid coarse pornography and sites boasting offensive crass jokes. But she learned to hold her nose while she navigated her way to medical websites, subscribed to bulletin boards on cancer research, set herself up to receive alerts on clinical trials. And she got answers the real live doctors would not give. How does cancer kill? How does chemo work? What really are the odds of remission for a particular type of cancer at a particular stage? The amount of available information was massive, the presentation was sterile and, in her father's case, the news was bleak. But it was knowledge, there for the taking—and in the end it was valuable to really know. Lola had embraced the full possibilities of the internet before many of her cohorts had learned to use email. By 2009 she considered the internet almost an appendage.

She typed "Nigeria history" into her favorite search engine at lunch and studied the various ornate and enticing doorways into her new world. Pick a door, Lola.

Well, for starters, door number one informed her that there was no such place as Nigeria. <u>Not until recently anyway</u>. There were groups, tribes, clans—some loosely affiliated and others sincere enemies—all trying to live their lives as best they could, to care for their own, eek out what small comforts and joys they were able to. Then along came these strange pale-skinned people willing to provide lavish gifts in exchange for enemies captured and provided to them. Less enemies around? And lavish gifts as well? What was not to like about that arrangement?

And so what started out as an apparently sensible response to an offer grew into a situation where, for about sixteen generations entire kingdoms became rich by selling to the white people far more Africans than they could ever have procured for themselves. Over those several hundred years, somewhere between thirty and <u>three hundred million</u>, that's right - three hundred million, of Africa's hopeful and strong young people were shipped off of the continent never to return.

And then, one day out of the blue, some of the strangers arrived and declared, "Selling people is morally wrong. It is bad to sell people of any kind. You must not do it any more." This would have been confusing enough after all of this time but some of the other strangers, the ones from a place called the New World, said, "Do not listen to them. They are British. We have a great large land that needs more and more of you and we will pay an even better price if you bring us more enemies." And so they did, paying much better prices for a few generations.

Then the British army arrived, angry and with many soldiers, and took control of all the lands saying, if you cannot stop this horrible immoral slave trade then we will do it for you. And once the British came, they never left. Eventually they took all the tribes that hated each other and those that liked each other and those that did not know and could not speak to each other and said, "You are now all one country, and we are in charge of you." And then there was a Nigeria.

Whoa. Lola looked cautiously across the hall at her coworkers. They were two young Nigerian men, both experienced geologists, both with easy smiles and helpful natures. If they were pissed about how their country got formed, they were hiding it well.

"Lola. Staff meeting at one." This message delivered in a walk-by from Bob, the older American engineer who was loosely in charge of the technical staff. Right. She closed the internet quickly and thought, *Have I got a lot to learn.*

Djimon seemed surprised at the request, but he agreed to come back to the Ebonyi region where Ikenna lived and meet Ikenna at one of his wives' houses for tea and more conversation. He drove in on a Saturday morning just after the clearing of the land had begun for the year's yam crops. After exchanging pleasantries for a full cup and a half, Ikenna took a small sip and a small breath and did his best to tactfully share with Djimon, father to father, his concerns.

The Yoruba man could not have been more understanding. Yes, of course, he already had three children with his first wife and one was a daughter. What had he been thinking, expecting a good father like Ikenna to agree to a marriage so quickly and with such little information. He should clearly have expected more questioning.

Djimon went on to explain to Ikenna that his own mother had come from far away, a Fulani woman from the far north of Nigeria. She had moved to the southwest to marry a Yoruba man, and as Djimon believed himself to be particularly gifted in every arena, he credited his own ample genetic advantages to the mixing of the blood from two such separate regions.

His own first wife had been a local girl selected by his parents, of course, and he had of course respected them and accepted the wife. But now that he was older and had means of his own, he wished to duplicate the wisdom and good fortune of his own father and secure a bride from yet another corner of this fine nation, in hopes of producing sons, and yes even daughters, as physically and mentally gifted as he himself. The specific charms of the girl in question mattered not, as long as she came from a line of fertile, strong, smart people, which Djimon could clearly tell was the case just by meeting Ikenna and seeing all of his fine young children playing in front of the house.

Ikenna nodded at that. Yes, indeed there was a fine strong group of youngsters in his yard. The wife who had just brought in more tea smiled in flattered agreement as well.

"So she is perfect," Djimon explained. "She is young and healthy, not spoken for, and most importantly she clearly brings excellent lineage." He paused, hoping for Ikenna's concurrence. When Ikenna stayed silent, he continued.

"As I explained to you earlier, unlike in your culture, the idea of bringing her into my home to live for awhile as a guest in order for us both to evaluate the situation just isn't accepted, sensible though your custom is." He paused again.

"I've become rather taken with the idea of marrying her, and if it would help to reassure you of that then I am willing to increase the bride price. Say by twenty percent? And as we discussed, to pay the amount to you in full before the marriage."

Still silence. Unbelievable. An Igbo man who was hard to buy. Djimon hesitated, trying to figure out what possible remaining objection Ikenna could have. There were many seconds of silence.

"Will you be good to her?" the father finally asked.

"Oh. Why yes. Of course. Very good to her. I promise."

And with that, Ikenna was satisfied at last.

When Djimon left a bit later after necessary matrimonial arrangements had been made, Ikenna turned to find the wife and share his relief that this marriage would take place after all. But she was nowhere to be found. She had run over to her co-wife's house, bursting with news at the amazing, even-better bride price their brilliant husband had negotiated. The two women jumped and hugged with joy.

Somadina had of course heard through the other women, but she had the manners and sense to keep the information to herself as she served juice to her father the next day. She inquired after his health, his wives' health, his children's health. Finally, as though as an afterthought, he said, "I have been thinking lately about Nwanyi's future." By unspoken agreement they never mentioned Nwanyi to each other, so Somadina was sure that her father was going to give her the news.

"She will be sixteen years old in less than a month," Somadina remarked.

"Plenty old enough for marriage," her father replied.

"No, barely old enough," Somadina corrected. "But a suitable suitor is not always easily found."

"True. Sometimes a father must be more creative on behalf of his children," Ikenna said.

"True," Somadina offered back, at which point Ikenna knew that Somadina knew, and that at the very least she would not fight him on this.

"The stranger about which you have no doubt heard talk has given me his word that he will treat your sister well." This yielded only a stony silence. "Your sister is closer to you than anyone, closer than to her aunts or to my wives. I was hoping you would talk to her. Prepare her a little for what will happen. You know."

Yes, Somadina thought. *I know.* And she assured her father that she would be there in every way for Nwanyi. As always. "Have you told her yet?"

"No," Ikenna sighed. "That is next." And he finished his juice with resignation.

Somadina generally worked hard during the day, caring for her small son and husband with diligence, if not with enthusiasm. She almost always fell asleep early and easily, tired from the work and heat and happy to stretch out on the giant double bed that she shared with her husband and son and content to cool off under the large fan in their small bedroom. However, during the night Somadina's mind seemed to work overtime while she slept, and she often had trouble staying asleep until the morning.

That particular night, Somadina slept poorly and, as was her way when she was worried, she became even more restless as the sky took on the faint dull grey of first light. Dozing and waking, tossing and turning, she kept thinking of the various horrible ways a marriage could go wrong for a shy woman who was far from her family and whose husband had been chosen quickly and unwisely.

That particular night, in the comfortable king-sized bed that she shared with Alex, Lola tossed and turned. She was someone whose body naturally wanted to stay up past bedtime each night, and who therefore always had problems falling asleep. She knew that she tended to do her worrying when she went to bed, and she'd had more restless nights than usual over the past few months, mostly worrying about money.

Alex was a good teacher, he had been a good coach, and he was a man doing exactly what he was meant to be doing. She admired him beyond belief. But he also was not making the salary that was putting kids through college. Zane, turning twenty-three in just a little over two weeks, had finished his bachelor's degree over a year ago at one very expensive Ivy League school. They'd been so proud of him for even getting in that they had sworn to find a way, and every bonus and extra bit had been funneled into his education. Until lively, capable Ariel had gotten into a very prestigious school two years later, with dreams of her own. Then every extra penny had been split between the two.

Now they were still paying on both educations, while Zane was working and trying to save his own money in hopes of returning to graduate school in a year or two. Alex was still driving his 1996 Taurus, and her 2000 Camry wasn't far behind on its journey to the scrap heap.

And then, she'd found herself unexpectedly unemployed, with little debt but also no savings to speak of, and a mass of regularly occurring bills that could not be ignored. The severance package had helped get them through the last few months, and they would manage okay, if she could keep this job for at least a few years xº

no matter what happened with the economy. Geez, she was trying.
...

But tonight's restlessness was different. Not money. Safety? She ran through her loved ones. Alex was next to her and Teddie was asleep upstairs. Yes, she was sure. The cats were quiet and so was the house. She tried hard to hear a subtle background noise that might be sending her signals of which she was barely aware, but there truly was nothing.

Sometimes she still worried about her mom, before she remembered. Right. No mom to worry about now. So not that. And on a weeknight in January, Zane should be sleeping, and Ariel studying. So who? Well, there had been an odd conversation with her sister today.

She and Summer had been very close growing up, in spite of their five-year age difference. It had been just the two of them, with big sister Lola serving as adviser and protector to sweet but far more mischief prone Summer. Lola smiled to herself, remembering how at eight years old she had promised her little sister that she would always protect her. And in fact she had done so, for years shielding Summer from a stern no-nonsense mother, from the Foley brothers next door, even from the dog down the street.

Then their lives had gone very differently. Lola, in Houston, had pretty much gone straight from grad student to married woman and professional while Summer spent years more enjoying life, dating and partying, and had finally, only a decade ago, married an older man with considerably more means, two ex-wives and a handful of grown children of his own. Each sister cheerfully shared and took vicarious joy from the others life, and Lola felt for years that she and Summer had somehow complemented each other well.

Then when Summer married and moved to Denver where Gregg had his primary residence and most of his businesses, she passed on having kids and embraced a life centered around entertaining, caring for her husband, keeping herself attractive, and overseeing a clothing boutique, which her husband owned, an employee ran, and she played at when it suited her. As the years passed, Summer had more trouble understanding Lola's long hours at work and at PTA school carnivals, and Lola had not understood Summer's dedication to pampering herself and Gregg. But beneath the growing lifestyle rift, they still loved each other.

When they had spoken briefly today, Summer's normal effervescence had been a little too bubbly as she avoided questions and turned the conversation back to Lola every time. The more Lola thought about it, the more sure she became that something was wrong. Damn it, she should have persisted and gotten some answers. She was still big sister and protector.

Images of Summer's fluffy blond hair and Gregg's well-trimmed mustache floated through her barely dozing consciousness as she tried to drift off to sleep. It was their images, right? Gregg was a basically friendly man, but he looked harsher than she'd ever seen him. Darker, too. That was weird. And Summer had always been a beauty and had known it. Had she ever seen Summer look that hesitant? It was like she was seeing them, but she wasn't. This was just goofy. Lola fell into an uneasy sleep, promising herself she would call again this week and ask more direct questions.

Djimon knew that the next few days would be crucial and difficult. Money and flattery had eventually won over the old man, though it had taken more of both than he had anticipated. Word had been that the father cared not at all for the girl, which is what he had been seeking, but some vestigial sense of duty must have kicked in and prompted him to become uncharacteristically concerned about the girl's welfare. It did not matter. It had been handled. And some of what Djimon had said was even true. His mother was Fulani.

But at the engagement ceremony, which Djimon had gotten the old man to agree to hold just days after consenting to the marriage, he would basically be on display to the whole village. Suspicious behavior on his part could still void the entire arrangement. It was bad enough that he was an unknown stranger with no family at all attending and acting as his own officiating elder, but at least it was less of a breach of etiquette here than it would have been in his own mother's village. And he had gone to pains to excuse it with a combination of his age, the story he had invented about seeking a wife from afar, and the distance he had traveled.

The greater danger was that someone would see through to his complete lack of interest in the girl. No, more accurately to his repulsion to her. For the biggest lie he had told Ikenna was that he believed that the mixing of genes produced advantages. In fact, Djimon opposed such unions on many levels, and was hoping that he could count on the repulsion he naturally felt towards the unrefined-looking southern Nigerian woman's features to keep him from ever once losing control and planting his seed within this new bride.

It was true that he had searched hard to find the perfect Igbo woman for his needs. He required a girl with no close ties to parents, one whose family for one reason or another might find it expedient to send a daughter elsewhere and would be willing to ultimately lose track of her. In other parts of the world an unwanted pregnancy might suffice for that purpose, but among the children-loving Southeastern Nigerians there simply was no such thing.

So he had been left to find an Igbo daughter who truly was not wanted. Word travels. He had found Nwanyi. And as soon as he set eyes on her he knew she was perfect. But for the next few days, he did need to convincingly play the eager husband to the probing eyes of her kin.

On the night that had been selected, he arrived at her father's house in his best clothing, and knelt before her father. He and Ikenna had agreed to honor some of each of their customs, while improvising a bit to accommodate the particulars of the situation and to move things along a little faster than normal, as he was understandably anxious to return home.

He presented a handwritten letter of proposal tied with a pink ribbon to Ikenna who sat against one wall, with his two wives, his two oldest sons, now both fourteen, the two sisters who had taken the largest hands in raising Nwanyi, and Nwanyi's older sister. All were smiling for joy, except for the older sister who eyed him quizzically. Okay. That was the one with whom he needed to take special care. Everyone else was clearly all for this marriage.

At the father's gesture giving permission to rise, he stood, opened his letter and read aloud his desire to marry Nwanyi. He thought he gave it a good read, but big sister's eyes stayed puzzled. Nwanyi was then brought from the kitchen and presented to him. He had asked that she be veiled, as was the custom of his people, and that no alcoholic wine be drunk, though he knew many a Nigerian Muslim who would forego the prohibition against alcohol for such an occasion. He thought that both the veil and the lack of inhibition-reducing liquor would work in his favor. In the spirit of give and take, he had agreed to present the father with the traditional kola nuts, which he happily did now with a flourish.

When Nwanyi nodded her consent with her face still covered, Djimon had no idea whether it was with eagerness or reluctance, nor did he much care. Ikenna voiced consent on behalf of the rest of the family and Djimon produced an envelope with cash which would suffice as the owo-ori-iyawo, to a Yoruba, or the ika-akalika, to an Igbo, either of which was basically a gift from the groom to allegedly compensate Ikenna for the very great expenses he must have incurred to raise such a magnificent daughter.

Food was produced and tables began to fill and overflow as neighbors now arrived and additional kin showed up. The strong smell of pepper soup mixed with the aroma of fried plantain. Cooked goat and chicken was lavishly provided. Djimon helped himself to the jollof rice, savoring the thick tomato taste while he watched a particularly large man deftly fashion a big helping of stiff white pounded yam into an eating utensil which he then used to expertly scoop up a large portion of the hearty greens-laden fish soup.

Wine was being poured, albeit somewhat discretely, in spite of Djimon's request, which annoyed him. He did not like having his wishes disregarded. But he forced himself to bury his irritation deep, reminding himself that this was all a charade anyway, merely a means to an end, and what was one more tiny piece of play-acting in the grand scheme. Nwanyi's more astute relatives noticed his brief disapproval and his tactful decision to ignore the wine, and it bought Djimon a small measure of approval in their eyes.

x^0

As the evening progressed Djimon was hugged and greeted and inquired about by many guests. He assured all that he could not wait to return for the wedding itself in a month. The hospitality here was tremendous. Oh yes, it was all terribly rushed, but what was a busy businessman like himself to do? And really, why delay when it would be such an auspicious start to the marriage for it to take place on the feast day of St. Valentine, celebrated in so much of the world as a patron saint of love. Wasn't that indeed a fine day and one worth rushing the wedding for? Djimon had been very proud of himself for finding that reason to push the marriage ceremony into the month of February instead of delaying it for months like Ikenna had wanted.

Yes, he agreed, it was indeed true and so very sad that his own mother was ill and his sister attending to her, and they would be unable to make the wedding next month. Mom just was not strong enough to travel. Yes, it was true that his friends and family were mostly busy or gone, so yes he had told Ikenna not to plan on many of his own people there, but then again that was all the more reason to embrace Nwanyi's lovely family, right?

Of course his own kin would host a wonderful welcoming feast for Nwanyi in Lagos once she arrived. What? Umm, yes, of course Nwanyi's kin here would be welcome to attend that feast if they were willing to travel all the way to Lagos. He'd send an invitation, as soon as it was all arranged. Of course.

A fair bit of time passed before he saw that his wife-to-be had removed her veil, to eat of course—how could he object to that—and she was eyeing him with nervous anticipation and just a bit of fear. He nodded with satisfaction. That is a good start, he thought, pleased. I can work well with nervousness and fear.

On January 21, 2009, Barack Obama was sworn in as the forty-fourth president of the United States. While most of Lola's Texan acquaintances were loudly unenthused about the event, Lola's Nigerian coworkers were genuinely pleased by it. Lola herself was quietly hopeful that this multi-racial intellectual with an apparently kind heart and African roots would be just what America, and maybe the world, needed.

On Monday January 26, <u>The New York Times</u> reported that in one day alone U.S. companies announced over sixty-two thousand job cuts in their offices worldwide. <u>Reuters</u> added that Iceland's prime minister said he would resign as his coalition government had fallen apart under the pressures of the bankrupt country's financial crisis. Lola marveled that an entire country could actually go bankrupt.

That same day, Lola celebrated her forty-ninth birthday at a favorite local restaurant. She and Alex toasted to her being employed again. Teddie, always her sensitive cheerleader, gave her a small magnet to keep near her desk at work, and Lola smiled as she read it. "Everything is okay in the end. If it's not okay, then it's not the end." Wisdom from a wise thirteen-year-old.

This could be so much worse, she muttered to herself, wondering how many others could not, would not find work as easily as she had. Times were tough. She resolved quietly to appreciate what had gone right, move on from what had gone wrong, and to do whatever it would take to make this new job work out well for a few more years.

x^0

Chapter 4. February 2009

Q: What else is easy to communicate telepathically?

A: In modern society, popular music seems to have a surprising ability to transmit directly from mind to mind. One may hear a song "playing" in ones head, only to find that another person with mild receptive abilities will "hear' the song also and start to whistle or hum it. This is frequently unsettling to people, and is often a person's most concrete encounter with telepathy.
(from "FAQ's about telepathy at
http://www.tothepowerofzero.org/)

Over the next few weeks, Lola finished working her way through the interpretation of the small structure located in one corner of her company's lease. As happened so often in the oil business, her company had subleased the drilling rights from another company which had done so from another company, and now the term of the lease was near expiration and either a well would need to be drilled soon or the lease would need to be relinquished untested.

Because of the convenient fact that oil floats on water (check your salad dressing), one looks for oil in high places where the tiny coarse rock grains have enough spaces in between them to hold a good bit of oil. A rock with ten percent of its volume as space is a good rock to someone in Lola's profession. Find the highest spot in it, put a nice tight rock like shale above it, which has virtually no spaces into which the wily oil can sneak out over the eons, and someone like Lola gets the message. Drill here.

This part of her job sat somewhere between treasure hunting and puzzle solving, and Lola had to admit that her day-to-day work would not have made a bad 3D video game if someone added a little bit of music and some glossy effects. And, okay, maybe a car chase or two. Lola enjoyed herself as she twisted and turned her 3D visualization of the rocks on her computer screen, humming as she looked for shifts in the rock layers known as faults. Then she had to laugh when she realized what song she was humming.

Cyndi Lauper's 1984 hit *"Time After Time"* had once been a favorite of hers, and now that Lola thought about it, it made rather good music to prospect by, given how the lyrics seemed to reassure her about finding something or someone. She was surprised she hadn't remembered the song sooner. She sang a little louder.

"Time After Time." Bob, the older engineer in the group, identified the song as he walked by her door. "Geez Lola," he said, "I've had that song in my head all damn morning. What are you doing singing it?"

"No idea. Maybe we listened to the same radio station on the way to work?" she guessed.

"I only listen to my iPod," he replied.

Lola shrugged and went back to looking for indicators of what filled those tiny spaces in the rock (Oil? Natural gas? Salt water? It was never anything interesting like tequila or bubble bath. …) and worked until she was satisfied.

Meanwhile, of course, personal life went on as well. On February 1, 2009, the Pittsburg Steelers beat the Arizona Cardinals twenty-seven to twenty-three in Super Bowl XXXXIII. An estimated ninety-nine million viewers watched, including Alex. Lola passed on the football, but did watch some of the commercials.

February also brought a special evening Skype session with Zane, with the three of them singing an enthusiastic Happy Birthday. The family songfest clearly embarrassed Zane as his housemates laughed and made faces in the background. He lived with an odd mix of four other recent grads, each one bright and more than a bit unusual. Lola had met and liked every one of them. Zane, who had been an almost scary-smart child and adolescent, had generally had few friends growing up, and in some grades it had seemed he really had none. Yet here it was clear that behind all their good-natured teasing of Zane, these people genuinely liked and appreciated her unique son. Lola suspected that there would be some sort of birthday celebration there as well, after the phone call was over.

Meanwhile Summer and Lola played phone tag, each leaving

the other cheery warm messages to have a really good day and call back soon.

On February 14, actress Salma Hayek married her beau in a "romantic civil ceremony" according to the celebrity-wedding website. NBA player Marko Jaric also opted for a quiet Valentine's Day wedding with supermodel Adriana Lima, while skiing in Jackson Hole, Wyoming. And, the morning of February 14, 2009, Nwanyi relaxed in the ritual pre-wedding bath and enjoyed the sensation of her older sister and two aunts scrubbing her back and her legs.

She could not remember a single time in her life when she had been the center of attention like this, and in fact most of the time she had the odd suspicion that people just wished she would go away. Somadina tried to tell her that if she believed that then it would become the truth, but that was easy for someone like Somadina to say. But today, just today, was all about her and she had never been happier in her life. "You are glowing just a bit, little one," an aunt had said with surprise and approval. Somadina beamed.

The wedding day began at Ikenna's house, with the ceremonially bathed Nwanyi draped in a beautiful gold brocade, which would match the brocade worn by her new husband to the ceremony. Nwanyi had wanted the two of them to wear lavender, her favorite color, but for some reason Djimon had objected, and gold had been selected instead.

Nwanyi was decked with ornate necklaces, bracelets and anklets, and an elaborate gold headdress with a semi-transparent veil. As was the custom with her particular kin, once the guests arrived at the house Nwanyi was expected to engage in a playful tradition of selling eggs to them. While the custom was intended originally to show one's new husband that one would be an enterprising asset, in today's world it was of course really just for fun and the guests gleefully bought the eggs, to Nwanyi's delight.

The next tradition involved Nwanyi offering palm wine to her husband, but in this case Ikenna had agreed to mango juice instead. Nwanyi, with a large, ornate goblet of juice in hand, nervously began her hunt for Djimon. She knew that this part of the ceremony also involved the guests playfully distracting both her and Djimon to prolong her efforts to offer him the drink. But as the game wore on, although the guests were increasingly enjoying their role, Nwanyi began to get genuinely nervous. The guests may have been less playful if they had understood the degree of Nwanyi's growing distress. She wasn't just a jittery bride. The joy of being the center of attention had started to wane and she was now a hesitant soul realizing that she was about to leave the only home she had ever known in the company of a man to whom she had never spoken.

By the time Nwanyi found Djimon, she was visibly shaking. From across the room a worried Somadina looked up. Timidly, Nwanyi approached the man she was about to marry. He looked up at the goblet with feigned surprise. As she reached the goblet out towards him, he playfully reached to take it from her, then withdrew his hand an inch in pretend nervousness, with just a touch of fake jitteriness which was almost but not quite a mock of her own behavior. The crowd chuckled good-naturedly. But Nwanyi's hands, shaking with real nervousness, could not respond so fast, and the ceremonial juice went crashing to the floor.

Given the traditional importance of the offering of the goblet, under other circumstances the crowd might have gasped. But the momentum for laughter was already there, so instead of gasping, the uncomfortable wedding guests laughed, and an overwrought and mortified Nwanyi burst into tears. As Djimon looked closely for the first time at Nwanyi's lowered eyes that she now dared not raise to him, he saw her deep embarrassment, and sensed the self-loathing behind it. And he thought, *This could not be more perfect.*

It took both aunts, Somadina, and another cousin to calm Nwanyi down enough to get her to the church. "That goblet nonsense is a silly piece of fluff that doesn't matter a bit," the kinder of the two aunts assured her.

"They laughed because they did not know what else to do," Somadina insisted. "Forget it. You are the beautiful bride today. Let's go." But Nwanyi did not feel beautiful anymore, and the attention of the crowd no longer felt warm or made her happy.

Thus the teary-eyed bride and the mostly silent groom met in the local church that celebrated both Christ and Chukwu and was friendly to Allah as well. It was agreed that the once-again veiled Nwanyi would present her husband with a Bible, and he would present her with a Qur'an, and a local official would pronounce them wed in the eyes of all Gods and all people, which he did. And so, they became husband and wife without ever once truly looking each other in the eye.

The church ceremony was followed by more food, more drink, live music, and much dancing. Djimon apologized profusely that none of his kin had been able to attend after all, being all aging and ill, or scattered and busy. Nwanyi's people found the absence exceedingly odd, but fortunately Ikenna had many friends, and his wives both came from big nearby families happy to contribute to the celebration with hearty consumption and lively participation. Ikenna could have sworn that the larger of his brother-in-laws had consumed an entire goat at the wedding feast.

As <u>the celebration</u> wore on, Ikenna watched as his tall and stately daughter Somadina carried her one-year-old son Kwemto on her hip as she visited with relatives, and watched with even more interest as eager husband Azuka attentively brought his wife food and drink. Although Azuka had always been clearly more smitten with Somadina than she with him, Ikenna suspected Azuka's unusually generous behavior today might have been because Somadina was pregnant again. Could he, Ikenna, really be that lucky? This would be not just a second grandchild, but given Nwanyi's impending departure, also a happy distraction which would make life easier for all.

Although the dancing would continue on into the night, it would normally be expected that at some point the bride and groom would exit the celebration to do what brides and grooms are expected to do the world over.

However, as Djimon had no suitable home of his own or of his family's to which to take his bride that night and accommodations for travelers in Ikenna's small town were meager, it had been agreed in the initial discussion that Djimon would continue to lodge with the local family who housed strangers, and that Nwanyi would be permitted to spend her last night there in her sister's house to say goodbye. Their married life would truly begin after they left the village. Djimon considered the success of that particular piece of negotiation, viewed by others as a concession on his part, as a stroke of immense good fortune.

    Azuka was generally an easygoing and considerate man who had eyed Somadina ever since he was a boy. His parents were kindly, and inclined to indulge their quiet, well-behaved only child who had, after all, asked for very little. So they had saved money and worked hard to set his marriage to Somadina in motion because they recognized that there was nothing that would make Azuka happier. Fortunately, Ikenna had no other particular plans for his eldest daughter and had, in fact, been smart enough to recognize that having a devoted husband was a fine situation.

    Young Somadina, strong and independent, had neither objected to nor been enthused about the marriage. She had been pragmatic, accepting the duties and responsibilities of being a wife without complaint or apparent resentment and giving Azuka no cause for complaint either. And yet Azuka knew that his ardor was not particularly returned.

    And because he was not only physically attracted to Somadina but he also truly cared for her, he responded by giving her ample space, asking for little of her time and attention and keeping his physical demands to a minimum. She seemed to recognize his adjustments on her behalf, and had slowly over the past two years responded to his behavior with a growing appreciation and, maybe, even something that approached friendship.

    The night of Nwanyi's wedding, however, Azuka had danced and drank and danced some more and now he dearly wanted his wife in the most basic of ways. But he also realized that this was one time in which his needs would be less welcome than usual. As he approached the small house that had been given to him on his own wedding day, he saw the two sisters sitting on the porch step, arms around each other, a set of hands entwined. His Somadina was talking softly, chiding Nwanyi into blushing giggles, and he thought, *No. Definitely not. I best leave them alone.*

With a touch of sadness, he headed back to the music, admittedly open to whatever temptations might come his way.

Given all the differences in their natures, it was hard for anyone else to understand why the two sisters were the best of friends. Some thought it had to do with the loss of their mother, each representing to the other that missing piece of their lives that no aunt or stepmother had been able to fill. Others, if they were more perceptive, noticed that Nwanyi needed encouragement, love, and a protector and that Somadina needed to give encouragement, love, and protection. The cynical might add that from such complementary needs the deepest of human bonds are formed. But the simple truth was, well, simpler. They enjoyed each other. For under Nwanyi's insecurities and Somadina's stunning poise, they laughed at the same jokes, generally liked the same foods, clothes, and people, and shared many of the same ideas about life. They had fun together. And while motherhood had, of necessity, turned much of Somadina's attention elsewhere, she was still deeply aware that her best friend was leaving town and entering into a situation where contact could be infrequent.

Protector that she naturally was, however, that night she worked hard to keep Nwanyi laughing and brushed away any return to sadness with reminders of how cell phones and computers had made the country, indeed the world, a much smaller place. They were not so poor, they could both access such items, and then they would laugh every day like they were now, and visit often in person as well. She, Somadina, had plans to start earning income soon, once the baby was just a bit older and suckling less, and so they would be able to talk and be together often. Somadina promised.

They slept side by side that night with the baby Kwemto between them, and the next morning Somadina worked particularly hard to make her thoughts and feelings strong and cheerful as she bid goodbye. She tried to reach out to Djimon with a farewell that was both accepting yet a bit cautionary, but as she clasped his hand all she could feel was a sort of cold, slick metal sensation. How odd. "Take good care of my baby sister," she tried to keep her voice light.

"Oh I certainly will." His voice was equally light when he replied, but it filled her mouth with a taste of the same malleable metal that she could almost feel sliding around uncomfortably between her back teeth.

Then as Nwanyi got into the passenger side of Djimon's car and the car pulled out onto the road, two things happened. One, Somadina saw a disheveled Azuka out of the corner of her eye as he tried to unobtrusively enter their house. Two, she felt the odd sensation of a window opening in her head. Just a crack, but she could swear that she could feel a cool breeze blowing in information, where there had been none for a very long time. So as the car drove away and she fought back tears, mixed in with her questions and her worry and her sorrow, she felt wonder. And a growing sense of power that she had not felt since she was a very small child.

Lola woke from a sound sleep, with a sharp pang of sorrow. She shook her head, trying to remember what the dream had been but she could find no dream. Just worry. Questions. Frustration with someone. Alex? Why? There was sorrow, draped over her like a heavy blanket. Her best girl friend was leaving town? That wasn't possible. ... she didn't have a best girl friend here, really. Nonetheless Lola found herself fighting back tears as she lay in bed. It was so strange that she started to laugh. Then, she felt something else. A breeze, in her mind, and with it a sense of power that was familiar. Lola felt like an old skill was being reawakened. What was it that she was remembering how to do?

Somadina paused before she entered the house. *No, not now. I will only miss Nwanyi and fight with Azuka*, she thought as the idea of both activities made her heart sink. So on impulse, Somadina rearranged her half awake baby boy onto her hip and walked the short distance over to her father's house, looking for one of her maternal aunts. Both aunts were certainly going back home today, and if she could get a ride with either family, she could borrow plenty of clothes for herself and Kwemto and have a short visit. A few days away might do her a world of good, and given how close they all knew that she was with Nwanyi, neither aunt would ask about her lack of packing but would just accept her as a welcome guest. It was good to have relatives like that. And better yet, both aunts had access to cell phones, so she could call Azuka's father and ask him to let her husband know not to worry. In a few days, when she would get around to making the phone call.

Although oil seeps were seen in the Niger Delta in the 1900s, no one then could have predicted how the discovery of massive quantities of oil would eventually shape the futures of entire countries such as Nigeria and, in fact, would help shape the politics of the world. Shell Oil made the first commercial discovery west of Port Harcourt in 1956 and Nigeria first shipped crude oil to the international market in 1958. A year later the Nigerian government made what was arguably one of its single smartest moves ever and introduced regulation of oil industry profits, originally mandating a fifty/fifty split between the government and the oil company. On October 1, 1960, when Nigeria gained its independence from Britain, it was producing <u>seventeen thousand barrels of oil per day</u>.

Bob was looking over Lola's presentation materials when he stopped and squinted at her stratigraphic column, designed to show the various important rock layers to her audience as she made her arguments for her drilling location.

"Where did you get this?" he asked.

She explained that she had copied it from somewhere in the publicly available literature, the way folks in her profession usually did. Why?

"We just don't usually refer to it as the Biafra formation here, that's all," he said. "You might want to use an alternative name for it."

That was odd. So Lola went back to the internet.

In 1966 and 1967 there were two consecutive revolts as the various larger ethnic groups in Nigeria vied for control of the government. The second one put the Northerners in charge and rather than keep on fighting, or accept this new rule, the southeastern Igbo chose to secede, and they formed the independent nation of Biafra. After a protracted battle and a brutal blockade, somewhere between one and three million Biafrans died, mostly due to starvation and disease. The death toll was of course the highest for the children, the elderly, the ill, and the pregnant and nursing women. Biafra surrendered in 1970.

Médecins Sans Frontières, or <u>Doctors Without Borders</u> as it is called here, was one of the few charities the Zeitman family had supported enthusiastically over the years. Lola was surprised to learn that this international medical humanitarian organization, which provides aid worldwide to people whose survival is threatened by violence, neglect, or catastrophe, was founded in response to the painful ordeal of Biafra by frustrated French doctors who were prohibited from speaking out during the conflict. Today, while Doctors Without Borders remains firmly apolitical, it allows and even encourages its volunteers to speak out on behalf of victims anywhere. In 1999, MSF received the Nobel Peace Prize.

Some speculated that the rich oil resources in Biafra's portion of the Niger Delta were part of the reason both Nigeria and Britain fought so hard to prevent Biafra's secession. "You think?" Lola muttered as she read on. And, in fact, oil production had risen from seventeen thousand to more than a million barrels of oil a day by 1970. Nigeria joined OPEC in 1971.

Since then, hundreds of billions of dollars have flowed into Nigeria from oil, making up the vast majority of the country's economy. Although over the decades the government has upped its share of the split to as high as eighty percent on some leases, residents of the Niger delta continue to complain that they receive a disproportionately small amount of that revenue while bearing the brunt of the environmental damage to their land and fishing areas.

Biafra remains a difficult memory for all Nigerians, and to a lesser extent to the British and Russians who supported the highly criticized blockade, and to the Canadians and French who sided and even fought with Biafra. Some Americans remain embarrassed at how easily their own nation was persuaded to look the other direction. After ten minutes on the internet reading about Biafra, Lola agreed with Bob and found another name. It was a matter of simple respect for anyone in her potential audience who might have lost a loved one in the conflict forty years ago.

  The well that Lola and her coworkers were proposing had to be approved next by their partner company, an indigenous company headquartered in Lagos. Lola was told to be ready to present the following Monday, when the appropriate parties would be in Houston on other business and wished to see her work while they were nearby. It had been a long time since she had made a real presentation to anyone. These days, in smaller companies it seemed that every layer of management generally just wandered by an individual's work station for a live update, or one emailed specific slides (okay, they weren't even slides anymore, they were files) to whomever needed a piece of particular information, cc'ing (okay, there wasn't any real carbon copy involved here) anyone who might be vaguely interested. The good news was that she no longer spent days overseeing the drafting, coloring, and labeling of paper displays to show her ideas. The bad news was that she, and everyone she knew, had to make time to sort through masses of emails with dozens of pieces of information each day.

  But these particular Nigerian dignitaries wanted a formal presentation, so a formal presentation they would have. Lola knew that exhibiting her work to a room full of people had always been one of her strengths, and she welcomed this opportunity to show off just a bit for her new employer. Yet even she was taken aback when she walked into the conference room to get set up.

  American meetings had long since become smaller, more informal, and had a tendency to inch into starting later than scheduled, with the occasional self-correcting gimmick like fining the last participant to show up, which would have the effect of setting the "late" clock back to zero so that the creep into lateness could begin again.

  Oddly this phenomenon had nothing to do with laziness or lack of promptness, but rather was a function of everyone trying to be more efficient. Because no one wanted to waste their own time waiting for the other attendees, everyone tried to time their arrival to right before the real meeting would start. Thus, time-conscious Americans tended to start their meetings later and later as they each strived to waste less and less time.

So Lola was more than surprised to walk into a room filled with twenty or so people, all more than fifteen minutes early to the meeting, many of them dressed in full formal African regalia and the rest in impeccable Western business attire, both males and females, all sitting respectfully and quietly with their hands folded in their laps, waiting for her. Watching her. Acting courteously like they had not a better thing in the world to do than to listen carefully to everything that she had to say. She smiled nervously and began to hook up her laptop to the projector, explaining that it would be just a few minutes before she would start. No one seemed in any hurry, and of course everyone knew that they had to wait for the Americans who would rush in five minutes late.

Lola regained her usual composure and the presentation went well. A few of the attendees, Lola suspected, had been invited along as a courtesy and were largely disinterested in what she had to say. They simply listened politely, unlike Americans who would have been far more likely to be texting messages. Others, however, asked excellent questions and contributed helpful information in a spirited yet respectful style that Lola found she enjoyed.

As always, she smiled often and adapted her style to the cadence and tone of the audience. Over the years she had learned to keep this latter tendency in check, only because if she was not careful she knew that she would soon be imitating the accents and gestures of those to whom she was speaking. This rather annoying tendency of hers had embarrassed her deeply more than once, and she was afraid that various parties throughout the years had suspected she was making fun of them. Nothing of course could be further from the truth, but Lola had learned to be more careful with this empathetic ability of hers that seemed to sometimes turn into a force of its own. In the end, she kept the empathic thing in check and knew that the presentation had gone smoothly. The well would be drilled. She did not, however, expect the next turn of events.

In the days that followed, Djimon discovered how extraordinarily fortunate his choice in a second wife had been. Throughout the drive southwest toward Lagos, sometimes over major highways and twice over bad roads as he detoured for "business meetings," Nwanyi was not only timid, she asked for almost nothing and did not even seem to expect kindness from him. She stopped her attempts at conversation early on when they were met with stony silence, only asking twice to use his cell phone to call her sister. He informed her curtly that his charger worked poorly and he was saving the battery for important calls. After the second time she did not ask again.

And she appeared to be fearful about sex, or at least shy enough about it that although they slept in the same bed at night, she never brought up his lack of interest. As they traveled he saw to it that she stayed covered and had whatever meager food and water she required, and in return she simply did not complain to him. He figured with satisfaction that she was scared of him and vowed to see that useful condition continue throughout what he had come to think of as "phase two." Phase one, of course, had been finding and procuring her.

Four days later they arrived at his home, where Mairo (May row), his true and beloved wife with her beautiful Fulani features, dutifully got Nwanyi settled into a particularly cramped and poorly ventilated room in the rear of the house, and promptly assigned her a sizable share of the less desirable household chores that would normally have fallen to the servants. Djimon had to smile. Even though Mairo understood all too well how important Nwanyi was to their plans, and what little husbandly interest Djimon actually had in the woman, she still was apparently not inspired to exhibit the least bit of kindness to the Igbo. Which, now that Djimon thought about it, was just as well.

It had never occurred to him that the two women could actually become friends, given Mairo's tough Northern heritage and deep devotion to their cause. However, if such friendship were to happen, it would throw a major kink into the plans. It was just as well that he let Mairo inflict all the petty insults that she wanted.

"You're going where?" It was one of the rare times that Alex was genuinely annoyed with her. "I thought travel was not part of this job. Come on Lola. Be sensible. They kidnap people in Nigeria. This is not some youthful canoe adventure of yours, or backpacking across Europe with your college boyfriend."

"We didn't go to Europe. We went to Canada."

His scowl prevented further comment. Instead, "Just tell them no. You are not available."

"In my profession you don't tell your employer that. It's not like I work for a school district where they can't fire you, dear!"

Instantly she regretted saying that. Damn. She felt the flash of hurt on his face herself. But the simple fact was of course that she wanted to go. She loved to travel, absolutely anywhere, and travel opportunities that did not involve visiting relatives, attending conferences for work, or cheering on children engaged in kids' activities, had been few and far between for too many years and all had been predictably tame. She couldn't remember the last time there had been even a little adventure involved in going somewhere, and this from the geeky girl with the thrill-seeking side to her who had once spelunked through caves, rappelled off of the side of her dorm building, and jumped out of an airplane practically the minute she turned eighteen. And yes, she did have a bit of an issue with Alex telling her what to do even if he actually wasn't.

"My company has excellent security," she lied. In fact, her old company had excellent security worldwide for its traveling employees. Her new company, well, she was under the impression that she would have some sort of an armed escort and a driver while she was there which would certainly be plenty. And she did not want Alex to worry. Really.

"I will be flying there and then whisked from the airport to a perfectly predictable hotel chain which you have heard of and stayed at yourself. I will go to the office, make my presentation which I honestly had no idea they would like so very much, spend another night at the nice hotel, get escorted back to the airport, and come straight home. I promise. You'll barely have time to rent and watch one of those inane movies about a bad sports team that develops a lot of heart and finally wins that I know you watch when I'm gone."

"Teddie and I watch them," he said a little defensively. "She likes the heart part. I like the sports part. It works."

"Whatever. You won't even have time to miss me."

Chapter 5. March 2009

Somadina stayed away longer than she had planned, trying to sort through the strange mix of emotions in her head and working to get a grip on the influx of new information which she was picking up from those around her. She spoke to Azuka twice during the two weeks she was gone, assuring him that she and baby were fine and she would be home soon. Finally she knew that she had to go home if for no other reason than the fact that both Kwemto and Azuka missed each other so much. It was unfair to continue to keep them apart. She caught a ride from her uncle's brother who was traveling that way anyway, and came home unannounced late Sunday afternoon. She headed to her kitchen, thinking to make a cup of tea and to just sit by herself for a few minutes, but Azuka was already at the kitchen table, his head in his hands and a cup of tea in front of him. To his credit, he made no effort to avoid her, and as she took the chair across from him he met her look. "I'm sorry," he said simply.

"For what?"

"Don't be childish Somadina. Please. I know you know. It was your sister's wedding and your last night with her and I went out and had sex with another woman. It was a very selfish thing to do."

And of course she knew, and would have known by his behavior even if she could not have felt the shame radiating from him in waves. "Who?" she asked. Oddly enough she was curious.

"Chika."

Great. Chika had sex with any man who was willing, which was bad enough. She and Somadina had never particularly liked each other, which was probably worse and Somadina suspected that Chika's enthusiasm for Azuka might have had more than a bit to do with that, although she would not insult Azuka's pride by telling him so. But the real problem was Chika's husband. He traveled often on business and everyone in town knew that he bragged about the prostitutes he bought in the bigger cities. Somadina felt a small sharp worry grow. "Azuka, did you?"

"No," he sighed. "I did not. I did not have one. And I was too drunk to care."

"So there could be a child? A disease?"

"Yes. There could be both."

They sat in silence for several minutes. Azuka got up and poured himself more tea and without asking poured her a cup as well.

"So," Azuka offered, "I have decided that I am going to divorce you."

"What? Don't be ridiculous. It was one night. Even I do not wish to overreact like that."

"I'm not overreacting. I understand what a poor choice I made and what a very poor choice Chika was. So it is just a temporary divorce and it is only between us. We will speak of it to no one. I have some money saved. After enough time has passed, it is three months I think, I will go to the clinic and I will get the test. We both know <u>the disease</u> to be feared. Then when I get the results I will bring them to you."

"I have never heard of a man behaving in such a way."

"Well it is the way I wish to behave, Somadina. I would not pass this disease on to you, possibly to our unborn child, because I did one stupid thing. Think about it. And if the worst has happened then we will make the divorce permanent."

Somadina could not believe that Azuka was volunteering to do this most unusual thing for her. So it was only fair to tell him.

"My body began its monthly cleaning at the wedding, Azuka. I do not know why it always seems to happen to me on special occasions, which is so annoying. But I did not have a chance to tell you in all the excitement. I am sorry, but it looks like I am not pregnant after all."

Azuka nodded slowly. "Perhaps, given all this, it is for the best," he said. He smiled a little sadly. "We remain privately divorced nonetheless."

"So what happens if your test comes back positive?" Somadina asked.

"Then we make the divorce public and real. You can tell everyone it is my fault. I won't care. And my family will not ask for the bride price back, of course. I know that my parents will be okay with that, and if they are not, then I make good money in the repair shop already. I can pay them back. Your father can keep his share, you can keep yours."

"No Azuka. I won't do that. You will need medicine. After awhile you won't be able to work."

"And you Somadina will be raising our wonderful son. You have no real way of making a living, you've spent the past two years mostly pregnant and nursing. I want you to open a shop of your own, or learn to make something to sell. You are very resourceful and that money needs to start you on a new life. Unless of course," he added with more sorrow, "you wish to remarry right away. Then if he is particularly rich, yes I might take the money back after all."

Somadina had to smile at that. "You know, Azuka, odds are very good that after one night you are fine. Especially if you didn't do anything particularly, uh, unusual with her."

He laughed a little. "No dear. We had one very quick and not particularly good bout of the most normal, basic sex imaginable. It was over before it had barely started."

"So," she asked, admittedly just a bit comforted by that news, "what exactly is your plan if the test comes back negative? You reclaim me as your rightful wife?"

"No," he answered very seriously. "We remain divorced."

"What?"

"Yes. And I propose to you. All over again. And you may say yes or no."

"Azuka, don't be daft. I already said yes once."

"No you didn't, Somadina. Your father said yes. What you did was not object."

In fact, Somadina thought, that was exactly what had happened. She knew quite well that at eighteen heading into nineteen, her father was going to find someone for her and soon, and the gentle boy Azuka seemed like the lesser of many evils. She could count a dozen worse types of husband without even trying. Why she could have ended up herself with Djimon, or someone like him. Clearly her father was not particularly adept at choosing husbands for his daughters. So she had accepted an acceptable situation, when it chose her. What was wrong with that?

"Somadina, I have wanted you for my wife as long as I can remember. My parents indulged me mightily by seeing that I got to have you. But now I understand, that one can have a woman, but not have her. So this time you will really get to choose. If you say no to me, we will divorce quietly. You and your father can both still keep your money. You should still use it to find a way to support yourself and our son. I will still help to raise him. Tell people whatever you want. Tell them I was unfaithful. Tell them I treated you poorly. Tell them I am impotent. No. Wait. Don't tell them that."

"You can always disprove that rumor for yourself," she laughed a little in spite of herself.

"And finally, you should know that I also want you to take your share of the bride money and find a better way to support yourself even in the unlikely event of the remaining third alternative. All women should have a livelihood in this world Somadina. And you are talented. Learn to do whatever suits you."

"Wait," she was confused now. "What is this unlikely third alternative?"

"You know. I am fine. I ask you to marry me. This time, you say yes. And you mean it."

Mairo was quite happy with Djimon's choice in a second wife. For starters the young woman did not seem overly bright, but of course to Mairo most of the southern women seemed less refined and even less intelligent. This girl was also uneducated, which was a plus, having never been to formal school at all although unfortunately a sister had taught her to read and write English fairly well. She was mostly docile, with unbelievably low self-esteem and expectations. Finally, and most importantly, she was unattractively short and scrawny, with small furtive eyes and a particularly flat, broad nose which Mairo thought made her thoroughly ugly. Mairo's heart had lifted the second she had set eyes on her.

Over the first few weeks Mairo applied herself to ensuring that Nwanyi remained housebound, as was common enough for women in some of the more traditional households. In order to arouse no suspicions, Nwanyi was allowed a short weekly cell phone call home, which Mairo supervised, encouraging Nwanyi to explain that Djimon wished not to waste money on unnecessary or lengthy contact, and telling her bluntly to be positive if she wished to have dinner. Nwanyi was smart enough to comply.

Mairo also went out of her way to see to it that Nwanyi was pretty much accepted and ignored by her own three small children, who quickly categorized the new woman as an unimportant servant in their own minds. Other nearby kin, neighbors who visited, and even the few household servants which they employed were all told that the new wife was "odd", a sort of charitable project of Djimon's. Mairo liked to laugh that she could not imagine what the man was thinking, but all were advised in a friendly conspiratorial whisper that the strange, quiet woman was just a little unbalanced and best left alone. And strangely enough, being ignored seemed to be exactly what Nwanyi was used to.

Djimon had seemed just a little surprised and slightly amused to notice that Mairo was taking such a strict hand with the submissive Nwanyi, even intimating to her that maybe for starters her treatment bordered on the unnecessarily cruel. As far as Mairo was concerned, she didn't need all that book-learning to understand how to control someone. She had small children. She had female relatives. If you don't give anyone an inch right from the very beginning, then they can't find a weakness in you to exploit. Mairo personally thought that one did not need all that schooling to understand psychology.

On March 9, 2009, all the major indices on the New York Stock Exchange hit new lows. Most traders had thought the market had bottomed in late November, but after bouncing back a little in early 2009, stocks had proceeded to fall off a cliff. Though there was no way of knowing it at the time, for years later the stock price chart of virtually every stock publically traded in the world would make a jagged, irregularly shaped *V*, with March 9, 2009 sitting at the very bottom of the shape.

This particular evening, it was Teddie who greeted her at the door with a hug, her head of thick curly dark hair burrowing into her mom's shoulder. Lola tried to muster the energy to hug back with equal enthusiasm. She had been on the new job now about two months, and she was still exhausted each night. She had forgotten how being totally out of one's comfort zone just wore one out. From figuring out parking and lunch to learning new software and email protocol, she had been making a series of small adjustments every time she turned around. The past week had been made worse with the arrival of her new computer, and the resulting software upgrade when they migrated her project to the new machine. Now the damn icons were all a little different and she had just been starting to figure out what was where. She just wanted to sleep all weekend.

But Teddie's hug had a purpose. "I was hoping we could go shopping tomorrow? Maybe get a few new things to wear to school?" Teddie's big dark eyes were hopeful and pleading.

Ah yes, now that mom was making money again. Lola told herself not to be so cynical. It was, after all, the start of Teddie and Alex's spring break, and this year they had opted for a quiet stay at home, with both of the older two staying put as well. Surely they could at least afford a little shopping trip.

"Of course Teddie. Let's make it in the afternoon, okay? Mom wants to sleep in." And she told herself that she should consider herself lucky that her thirteen-year-old daughter still wanted to be seen with her. Best get a good night's sleep, wake up refreshed and enjoy the time together with her youngest child while it lasted.

But sleep that night would not come. At first Lola thought she was just too wound up from work. The bottle of wine and rented movie that she and Alex shared had not done their job of relaxing her, and Teddie's request that two of her many girlfriends be allowed at the last minute to sleepover had precluded the intimate ending to the evening that Lola would have preferred. Now Alex lay snoring quietly once again while she and her pillow did their dance. Flop. Punch. Tilt. The pillow was never right these days. Lola finally just started to doze.

"You hit me!" Good grief. Lola sat upright, completely awake. It was Summer's face she had seen, in the start of what seemed like a dream, and it had been contorted with anger and shock. At Lola? At Gregg ? Lola could not even imagine him doing such a thing. But she felt the fear. Summer's fear? Her own fear? Actually, for the life of her it seemed like someone else's fear, but that made no sense whatsoever. She stared up at the bedroom ceiling fan, calming down.

Then she remembered staring up at a ceiling fan once before, having had a very similar sensation. That had happened, hadn't it? Except there had been no punching or fear involved then. It had been something more pleasant. And hadn't she been almost asleep that time as well? And also overly tired, and overwrought about work?

Of course. The night before she made her first big lease sale presentation. Massively pregnant and highly emotional. At the time it had seemed so real, and lying in bed trying to fall back asleep staring at the ceiling fan, she had decided that it was her baby, little Zane, whose mind she had heard. So. It was happening again.

Somadina remembered as a small child taking for granted how easily she had sensed the feelings of others. After Nwanyi's birth she guessed that she must have taught herself to muffle the input, although she had no memory of doing so.

Now that Nwanyi was gone, she felt the ability coming back. Somadina lived in a world in which she had easily accepted unexplained phenomenon, and being unusual did not frighten her. She found the feelings of those around her to be mostly vague— unfocused joy, fear, anger, discomfort—all of which she was learning how to ignore with only a little concentration.

But Somadina's worries about her sister remained only a nagging notion. Even as Somadina found that she was picking up more and more from those around her, she still could not get a good grasp on Nwanyi and how she was doing. It frustrated her. Maybe it was because her sister was so far away?

Nwanyi had already made a dutiful call to her father's cell phone on the two previous Sunday afternoons, the first time to let him know that she had arrived safely in Lagos and the second time to assure him that all was well. After hearing of the timing of the first two calls, Somadina made a point of going to her father's house on the third Sunday, and, as she hoped, she got to speak to her sister herself. The conversation had been short. It appeared that phone time was unusually closely monitored in the household and, Somadina sensed, it was not a private conversation. Nwanyi sounded more quiet and restrained on the phone than Somadina had ever heard her.

Then, on the following Saturday morning, four weeks after the wedding day, Somadina lay in bed barely awake, as Azuka had taken Kwemto outside to play so that she could sleep. She sat up in bed and felt a surge of confidence and determination, as though she had made up her mind to confront someone with a well-thought out and entirely justified complaint. She felt strong. She felt certain. And then, she felt surprise. Hurt. Physical pain. Complete confusion. What had gone wrong? Where she had expected a little sympathy and even a little affection, there had been none. Nothing.

Somadina got out of bed with her face stinging and a strong feeling of nausea. She stood by the side of the bed, saw Nwanyi in her mind, and felt tears on a burning cheek.

The next day the rains started, coming earlier this year than usual. She walked to her father's house anyway and waited all Sunday afternoon. There was no call from Nwanyi.

They had been married exactly four weeks when he lost his temper with her, and that really annoyed Djimon. He prided himself on better self-control. Did not he of all people know that it was so important to stick to the plan? Completely?

He considered this to be the time period during which he wanted Nwanyi to feel isolated and lonely but more or less safe so that she would not feel the need to make an unexpected escape or call for help. This was the time during which her family was supposed to be getting complacent about her safety.

But the truth was that she had startled him by speaking early that Saturday morning while she was dusting in his private office. She was almost never left alone with him, Djimon noticed, but Mairo hated dusting or even being near anyone dusting, because it aggravated her allergies, and of course Nwanyi could not be allowed in the office by herself. So Nwanyi had been sent in to dust while Djimon worked.

She broke the silence tentatively and even respectfully, but once he raised his eyes up in response her words began to tumble over each other uncontrollably, like they had been rehearsed often and held in for far too long. He found himself listening to a surprisingly bold tirade about the distribution of household duties and it was clear that this woman actually felt like Mairo was the one in charge of her. It seemed to Djimon that she saw him as the weaker partner, the one who might be willing to give her some rights in the household. Like he might lower himself into the sphere of domestic chores and make things better for her!

Djimon was not a particularly cruel man, as he often reminded himself, and he took no joy in violence. But Nwanyi's turning to him in hopes of fairer treatment had surprised and insulted him, and he would not be insulted. His first response was to administer an instinctive face slap like he would to a sassing child, except that the slap came out considerably more forceful. And when that seemed insufficient for the boldness of her crimes, he added a hard jab into her abdomen with the book he was holding in his other hand, accompanied with a curt "Don't you dare ever complain to me again."

As the corner of the book punched deeper into her flesh than he had perhaps intended, Nwanyi's baffled eyes widened with pain. Then came understanding. Good. She realized completely that his disinterest in her was not to be mistaken for some sort of distracted, preoccupied affection.

"Summer? How are things?" When the two sisters finally connected the next morning the call was weeks overdue. "It is so good to hear from you dear," Summer sounded better. "You have just been on my mind lately."

Lola loved how Summer didn't get pissy about it when they didn't talk for awhile. "And you've been on my mind, believe me," Lola answered truthfully.

First they went over Lola's new job, then Summer needed updates on her nephew and two nieces. Finally, they got to the part of the information exchange that Lola had been anxious for.

"So how are things with Gregg?" She worked at keeping her voice light.

"Oh same old same old," Summer laughed, but Lola was sure that she heard some tension there. "His golf game keeps getting better, his diet keeps getting worse."

Lola persisted. "Uh, you two doing well?" Damn. There was a bit more edge in that last question than Lola intended.

"Yeah. We're doing fine, dear. Marriage has its ups and downs you know. How are you and Alex?" Summer's answer had a bit of edge back.

Oh hell. Lola just dove in.

"Okay. Look. I had, okay, I had this kind of weird dream about you. I know it's crazy, but, well, hey, I am your big sister. I can't help worrying. I dreamt he hurt you. Hit you. I know this is dumb and Gregg's a great guy. But well …" Lola let her voice trail off.

"Lola?" Now Summer did sound just a little bit pissed. "You have this thing where you really think you know what people are thinking and feeling and you know, you're really not always right. In fact, you are sometimes way off base. Gregg and I have a wonderful relationship. It does happen to be in a bit of a rough spot now and okay it's not your and Alex's relationship, and maybe I am not so independent like you think I should be, but we're working things out, and you are not even in the ballpark about Gregg doing something like that to me. Your weird dream things are something you should probably keep to yourself. Okay?"

"Of course. I am sorry I brought it up. It was just such a vivid dream. I didn't mean to offend you, honestly." *Sheeshh, that had been a bad way to handle it.* What a shame there was no way to unsay something, no way to hit the "undo" button like she did all day long on her computer.

What Lola really wanted to tell her sister was that she was there for her no matter what was going on, that she was happy to listen if need be. But, as was Summer's way, she changed the subject so quickly and thoroughly that that was the end of that. Even the cat got off of Lola's lap and walked out of the room like the interesting part of the conversation was over.

Once Somadina had trouble getting any sort of sense of Nwanyi's state of mind, she started using her own mind to look for help. It wasn't a conscious choice, it just sort of happened. Like asking passing strangers on the street, "Have you seen my sister??" And at one point, she felt like a stranger had stopped and answered. She had no idea why this particular person had responded, and she could not even say exactly how she knew the person was there at all. But Somadina was certain there was someone out there who had heard her, that it was not anyone she knew, that it was not even anyone she had ever met. Not, in fact, anyone who had a life even remotely like hers. Yet also not an ancestor nor an evil spirit.

In fact, she was certain that this person was basically kind and not only posed no threat to her or Nwanyi, but that this unknown person might have the means to possibly help the two of them. She was a she, Somadina was sure, and she had power and resources at her disposal of which Somadina could only dream. But, in many important ways this person was also like her. She picked up people's feelings easily. She wanted the world to be fair and right and better than it was. She worried about others.

After that, Somadina concentrated her thoughts and feelings on two things. One of course was sending Nwanyi messages of comfort and support, assuring her that she would get her help somehow. She was not sure at all if Nwanyi received those messages in any way, but she tried to send them as hard as she could.

And the second was to reach the other woman. "Help me. I need help. Help me." She sent the thought over and over like a radio broadcast and hoped that when the other woman received her cries for help she wouldn't be too baffled.

The night before Lola left for Nigeria, she fell asleep with wonderful ease. Then—

"You will be okay. I promise. I will find a way to help you. I promise. Your big sister still loves you, still cares about you. Knows you are hurting. I am finding a way. I promise. I will help you."

Lola woke to tears wetting her pillow. Thankfully Alex had not heard her sobs. She saw no faces this time. She just felt sorrow and a sense that she absolutely positively had to find a way to help. Okay. Help whom?

Alex insisted on driving Lola to the airport, an act that Lola thought was both considerate and mildly patronizing. It was like Alex felt like she needed one last bit of being cared for before being sent out into the wild. Lola tried to focus on the considerate part because she and Alex really did not need to have a fight before she left. So Lola and Alex actually held hands that Sunday afternoon while he drove her to Bush Airport's international terminal, and they alternated between exchanging pleasantries and traveling in comfortable silence.

Lola was not particularly nervous about the trip or the presentation, although she did have a concern that she was certainly going to keep to herself. She was worried about sleeping. It seemed like since the start of the year she had slept far worse than usual, waking often from odd dreams filled with fear, anger, and tears. For all of her fierce independence, she found that the presence of Alex's sturdy body and gentle snoring helped her get back to sleep. Yes, the days in Nigeria would be fine. She was just a little apprehensive about the nights. But Alex did not need to know that.

Lola boarded the plane and settled in, opting for two glasses of a nice red wine with dinner, followed by two Advil. It worked. As the plane began its descent into Paris, she woke up to the smell of airplane coffee, feeling surprisingly refreshed, and by the time she boarded the plane for the six-hour flight to Lagos she felt a lightness and a sense of purpose that was a bit hard to explain.

Lola was not a woman taken to what she thought of as silliness. She was a more or less lapsed catholic with vague spiritual beliefs that never quite made it to the extreme of agnosticism (much less atheism) and yet also never made it to the other extreme of deep religious faith. Rather, her view of life encompassed a vague sense of some sort of higher power and a universal code of ethics, but not a lot of detail beyond that. If asked in a survey if she believed in God, she would have said yes. But, she did not fill her days believing that God had a plan for her, and in fact she shook her head at acquaintances who prayed for amenities like good parking spaces at the mall, and outright shuddered at those of all faiths who implied that they were on the correct side of some almighty battle and those of other religions were going to be really sorry someday.

She thought that today's overwhelming sense that she was suddenly exactly where she was supposed to be, doing exactly what she was meant to do, would have been easier to accept if it had been her nature to put it in a religious framework, believing that for some reason arriving in Nigeria was part of God's plan. Or, for that matter, it would have been easier to dismiss outright if she was certain such feelings were utter nonsense and she was just being a little bit crazy. The problem with trying to keep an open questioning mind, she acknowledged, was that one did not know what to make of sensations like the one that she was having. She did not carry around a framework for easy classification of the unusual.

She did, however, carry around a sense of getting the job done, and so she put aside her newfound sense of purpose as surely as she had put aside all of her recent nighttime disturbances, and sought out her driver and armed escort in the cacophony of colors and noise awaiting those who had just cleared customs and immigration. There they were—the escort was armed and serious, the driver was holding up a sign that sort of looked like her name.

She realized that Alex would have been so relieved if he could just see the front of the <u>Sheraton Lagos Hotel</u>. It was near the airport, which would have reassured him, with palm trees that could have been found in Houston and the familiar red logo clearly displayed.

Then, she realized, Alex could see it. Sometimes she just plain forgot that she now lived in a world where such was not only possible, it was common. So she reached into her purse and snapped a quick picture with her phone, rather hoping that the two men with her did not notice her taking a picture of something so stupid. And while it was true that Alex did not know how to text, she could now send the photo to Teddie to show to her dad. Wait. It wasn't quite six p.m. here so it would be just before noon in Houston. Better not send it now. Teddie was not supposed to have her cell phone with her at school, much less turned on, but one never knew. Lola did not want to have to go to the principal's office a second time to reclaim a child's cell phone. Reassuring Alex by photo could wait.

  Lola was lucky to get one of the refurbished rooms at the hotel. Though it was fairly basic with only a small window, it was clean and everything worked well. Others had advised her that as an American she might find the Nigerians unhelpful and even surly, but as soon as her smile erupted of its own accord she found the hotel personnel warm and helpful. Later that night, with room service eaten, photo finally sent, and assorted loving messages exchanged by email, Lola found that jet lag and travel fatigue did what she had feared they could not, and she slept in relative peace.

  The next morning she was met not only by her familiar driver, but also by Jumoke, an operations engineer who headed up the small technical team in Lagos and had been apparently assigned to see that she reached the office safely and adequately briefed. Tall and thin, in his late thirties, with remarkably dark skin, he spoke with a precise and strong British accent. "Driving here is a bit more chaotic than you will be used to," he explained. Lola, having been to Jakarta, Mexico City, and Cairo on business, smiled. "No, I am serious," he added. "It is not like other places you have been." Lola found the comment odd, but, as she discovered in mere minutes, quite accurate.

  As the car made its way, alternating between rapid acceleration and lurching stops, Lola watched and listened to <u>her surroundings</u>. Indeed, the extreme poverty that had sprouted up between the more developed areas of Lagos was as dire as she had been led to expect. And the interaction between Nigerians talking to each other along the street was louder and more aggressive than she was used to. She had been told it would look like everyone was arguing, and she could see why. But it didn't feel like they were arguing. Lola had no trouble sensing the camaraderie and even affection underneath much of the boisterous behavior.

Yes, some of the license plates really did say "Center of Excellence," a subject of amusement among Americans back in the office. And she must have heard "No wahala" a dozen times. It was like going to Australia and hearing "no worries," or to Jamaica and hearing "no problem mon." When one visits a place for the first time, it's nice to have those little expectations met.

At the Lagos office, Lola's audience consisted largely of investors involved one way or another in the offshore mineral lease. They were a mix of South African, British, and Nigerian businessmen who, Lola quickly discovered, had the fairly common non-technical person's interest in hearing about the technical parts of their own industry. So Lola allowed herself to wax a bit eloquent about the components for a successful well.

One needed not dinosaurs nor even remnants of ancient swamp plants so much as one needed millions of years worth of tiny sea creatures to live and die and settle their little organic carcasses into the ocean floor to be buried beneath more sediment and then, more slowly than a human brain could imagine, be turned into a dense, organic, rich shale. Roll the tape for millions of more years of heating and burial, cooking like an incredibly slow casserole.

Lola's mom had once asked her how we could possibly run out of oil when certainly the earth was making more all the time? She had wanted to answer, "Sure, and whatever species is around, if any, in ten million years just might find some of the fresh stuff," but she drew the line at sounding like a smartass to her own mother. So she had settled on "The earth just cannot make it fast enough mom."

In fact Lola had often thought that if the average car owner really understood what it had taken for the earth to make a gallon of gasoline, not to mention for man to find and produce and refine it, he or she would treasure each gallon like the irreplaceable gift from the earth that it was. Twenty-plus years in the oil business had left Lola more in favor of conservation than many of her more liberal but less informed friends.

But from at least one point of view the Niger delta had been blessed, as had the Gulf of Mexico, with plenty of dead tiny sea creatures, plenty of time, and then plenty of nice sand dumped on top thanks to big, hearty rivers. A little tectonic activity to provide cracks and faults and some shale or salt moving around almost like a lava lamp over the eons, and the end result was high spots to trap the stuff and migration pathways for it to get into the traps and plenty of places to drill.

While the people of Nigeria had both suffered heavily and gained mightily from the odd confluence of circumstances which had put what Texans called "black gold" in their backyard, Lola focused on only why this well would be a good well. Why this well should be drilled. By the end of the presentation the room was nodding and smiling along with her. "Some days," she thought, "it is just a little scary how good I am at this."

"Do you think you are good at finding oil and gas?" Jumoke, her operations engineer escort, asked her as he and the driver brought her back to the hotel. He had insisted on accompanying her, and apparently planned to buy her dinner at one of the hotel restaurants. Lola had done her best to discourage him. First of all, she almost always preferred her own company to making small talk with someone she did not know. Secondly, for all she was now in her late forties she understood that she was often mistaken for being younger, and so she still avoided situations in the business world which could be misunderstood.

She and Alex had often laughed about how they could each have hardly picked a better profession in which to meet the opposite sex, he surrounded by a largely female teaching staff, and she in the very male oil business. But the fact was that they had both learned how to send out signals. And how not to. Friendly and warm, hopefully. But not interested. Not available. Busy signals, actually. Because if one just plain never got to the point where one had to decline, then, well, one wasn't going to make the mistake of not declining. Which meant that twenty-five years later one might still have a good marriage. At any rate, it had worked for them.

So Lola was a little annoyed at Jumoke's insistent hospitality, but she tried to answer his question cordially. "I'm capable at finding oil, but so are most folks who have survived in the profession as long as I have. I guess that I am faster at it than a lot of folks, particularly if there is a rush and I need to be."

"Then what is it you think you are so good at?" There he went again. Stop asking me these damn odd questions that make me feel like you are reading my mind, she thought with a hard slap of a thought. And saw him smile slightly. Okay. This was getting weird.

"I'm sorry," he said. "I have a habit of reading people really well. A little too well sometimes. It makes them uncomfortable. I'm sorry. It's like I can—"

"Guess what they're thinking," they both said in unison aloud, her with a question mark at the end. And they both laughed uncomfortably.

"You need not worry about me," he added. "I am taking you to dinner to do you the courtesy of being a good host, without regard to your gender. Plus, to be honest, I wanted to talk to you because while watching you present today, I realized that we are somewhat alike. It's true that I mostly avoid people like me because at worst they make me uncomfortable, and at best they wear me out quickly. But I also can get a feel for them far faster than others, which is why I am doing such a remarkably good job of reading you. It is a strange thing to explain. And because I do not meet so many people like us, I wanted to talk to you Because I am trying to learn. So help me out please. I am curious. What is it you think you are so good at?"

Lola sighed. "I am good at selling things," she answered honestly. "I never wanted to be in sales, I have always valued my brain and, yes, my integrity. I think of sales as a profession in which one convinces someone else to buy or sell or commit to that which they would not necessarily choose to do on their own. Maybe with no harm done to them and maybe even, under the best of circumstances, with some good benefit to them. But they have been convinced just the same. And for some odd reason I have always been terribly good at convincing people to do things. Drill wells. Lease properties. Get me into a college class that is already full or reduce the property taxes on my house. I just know what I need to say and what they need to hear. It varies all over the place. It is not like there is a single formula or secret, but if I try, I can find what will work if anything will and then I can do it. I guess I gravitated towards science partly because I never liked that side of myself. So how was I supposed to know that in virtually every scientific profession, you sell your ideas?"

And Lola realized with a start that she had just shared more of her self and her honest feelings with this person she had barely met than she generally shared with friends or coworkers she had known for many years.

"I know," Jumoke agreed. "You just can't afford to share much of yourself when you are like us. I don't even understand why I work the way I work. I certainly don't expect anyone else to understand."

"Wife? Girlfriend?" Lola went ahead and asked.

"No." Jumoke paused. "A brother. He is like me but very different. No, not an evil twin. He is very nice, very kind. But he has the same gift, and yet he is a very different kind of person with it. It is hard to explain. We are very close in some ways and yet cannot be together very long. Friends and girlfriends both come and go. People seem to like me, but I tire of people easily. It is not always a joyful thing to have a feeling for what makes others work, you know? You know."

She did. Lola thought of all the casual friends who had disappeared over the years, largely because Lola let the friendships go. At some point she tired of listening to so many people, for inevitably she listened in relationships far more than she talked.

"It can be lonely to feel so close to people?" Jumoke offered. True. And so over a lovely Indian meal she and Jumoke found that they were indeed brother and sister of a special kind.

Finally, as dessert of some sort of milk pudding and a strange canned fruit was served, Jumoke asked a different question which stirred the feelings of unease that she had kept out of her mind all day. "You say you are married to a good man. I think you are very lucky in this."

She nodded. Given Jumoke's life story, she realized she might have been far luckier to find Alex than she had ever realized.

"But, he has not changed lately has he? He is not hurting you?" Then sensing but not understanding her startled reaction, he tried to sooth. "I am sorry. I do not mean to offend you. It is not my business."

"No. It is okay. Really." But the question troubled her in ways she did not immediately understand. Without discussion, they both let the conversation move back to the oil business and the upcoming well, and after awhile Lola took the opportunity to interject an assurance to Jumoke that he had overstepped no bounds with his question, and that in fact Alex was a prince of a man who treated her wonderfully and that she herself was more than fine. Jumoke had seemed relieved but puzzled, yet he let it go. They parted after dessert as old friends.

Lola realized as she headed to her room that while she had held back sharing her own odd experiences that dovetailed with Jumoke's question, this had also been the only question which Jumoke had uncharacteristically let her avoid answering. Why?

All she could figure out was that she and Jumoke had on some level each come to their own terms with their unusual interpersonal skill sets. They had each rationalized what they could do in terms that made sense to them, did not frighten them, allowed them to function without invoking any beliefs which might label them as kooks. They both believed that they habitually picked up tiny, barely visible and barely audible clues from others and used these clues to read people particularly well, to the point that, combined with a little common sense, they could almost appear to sometimes read minds. It was a fine line. But it invoked nothing disturbing. They were both okay with such a view of their world and their roles of being largely loners in it.

But Lola also realized that the idea of receiving some sort of a distant distress call from an unknown person who was in an abusive relationship challenged this view. It pushed the whole thing into a whole new realm for her, a realm that she was understandably reluctant to enter. And for Jumoke to ask such a question? It pushed him there too.

> Q: Do you have to be physically near a person to communicate with them telepathically?
>
> A: No. Of course reception and meaning are greatly improved if you can see and hear the other person and use visual and aural clues to provide a better understanding of what is being received. And distance plays a factor, which implies that some sort of physical rules apply even though emotional transmission does not seem to be as absolutely physical as the transmission of light or sound because it doesn't diminish with distance by a clear mathematical formula, and walls and barriers are not a factor other than barring other input as mentioned above. Also, a link forged between two minds remains for a period of time in spite of an increase in distance. If the link existed just briefly and was relatively superficial, then it will fade quickly once the people are separated. If on the other hand the link was strong, enhanced by a similar situation or an extremely common shared point of view, then the connection appears to be able to jump over large physical distances indefinitely, much like charged electrons can arc across space. Once such a strong link is made it is often permanent, but even that link will be stronger when the two people involved are in close proximity (from "FAQs about telepathy at http://www.tothepowerofzero.org/).

Somadina awoke with the wonderful feeling that the lady was coming physically closer. At first Somadina was confused. Then she realized. Of course. The lady was not Nigerian. That possibility had not occurred to her. But it made sense. And for some reason the lady was actually coming to Nigeria. At least to West Africa. Somadina was sure of it and so she sent thoughts over and over to tell the woman that she was now exactly where she needed to be. Somadina then spent two happy days feeling even closer to the woman, working to make her feel happy to be in Nigeria, and trying to find a way to better connect.

Then, two mornings later, she awoke just as sure that the woman was already leaving. What? Yes, she was heading to an airport. But she had just arrived! Who spends only two days in a country? *You're leaving? You just got here. You can't go!* Somadina knew that she was being immature, but she could not help feeling anger, and disappointment. In the strength of her own emotional outburst, she received the worst kind of confirmation that the mysterious woman had been hearing her all along.

With an evening flight home on Wednesday that required a late afternoon departure from the hotel, Lola had decided to sleep in as late as she liked, to spend a few hours by the pool relaxing (no solo adventures into town, she had promised) and to just have an easy day before the nineteen-hour sojourn home. Sleep came and went that night, with an odd blurry feeling of nervousness but nothing upsetting. It wasn't until morning, when she woke up naturally with no alarm clock, that she felt the sense of turmoil.

You're leaving? You just got here. You can't go! It was an unmistakable thought, as clear as if it had come from a distraught lover, needy parent, clingy friend. Anger and disappointment. Even a bit of panic. Who the hell cared if she stayed in Nigeria?

Impatiently, she got out of bed, began to gather together her toiletries. *Leave me alone*, she thought with vehemence. *I do not want to hear from you. Whoever you are. Get out of my head.* And then to herself. *Stop thinking this is real. It is not. You have a thirteen-year-old daughter and two other kids counting heavily on you and this is absolutely no time in your life to have mental issues. You are fine. Get a grip. Act like a normal person.*

She took a moment and sat in the uncomfortable easy chair and forced herself to use the simple mental imagery she had learned in Lamaze classes so very long ago. But instead of picturing a beautiful lake at sunset like they had taught her to do in order to relax, this time she pictured the giant steel doors to a vault, glimmering in a cold artificial light, clanking closed in her head. The doors seemed to work. She got out of the chair feeling better. As she finished packing and headed poolside for lunch with her email and her internet, she felt fine actually. Although strangely alone.

Leave me alone! Somadina heard the thought, felt the feeling and felt the vehemence behind it. *I do not want to hear from you. Get out of my head.* And then Somadina could feel the woman picturing giant steel doors, glimmering in a cold artificial light, clanking closed in her head.

No! Somadina pleaded. *Don't shut me out. Please.* But the doors were now closed tight, and Somadina, even as a small child, would never have dreamed of trying to force open the doors of another's mind. So she sat at her kitchen table, devastated by this unexpected setback, and feeling strangely alone.

Yet there was nothing to be done other than to be patient, to hope. Somadina smoothed the folds of her lightweight loose cotton wrap, working to smooth her own emotions as she smoothed the soft worn fabric. She would wait. It would be okay. Sooner or later the door would open, if even only a crack. And then she would be there and she would find a way to demonstrate that she was harmless. A supplicant. One who begged for and deserved help.

Chapter 6. April 2009

The U.S. State Department will tell you that Nigeria is a country of around one hundred-fifty million people living in an area about the size of Texas and Oklahoma, making it the eighth most populated country in the world. Lest you think it backward, note that it also ranks ninth in the world for internet usage and sixteenth in the world for cell phones. One might guess that perhaps this has something to do with the fact that the median age in Nigeria is about nineteen years old, as opposed to, say, Italy where the median age is more like forty-four. But no, Italy ranks thirteenth in the world for internet usage and eleventh for cell phones, so go figure.

The State Department also tells you that there are more than two hundred and fifty different ethnic tribes in Nigeria, and almost as many languages. Only English is spoken by all. A map of Nigeria shows the "Y" made by the intersection of the large Benue River with the even larger Niger River, which happens more or less in the center of the country. Most of us tend to forget that crossing wide rivers used to pose something of a problem throughout most of human history.

Americans must go past the government websites, however, and on to less dry sources of information like <u>Lonely Planet</u> to get the more interesting story. Here one discovers that before the dubious distinction of British colonization, in the area that is now Nigeria's lower western side of the rivers' Y, there used to be a patchwork of small states, often dominated by a group known as the Yoruba (your uh BAH) and containing the famous Benin Kingdom of old, an important centre of ancient trade and a producer of fine metal artwork.

Today the Yoruba and others in this southwestern part of the country are about half Muslim and half Christian and, judged by the standards of violence in the rest of the world, they coexist not so poorly. Examining a map also shows that this region contains the left half of the Niger Delta, which problematically turns out to contain large quantities of oil which are worth a lot of money to some and which do a lot of damage to the crops and fishing spots of others.

Meanwhile, in the lower right side of the Y, lived and still live the Igbo and other "agrarian peoples," who chose not to develop centralized empires before colonization, but did allow themselves to be overwhelmingly converted to Christianity, particularly Catholicism, and who continue to inhabit the eastern side of the Niger Delta.

Setting in the upper cup of the Y are the Hausa/Fulani. These people, due to religion (already converted to Islam), culture, and geographic isolation managed to remain relatively untouched by Europe. A closer look at the history of this arid northern cup shows that while the two tribe names are often run together today, they were at one time more distinct. It would probably surprise no one to discover that the Hausa and the Fulani did not always get along so very well. The Fulani were traditionally nomadic herders, and although they were mostly Muslim like the Hausa, there was some local animist religion mixed in. The Hausa, more settled into towns and more strictly Muslim, once considered the Fulani second class.

In the early nineteenth century, a Fulani leader named Usman dan Fodio created an empire which would later be known as the Sokoto Caliphate, which eventually centered around the northwestern Nigerian town of Sokoto, and which would become the largest sovereign state in Africa. After a rocky beginning of conquering and defending himself, Usman dan Fodio and his kin settled into ruling this area with peace and prosperity for many decades. The empire became known for its education and its arts, with the leaders themselves writing poetry and publishing discourses on religion, politics, and history. This, by the way, included Usman dan Fodio's wives and daughters, and particularly one daughter named Nana Asma'u who became famous as a writer, politician, and educator and today still serves as an example of female accomplishment for Muslim girls and women the world over.

Over time as the empire became more Hausa in character, even adopting the Hausa language, much of the animosity between the Fulani and the Hausa began to dissipate. In addition, thanks to the success of the caliphate, the population itself enjoyed an unprecedented level of safety from raids by Saharan nomads. That was until it was seized by the British in the 1880s, for reasons that must have made sense to the British at the time and probably involved, more than anything, Britain's ongoing pissing match with France. The British allowed the caliphate to subsist for awhile on British terms, at least until 1903 when the region was just plain divided up between the French and British.

Today, descendents of dan Fodio continue to fill the appointed position of sultan of Sokoto, who serves as the main religious leader of Nigerian Muslims. The Sokoto Caliphate remains an Islamic spiritual community in Nigeria. In 2006, a new sultan of Sokoto was appointed when his brother and predecessor was killed in a plane crash. <u>Colonel Sada Abubakar</u>, generally described in the press as a relaxed and easygoing peacemaker, was selected to serve as a symbol of good governance and Islamic unity, and to continue his brother's work of trying to ease tensions between Nigeria's Muslim and Christian communities.

Nigeria has approximately seventy million Muslims, sixty million Christians, and twenty million people who pray to other gods or not at all or to some of both. The vast majority of them get up in the morning just like most of the rest of earth's other seven billion inhabitants, hoping for peace and comfort in the day ahead.

Some of these Nigerians start their day filled with love, some with pain, some with hunger, some with ambition, some with boredom. A small but not insignificant percent would readily cheat another, at least a stranger. And a fair number carry anger of one type or another throughout their day. But the fact is that few are compelled to harm others. Legitimate religious groups there support coexistence, and it is the rare human who tries to justify inflicting more pain in a world in which they have already seen plenty.

But with a pool of more than a hundred and fifty million people to choose from, the violent and fanatic do exist. Like any other country, Nigeria has its predators, its bullies, and its extremists filled with such a sense of righteousness that they believe the goodness of their cause justifies actions which defy understanding.

Alex had a surprise for her of which he was really rather

proud. She could tell when he met her at the airport. Lola, organizer and planner that she was, did not particularly like surprises and Alex knew it. But because she was smart enough to never want to discourage a little occasional romance and intrigue in their maturing marriage, she kept quiet and bided her time. To wait was not her strong suit, but she would find out soon enough. She slept for fourteen hours once she got home, which helped with everything, then dragged herself through work on Friday, appreciative that it was the weekend already.

That night, over pasta and red wine, Alex casually reminded her that the following weekend was Easter. Indeed, she had forgotten. She remembered years of egg hiding and Easter basket making and picture taking in the park with Alex fooling with tripods and timers that never worked quite right, while she held in check squirming children who could not wait to get out of their fancy clothes.

"Teddie's friend Shawna's family is going to the lake for the weekend and they invited her along. I told her she could go." Okay. Lola wasn't all that crazy about Shawna's family for reasons she could not quite put her finger on, but this weekend trip would probably be just fine. She was also going to start seriously working on doing less needless worrying. Sure. Teddie should definitely go.

"That leaves you and me," Alex smiled. "And I know that you have next Friday off." Hmm. Lola was starting to envision a bed and breakfast getaway. A little romance. A lot of sex. Okay. That would work well. Good for Alex. Not part of his practical nature at all to plan something like that, but hey, it was good for everybody to behave a little unexpectedly every once in awhile.

"So let's get that camping stove out of the attic and make sure we still have all the pieces to your old tent."

"What? We are going camping?"

"Oh no dear. Camping is only a small part of it." Alex was clearly very pleased with himself. "Guess what I found out? I knew that one of the math teachers that I work with used to be a rafting guide. But what I did not know until this past week was that his real passion is doing whitewater in an open canoe. Just like you!"

"Alex, that was twenty-five years ago."

"He and his wife go every once in awhile. They've been dying to do the Big Piney River in Arkansas, but he was telling me how they really ought to have a second canoe for safety. It is only about an eight-hour drive from here, but we can leave right after school Thursday and get in by midnight. Be on the river all day Friday and Saturday. Drive home Sunday. Lola, it's what you wanted. Some excitement. Some thrills. You do not have to go all the way to Africa."

Okay, that's what this was about. "Alex, you've been in a canoe with me about six times over the past twenty-five years. I am really out of practice and while I will definitely give you that you are strong and athletic, you're not particularly experienced. We probably don't belong in anything past a class one rapid together."

"And that is probably what we will be in, dear. Ken says that one of the problems with this river is that it gets too low to run. We're more likely to be dragging our canoes over rocks than dealing with rapids. I told Ken all about your background canoeing up in the arctic when you finished your undergrad, and I could tell that he was impressed, but honestly I think Ken invited us along more so he'd have another big guy to help drag the canoes. And if we do get into a few riffles, you'll do fine. I promise that I will cheerfully sit in the front and let you steer. I trust my wife."

Now really, what could she say to that? The canoe trip was on.

Nwanyi called on Tuesday morning, and, according to a rather defensive Ikenna, it was short and uneventful. Somadina asked her father if she could please use his cell phone to call Nwanyi back, and only got a strange look and a painful worried feeling from her father. Odd. Yet in spite of the concern, almost panic, that she could clearly feel from him, Ikenna assured Somadina that all was well with her sister and asked her if she would please stop worrying. The following Monday afternoon Nwanyi called again, for another short and subdued hello to her father, who passed along the greetings. Again Ikenna brushed off Somadina's request to use his phone to call back. Somadina thought, *This is nonsense. I am going to take Azuka up on his offer. I am going to start to make money, and I am going to get myself a cell phone of my very own.*

As Lola and Alex enjoyed their meal, a giant low-pressure area was beginning to move slowly down from Canada, carrying an unusually large amount of moisture in its wake. The rains began in upper Michigan on Saturday, and by Sunday, Wisconsin and Illinois were drenched as well. As Alex and Lola gathered gear and clothing and supplies with increasing enthusiasm and anticipation, the low-pressure area expanded. By Monday night a large circle extending from southern Indiana to Biloxi, Mississippi was experiencing heavy rainfall. Even Houston got a few showers. The low-pressure area lost much of its momentum by Tuesday, virtually stopped moving, and continued to dump record amounts of moisture in the south-central to southeastern United States.

Early Wednesday evening, Alex emerged from the attic with one more item to bring. He had found her old canoe paddle, the one she had bought herself in 1982 when she had had almost no money, joining friends and dorm mates that summer for the adventure of a lifetime in Canada's Northwest Territories. It was a battered white with a yellow plastic handle. Just seeing it again made her smile. "I don't want to lose it," she protested. "Then don't use it. We'll tie it into our canoe as our extra paddle, and keep it with us for a backup, which we won't need, and just to make you smile the whole time you are traveling down the river."

Later that night, Ken called to let them know the good news that water on the Big Piney was nice and high so water would be plentiful and the odds of having to drag their canoes were almost nil. Better yet, the forecast for Friday and Saturday in Arkansas was cool and sunny, with highs in the 50s, blue skies, and the pesky rains due to be well out over the Gulf of Mexico. This was indeed going to be a very fine weekend to be on the river. Lola had to admit, once she had adjusted to the idea, that she was excited to go do this and appreciative to Alex for setting this up. Sometimes he knew her better than she knew herself. Anyone would go to a romantic B&B.

This was an adventure, one tailor-made for her. She was an incredibly lucky lady.

    Djimon was a man who started most days with a simmering anger. He had been raised to believe that his people, his mother's people, had created a paradise of beauty and enlightenment. No passing fluke, this wonderful Utopia had existed for nearly a hundred years before it had been washed from the earth by the unnecessary and unfathomable cruelty of those unable to accept that members of another ethnic group, his ethnic group, could create a superior and civilized society. And look what a mess the foreigners had made for them instead. Nigeria's most precious resource, oil, had been spilled without concern, squandered on foreigners and a few Nigerians too selfish to use the proceeds to rebuild a great nation. Corruption, scams, and sexually transmitted diseases were now his country's most famous exports.

    Djimon lamented every day to himself about how Christians the world over dressed their women like whores while Muslims the world over scared off legitimate converts by ruling like medieval tyrannical thugs who incited angry and ignorant youth to commit violence without plan or reason. Djimon thought that never was there more of a need than now for an enlightened ruling class, just like the Sokoto Caliphate had once been. And never was there a country more poised for it than Nigeria. He loved Nigeria. He loved all seventy-five million of its Muslims and all seventy-five million of the others. If he had his way he would not hurt a fly to rebuild Nigeria into this great new nation that he envisioned.

    Though Djimon was devout, of course, he did not consider his cause to be about religion. He was willing to allow any human their freedom of conscience, in hopes, obviously, that the freedom would eventually lead the more enlightened to Allah. No, this was about groups of people doing what they did best. Some farmed. Some built, manufactured, or sold goods. And some were destined to lead—to be the scholars, the scientists, the artists, and the intellectuals—like his people. They had so clearly been meant by their creator to fill that role for all of greater Africa. Their very minds and bodies evolved to be the born leaders of the continent. Until the outsiders had come and ruined everything. In their blurry vision, all Africans were alike, all Africans were less than they. The outsiders had robbed Djimon's people of their natural place, of their birthright. Djimon's anger simmered every time he thought of it.

But who would listen to him, to his small group of committed Fulani, and a few sympathetic Hausa. They met and they planned but they had no power. No voice. No avenue to get their message out to persuade except for the one avenue always open to the powerless, to those who will not be listened to any other way. And so what must be must be. What he was trying to rebuild, what he was trying to give back to this sorry, hurting world, surely was beautiful enough to more than justify a few acts of less than admirable behavior.

In a typical year, about two and a half million Americans die. That seems like a lot of people, but of course we are a lot of people. In more understandable terms this means that every year roughly eight out of every one thousand people die. Six of those are over sixty-five, and pretty much thought of as "old" by most of the population under fifty. Except of course when the dying person is one's own relative, in which case, depending on circumstances, the person might not have seemed that old at all. Cancer and heart disease claim roughly half of those "elderly" lives, and other diseases claim most of the rest.

Over any two statistically average years, three of the remaining four deaths would be folks in the forty-five- to sixty-four-year-old range, most likely being men or women who had the misfortune to succumb particularly early to heart disease or cancer as well.

The remaining death, a local tragedy of someone in the one to forty-four-year-old range, could have a lot causes but statistically it would most likely be an accident of some kind. After forty-five years of age, accidents become increasingly less significant as a cause of death, because disease becomes more prevalent and probably also because by the time one hits his or her mid-forties, one is supposed to have gotten a little smarter about not taking stupid risks that have a high probability of ending one's life.

Through a small local outfitter, they had reserved canoes and arranged for the initial ground transportation upriver to the put-in point. They arrived at the outfitters, as hoped for, under beautiful blue skies Friday morning. But the outfitter was hesitant. Water from all that rainfall, he explained, was just now reaching the Big Piney, and the river had yet to crest, even though the rains had stopped. The currents were strong and deceptively dangerous even in regions without rapids. So while normally a great river for canoeing, at least when there was adequate water, the Big Piney was really not the place for a canoe today. Perhaps they would consider an inflatable raft, which would be much more forgiving?

Lola was okay with the raft. Ken's wife Sara, a sweet outdoorsy woman from Maine, nodded her agreement. But Alex did not want to see Lola denied her adventure in a canoe, and Ken wanted this eight-hour drive to yield a new entry on the spreadsheet he kept on rivers he had been on in an open canoe. Neither woman wanted to be the one to insist. So the compromise was made to promise the outfitter and themselves to portage around any rapid which appeared dangerous, to scout frequently, to take no chances. Just do the fast flat water and walk around the rest. It would be fun.

As soon as they got on the river, Lola knew it had been a mistake. Alex, graceful and quick on a tennis or basketball court was big and awkward in the front of the canoe. His balance was off even worse than she remembered from years ago, and though she believed he had intended to listen to her instructions as promised, as soon as they entered the first little set of riffles he began to improvise, instinctively trusting his body because in so many arenas he knew how to use it so well.

But not here. She had argued with him unsuccessfully before that reaching far out of the canoe was a very bad idea, even in flat water, but, physics teacher that he was, he insisted that if she would just watch him and reach out equally far in the other direction at the same time, the combined effect would be to make them more stable. Sure enough, as they sailed through the first little shoot he spontaneously reached far out to his side. Damn. She needed to keep her paddle close in to steer and this was no time and place to have to argue physics with the man. She opened her mouth to yell, "Stop it you idiot," but never even got to "Stop" before the tilt of the canoe in the fast water set the canoe on its side and over, with the two of them flailing in water seriously deeper, faster and colder than she would ever have expected.

Unfortunately the riffles turned into bigger rapids around the bend, and as the water picked up speed and intensity, Lola found herself unable to even keep her feet downstream of her body, the most basic rule of safety, much less able to make her way through frighteningly strong water to either of the river's banks. A branch or rock seared into the side of her thigh, and her teeth started to chatter with shock and cold as she bobbed her way through the water.

"Get to the side." Ken was yelling at her from up ahead on the left bank with Sara, who was busy checking the runaway canoe which they had somehow managed to rescue.

Thank heavens these guys are good, Lola thought, doing her best to make her way over through the now slightly calmer water. *Alex. Where was Alex?*

With relief she heard his voice yelling from the right bank. *Okay,* she thought. *We were lucky. Let's get off of this damn river.*

They took an hour or so to dry off a little in the sun and to bandage up Lola's bleeding thigh as best they could. All agreed that this was probably a bit more than they had bargained for. Lola suspected that Ken and Sara probably had the skills to have gone on by themselves even in this fast water, and that at least Ken wanted to, but they recognized that Lola and Alex were definitely in over their heads and that aborting the mission, so to speak, was just the right thing to do. *Next time they will probably bring two more adept people,* Lola thought sadly.

Alex wanted to just try to get back to the road where they had been let off and use Ken's well-waterproofed cell phone to call for help. But Ken looked at his maps, and determined that there was just a short, maybe half a mile, stretch of absolutely flat water between where they were now and where a road crossed the river.

They could exit easily at that point at the bridge, where both they and the two canoes would be simple to retrieve. It made much more sense.

Lola had hung onto her paddle throughout her ride, but Alex had let go of his as soon as he was dumped. As the vintage "spare" paddle was slightly longer than her rented one, she insisted that he take it. As Lola and Alex, still damp and chilled, reluctantly got back in their canoe, Alex turned to Lola sheepishly. "You're not mad at me?"

And she could honestly answer, "No. I am just glad we're both all right. Let's get the hell out of here, okay?"

The American Canoe Association promotes water safety and provides a variety of colorful and easy to read pdf files which one can download for free. One, called The Paddler's Safety Checklist, details hazards on a river, including something called a strainer. It explains that strainers are "fallen trees; bridge pilings, undercut rocks or anything else that allows the current to flow through it while holding you. Strainers are deadly. "

Ken and Sara took the lead, moving quickly without incident down the middle of the river towards the new take-out point. Lola and Alex were a bit more wobbly, squirming in their wet clothes, nervous about another incident, and just anxious to be done. For all that Lola liked being on the water, she was not particularly fond of being *in* the water. She could barely swim, always got water up her nose and into her eyes, and her one attempt at scuba diving had been a claustrophobic disaster with her unable to remain under the surface long enough to even learn to use the equipment. Alex had completed the lesson on his own. No, give her adventure in the open air any day. Well, almost any day. She had enough adventure of any kind for this particular day.

When they rounded the bend Lola saw the pile of brush, leaves, and branches which had accumulated along the outside bend of the river. She tried to steer away into the middle, but most of the water, and most of the force of the water, was directed at the pile of debris. "Paddle harder," she screamed at Alex, hoping he could give their vessel more momentum with which she could work. But it was too little too late. Damn. They hit the mass of branches and twigs broadside, and the force of the water quickly tilted them sideways and then they went over. Again.

Lola started to pop back up, but could not break the surface of the water. The top of her head kept hitting the submerged side of the canoe which was directly above her. The current was holding the craft tight against the branches and debris behind her. Shit. She needed air. She pushed upward on the canoe. It did not budge. The water held it firmly, turning the flat piece of metal into the equivalent of a two ton object which was keeping her submerged. She tried again, this time pushing at it hard with both her hands and the top of her head. It still did not budge a fraction of an inch. Whoa.

She could see the sunlight hitting the water on the far side of the canoe, sparkling at her a mere two feet or so away. Plenty of space to come up to the surface out there. So she tried to move herself forward against the current to the upstream side of the canoe and found that there was no way she was moving upstream. She was in fact pinned tightly against the pile of twigs and branches, held in place by a current far, far stronger than she. She could not move forward at all, much less clear the twenty-four- or so-inch width of the damn canoe. And she needed air.

She tried to go left. No luck. Right. No. The water had pushed her hard into a concave wall of debris, flowing with extreme force to a point behind her and that was absolutely the only direction she was going to be able to move. Except that she couldn't. For while there was plenty of room for the water to go past her, the thick mass of twigs against her backside contained no holes big enough for a rabbit, much less a human, to pass through.

A strainer. She had heard the term, but never quite understood the name. Now she clearly saw a pile of spaghetti in her sink, water flowing through the little holes, pasta held firmly in the container. Oh yes. She was being strained like a cooked piece of tortellini.

At this point her brain calmly told her, *If you keep doing what you are doing, you are going to die. Soon.* It was a factual pronouncement made without any emotion at all, and Lola knew it to be absolutely true.

Then the voice split into two. One very calm, very soft piece began reasoning with her that dying right now just was not a good idea. Alex, the children, the guilt of the accident, people counting on her at work, friends, and neighbors, much left to be done and so on. Even at the time Lola found the soliloquy on staying alive odd. This was not a premise with which she was inclined to argue.

The other part of the voice began asking simple questions. *Have you tried up?* Yes. *Forward?* Yes. Left, really hard. She tried again, harder. No luck. *Right really hard?* Yes! *Think Lola*, it said. *What direction have you not tired?*

I've tried them all, she responded with frustration. *I cannot move.*

It asked again. *What direction have you NOT tried?*

Oh yeah. Down. She had not tried to go down.

The life jacket, designed to save her life, and without which she would not have dreamed of getting into a canoe, had kept her up just under the surface of the water, right under the boat. But now, if she took it off and used all her strength, particularly her legs, which were her best hope for sheer power, she thought that she might be able to wriggle downward. She could feel her hands quivering as she fumbled to loosen the buckle and tie. She had to hurry. She needed air.

She inched her way down while the current kept thrusting her hard against the mass of branches. The jacket slid off above her as she managed to slither and squirm deeper down the wall of muck, finally succeeding at least in turning towards it while she did so. The twigs and bark now scraped into her flesh in front .

But now that she was facing the wall of debris she could use her legs better and fight harder to go down. Finally, her one foot found the river's base, and then it felt an even stronger current moving along the river's floor.

She did not have to think about whether to lower herself into the current, because at that point the river grabbed her of its own accord and pulled her firmly along the bottom. She could no more have resisted it then than she could have fought its power earlier. Later she would wonder that no piece of clothing had caught on anything, and that in fact the space at the bottom had been large enough for her to get through. But at the time she just rode it like the ultimate water-park thrill and emerged seconds later on the far side of the strainer, eyes clear and nose miraculously empty of water and took a great gasp of wonderful, beautiful air.

Halfway through that gasp she was sucked back under again, this time beneath a second, much more shallow strainer. The current carried her under it without effort, smashing her head against the logs above as she traveled with no choice on her part, and she emerged from the second strainer choking and fighting to stay afloat.

It was then that she thought of Alex. Oh my god. He'd been dumped with her. He'd been under the canoe with her. She had not even thought of him. Had not even looked for him. Good Lord. She had been busy saving her own life, and he was still there. Probably now dead.

Lola was more upset than she had ever been in her life when she heard Alex's voice, loud and extremely commanding. "Lola. Grab the paddle!"

Coming up very quickly on her left was a sopping wet Alex who had clearly waded out way past safety and was reaching out to her as far as he could with her wonderful old canoe paddle.

Lola would later wonder how she ever managed to grab it. It seemed far away and she was coughing her brains out and had not an ounce of strength left. But somehow, the blade of the paddle was firmly in her hands, and Alex was pulling her in, now aided by a clearly concerned Ken and Sara. She sat on the shore and coughed up water for seconds more while they all gave her some space. Then, she just sat longer and let herself shudder.

Finally Alex came and put his arm around her silently, and Sara brought over whatever she had been able to find which was dry to put around her. Ken was looking for more bandages. Lola noticed that she was bleeding in multiple places.

Sara turned to Alex and said, "Amazing. All that and she is

sitting there smiling."

     The drive home was far more subdued, with a bandaged Lola huddled into all the dry clothing she had left in the car. Fortunately, no one cut was particularly deep, and the cold water had worked well to keep her from bleeding too heavily. Alex turned out to have been thrown from the canoe when his end hit with more force, coming up mid-river, and this time he had shown the presence of mind to hold on tightly to her precious paddle. Ken had watched with concern as she had failed to surface for more than a minute, knowing full well the dangers such a strainer could pose. Lola questioned his assessment of the time involved. She had guessed that it had been only a few seconds, moving in that odd slow way that time sometimes does during an emergency, only because she could not imagine that under any circumstances she would be capable of calmly holding her breath under water for a full minute while functioning in any capacity other than sheer panic. And yet …

     Lola also wondered about her survival odds if she had continued to be sucked downstream, choking and exhausted in the cold water which turned out to contain an ever-increasing amount of debris. It turned out that Ken and Sara had tried to talk Alex out of wading out into the water to get her, but as far as Lola was concerned, "Grab the paddle" had saved her life.

     Dinner that night was at an all-you-can-eat buffet found along the road. Ken, who was driving and pensive, had iced tea, but Lola, Sara, and Alex were happy to order a beer. Lola had three.

     A few days after Somadina decided to go into business, any business, she had a lucky break with her mystery woman. It was early evening of the Friday night before the Christian Easter. Azuka was still at the shop working. She was sitting on her porch listening to the songs of the crickets and rocking her son, who had woken up cranky from a late nap. As she stroked his hair and hummed to him to calm him down, she had a strong feeling of rising panic in herself. It was not seeing a snake kind of panic, or one of hearing a particularly loud thunderstorm. It was an irrational, deep, fear for one's life kind of panic. Her first thought was to find and help the sufferer. Who could watch Kwemto quickly for a few minutes? In which direction was this person? But before she could get out of the chair she recognized a familiarity to this victim. It was her lady. Dying, or at least in very real-life threatening trouble which Somadina could not identify. Could not do anything to alter.

"You must not die," Somadina said softly. "You must live. You are important. Others need you." And Somadina could tell that the woman heard her. Heard Somadina telling her she needed to stay alive. And that she found the words soothing. Soothing enough that the woman herself was calming her panic, had calmed it, and was trying to find a solution to her predicament. Somadina could offer no other help, for she had no idea what the predicament was. How did a fine, rich powerful lady get herself in a place where she had to fear for her life?

So Somadina just kept the soothing words coming. "Life is good. Now is not a good time to die. You must a find a way to live." And as she soothed she stroked her own son's hair, repeating the words calmly over and over until she knew that somehow the woman had found a way to live. She could feel the lady's exuberance, a temporary return of the panic, then more exuberance as everything was okay after all.

The next morning, as Somadina lay awake in her bed, she took her opportunity, knowing that if she dared waste such a chance, it might not come again. She concentrated as hard as she could and visualized the steel doors as gone. In their place she left an offering for the lady. She put the most beautiful bunch of flame lilies she could imagine, because she knew that the lady's favorite color was red. She added a couple of live butterflies, because the lady loved butterflies, and as an afterthought she added a platter of the best mango and some kola nuts, and spread the finest red and gold brocade she could imagine under all of it. There. Even if only imaginary, it was now a gift worthy of a queen, and hopefully the lady could see this and take pity on Somadina and her plight. But, just to be sure, Somadina concentrated hard to send a thought, a feeling, with it which she believed to be the most basic of messages between strangers. "I helped you. Now please help me."

That night as she lay falling asleep in her own wonderful bed, Lola felt a cool refreshing breeze blow. She had the sensation of looking up to see where it was coming from and could not have been more surprised to see in her mind's eye the pair of giant metal hinges which had held the big steel doors she had so carefully visualized closing while in Nigeria. But the doors were no longer closed. They were gone entirely. Vanished. What the hell?

And down on the floor in one corner was sort of a, what? An offering? There was a bunch of beautiful tropical red lilies of some kind. Two live butterflies softly perched on them. There was a platter of food, with some sorts of fruits and nuts. And this exquisite fabric lay under all of it.

And with it came a message, a feeling so basic that Lola had no trouble understanding it. "I helped you. Please help me."

Now that Lola knew more about Nigeria, she started asking more questions of her co-workers in Houston. She discovered that one geologist in Houston was Hausa and the other was Igbo, and noticed that the two young men seemed to be good friends. She thought about the tensions she had read of, and finally carefully asked Okocha (Oh KOH cha) the Igbo, about whether the tribes were still hostile to each other. She got a careful silence. Not the educated, he explained. In fact many of his closest friends were from boarding school and from his year in the National Youth Service Corps and in both cases, they had roots very different from his.

"National Youth Service Corps?" Lola was surprised to discover that all university graduates in Nigeria, male and female, are expected to spend a year working in a sort of internal Peace Corps program in which they are posted in any part of Nigeria except where they are from with the expressed purpose of reducing prejudices and hostility.

"What a great idea. When did they start this?"

"1973." Okocha said, then added when Lola laughed in surprise. "I know. It has been awhile. It was in response to the Biafra secession, and it had a very long way to go to accomplish its mission. It has probably made more inroads than you think. The real problems today are often caused by outsiders, usually just kids brought in from neighboring countries to make trouble, and by our own uneducated. Those are hard issues to fight."

Indeed they were, Lola thought. Anywhere.

"But we are all still proud of the tribes that we come from, and we try to keep our customs and languages alive," he told her. She recognized an opening. "So what is unique about the Igbo?"

Okocha chuckled with pleasure at being asked. "We are the business people of Nigeria. In my home town, everyone is expected to get up in the world, to amass some means of their own and build a good reputation. We work hard and look out for each other, but we also expect everyone to strive and compete."

"Sounds a lot like the ideals I grew up with in West Texas."

"Good. I think the Igbo and the American West have a lot in common," he agreed. "Community cooperation, but a strong expectation of individual accomplishment."

"That's Texas," Lola laughed.

"But we are a stubborn people, too. We do not choose to fight, but we will not be pushed around."

Lola nodded to encourage more.

"You know how they packed the slaves from Nigeria onto the ships, shackling them together for the voyage?"

Lola didn't. It was an uncomfortable part of history she had not gone out of her way to study and she would not have dreamt of bringing up the subject with someone from Africa. But Okocha proceeded as if slavery were a perfectly fine topic for conversation.

"Well there was one ship with just Igbo men on it. Some say a thousand of them. Worth lots of money. And they made a pact among themselves on the voyage over. Everyone had to agree. When they finally took the men off of the ship on the beach in South Carolina, all one thousand of them turned and walked together into the ocean. And drowned. That's how stubborn the Igbo are."

Lola saw the light of pride in Okocha's eyes and felt his overpowering emotion at this story of inspiration which he must have been told from childhood.

"You know, after that they tried to get slaves from other tribes and avoided the Igbo. And that's what my people are capable of."

Although Lola shuddered involuntarily at the idea of being trapped under the waves, drowning while shackled to a thousand other human beings, or even a dozen, she had to wonder, even if the story were only partly true and had been exaggerated over time, why hadn't such an amazing tale of heroism made its way into her history books too? Over the course of her childhood she had been forced to memorize every detail about the Alamo. Were her historians that blind to the bravery and self-sacrifice of others?

Nwanyi had lived in Djimon's household for about two months, and one of the very few joys she had been allowed was a call home every week. This call had gone far to help her maintain, so she was understandably disturbed when after two months the phone privileges stopped. This of course was part of Djimon's careful planning, but Nwanyi thought and hoped that it might have been a mere oversight which could be easily corrected if she could only find the courage to speak up.

It took her two days of carefully planning what she would say. Then, while she was clearing breakfast dishes the next morning Nwanyi began, albeit meekly, to remind them that that she had not been allowed her weekly call home now for over two weeks. Mairo looked up in genuine surprise at the sound of Nwanyi's voice and Djimon thought with just a little satisfaction that Mairo must have assumed, in error of course, that Nwanyi was already completely subjugated. Like such could be done so easily with any human, no matter how pitiful.

Djimon, who had actually studied human nature at the university, had carefully planned for years now how he would break this person down completely once the opportunity arose. But, he reminded himself, he had not shared that plan fully with Mairo, and so Mairo was merely operating on no more that just a set of naturally cruel instincts. He should not fault his wife for being, after all, just an uneducated woman who shared his goals. She was lucky to be paired with such a capable and informed husband, who in this case had successfully anticipated Nwanyi's next move. Djimon had given careful thought to his response, as he knew how very important each part of the choreography truly was and did not want to react merely in anger this time.

"Would you repeat that?" he said in a very neutral tone. When Nwanyi hesitated, he actually gave her just a bit of a smile. It was all she needed. Her eyes lit up a bit, and she started again, slightly louder, slightly bolder. Within her first few words he had in his hands the garden shovel he had brought inside and placed within easy reach. Halfway through the sentence he had used the handle of it to smack her as hard as he could across her left cheek, swinging it with both hands as if it were a baseball bat. He thought he heard cartilage, maybe bone, crack. Mairo's mouth dropped open. "You should learn some better techniques with her yourself," he said to Mairo dismissively as he walked out of the room, leaving Mairo herself to deal with the aftermath.

There had been no call this time for over two weeks. It was a Tuesday morning when Somadina was making a little breakfast for Azuka and Kwemto, humming softly to herself with her other worries temporarily forgotten, when suddenly she let out a blood curdling scream. The little boy ran to his father's lap in terror, and Somadina collapsed on the floor. Two neighbors ran in to see what was wrong and found Somadina crumpled on the floor, apparently just fine but rubbing the side of her face with a look of disbelief in her eyes. Azuka was holding the boy, standing yards away, looking equally baffled.

"'It's the spirits. They speak to her," one of the older neighbors declared with certainty.

"She always has been a bit chosen by the spirits, even as a little girl," the other nodded.

And so Somadina not only had a second, unfortunately horrible contact with her sister, but from that contact she gained the source of income that she had been seeking.

Lola woke up with a scream. A baffled Alex stretched out an arm in reassurance. "Bad dream?"

"I guess so. I can't remember much about it. Blinding pain. Sorry dear. Go back to sleep."

x^0

Chapter 7. May 2009

Word spread quickly throughout the neighborhood that the spirits were once again talking to Somadina, who everyone clearly remembered now had been most certainly touched by the spirit world as a small child. When the first girl showed up the next day at Somadina's doorstep wanting her fortune told, Somadina, at first, did not even consider it. Somadina was an honest woman. She had never had a vision of the future in her life; she had not the faintest idea of what was going to happen tomorrow.

But as the girl pleaded, Somadina realized something odd. The girl really did not want to know the future as much as she just wanted reassurance now about the things she was feeling today. It seemed to Somadina that what an adequate fortune-teller needed was compassion, common sense, and a strong ability to know what the seeker was worried about at the moment. And she, Somadina, was very good at telling what was worrying somebody. She already knew what was worrying this girl. So in return for a very small contribution, she told the girl she was willing to give it a try.

She seated the young lady in the simple main room of her little house, in wooden chairs that she moved close together and facing each other. She grasped the girl's two hands in each of hers, as she had seen others do. "I am totally making this up," she muttered to herself. She closed her eyes like she was concentrating, when in fact there was nothing on which to concentrate.

"You are concerned. There is a boy you like." She began tentatively, opening her eyes. The girl nodded eagerly. "You are afraid he does not like you." The girl nodded again. *This is not a particularly impressive performance*, Somadina chided herself silently. This opening would probably work with most of the unmarried young women around. But now was the part that required the compassion and the common sense, which was harder. Make no predictions. Reassure. And say what was most likely to achieve positive results.

"You must understand that you are a pretty and fine young lady. And confidence is attractive to others. Whether this boy will care for you or not depends on your own actions going forward. If you are kind, but also behave like you are worthwhile and not to be easily had, then it is more likely that he will be yours. Your fate here is undetermined yet, but if you believe in your own worth, then it is more likely that he will believe in it as well."

The girl thanked Somadina with genuine gratitude in her eyes and Somadina felt just a bit guilty for taking the money. *Relax, you may have helped this child,* she told herself. *And advice that is paid for is valued far more than advice that is free. Charge just a little and say good things that cause no harm.* So Somadina thus allowed herself to become a fortune-teller.

The girl told others of Somadina's impressive abilities and soon a small trickle of worried souls was making its way to Somadina's door. Those with ailments were comforted and advised to take better care of their health and to consult medical experts as this would provide the best chance that all would end well. Those with conflicts were calmed and told that the future would be bright if they just forgave both themselves and others. Those with money troubles were charged even less than the rest and assured that if they continued to work hard their luck would change. And every sort of problem resulted in the prediction that being truthful and kind improved the probability of a good outcome.

Azuka and his mother both spent more time caring for Kwemto, as Somadina's reputation grew and she became almost a full-time fortune-teller. Although this was not the sort of profession he had envisioned for her, Azuka found that he did not mind. Somadina seemed to be less worried about her sister, now that she was more occupied, and now that she was doing something that would give her the means and power to help. Somadina's cell phone fund was growing in tiny increments every day. And, oddly enough, something else was changing as well. Azuka could not help but noticing that as Somadina told more and more fortunes, the village itself seemed to be becoming just a little more happy, a little more healthy, and a little nicer place to live. Odd how that was working.

Nwanyi's life had never been particularly happy, and it was hard to tell whether problems sought out Nwanyi or, in hope of attention and comfort, it had become the other way around. Certainly the girl was a gentle soul who wished no ill to others, but she desperately wanted to be liked, or at the very least noticed. But now her life had changed dramatically, and it was filled with nothing but misery.

At first Nwanyi had wallowed a bit in her mistreatment, storing indignant stories to share with those back home. But as contact with her relatives was reduced to almost nothing, she found herself even deprived of the small joy of daydreaming about sharing her troubles. The day after the incident with the handle of the shovel, as her face throbbed horribly and she threw away with sadness the tooth that had become dislodged completely, it finally registered with Nwanyi that she was actually stuck. Not stuck in a bad situation, but stuck in a horrible situation. For the first time in her life she thought about running away. True, she knew that life was not generally kind to young women in her world who did such. This made such an attempt, for her, an act of courage and defiance beyond anything she had ever done before.

She toyed with elaborate plans that would brand her as brilliant as well as brave, but in the end she simply waited until the others were all busy, and then she walked out the servants' entrance in the kitchen, where she had sometimes been allowed to do chores. She closed the door behind her quietly and left quickly, before someone could see her go. Then she took a deep breath and purposefully walked as fast as she could several hundred feet without looking back. She noticed as she walked that she was in a more affluent area than any which had existed in her hometown, with big houses with beautiful red clay roofs and yards surrounded by high and ornately decorated adobe walls. The yards themselves were so large that she had only passed three homes before she paused for a moment to rest on the far side of a large flowering bush. <u>She sat on the ground.</u>

"What am I doing?" she asked. " I have absolutely no money. I do not know where I am. I do not have the means to reach anyone who could help me. I could ask a neighbor for help and they might let me use a phone but then again they could be Djimon's best friends. How does one find help in such a quiet, pretty place?"

She decided that as soon as her heart calmed down, she was going to get up and just start walking as fast as she possibly could for as far as she could possibly go. That would be best because at least she would be far away from Djimon. But before she arose, she felt a child's arm slip around her shoulders and she looked up into a young boy's grinning eyes. "Here she is mama. I caught up with her."

Running down the street after the boy was the heavyset cook with whom she had occasionally done chores. The woman must have seen her leave after all. "Nwanyi. Nwanyi," the woman ran towards her. "It's going to be okay child. You don't want to do anything stupid, dear. There there." The woman got close enough herself to put her arm around Nwanyi. "I'm a second wife too. I know it is not always easy. Sometimes it takes awhile to fit in. These are good people. I've worked for them for years. I know it has been a rough start. But you're going to be okay."

The large woman began herding a confused Nwanyi back to the house. "You'll see. It will all work out fine. Things always do." The sympathy worked to bring Nwanyi back to her usual compliant self, as the woman walked her back home with the eager, fast little boy following behind. "Here. In you go. You just needed a little air. Of course. You need to spend more time outside."

And before Nwanyi could sort out her thoughts there was a warm cup of fragrant tea in front of her. "This will help."

Ibrahim, the gardener, watched Nwanyi's return with apprehension. He almost wished that the girl had gotten away. He had worked for Djimon and Mairo for years now and never seen either treat anyone the way they treated this young woman, supposedly part of their family now. He had always considered them good people. But this new second wife was worked like livestock, barely fed scraps, kept in a servant's room, and hardly spoken to. For the life of him, he could not imagine why she had been brought into the household. He almost felt like Djimon and Mairo were having some sort of warped contest to see who was capable of treating her the worst. He shook his head helplessly. It was not, of course, his place to intervene. As he watched the cook, a fine and caring woman, offer comfort to the girl, he suspected that her simple act of kindness would cost her dearly.

Djimon just shook his head as he watched the women return through a front window. It was a shame but perhaps to be expected. Every plan had its minor bumps. This was a good warning that Nwanyi needed to be secured more carefully. Perhaps the servants and neighbors could be told she was trying to run away because she wasn't quite right in the head. Please alert us if there are any, you know, problems. Something like that.

The real shame was the cook. She had been with him and Mairo since their marriage, and was particularly competent and helpful. Damn. Too helpful. She would have to be fired tonight, before Nwanyi felt she had even the slightest chance to develop a confidant.

Lola found herself oddly haunted by the vision of a thousand Igbo slaves walking into the sea. As the days passed she had to face the fact that besides her fascination with the heroic self-sacrifice intended to protect those still back home, she was also oddly absorbed with the idea of the drowning itself. In fact, as the week wore on she realized that she got a strange sensation from the very sound of running water and that she was spending a lot of time thinking about being submerged.

Her first solution was just to be particularly gentle with herself. For the next couple of weekends she spent all of her time planting flowers in pots on the porch, which now overflowed with geraniums, begonias, and salvia in pinks, whites, and especially in her favorite, reds. After work, she sat on the porch in the evenings, looking at the flowers and sipping wine, generally for hours. Most evenings she thought for a while of her mom as she sat and wondered what dying had felt like for her mom.

A few times she called Summer, who was often out, or just heading out for the evening, but who a couple of times felt like a sisterly talk and seemed to be doing better herself these days. Sometimes Alex would come out and join her, bringing chips and homemade guacamole with him, drinking a beer as he sat next to her on the porch swing. Other times, Alex would fall asleep on the couch waiting for her to come in, giving in to the general exhaustion that seemed to overtake him by the end of every school year.

Sometimes Lola stared at the flowers and thought about her children. Zane, who had finally found a job in the science field with just a bachelor's degree, but remained somewhat underemployed now in Chicago with his Ivy League diploma, struggling with his lack of contacts in a job market filled with so many young people. Few had stepped easily into the impressive entry-level positions they had all expected.

It was painfully apparent now that his public school education in Texas had not in the least prepared her son, socially or academically, for his future. Zane had survived, it seemed to Lola, by befriending the kids in his class who were there on a scholarships. They had filled the Zeitman's home on two spring breaks now, his junior and senior years, and it was ironic to Lola that in a school filled with the children of the rich, Zane had managed to find the one possible group of friends who actually considered the Zeitman family to be wealthy.

Luckily, Zane was coming home for a visit in June before his entry-level training program rotated him into a new part of the company. He would temporarily leave behind washing Petri dishes and organizing lab equipment to do a stint in the marketing department, something she would have guessed that Zane would have hated. However, her low-key son seemed to be rather eager for the change of pace.

Meanwhile, highly driven Ariel had just finished her junior year at a prestigious private school, and while her proud daughter would not have dreamed of complaining, Lola knew that she had struggled as well. She had landed in the middle of a very different crowd than Zane, and so had joined a sorority along with all of her dorm mates and hung with girls who, Ariel herself had laughed, would not dream of borrowing her clothes.

Lola suspected that her enterprising daughter had traded help with homework for the use of her friends' expensive make-up and accessories, and even if the exchange was an unspoken arrangement, Ariel had also shown herself to be adept at finding ways to thrive in a world for which she was not well prepared. Internships had been almost non-existent this year, so Ariel would be home for the whole summer again, looking for some sort of routine job at the mall.

But the one having the toughest time at the moment seemed to be Teddie. A born hugger and listener, she had always been the one to reach out warmly to her mother, particularly when her mom was having a difficult time. It was only in the last month or so that Teddie had become aloof and irritable. "She just turned fourteen," Lola reminded herself. "You ought to know by now that this happens and usually sooner." Yet, Lola missed Teddie, the old Teddie, almost as much as she missed her other two children.

For part of each evening, Lola allowed herself to just sit on the porch and imagine the sound of rushing water and to think about how she now had trouble washing her hair without cringing. This puzzled and even intrigued her a little. She would never have guessed a brief experience like the one she had, which ended perfectly well with no harm done, at least once all the minor cuts and bruises had healed, could linger on in her mind with such intensity.

The sense of panic could be set off by sunlight glistening on a liquid the way it had glistened through the water on the unreachable other side of the canoe, or even by just feeling trapped by riding in the back seat of a two-door car. To a woman who, for most of her forty-nine years had reacted to the idea of mild mental problems and syndromes of all types with "why don't you just get over it?" it was, well, informative to discover that some things were surprisingly difficult to get over.

When all those doubts and fears would no longer keep her mind busy, Lola's thoughts would invariably wander off to the strange woman with whom Lola had agreed, bizarre as it seemed, to listen. In spite of that, she had not acquired much more useful information. The woman seemed to be younger, less educated, and probably more superstitious. She also seemed foreign and based on her not wanting Lola to leave Lagos, Lola was assuming she was

Nigerian. She had a younger sister, of that Lola was certain. She was very worried for the sister and lacked the means to help her. Lola supposed that meant resources, maybe money, but also the woman seemed to lack the knowledge to help as well. Was the sister lost? Kidnapped? Had she run-away from home? Certainly she was gone and could not be found.

 Sometimes Lola tried to sort of mutter comforting things back to the woman in her head, but that never seemed to help. Lola had not a clue what else she could do.

 Other times she just sat and thought about nothing at all. It was one of those times, when her mind was sort of on water and sort of on nothing, when she heard an elderly gentleman's voice clearly in her head.

 Lola? Little Lola Conroy? Good heavens dear, is that you?

 She searched her mind for knowledge of any older man who might have known her by her maiden name.

 It's okay honey. You're fine. I didn't mean to startle you. It's okay. She could almost see an elderly man backing out of her mind with great care.

 Good grief, she thought. *Now what?*

 Mairo spoke to him less after the incident with the garden shovel, and he saw the change in her eyes. Good. A little fear of him would be beneficial. Nwanyi's face had swollen horribly and turned awful colors, and the servants had to be told a story about an accident. Djimon largely avoided both women and turned his attention more and more to the planning of the "big event," as he had come to call it in his own head, and much more importantly to the handling of the aftermath, that brief period when he would be able to command attention and even, in some circles, respect. The importance of that time, and the wise use of it, could simply not be overstated.

 So he was caught off guard when Mairo informed him that she was going to visit her ill mother, who had moved down from the North a few years ago to live outside Lagos in a nearby town with Mairo's sister and family. Her mother was ill?

"Fine, just take Nwanyi and the children with you," he muttered in dismissal.

"The children, of course. But Nwanyi? I cannot. My sister is a nurse and she will know what sort of thing happened to Nwanyi's face. It will raise questions. About you. About Nwanyi. It is not a good idea," she responded. Djimon realized that Mairo also wanted the break, probably just from looking at Nwanyi's damage. Okay. She had earned it.

"Fine. Can I lock her in her room?"

"There is no lock on it. We discussed it. Remember? The servants would talk."

"Right. Look, I do not have a lot of time to watch her. Send the servants home, make sure they do not come back until you are back here, and take the kids, and I will think of something."

When Mairo left early the next morning, driving herself like the modern woman she was, Djimon headed straight into Nwanyi's room. Nwanyi pulled her covers over her body in surprise. Then smiled shyly. *Of course*, she thought, *the first wife has left*.

She had been expecting this moment ever since the marriage day. Sometimes she had dreaded it. Early on she had also, occasionally, hoped a little for it. Somadina had made it sound not so bad.

But as Djimon had ignored her, a third reaction had come into play. For all that she had no affection for him, she resented Djimon's complete lack of interest in her. What was the matter with her anyway? She was healthy. Young. Female. She needed to get pregnant like any other woman. It was time. That was his job. He should do his thing already. Making her wait seemed like a particularly cruel rejection that she did not deserve. Frankly, for all that she thought he was a fairly awful person, she resented his lack of interest in her even more than she disliked him.

So she stood, slowly let her nightgown fall to the floor, and smiled as seductively as she could manage with her swollen face.

Oh no, Djimon thought. *She actually wants me to, to …* With her he could not even find a word for it. Finally. *She wants me to mate with her.*

He was as horrified as if a female monkey had presented herself to him. And then, just as if a female monkey had presented herself, he was a little amused. Okay. Who could understand women? But wait. Under no circumstances could this one be carrying his child when she was forced to do what she had to do. He could perhaps have anal sex with her? No, even that sometimes ... backfired.

Well, it was probably time that he began phase three anyway, he thought. And that meant that he needed to begin to cause her physical pain, to beat her regularly. He looked clinically at her backside. He could think of no reason for keeping the beatings from being somewhat sexual. His bare hand. Her bare body. Maybe occasionally crossing that fine line between pleasure and pain. Perhaps it might be crossed for her, which could be helpful. Certainly he could cross it a little for himself and make this less of a burden. In the end she might come to love his rough touch. Or to hate it. It did not matter. Everything he had been able to learn on the subject left him believing that confusing her inexperienced budding sexuality with naked beatings would increase his physical dominance of her, and that would only, ultimately, help his cause.

When people asked Lola if she "believed" in global warming, as they often did, the tone of the question always reminded Lola of being asked if she believed in Santa Claus. As someone who worked in the oil industry, she was aware that the questioner, like this neighbor who had just wandered over to interrupt tonight's porch ritual, usually had a preferred answer that he or she was hoping to get, one way or the other.

Lola preferred to stick to what she believed were the facts. I believe that the earth's temperature is slowly rising and we are seeing changing weather patterns due to that temperature increase. Check the rates of glacial melting if you do not believe me. Yes, I believe that the earth's temperature and weather patterns vary naturally over time and it is hard to isolate a single cause for the changes. I know that burning hydrocarbons emits carbon dioxide. I know that that the emission of significant carbon dioxide into the atmosphere will affect the earth's temperature. I believe that we are now emitting a significant amount. Yes, I believe it is possible we are overestimating the effect and the earth's ecosystem is more stable and healing than we give it credit for. Yes, I believe it is possible we are underestimating the effect and the earth's ecosystem is more delicately balanced than we understand and we are all already doomed. I do believe that it is sensible to plan for something in the middle and make a realistic but rapid transition to burning fewer hydrocarbons. Yes, I work in the oil business. No, I don't want to turn an uninhabitable world over to my children or theirs. No, I don't want to go broke and yes, I'd like to more or less maintain my standard of living. But seriously, having a world economy largely based on extracting a messy, even toxic nonrenewable resource that we are going to run out of sooner or later was probably a bad idea anyway, wasn't it? So what am I doing about it? I'm working hard to keep the lights on, the computers running and the coffee pots full, while those trained to find better solutions find them.

"From what left wing radical groups are you getting *your* facts?" the neighbor asked, shaking his head. Lola was guessing this meant that the man had not gotten the answer he had wanted.

"NOAA. <u>National Geographic</u>. The New York Times. The Journal of Atmospheric Chemistry. I can get you a complete list of scientific references," Lola offered cheerfully. It didn't surprise her that he declined, and as he left she heard him mutter something about how those very people were going to eventually put both him and Lola out of business. To which Lola muttered back, *we better hope so …*

Nwanyi had not called now in weeks. Somadina knew that her father was avoiding her, because he did not want her to know how worried he was. She, for her part, felt better only because she was now doing something concrete to amass the resources to tackle the situation on her own. Somadina managed to stay calm and hopeful during the days, but sometimes at night she still became agitated, swearing she could hear Nwanyi whimpering in her sleep like Nwanyi had done when she was a very small child. When this happened Somadina would try to whisper comforting things to Nwanyi as she herself fell asleep.

Meanwhile, Somadina did her best with those who came to her for help. Today it was a woman who had yet to conceive, who wanted reassurance from the new fortune-teller that a baby would come soon. Or at least eventually. This was a difficult problem for a well-intended fortune-teller like herself. "Eat well. Rest. Spend time outdoors. Relax. Have sex often. Don't worry." It frustrated her that there was nothing she could actually do to help. Some days the banal advice she gave seemed so inadequate. So many troubles in the world. So very little she could do about them.

Finally, as the end of May neared, Lola realized that she was soon going to have a husband off work for the summer and a college-aged daughter home. She also had a young teenager to whom perhaps she should be paying more attention, not less. Sitting for hours every night on a porch starring at flowers and sipping wine was maybe not such a good long-term plan.

She needed information. She needed it about a couple of things. So the Thursday before Memorial Day weekend, Lola poured a particularly large glass of her favorite pinot noir and took her laptop out to the porch with her. Alex raised an eyebrow at this new development, but said nothing. With a determined air, she opened two tabs. Her search engine tried to direct her towards geology, or Africa, or others items of peripheral professional interest. But tonight one window was going to be devoted to post-traumatic stress, and the other had already provided her with 1,350,000 results for "research facts telepathy" in under 0.23 seconds.

Apparently telepathy means distance feeling, and the term originated in 1882. Feeling. That explained why it kind of sounded like empathy and sympathy and other feeling words. And like telephone and television and telecommunication and, enough, Lola told herself, keep searching.

It turns out that post-traumatic stress disorder, commonly called PTSD, is a type of anxiety disorder that can occur after you've seen or experienced a traumatic event that involves the threat of injury or death. It is classed as "acute stress disorder" if it only lasts fewer than thirty days.

Been more than thirty days now. Damn, I have official post-traumatic stress disorder. Go figure.

It turns out that people really like to deceive each other concerning psychic powers even when no real money and only minor notoriety are to be gained. The internet provides a long list of ESP scams over the last couple of hundred years and details ways that charlatans have used non-verbal signals to discretely communicate, while giving the appearance of psychically transmitting information. The list includes looking up, down, right, and left for the four suits of a deck of cards, coughing, sighing, yawning, sending Morse code with jingling coins (*now that cannot be easy*), and gesturing to various body parts which have been given a prearranged meaning. (*Now that could be funny to watch.*)

People with PTSD re-experience the event again and again in at least one of several ways. They may have frightening dreams (*nope*), may feel as though they are going through the experience again (*okay, I got that one*), or they may become upset during anniversaries of the event. (*Oh great, something to look forward to.*)

One particular type of modern research into telepathy particularly intrigued Lola when she came across it. It involved something called the Ganzfeld ("total field") effect and it used a person designated as the receiver, who was placed in a calm soundproof room filled with white noise. Another random person was selected as the sender and placed in another soundproof room. Instead of using playing cards or sheets of paper with easy to classify but emotionally sterile information like blue circles and yellow squares, the sender was given a packet containing a group of related pictures and/or short video clips which had a certain emotional theme or feel to them, and the sender was asked to try to telepathically communicate the feeling of the images and sounds from the packet to the receiver. Then the receiver was shown copies of four such packets, each with a very different theme, and asked to rate the degree to which each packet matched what he or she had just experienced. If the receiver assigned the highest rating to the actual packet which was used, it was scored as a "hit." *Okay, this at least makes more sense,* Lola thought, *because it involves feelings people might care about sending and receiving.*

Those who analyzed the results of such experiments run over many years found a hit rate of somewhere between twenty-eight and fifty-one percent, depending on what was thrown out or included, which depended mostly on the analyzers predisposition to the subject. Lola was surprised to read that even twenty-eight percent, while not impressive, is, if accurate, statistically significant for such a very large number (over six thousand) of tests. However, The Straight Dope explains how this hardly constitutes "amazing ESP proof" and The Skeptics Dictionary, which they reference, goes on to concludes that "the actual size of this psi effect is so small that we can't detect it in a single person in any obvious way. We have to deduce it from guessing experiments. What hope do we have of isolating, harnessing, or expanding this power if a person who has it can't even directly recognize its presence?"

And what, Lola thought, *if a person who has it recognizes it all too well?*

There are no tests that can be done to diagnose post-traumatic stress disorder. Though at the far end of the spectrum its existence cannot be denied, it appeared to Lola that in any one particular case it was basically in the eye of the beholder. Treatment to reduce symptoms appeared to include encouraging one to recall the event and express one's feelings about it, in hopes that one might gain some sense of control over the experience. It was noted that support groups could be helpful. Medicines that act on the nervous system could help reduce anxiety and other symptoms of PTSD. The best outcome depended on how soon the symptoms develop after the trauma and on how quickly one got diagnosed and treated. One should call one's health-care provider early. *Got it.*

According to a 2005 Gallup poll, thirty-one percent of people in the U.S.A: believe specifically in telepathy and forty-one percent believe in some sort of extrasensory perception. Most amazing to Lola was that the poll showed no statistically significant differences about this belief among people by age, gender, education, race, or region of the country.

Djimon was not cruel; he told himself that over and over. He did not delight in death like the thugs who had brought such embarrassment to his beloved religion. He did not even wish harm to the pitiful woman he was now beginning to train so that he could confidently use her to send his message. No, he was just doing what he had to do. In the name of his beloved country. His mother. His children's future. And if the feel of her fresh taut skin under the palm of his hand brought him a glimmer of pleasure now and then while he did what needed to be done, well then didn't even a hero like him deserve a bit of joy in the middle of such a laudable struggle?

After their first weekend alone, Djimon sent Mairo and the children off almost every weekend there after to visit relatives, so he could have the house to himself for "training" Nwanyi, which, as he pointed out to Mairo, was best done in isolation after all. Mairo went willingly and said little. Nwanyi soon had visible sores around her wrists and ankles, which Mairo could only assume had come from struggling against restraints. Mairo shuddered. Djimon could do this?

After the first weekend alone with Djimon, Nwanyi became so withdrawn that she often appeared to be sleepwalking. But occasionally, Mairo would catch Nwanyi's alert eye with a look that was, what … victorious? That was it, Mairo thought. Nwanyi looked at Mairo like she had just beaten her in a contest. And, Mairo thought sadly, in a way she had.

The receptionist gave Lola a clipboard of paperwork to fill out while she was waiting, and along with the usual requests for medical history and contact and insurance information Lola found herself with a personal questionnaire.

"Have you gone through a divorce, separation or break-up in the last year?" *Thank heavens no.*

"Has anyone you are close to died in the past year?" *Well, yes my mother. May of 2008.* It seemed like forever ago, but it was really almost a year to the day. "Was it unexpected?" Yes, a heart attack at seventy-two had been unexpected. Working in her yard, doing what she loved. But still too young. Not yet old.

"Have you lost a job in the past year?" *Hell yes. December 2008. Along with what had seemed at the time like half the country.*

"Do you have any serious physical illnesses?" *No, healthy as a horse.* "Do you have any chronic health problems which, while not life threatening, affect your quality of life?" *No, healthy as a horse.* "Have you experienced any traumatic events that involved the threat of injury or death in the past year?" *Yup. That is why I am here.*

Dr. Walker was a small middle-aged man with a kindly face. Lola's primary physician, who she almost never saw, had referred her to this particular Ph.D. psychologist, assuring Lola that if a prescription was recommended he could prescribe it himself. As she entered the small, comfortably furnished but not lavish consultation room, she saw that Dr. Walker was glancing over her questionnaire.

"Lola, right? You've had quite a year Lola. Hmmmm. Mother passed away suddenly about a year ago. Recently let go by your employer of twenty-four years? Hmm. How were you doing before this car accident?"

"Fine. I was doing fine. But I wasn't in a car accident."

Dr. Walker squinted at the paperwork. "I see. A canoe accident." He gave her a puzzled look. "What were you doing in a canoe that could possibly have killed you? The other canoe was going too fast?" He chuckled a little.

"It's a long story. I'm here because the sound of running water kind of sets me on edge these days and I get a little frantic if I cannot easily get out of where I am physically."

"You mean you get upset if you are trapped in an elevator?" He smiled again, clearly enjoying his own streak of wittiness.

"No, I mean I have to now sit at the end of the row in a movie theater. If it is a booth at the restaurant I have to be on the outside. And these days you can absolutely forget about me sitting in the middle of the back seat of a car."

"I see. Some people are like that. It's a control issue. Do you feel like you lack control in your life?"

"Everyone lacks control in their life. I just never used to care at all where I sat and the change is a little, odd." Lola was having an exceedingly hard time getting this man on her wavelength, getting him to understand.

"So it's not really causing you a problem?"

"Well, I don't wash my hair as much. Is that a problem?"

"I don't know. Do you think you used to wash your hair too often?"

Lola decided that if she gave Dr. Walker the benefit of the doubt, she would agree that he was well-meaning. But she had seldom met another well-intended and alert human with whom she could communicate less. And she was paying him how much for a fifteen minute appointment just so she could communicate to him?

Dr. Walker must have felt the same way. "Lola? Lola. Look, you don't need to talk to me about everything that has happened. It is clear that you have had several stress-inducing events of varying severity over the last year. So, I am going to recommend that we treat you for a mild anxiety disorder and that we start you on a low dose of a common antidepressant. It is the one I think is most often prescribed for anxiety issues. It's very safe, it's been around for years, and I and Dr. Hayes will monitor you closely."

"But I am not depressed."

"These types of medications are called antidepressants, but they are actually used to treat a wide variety of conditions. I just read somewhere that more than half the time now they are prescribed for something other than depression. There is no stigma here. You should know that at least ten percent of Americans now take some sort of selective serotonin reuptake inhibitors, which is the type of medication which I am going to ask Dr. Hayes to prescribe for you."

"But I don't want to be medicated."

"You need to let us help you Lola. Give the receptionist information on your preferred pharmacy on the way out. I'll have Dr. Hayes' office call the prescription in now. You should know that this is not like taking aspirin. You have to take it consistently and let it build up. So it will take several days before you start to feel an effect. So let's say I will schedule you in again in two weeks. Call Dr. Hayes' office if you experience any side effects."

"There was one other issue I thought I should maybe mention," Lola said hesitantly. She saw Dr. Walker glance at his watch.

Lola took a deep breathe and exhaled with deliberate slowness. "I've kind of been experiencing this sort of, uh, affinity for this other woman."

"You are having lesbian sexual fantasies?"

It was Lola's turn to chuckle. "No, no nothing like that. This isn't anybody I even know."

"Fantasies like this are not uncommon, even among otherwise completely heterosexual women," Dr. Walker assured her. "And fantasies about people one does not know are much more common, especially in women, because they feel much safer."

"I'm not having fantasies about her."

Dr. Walker looked at the watch again. "Lola this is very interesting but unless you are actually hearing voices in your head," he smiled, " I am going to ask you to defer this topic to our next meeting, okay?"

Lola looked at him oddly.

"You aren't hearing voices in your head telling you to do things, are you?" he said in a mostly amused tone.

"No. No one is telling me to do anything."

"Okay. Good. We will talk again in two weeks then and I think you will be surprised at how much more calm and in control you will feel. Thanks for coming in Lola," he said as he stood up and shook her hand warmly and began walking her to the door.

The next morning before work Lola sat at her bathroom vanity for a while staring at the small green pill with the product name on one side and the 25 mg dosage on the other. She had never been on medication in her life except for the occasional antacid tablet, head-cold remedy or over-the-counter analgesic for a rare headache. And now she was expected to take this every morning point forward and had been warned by the pharmacist absolutely not to stop taking it once she started without speaking to her doctor lest she suffer withdrawal. (Withdrawal??) That alone was giving her a slightly claustrophobic trapped feeling.

Let's not over-react here, Lola told herself. *You were on birth control pills at two times in your life for years. Probably would be now still if Alex had not volunteered to get a vasectomy after Teddie was born. So you can take medication if you need to.*

Thanks to all the commercials on television, she expected the laundry list of unpleasant side effects that would be printed out for her to read, and she was not disappointed. Particularly alarming however was the instruction to tell her doctor immediately if she experienced agitation, hallucinations, or coma among other things, as this might be a symptom of a life-threatening condition called Serotonin Syndrome or Neuroleptic Malignant Syndrome. *Coma? Call my doctor if I go into a coma? Okay.*

She was also expected to contact her health-care provider if she experienced thoughts about suicide or dying, attempts to commit suicide, new or worse depression, new or worse anxiety, feeling very agitated or restless, panic attacks, trouble sleeping, new or worse irritability, acting aggressive, being angry, or violent, acting on dangerous impulses, mania, or other unusual changes in behavior or mood. Great. And she was taking this medication to prevent what?

The kicker came when she read that the medication could affect her ability to make decisions, think clearly, or react quickly, and finally that drinking alcohol while taking it was not recommended. Lola almost threw the whole damn bottle in the trash at that point, until she thought of Ariel coming home that night and how Lola truly wanted to be more like her old self for her daughter's sake. Okay, she thought, I'll give it one chance. This little green pill gets four weeks.

Chapter 8. June 2009

Within a few days the Zeitman house was at its usual level of summer activity. Alex, now out of school, was enrolled in two different training programs, a district one for high school science teachers and a seminar on young people with emotional disturbances to keep current his second certification in special education. In between the training he would take on a list of household improvement projects, shuttle Teddie to a summer volleyball workshop, get each of the aging Zeitman cars in top working order, and handle at least half of the stuff on their mutual back burner.

Teddie was slightly more pleasant now that her big sister was home, and Lola noticed with joy that for the first time their over seven-year age difference was not so great. As the two sisters sat huddled together in front of Ariel's laptop laughing, Lola noticed how much Ariel's thin straight coppery red hair contrasted with Teddie's almost black curls. How Ariel's lanky body differed from Teddies already soft curves. How Ariel's narrow, challenging light blue eyes differed from Teddie's round warm dark ones. Now that she thought about it, the girls had as little in common in other ways as they did physically. So it brought Lola joy to see the two of them head off on a shopping expedition together, and to hear that they were going out to lunch, or that they were renting a movie to watch together. This was good.

Lola felt like her employer had been getting less than her full attention since the canoe trip, and so now that her clan was together looking out for each other, she tried to focus harder on her work. The success of this well was clearly important to her tiny company. The location had been approved in theory, and now the engineers were developing a specific drilling plan while all of the necessary permits were being obtained, a drilling rig was being sought, and the drilling materials were being procured. All were vital and time-consuming parts of the process, but from Lola's point of view the main work was done. A reprocessed seismic data set had arrived over the area, and her job now was merely to double and triple check her own original interpretation.

Near as she could tell, the medication was having absolutely no effect. Zilch. No scary side effects, no change in her symptoms, no nothing. But she continued with the morning swallow of the little green pill, hoping for the best. She had to reluctantly give up her evenings sitting on the porch anyway, as the Houston nights became too hot and clammy. She opted instead for the air-conditioned comfort of her easy chair in front of some mind-numbing television, where she most often joined Alex for reruns of crime dramas while they both ate the lavish salads Alex tended to make in the summer.

By the time Zane came home to visit it was almost mid-June. Lola picked him up at the airport that Friday evening after work, surprised at how pale and almost chubby he seemed, with his ill-behaved medium brown hair cut shorter than usual. "You really need to get some sunshine after all that time working in a lab" she kidded. He seemed embarrassed, and she let it drop.

Zane had always been a little self-conscious of his body, reacting defensively when Lola had chortled about his sprouting facial hair years ago or when she continued to marvel at his odd eyes that always seemed to be the color of the fabric of whatever shirt he was wearing. Oops. It was hard to be a mom.

"Good to see you dear," she changed tack. "Dad's got quite a meal waiting at home. His eggplant parmesan and Caesar salad special."

Zane's major in neuroscience had always been a safe subject, as he was as fascinated by the workings of the brain as Lola herself was by the processes of the earth. So she pressed him for more information about the job. What was it like being part of a pharmaceutical company? He had called his work as a lab assistant grunt work, but wasn't he getting exposure to some of the leading edge research into new medications? Just to be around it would be so informative. Yes, Zane reluctantly agreed, some of the research itself was exciting.

Lola hesitated for a minute, not wanting to worry her son, then decided why the hell do you have kids if you can't talk to them at all? So she shared her most recent medical experience with him, keeping the information light and vague. She did not have to. Zane was surprisingly supportive, understanding very well based on his own studies, he told her, how even a short trauma could have surprising ramifications and how getting help was absolutely the right thing to do. "Too many folks in this world don't even have access to mental health care," he said. "We have a well-developed system in the U.S. and yet many are too proud or ill-informed to get the help they need. Actually Mom I am proud of you for taking care of yourself."

"Oh." Lola had not expected that. "Thanks."

This was probably why three days later, when Lola arrived for her follow-up appointment with Dr. Walker, she allowed him to talk her into doubling the dosage.

"I started you on a very low dosage, fully expecting this," he explained. "Fifty milligrams is what I would expect to be the appropriate dosage for you but I always like to start out cautiously. Now, you should have twelve or so tablets left at the old dosage and I want you to dispose of them safely.

"Why can't I just take two at a time and use them up?"

Dr. Walker smiled like one would at a particularly cute and precocious child. "In my experience it is best to keep this very simple and leave no room for a patient to go deciding to raise or lower their own dosage. Please dispose of them as I have instructed, and I will have Dr. Hayes call you in a new prescription that will be ready today."

So now Lola had little blue tablets that said 50 mg. And as days wore on Lola decided that they did not seem to do anything either.

Somadina had made no secret of her intent to buy a cell phone so that she could talk to Nwanyi as often as she pleased. By mid-June, just after the last of the yam crop had been planted, she figured that with the small coins she was charging her clients she had saved half of what she needed for a disposable cell phone with minutes, which she knew could be purchased in a nearby city. Her plan was to ask Azuka's father to please drive her to Abakaliki, or to lend Azuka the car so that he could do so, and she was trying to figure out how many more days needed to be worked, when Ikenna knocked on her door. He walked in without greeting and gruffly handed her his cell phone. "Do you know how to work this thing?" he asked.

"Yes. I have used others just like it many times before. Why?"

"Call Nwanyi," he answered. She found the phone's directory, saw that the only entry was her sister's name. It must have been entered by someone who was not her father and much more adept with small electronic devices. As she pressed the call button he offered, "Djimon typed in the name and number for me when he gave me this new phone before they left."

Bing ding bing. The little chimes played softly. "We are sorry. This number is no longer in service."

"It has been saying that since yesterday," her father told her.

"How often do you call Nwanyi?" Somadina asked surprised.

"Every day," he mumbled. "The very first time she called I tried to call her back to ask her a question I had forgotten. I don't even remember the question now, but I got this strange message saying my call could not be delivered to the number I had dialed. It bothered me, so I have tried to call her number every single day since. Until yesterday, I always got that message, every time, saying my call could not be delivered to the number I had dialed. What kind of message is that? But I never asked her about it and I know I should have. I was afraid that I was misusing the phone and I didn't want to look stupid. And she just never seemed like she wanted to talk when she called me. So to answer your question completely, yes I have tried to call her every day since her first phone call to us. And no, I have never gotten through to her once, although she has now called me a total of six times in the two months she has been gone."

Somadina sighed heavily. She did not know whether to be happy that her father had been making this effort or frustrated that he had not shared this with her. "That message you were getting means your number was blocked. Why didn't you try calling her from another phone? One you could have borrowed from someone else?"

"I did not realize that would work," replied a puzzled Ikenna.

"It doesn't matter now," Somadina said in frustration. "The number you have is now clearly disconnected. Do you have another number? Djimon appeared to have means. Perhaps his house has a landline?"

"If he does have such a thing I do not know of it."

"Okay. Do you have an email address for him? You know quite well that Nwanyi isn't that good at reading or writing, but I tried to talk her into getting email anyway once she got to Lagos. I told her that way we could at least send each other photos once in awhile. But I do not think she has done so. I have been able to get online twice since she left, and there has been no message from her. So perhaps we could email him instead?"

Ikenna shook his head sadly. "I have already asked both of your oldest half brothers to help me. Udo is especially good with computers. He is really very smart, Somadina. I took him with me to Abakaliki myself." Ikenna sighed. "We spent the day. I had him search all those things he knows. Yahoos and Googles and Facebooks and there is no such man in all of Lagos in any directory or anywhere to be found on the internet."

This was worse than Somadina had even imagined. "Well then let's take your car and drive to his home address. We can confront him in person and demand to see Nwanyi. Who does he think he is to deny a woman contact with her own father and sister like this?"

"Do you not think I would already have done this daughter? I have handled this badly. I should have gone with her to Lagos in the first place. Demanded to meet his family before the marriage ever took place." Ikenna looked sad beyond belief. "The address he has given me turns out to be that of some random government building. No one lives there. Udo pulled up a picture, it was amazing, he pulled up the picture right there on the computer, a picture of what is at the address Djimon had given me. It is a big office. Ugly, and very clearly nobody's home."

"Do you have any other contact information at all? Surely you got more?"

"Of course. I did try to be a good Igbo parent, even though

the situation was odd. I have names and addresses of all of his family. His mother. His brothers. He went to great lengths to show me their photos, and to assure me that Nwanyi was entering an honorable and welcoming family."

"And?"

"And Udo was in every case able to find no such people. Well he found two teenage girls on the Facebook with the mother's name, but obviously that is just a coincidence. It is certain that neither is Djimon's mother. No address he gave me was real. No phone number reaches a working phone. Probably nothing he told me is real. He may not even live in Lagos." Ikenna hung his head.

"And you have nothing else?"

"Just one more thing," and with this admission Ikenna looked as upset as Somadina had seen him in many years. "He gave me a mailbox to which to send her passport, with an addressed, insured box in which to put it, with all the postage paid. He paid to have the application rushed, too. I received the passport in such very good time, and I was so proud of that and so hoping it would make him happy that I sent it on to him as soon as it arrived last week."

"What?"

"Yes. He should have received it from me in the last day or two. I thought maybe I should have waited and confronted him about talking more with Nwanyi before I sent it. But I didn't want to lose it and didn't want him to think I was not keeping up my end of the bargain. I hoped that if he was happy we might hear from Nwanyi more. So I mailed it the same day Udo and I went to Abakaliki. In fact, I mailed it on the way into town. I had no idea our day would turn up such troubling information."

"Wait. Back up." Somadina had listened to this last confession with growing confusion and concern. "You got Nwanyi a passport?? Why??"

"It was the only thing that Djimon asked of me, other than to have a very quick wedding. He said it was very important to him, that he traveled often and understandably wished to have a wife with him on those occasions when he was gone for a lengthy period of time. He said that his first wife had some issues trying to get a passport because of some political group that her family members were involved in. Nothing she has any part in of course. But Djimon had given up trying and so he was particularly happy to have this Igbo wife now with no past to cause problems in this area. He asked me as a personal favor. Just to be sure that association with his first wife, Mairo, did not cause issues in Nwanyi's case as well, he asked me to get the documents under Nwanyi's unmarried name and have them sent here and then to forward them on to him just as soon as they arrived. It seemed so reasonable. He was a good man who just wished to have a wife with him to help him avoid temptation while he was away from home. I admired that."

It was Somadina's turn to sigh deeply. What she really wanted to do was to scream at her father, "How could you be so incredibly stupid??" but in her world, as in many, such behavior would have been unacceptable beyond belief for a twenty-one-year-old daughter. So she said merely, "He must have received the passport yesterday."

"I know." Ikenna muttered. "I know. Because I also am sure that is when he turned off the phone."

"Nwanyi may be in more danger than that of just common mistreatment from a bad husband," Somadina added.

"I agree," her father said. "I too am saving money now. As of this morning both of my wives are on a very strict budget and not terribly happy with me. But I need to hire a detective. I need to find my daughter. I just came here, well, because I did not want you to waste your money buying a cell phone. You may use mine all you like and you could have used it all along. I just kept it from you hoping that not being able to get through was some sort of misunderstanding, one that I could fix before you got involved."

He paused, as if he was considering whether to say something or not. He decided to go on. "Somadina, please understand that I did not involve you sooner only because I did not wish for you to think any more poorly of me than you already do."

"And that worked well," Somadina muttered.

"Since your mother died I cannot seem to do anything right in this particular area. But it is not because I am not trying." And he thought, with fear, of how over the years Amaka had occasionally appeared to him in his dreams, always beseeching him to do better by the two daughters she had left him, and never satisfied with his meager efforts which she always judged to be too little too late.

"Then let's work together," Somadina said with whatever graciousness she could muster on behalf of her sister. "Nwanyi needs us to be as smart as we can possibly be. Smart together. Not stupid alone." It was the closest she could allow herself to get to chastising her father, and though he noticed it, this once he let it pass.

"I agree," he said. "Let's combine what we know and what we can do and get her back home."

He started for the door, then paused. "You can't really tell fortunes can you? That could perhaps be useful."

Oh dear. "No father, the truth is that I am a pretty weak fortune-teller. Please don't pass that around. I, um, have enough skill to help the lovelorn, but not enough real skill to help us here. But you know, I do have some other unusual abilities. Maybe I can use them better, now that I know how serious the situation is."

As her father walked out the door, she resolved to also start using her abilities in earnest to make sure she was getting the entire story from her father point forward.

In 2002, Lola made her one and only attempt to write an article for publication. It was called "Face Painting for World Peace." After dozens of revisions, it still sounded embarrassingly naive, and therefore it still lived in the bottom of a desk drawer awaiting additional inspiration or perhaps just more sophistication. The odd thing about the article, though, was that Lola knew its basic premise to be utterly true. She just lacked the skills to express the concept.

Over the years Lola had made a significant effort to be involved in her children's lives because she thought it was important. To them, to her, to their future. But a full-time career meant she had to pick her spots wisely. Half-a-day off to drive the van on a field trip. Yes. That one was a real kid pleaser. Joining PTA committees which would hold endless meetings, usually during the day attended by moms in no particular hurry and about which the kids could care less? No.

The annual PTA carnival, a huge event at her children's grade school, had lots of opportunities for attending such lengthy meetings. But by sheer luck, back when Zane was in first grade she had signed up for the face-painting booth. Turned out she had a bit of an artistic streak and a talent for inventing kid-beloved designs. By year three she was running the booth, featuring Ninja turtles and unicorns, and she had become one of the coolest moms at the school, which was interesting because she'd never been cool at her own grade school. Apparently, it was never too late …

As a completely unintended side effect, face painting changed Lola. With a husband teaching in the public school system, Lola and Alex made the principled decision to fight the "white flight" into private schools, to put their children and their energy into the public school system and their resources into a college savings account. So all three little Zeitmans had been sent to a magnet elementary school attached to a local intercity grade school and had grown up with groups of friends who looked like a junior United Nations delegation, which Lola and Alex were fine with, of course. Theoretically. But Lola at least had grown up in a time and place in which everyone around her was very white. It is one thing to believe something about how the world should be. It is another to actually be comfortable with it.

Then Lola found herself holding little black girls on her lap, dressed in the stereotypical frills that she used to scoff at. She painted rainbows on their arms while they giggled in delight and pretty soon she was giggling too. The little boy whose parents were newly arrived from India wanted the Batman logo on his chin. The little boy from Vietnam wanted a flower. The little Latina wanted a heart on her face and a lightning bolt down her arm. As Lola held the children, touched the children, enjoyed the joy of the children, year after year, somewhere along the way a funny thing happened. They went from being *those* people, to being people.

Once you make that transition, you don't go back.

A few years later when Lola's employer sent her to interview grad students as prospective new hires, she listened to the hopes and dreams of aspiring geoscientists from Jamaica, Croatia, Pakistan, and China. The HR department asked her to please stop recommending so many foreign students. It was then that Lola had penned her article. We need massive amounts of card tables and millions of gallons of tempera paint. A billion little paint brushes and a ton of old newspapers. Let's send every adult on the planet somewhere else, and have them paint children's faces for a day. Then have them interview the young adults for a day. Then have them paint faces for a day more. Let's do it once a year. Everybody goes somewhere different each year. We can do this. Given the time and resources, we can do world peace.

It was meant in jest of course, but only kind of.

She looked across the hall at her new friend, the young Nigerian geologist Okocha. A kindred spirit of Lola's had certainly designed that National Youth Service Corps with the wild idea of achieving peace in Nigeria. For all of its flaws and troubles, who knew what chaos that country might be in today without that oddly idealistic plan.

So how about just getting people working together in an office for world peace? Exchange students? Pen pals? She thought of her group of word-game playing internet friends. A Mormon grandmother with a delightfully earthy sense of humor. A Muslim physician who had been kind enough to explain to her what all the racket was about when she found herself in Jakarta on Eid al-Adha, which turned out to be a holy day for giving to the less fortunate and feeding the poor. Given that, how could one possibly complain about the music coming from the mosques?

So, internet games for world peace. Everybody grab a mouse and play something. Come on people. We can DO this!

Phase three, according to Djimon's plan, involved several weeks of moderate physical pain and mild verbal abuse on the weekends, combined with confinement and lack of attention during the week. It was important that the situation be well-orchestrated, and that Nwanyi not be made so afraid that she was pushed into rash or desperate behavior. The mild ongoing abuse had to become her new sense of normal while her self-esteem slowly eroded.

At the same time, it was also important that she have no friendly contact whatsoever, so that she would slowly, almost unnoticeably, learn not to feel any sense of hope. Djimon pushed Mairo to work with him on this latter part, to keep the children away, to slap down Nwanyi's brief meals personally, to limit toilet access, to keep her chores indoors, isolated, simple, and boring. There must never be panic, but rather an ongoing sense of discomfort that was never interrupted by joy. After six weeks of such, Djimon determined to his own satisfaction that Nwanyi was ready for phase four. This phase, which would feature more intense humiliation and discomfort, would begin this weekend.

Djimon waited until he heard Mairo's car leave the driveway before he insisted Nwanyi assume a crawling position on the floor of her tiny room, like a dog. He often did not need to bind her hands or feet anymore, depending on his plan, as she would now generally do as he ordered in hopes of making the sessions briefer. He took pains to assure her that her compliance indeed bought her shorter sessions. He knew this violated his own edict against giving her any sense of power over her own life, but it did make her less difficult to control, and on some level he enjoyed watching her strip and willingly assume any bizarre and even sexual position that he ordered.

Tonight, as she knelt on the floor like a scrubwoman, he took his time waiting and watching. He had learned that anticipation of what was coming was one of his most potent weapons. After a few moments, he would approach her quickly, and watch her tense, expecting the blow. Then he would wait some more. Until she relaxed. And then, sometimes, he would strike. Other times he would just walk away feigning disinterest, often pausing within her field of vision to eat a small snack out of his pocket, some delicacy he hoped she would crave, while she watched. Or, alternatively, he would return to her side immediately and administer her punishment. Or not. Thus he found he could inflict the maximum amount of anxiety and misery on her, with the minimum physical effort on his part. It was a particularly good technique on days when his back was bothering him.

x^0

Luckily, however, his back was doing fine this evening, which was good because this was a particularly important night. He made her watch from her position on the floor as he slowly put on his steel toed boots. Then he walked towards her from the rear and paused to give her time to wonder what nature of torment was coming. Then, using his stronger right leg, he kicked her as hard as he possibly could right in the center of her female parts. The "oof" sound she made was more of a groan than a scream. He kicked again, this time her right buttock. Then once again to her left lower thigh. They both know that this was rougher, faster than his usual style, but of course only he knew that it was for a carefully calculated purpose.

"I will stop," he whispered loudly, "when you say exactly what I tell you to."

Another fierce kick, this time aimed a little higher.

"Anything." She coughed out the word softly. "I'll say anything."

Good. At this point he had expected such compliance.

A slightly softer kick to the left buttock, its relative gentleness meant to acknowledge that she had acquiesced. "Tell me 'I am worthless. I do not deserve to be alive.'" Nwanyi exhaled loudly, then repeated it without emotion.

A bit rougher kick to the back of the right thigh. "Say it again like you mean it."

"I am a worthless. I do not deserve to be alive."

Another kick. "Again. With more feeling."

"I am a worthless. I do not deserve to be alive."

Another kick. "Again."

And so it went for almost an hour. At the end of it Djimon made Nwanyi scrub the entire floor of her bedroom, her bruised naked backside toward him while he supervised her from the hallway as he sat in one of the children's little bean bag chairs eating popcorn, using the power of its smell. The child's chair was slightly uncomfortable, but he pretended to be relaxed and even bored as he sipped his sweet soda loudly and occasionally administered an order to scrub harder or to redo a particular section of the floor.

Up until the middle of June, Nwanyi had given the servants little to remark upon, except of course for the broken face which no one thought for a moment was an accident. But now they gossiped to each other and to their friends and family with great animation about how the new second wife who always stayed in the tiny little room in back seemed to be getting stranger every day. And how sometimes, if she fell asleep before one of them left for the evening, they could hear her whimpering loudly like a hurt animal in her sleep.

After her talk with her father, Somadina tried to reach Nwanyi with renewed efforts. It frustrated her that she so easily picked up the mundane and irrelevant emotions of those around her, but all she could feel from Nwanyi was a muffled sense of misery and hopelessness that seemed to get worse with each day.

Somadina also tried reaching out harder to the mystery woman, who now often offered her feelings of comfort and sympathy but who had yet to prove to be of any use whatsoever. However, she was able at least to learn a little more about the woman. This lady had a husband, a good man whom the woman loved, and there were children. More than one. That was nice. And yes, the woman worried about all of them and she worried about someone else.

Then Somadina got the connection. There was a younger sister, almost exactly five years younger, who was now far away, whom the woman had looked out for and protected throughout childhood. The woman loved this sister dearly, and was worried about her. Somadina had to laugh. Wasn't it the way this gift of hers seemed to work? Instead of finding someone who could help her, she had found someone who would understand her.

Phase four was going as well as Djimon could have hoped, although he was a bit concerned that each week he spent more time than needed planning the specifics of the coming weekend's activities. To be completely honest, maybe he even occasionally dwelt on his plans for Nwanyi more than he should, particularly at

x^0

awkwardly inappropriate moments, like in the shower. And while he had to admit that the unexpected interest he had developed in his role as Nwanyi's chief tormentor was a bit disturbing, he assured himself that for the most part it was just a psychology student's clinical interest in the unusual combined with an admirable zeal for his cause. It would surely pass when his need for such behavior was over and done.

Zane left Father's Day afternoon, after the kids spent the morning indulging their dad in the spirit of the day by playing basketball with him. Zane had never been the athlete that his father had hoped for, more due to lack of interest than lack of ability, and though that had induced some frustrating moments for all over the years, Alex had eventually accepted that Zane was just the kind of kid who preferred video games and books and had satisfied himself with being proud of the unique achievements of his National Merit finalist son.

Ariel, on the other hand, had been something of a high school athlete and had a fiercely competitive streak. Had she not been also trying to match her brother academically, her girlfriends socially, and fill in part-time for her mom around the house, she might have been something of a volleyball star. Even giving it only a quarter of her attention, she was still good.

Teddie, who Alex thought had the best innate physical skills of all three, turned out to have the worst sort of personality for any contact sport. She was hanging in there with her junior high volleyball team, but hated it when the other team was mean, or when her own teammates criticized her or each other. She had already almost quit twice, once when the coach had actually yelled at the girls and once when the other team's cheering section had singled Teddie out for some mild verbal abuse from the sidelines. Lola doubted Teddie would last long at the high school level.

As she looked out the kitchen window at her clan while she whipped up waffles for a father's day brunch, she could hear a happy Alex coaxing the best from teammate Teddie, while Ariel struggled to not mind losing, and Zane struggled to care enough to make an effort for his dad. Ah well. Her family. She loved them.

Jumoke, the engineer from the Lagos office, surprised Lola by calling her directly at her office in the middle of an otherwise quiet Wednesday morning in late June. Lola was genuinely glad to hear from him, and they spent a few minutes getting caught up on company issues and life in general. Lola was sure that there was a point to the call, however, so she wasn't surprised when he said, "Lola, there is somebody who would really like to have lunch with you next week. I am going to ask an outright favor of you and ask you to please do this."

Lola assumed it was a friend looking for a job. "Of course. I'll be happy to talk to him. Who is it?"

"No, it's not professional. More, uh, personal."

"I'm not really looking to make new friends, Jumoke."

"Neither is he, dear. He is eighty-four, and I think he might have known your parents. At any rate he is from the Midland area, and he is a friend of my brother's."

"Well that alone has got to be an interesting story. Sure, of course I will. But why?"

Jumoke hesitated. "My brother dropped by last week and we got to talking and I mentioned your visit here last March. The more I described you the more adamant he became that you needed to meet his friend. The man's name is Maurice and he doesn't drive much any more, but he is coming to Houston on some other business. I'll email you details."

And Lola remembered the old man's voice she had heard in her head while sitting on the porch, asking about Lola Conroy. Damn. She knew now with absolute certainty that it had been Maurice.

On June 25, Michael Jackson died. Although none of the Zeitmans were devoted fans, all five mourned the loss of a talented, troubled man who had written songs that they had enjoyed. Lola noted with interest that so many people accessed the internet in search of more details about his death, or even just in search of shared comfort, that several major websites became unusable for a while. What a force we can be en masse, she thought.

While she found herself humming snippets of his music for days afterward, she mostly sang to herself the one song of his that she had liked best of all. Forty-three other musical stars had joined in to sing his 1985 collaboration with Lionel Richie called "*We are the World*", with over sixty million dollars in proceeds donated to fight starvation in Africa.

She could still see in her mind the video of Michael in the black jacket with the gold sequins, his sparking white glove undulating to the music while he sang the first rendition of the chorus. Lola thought that when Cyndi Lauper quipped that the lyrics sounded like a Pepsi commercial, she had a point. There was no deep meaning here. Just a hell of a great idea. "<u>We are the world.</u>"

Part II. x^0 Equals One
Chapter 9. July 2009

The Yoruba man Olumiji arrived in the village at the beginning of July, seeking the local woman who was performing magic. The villagers were defensive, for they basically liked their new fortune-teller who gave generally sunny, if somewhat vague, predictions that so far had a pleasant way of working out to be true more often than not. They were concerned that Somadina had violated some unknown law or perhaps offended some religious person and now would be asked to cease her soothsaying on their behalf. But the stranger assured everyone that Somadina was in no trouble.

Somadina, of course, had an entirely different worry when Olumiji came to her house. She was afraid that word of her talents might be spreading and that she would be required to predict the future for a less gullible and more serious audience, which she absolutely did not wish to have to do.

"I am not much of a fortune-teller," she greeted the man at her door. Azuka was still at the shop, and Kwemto was playing in the yard.

"I know you are not," he smiled. "But what you are doing is harmless. I have no quarrel with it."

"You have a quarrel with something else?" she asked.

"In fact, yes. May I come in please?"

Somadina nodded and hastened to make some tea for the stranger. He sat at the small kitchen table as she motioned to it.

"I am here in the rather awkward capacity of the neighbor who has been selected to ask you on behalf of all the other neighbors to please make less noise."

"I don't understand. You are not my neighbor, and I do not make noise."

Olumiji smiled. And then he softly touched her mind with a gentle hello.

Oh.

"Oh indeed." He spoke aloud. "Somadina, you know you have a gift. It should not surprise you that while it is rare, you are not completely unique. Many people have this gift to some minor extent, but like our relatively bad human sense of smell, they just ignore it in day-to-day life because it does not do them very much good."

Then, in response to a feeling he got from her. "Yes, it turns out that you are particularly talented, in fact you are probably at least as capable as anyone I have met. And I have met quite a few folks who can do this well. You might like to know that I am extremely gifted in this area also. And yet, you and I would find it quite difficult to hold this complicated conversation effectively between us, even here at close distance with eye contact and facial clues to help us. So ... I personally choose not to call this ability telepathy, although that is how some of my colleagues do refer to it. Extreme empathy? Maybe, although it seems to go beyond that. And while it has its uses, sort of like smell, it can be a nuisance at least as often as it can be helpful. Don't you agree?"

Somadina had to nod.

"But you are particularly troubled about something lately, and you have recently become exceptionally adept at giving off distress signals. Almost continuous distress signals. The rest of your village is largely deaf to the noise you are making, but those of us within mental earshot, if you will, can hear the racket and are starting to get both concerned and, to be honest, tired of the noise."

He felt Somadina's panic that she was going to be told to stop seeking help. "No. Hold on. No one wants you to walk away from someone in real distress if that is the case. We believe this is about your sister, but it has been hard to tell just what is going on. So, why don't you start at the beginning and tell me in words the actual situation. That way, perhaps, we can give you both a hand and a reason to calm down."

Somadina trusted the man. She already could tell on a very deep level that she could. But she would likely have told him the whole story anyway because there was little to lose. Ikenna had priced a private detective in Lagos a few weeks ago. It would be weeks more before they could afford even the most basic of searches. So any help that came more quickly would be welcome. And any reasonable chance to get such help was a chance to be taken.

Somadina's story started at the beginning with Nwanyi's birth and went on for quite a long time. While she talked, Azuka came home, met Olumiji, and gathered up their son and tactfully took him to visit his grandparents well before the story was half-finished. It was clearly more involved, and more serious, than Olumiji had expected, and it clearly was doing this young woman a world of good to talk through the events.

Olumiji listened patiently until he had to finally, reluctantly, explain that it was getting late and he had to go. He was so glad he had gotten the information. So glad that he understood now what was going on. Of course he would try to help, and others he knew, they would try as well. This awful man and Somadina's sister must be found. Her distress was understandable.

When Olumiji left, he gave her an email address and cell phone number on a dark red business card. "Tell your father about me," he instructed. "Explain to him that I will send text messages to his phone if I learn anything important. His son Udo can read them to him and should pass the information on to you. And I will also email you about any progress, so try to check your email. I promise that you have been heard and you are not alone."

He smiled, catching Somadina's amused notice of the reference to the meaning of her name. "Yes," he agreed. "Most telepaths are loners who need time by themselves to recharge. The choice of your name is indeed ironic. But it is a beautiful name. Meanwhile, please understand that you have been heard."

"I will try to ease up on broadcasting my worry," Somadina promised. "I can be quieter, so to speak. I just had no idea that there were people like me who heard me. I am sorry." And Somadina clearly felt Olumiji's assurances that no apologies were necessary.

"What is this odd thing on your business card?"

It was the letter "x" with a little circle by the upper right corner of the "x", sort of like the way Somadina had sometimes seen people write the temperature. "x degrees?" she tried.

"No, it is a mathematical term. It would take some explaining, but what matters is just that it is the name of a group of us who all have this talent like yours, and we get together and try to understand it and to help each other work with it and occasionally even just help people in general by using it."

"Like a club?" Somadina asked.

"Yes. Just like a club."

"Then how do you pronounce the name of the club?"

"Oh. We just call it One. Like the number."

"Well, that is easy enough to remember," Somadina laughed. Just knowing that One existed, she felt slightly better than she had in months.

And so the first week of July Lola found herself on the west side of Houston at a small Mexican restaurant, approaching an elderly fair-skinned man with faded freckles, a shock of white hair, and a huge friendly grin. "Thanks for coming young lady. A pleasure to see you." Maurice was as healthy an eighty-four-year-old as Lola had ever seen, and he rose surprisingly quickly to pull her chair out for her.

Oh good grief, Lola thought, but she said nothing.

Maurice beamed, "You have grown into quite an attractive young woman."

"You knew my dad?"

"I knew you. The little girl that rode around west Texas with her dad while he fixed two-way radios. Trucking companies, oil companies, every county sheriff's department, we all depended back then on two-way radio communication for all the places a phone line didn't reach. Which was most of the places. So practically every little hill in West Texas had some sort of base station or relay station on it back then."

"Yes, and a third of them went out every time we had a thunderstorm," she laughed as memories she had not recalled for decades began to resurface. And she started to warm a little. "My mom used to send me along with dad to keep him company on the road, especially if he had been out the night before trying to get some sheriff's department back on the air. She was always afraid he might fall asleep at the wheel. I missed a fair amount of school in those days, but I got a heck of an education."

"I bet you did," Maurice laughed as well. Lola was starting to have the odd sensation that she and Maurice had been friends for years.

"You, know, everybody I met always treated me very well. Those oilfield guys were incredibly sweet. Mudloggers would give me soda pop, the company man always had some kind of candy or cookie stash he was willing to share, and my dad was too busy to enforce rules about eating sweets. Sometimes they'd forget to take down their calendars. If I got left in the office by myself, I'd play with the ones with the transparent page on top that covered the girl with a little nightie, and I would lift up the page and she'd be naked."

"You played with those calendars?" Maurice seemed awkwardly amused and Lola thought to herself, *what in the world am I doing telling him this?* She realized that she had felt so instantly comfortable with the man that her normal filters for what made for appropriate or inappropriate conversation seemed to have disappeared.

"It's okay," he assured her, as if he somehow understood the dynamics.

"I mean, it was like dressing and undressing my dolls. I thought they were fun." She tried to turn the conversation onto a more normal track. "But luckily I never came across a single creep. Which is why I suppose to this day I have a greater comfort level in places that would make most women uneasy. It's served me pretty well in my profession."

"I bet so," Maurice said. "I heard you were a doodlebugger."

Lola had to smile at the outdated term for a geophysicist. "Mostly on a computer these days. But yes, I've spent my time in the field."

"Well we have a mutual friend in the oil business. Sort of. You work with a Nigerian company now. I understand that one of your engineers in Lagos showed you around a bit during a visit in March."

"That's right." Lola was all ears.

"This may seem odd for an old guy from West Texas, but I

have a good friend in Nigeria myself who is your friend's brother."

"Well that is what I heard. You guys worked together in the past?"

"Actually no. Our relationship has absolutely nothing to do with our profession."

Lola waited.

"We both belong to an organization. Kind of a loose worldwide group. Jumoke has been invited to join too, but he rather vehemently declines. His brother, on the other hand, is one of the leaders, so I think there is a little friction there."

"Jumoke mentioned that he and his brother had some sort of issues. He was pretty vague about it." Lola said.

Maurice smiled but said nothing.

"What is this about?" For reasons she could not quite pinpoint, this whole meeting was starting to make Lola nervous.

"Raise your left hand," Maurice said. "Just an inch or two. Please."

Lola rolled her eyes but she complied.

"Very nice. Now please but it back down." Maurice paused. "Do you have any idea whatsoever of what a miracle you just performed?"

"What are you talking about? I lifted my hand."

"And could you please tell me just how you managed to do that? How you succeeded in wishing your hand to go up and it actually did it, in just the way and the amount you wanted?"

"I …" Lola was going to start in on muscles and neurotransmitters and realized that her ability to explain exactly how she raised her hand upon demand was outside of her ability to explain. "A neuroscientist could explain it," she said lamely.

Maurice laughed. "I've got six trees outside this window who would consider it magic, if they could consider. And a baby four tables down who is in the process this very moment of desperately trying to teach himself to do that very thing, and he is finding it incredibly difficult. But even though you, a trained scientist and logical woman, cannot explain to me how you do it, you most certainly do not consider your ability to raise your hand to involve any kind of sorcery?"

"I do not."

"That's good. And I suspect you do not consider the cell phone in your purse magic either?"

"Of course not."

"And yet in both cases you largely have taken the word of experts that the powers involved obey the natural laws of this universe, because you believe in those natural laws, not because you can convincingly explain these natural laws yourself?"

"Well yes."

"Then would you be willing to consider that your abilities to connect mentally with others might also involve perfectly reasonable, albeit less understood, laws?"

So. That was what this was about.

"I don't know. I have been doing a little research of my own on the subject. I never used to give it much thought to be honest, but recently I've become, well, more curious about it. I'm not sure what I think right now."

"And that's a good start," Maurice said. "I know that you understand electromagnetic radiation. Tell me about the visible spectrum?"

"Okay. Sure. This stuff I do know. Our eyes see electromagnetic radiation with a wavelength as short as about four thousand angstroms—that's purple—to as long as about seven thousand angstroms—that's red. Even longer wavelengths are called infrared. They look black to us, but they exist and transmit heat. Wavelengths longer than that are microwaves, and really, really long wavelengths are radio waves. Like what you still receive with your car radio. We do radio stations in cycles per second, hertz, but given that the speed of all electromagnetic radiation is constant—thank you Albert Einstein—that's really just another way of expressing wavelength. Oh, and shorter wavelengths are called ultraviolet—they look black to us also but cause sunburn, among other things, and even shorter ones are x-rays. Then radiation gets really dangerous beyond that."

"Excellent. You passed your physics test," Maurice chuckled.

"And, scientist that you are, I suspect it would not surprise you in the least to learn that while most people do not see <u>electromagnetic radiation</u> with a wavelength longer than seven thousand angstroms, you do find people who can actually see a very deep shade of red at wavelengths past ten thousand angstroms. They can see it. You can't. Are they performing magic?"

"Of course not," Lola said. "Everything works on a bell curve. There are always outliers."

"Exactly. My dear, it seems that the human brain has a very mild and not particularly well-developed ability to send and receive emotional information by means that are at best poorly understood at this point but which we have no reason at all to suspect in any way defy the laws of physics. It has nothing to do with electromagnetic radiation by the way. As far as we know. All we do know for sure is that we just don't happen to fully understand all the laws of physics and particularly the ones that govern this phenomenon.

"And of course, just as with eyesight and the visible spectrum, there are outliers at both ends. Some folks are particularly inept at this process. Others are the equivalent of those who can see a deep and beautiful shade of red at eight thousand angstroms. And you are one of them."

"I see deep red? Metaphorically?"

"You see deep red at eight thousand angstroms rather well. Metaphorically. This makes you unusual. But you already know that you are."

And Lola acknowledged to herself that that was true, and Maurice seemed to understand her agreement as well. He went on.

"There is a sort of threshold, let's say the equivalent of seeing deep red at wavelengths greater than ten thousand angstroms, at which a human starts to possess some rather significant and impressive skills. It's a gradational situation, but unlike with the ability to see light, which we've been using as an analogy, this isn't a completely fixed genetic trait. He leaned forward like it was very important to him to communicate this idea.

"To use our analogy, folks who just see in the normal

spectrum tend to keep on just seeing in the normal spectrum. But folks who see deep red at eight thousand angstroms have this tendency, when stressed or otherwise somehow pushed or encouraged, to grow that ability into being able to see all the way to ten thousand angstroms. Jumoke, who usually stays out of our affairs, gave his brother the very strong impression that he believed that you were in the process of doing just that. Which is why I was asked to drive over here, make contact with you, and ask you to consider becoming at least loosely involved with our group."

Lola was a little overwhelmed. Yes, things were changing, but she thought of this as a rather private problem. "You want me to join something? Are we talking monthly meetings? Initiation rites? Membership dues?"

"None of that really. We'd just like to be in contact with you."

"Like you want me to open my mind to you?"

Now Maurice rolled his eyes. "Like we'd like your email address. Maybe your cell phone number. We share ideas and information, through normal channels. You may have noticed that this gift you have is not particularly great for passing along facts like the exact amount of our membership dues."

"So you do have membership dues!" Lola joked.

He went on. "We are just a group of folks trying to understand what exactly it is that we are good at. We try to help each other when the rare need arises. We occasionally try to quietly debunk fears and myths about telepathy if and when they get going. We do have a password-protected website that we would very much like for you to visit so you can learn more about us and we more about you. We keep it to members only, not so much because we're trying to be a secret society as much as—"

"Never mind explaining that," Lola laughed. "I do get it. It would hardly help my credibility at work or at my daughter's school for someone to find me listed on any kind of ESP website."

"Exactly. We're secretive only because none of us can care to be categorized as kooks. We're normal, sensible people trying to figure out why we seem to be able to do unusual things."

"You know," Lola offered, "while I was looking around on the internet I couldn't help but notice that a lot of the research has been about transmitting an image like a blue circle. And yet what I have seems to be a lot more about transmitting feelings. Less like eyesight, which is definitive and precise, and much more like, I don't know, fear being sent as a pheromone."

"Very good," Maurice said. "The human sense of smell, while basically understood, is really one of the closest analogs we have for this ability. Like smell, it is largely ignored on a day-to-day to basis. It can provide extremely useful information to a human—yikes, why does my apartment reek?—but even at best it usually requires additional information. Oh, yes, I see a dead mouse on the floor. Or, it looks like the dog pooped in the hallway. I mean one can smell the difference between dead something and dog poop, but you are going to want to look with your eyes and see what the problem is. Your nose has only told you for sure that there is a problem."

"So true," Lola agreed. "Or for that matter the things I sense seem to be a lot more like seismic signals. They are possibly caused by any number of things because they are big, diffuse pieces of information from which I am trying to get a precise interpretation."

"That's it exactly," Maurice laughed in agreement. "And here you've got a drilling engineer who needs to know when you are going to hit that pressure transition to the nearest foot, and an operations geologist who wants the tops of rock formations that accurately also. And your information is coming in a big one hundred foot high waveform, and you're not even sure if what you are seeing is the top of a rock formation or an echo bouncing off of another interface. Yes indeed. Telepathy is very much like that. If I'd ever met a telepathic doodlebugger before I might have recognized the similarity."

"So how long has this organization been around?"

"It has a complicated history. In its current form, since the late eighteen hundreds," Maurice said. "There was a surge of interest in psychic powers around then and several different organizations originated."

"I read about a few of them on the internet."

"Yes, well, the others all seem to have centered around

proving telepathy exists, and they either approached the problem by trying to substantiate claims—which means they spent a lot of time investigating frauds and cheats, or they focused on things like card reading which seems a little bit to me like asking folks to emit an odor on demand to represent a three of clubs and then asking someone else to interpret that odor. Not the right tool for the job."

"So how did your organization approach this?"

"Well for starters we just accepted our own empirical evidence that telepathy did exist, so we never bothered with public claims made by those wanting to gain fame or to entertain. Instead we focused on figuring out how, why, and when it really does work, and spent our energy looking for people like you, and like me for that matter."

"I see. And what have you found out?"

"We have a huge anecdotal database, but I think the most interesting thing is the extent to which the phenomenon seems to be increasing."

"Increasing? In an age in which we seem to be finding more ways every day to send information to each other already? Why?"

"Well we have a lot of heated discussions going on about that. In fact, as you'll find out, we're a group of people who likes to have heated discussions about a lot of things," Maurice chuckled.

"On this particular issue, one group holds firmly to the idea that all of this electromagnetic information we are sending around the planet is starting to hit unhealthy proportions. Or it will in the long run. Throwing off the birds and the bees, literally, so that eventually flowers don't get pollinated and the whole ecosystem breaks down. They see humans as part of some larger organism that includes the earth and every living thing on it, and they believe that this organism is trying to grow its own organic ability to transmit information in a way that is safer for all life on the planet."

"Wow. Now that's a wild theory I would not have thought of. Do you believe that?"

Maurice laughed. "I try to keep an open mind, but frankly it's a little too New Age for me. I'm an old Texas geologist from the oil patch. But I will admit that it is an interesting idea."

x^0

"So what do you think is causing it?"

"Well, it could just be natural evolution. I'm proud to be a born-again Christian, but I am a man who spent my career working as a paleontologist. You know, the guy who dates the scraps of rocks that come up in the drilling cuttings by looking at the fossils of the little dead bugs found in them."

"I know what paleontology is," Lola reminded him.

"Of course you do dear. It's just that being a fundamentalist Christian paleontologist is kind of an oxymoron—only it is one most people wouldn't get. The point is that over the years my education and profession have left me to conclude that I have no reason to quarrel with evolution or with the idea of God creating the earth in four billion years. So along with that, I have to figure that we're still probably evolving because why would God be done with us now? So I personally figure this whole telepathy thing is just part of God's plan. Making us better, you know. Maybe even more like him."

"Okay." Lola wasn't going to debate religion with this man. She liked him and he was as entitled to his view of the universe as she was.

"But I can tell that's not your cup of tea. There is another theory I do like," he went on. "It has to do with the fact that as we have more telepaths in society we get better at transmitting the one thing we cannot communicate well electronically. How we feel. Maybe with email and chat and text messages and all the social networking tools out there, we actually have a much greater need now to be able to send a sense of our feelings than we ever had before. We already know that evolution is a little clumsy and goes in fits and starts at best. Maybe we are trying as a species to grow, as quickly as we can, a tool to complement the quick growth of our own communication technology."

"You know," Lola said. "I do like that theory. And, in fact, I like your organization. Question, think, debate. Good approach. Go ahead and count me in, or whatever you are supposed to say when you join a secret club. By the way, what is the name of this secret club I am joining?" she smiled.

He handed her a card. It was deep red. It simply said "x^0."

"Deep red for metaphorically seeing ten thousand angstroms of light?" she asked.

"Very good."

"But why x to the zero power?"

"That's another whole long story. Another time, okay?"

"But isn't it kind of a mouthful to say?"

"Oh no," Maurice laughed. We just pronounce it "One."

"Well, that is easy enough to remember," Lola said, smiling at the math. And just knowing that One existed, she felt slightly better than she had in months.

It was a Saturday night, and the household was still empty. Djimon had Nwanyi strip and kneel in front of him, her face awkwardly close to his covered crotch. He briefly considered letting her ease his growing arousal by demanding oral sex, but reason and good judgment told him he was far better off waiting and handling that matter himself later. Instead he stepped back, pulled off his belt and smiled. He bound her hands behind her back, knowing that otherwise she would not be able to keep herself from trying to protect her exposed face and breasts. He stepped back to give the belt room to swing, but had swung the belt only twice before she spoke up herself.

"I am a worthless. I do not deserve to exist."

Well now, that was easy. Too easy, actually. He felt oddly disappointed. No, these sessions needed to be intense. Memorable for her. To be effective. Now what? Improvising, he untied her wrists.

"Don't move your hands," he ordered. "Don't even start to move them to protect yourself while I am doing what needs to be done to you. You do not deserve protection. Not even from your own pathetic hands. Do you understand me?"

She nodded.

"If you even start to move them while I am being forced to discipline you, you will get two more strikes for every time you move. Tell me you understand."

"Do not move my hands." She said it simply without

emotion.

"Why not?" he asked.

She froze in confusion. He struck with the belt hard across her face, coming closer to her eye than he had intended. Damn. She needed her vision. He had to aim more carefully.

As the blow grazed her eye, her hands flew to her face in horror. "That will be two more," he said coldly.

Djimon stepped back a bit more and carefully administered one to each breast, taking artistic pains to carefully center each hit on her nipple, both for his own amusement and to assure himself that he could indeed aim a belt. She did not move, either time, but tears were pouring from her eyes, whether in frustration or pain or both he could not tell.

"Do you deserve the protection of your hands?" he prompted.
"No."

He could have sworn she was relieved at figuring out what she was supposed to say.

"I do not deserve protection, even from my own hands. I am worthless. I do not deserve to be alive."

"Very, very good," he smiled. And so it went. That night, the next weekend, and the weekend after. The process was going every bit as well as Djimon could have hoped.

Azuka knew that he should head over to the clinic and get his results, but he felt reluctant to do so. What if? He wasn't sure that he was prepared for the consequences of knowing. He also knew that he had perhaps been more dramatic than necessary with Somadina regarding the possibility. … She was right that his odds were good. He knew many men who had done much worse far more often and did not have the disease. … Well did not have it as far as they knew.
…

Absentmindedly, he watched Kwemto play. He enjoyed living in a house with only own his wife and child, the way modern couples did. He liked being a father and hoped for more children, but his favorite part of the arrangement was living with his wife. Of course he would remarry if this all went poorly, but Azuka could not imagine doing that right now. Women were not interchangeable parts to him. If one does not work out, he could not simply substitute another. He rather envied men who felt that way—it must have made their lives simpler. He looked up as Somadina came in the door with a determined look in her eye about something. Hmm … If he had wanted simple he should have chosen a different woman.

As the Houston summer went from a slow simmer to a full boil, the Zeitmans survived the July heat together, had some laughs, had some nice moments. Lola continued to think that her medication was not doing anything one way or another, but Dr. Walker cancelled her third two-week appointment due to a family emergency of his own, and Dr. Hayes renewed the two-week prescription with a month's dosage of 50 mg tablets based on her over-the-phone assurances to the nurse that she was experiencing no side effects.

So Lola tackled her problems pragmatically, avoiding bathing more than absolutely necessary and staying out of middle seats altogether. It reminded her of the old joke where someone says, "Doctor it hurts when I hold my arm this way," and the doctor answers, "So, don't hold your arm that way." Simple enough.

She also noticed that the pleas for help from her imaginary friend, as she came to think of the young woman, seemed to be softer and less persistent. Maybe the woman had given up on her sister? That was kind of a sad thought.

But maybe not. For in place of the general pleas for help Lola now felt a new urge, if she could call it that. A strong urge to learn more about Nigeria. She found herself increasingly curious about the country and found it increasingly satisfying to research anything about its history and geography on the internet. Not as odd as it sounded. She was enjoying her job and had always liked knowing more about the places she was working. She had always liked travel and learning more about foreign locales. At least that is what she told herself, but at some level she knew that she was being gently tugged by someone else, by someone who had decided to stop begging for help and to start doing something more constructive.

x^0

So, just as the cat would try to herd her toward the cat food when his bowl was empty or herd her towards the front door if he wanted out, Lola let her curiosity be herded by her imaginary friend. She knew it was voluntary on her part. She did not feel possessed or driven. But she deeply wanted to know more about the Igbo people of Southeastern Nigeria. She was also very curious about Lagos. So she downloaded maps of the country and studied them. Studied the roads. Studied the rivers. Studied the Igbo culture and beliefs and felt some nights like she was an Igbo woman herself. Which of course she was not. But her friend was. Lola was now sure of it.

She told herself that it was completely harmless and even kind of fascinating. Like being one of the folks in the telepathy experiments that had been conducted at places like at Duke and SMU. Why not? These were prestigious, sensible places. She was just looking at packets, picking the one that most matched what she was sensing. Igboland. They actually called it that. And it was home. A match. She had a "hit." And it made her curious. What more could she learn?

Lola turned to the major news outlets and found that British news, particularly the BBC, did a far better job of covering news from Africa that any U.S. source that she could find. Reading through BBC articles on the internet, Lola learned that less than a month ago, on June 30, Amnesty International had released a report calling the years of pollution and environmental damage in the Niger Delta a "human rights tragedy." The report claimed that the oil industry had caused impoverishment, conflict, and human rights abuses in the region, that the majority of cases reported to Amnesty International related to Shell, and that Shell must come to grips with its legacy in the Niger Delta. The report noted that Shell Petroleum Development Company is and has been the main operator in the Niger Delta for over fifty years and is also facing legal action in the Hague concerning repeated oil spills that have damaged the livelihoods of Nigerian fisherfolk and farmers.

Lola found Buffalo Springfield's 1967 hit "_For What It's Worth_" starting in her head while she read the news article on the internet on her lunch break. Was it because the song's haunting tune and warnings fit the troubled tone of the story? Or maybe she had just heard Bob whistling the refrain in the break room….

In the article, the BBC went on to report that Shell had defended itself in a written statement provided to the BBC arguing that "about eighty-five percent of the pollution from our operation comes from attacks and sabotage that also puts our staff's lives and human rights at risk. In the past ten days we have had five attacks." The Shell response added that "in the last three years, gangs have kidnapped one hundred and thirty-three Shell Petroleum Development Company employees and contractors while five people working for our joint venture have been killed in assaults and kidnappings in the same period."

The general insecurity in the area, according to Shell, is what prevents it from running maintenance programs that might otherwise be run. Meanwhile, militants in the Niger Delta say they stage attacks on oil installations as part of their fight for the rights of local people to benefit more from the region's oil wealth. Others argue that the attacks are staged mostly for the attackers' financial gain.

Lola read the article with sadness, feeling for so many individuals now trapped on multiple sides of a bad situation. She had no trouble believing that Shell had behaved poorly, maybe even abysmally, decades ago, destroying the livelihoods of Nigerians they probably had barely noticed. But today, she needed an armed guard in Lagos to go from the hotel to the office. Who was in the right? How did one solve this sort of mess?

Djimon instructed Nwanyi to begin to mutter herself to sleep each night saying, "I am worthless," over and over, telling her he would have Mairo verify each evening that Nwanyi was doing as told and that Nwanyi would indeed be punished more if she did not comply. Of course he did not actually ask Mairo to check, as he believed that the less he involved Mairo in this particular part of the process, the better. It seemed to him that while women could be plenty cruel mentally and emotionally, to both men and each other, they all seemed to be unnecessarily squeamish about physical violence and had what he supposed was an understandable tendency to band together, in spite of their differences, against brutality from men. So it was best to keep Mairo, who was normally no angel of mercy, at arm's length from all of this. No unnecessary risks were warranted.

He found it interesting several days later when he heard from Ibrahim the gardener that the second wife muttered in her sleep. "Can anyone hear what she says?" he asked nonchalantly.

"No one could understand her for a long while. It sounded just like an animal whimpering. But now the cook is certain that in the morning she has heard her saying, "I have no right to be alive."

At first this annoyed Djimon, because it was not the phrase he had instructed Nwanyi to repeat. She was supposed to be saying, "I am worthless." He considered beating her extra hard for this minor act of defiance. Then he remembered what he had heard of her story, back when he was seeking a suitable woman for this role. Her mother had died in childbirth. He had forgotten that. So the girl had possibly grown up believing that she had no right to be alive. Might have cried herself to sleep with just that phrase as a child. Perhaps the muttering was completely unconscious, in which case it should be encouraged. Worthless. No right to be alive. What did it matter after all? They both worked.

Ibrahim enjoyed his job as a gardener and enjoyed the better life that this good employment gave his family. Nonetheless, he had mentioned the muttering to Djimon because he was deeply bothered by what he saw. He opened his mouth to suggest that just maybe someone of a healing profession should have a look at the woman, because she seemed to look more unhealthy each time someone got a glimpse of her. Just a brief look to make sure all was well?

But before an actual sound could be made, he caught the look in Djimon's eye and knew that the suggestion would be most unwelcome. That knowledge made Ibrahim sad, because he had always considered Djimon an honorable man, and Ibrahim did not like the idea of working for a man he did not respect. But Ibrahim was a sensible man too, and would not do anything rash to hurt his family. Rather, he resolved to find other ways to help the young woman, ways that would put Ibrahim himself on the side of right, but, God willing, not get him fired.

About two weeks after she spoke with Olumiji, Somadina managed to get Azuka's father to take her to Abakaliki, the nearest city, to use the internet café. She told her father-in-law that she was going to try to search for Nwanyi or any of her in-laws on social networking sites, and that she was going to also gather material which could help her in her fortune-telling. Both were true. She persuaded him to leave well before the sun rose, explaining that in the very early morning she had the best chance of unlimited access and no power outage. That was true also. But the main thing was that what Somadina wanted more than anything was the time and privacy to explore the website x^0, and Azuka's father had plenty of other business of his own in town and would not stand over her shoulder curiously like the others. Leaving very early also meant that she could go alone. She felt nervous as she settled onto her stool and carefully typed in http://www.tothepowerofzero.org/.

"Don't be silly. For heaven's sake, it's a stupid website. No one here knows or cares what you are doing." Password? Oh yes. She typed exactly as instructed. She began to read.

"Welcome to the homepage of x^0. Now please relax. As this is your first time here we invite you to explore and learn more about us. Click here to continue."

The only option was to click the small dark red button in the corner. Okay. Somadina clicked and read on.

> Telepathy, also known as "feeling at a distance," is direct brain-to-brain contact. It is a poorly developed human sense somewhat like touch or smell but understood far less well, probably in part because the sense is only possessed by a small percentage of humans.
>
> It is most often an emotional feeling received from someone else which is sometimes accompanied by one or more of the following: a mental image, sounds or words heard in one's head including tunes or songs, the memory of a physical

sensation such as falling, nausea, or cold, or the memory of a smell, touch, or taste.

Somadina thought how wonderful it was to read a description by people who understand exactly what it was she could do.

Just over a week after her meeting with Maurice, Lola sat alone with her laptop. She had avoided going to Maurice's website for a lot of reasons, one of which she supposed was discovery by her family. But tonight Ariel was out with friends, and Alex and Teddie had both gone to sleep a good while ago. It was the perfect time.

She turned the small deep red card over and over in her hand. On one side was the enigmatic "x^0." On the other side were Maurice's carefully scrawled handwritten instructions for logging on. She felt oddly nervous. *Don't be silly. For heaven's sake, it's a stupid website. You can delete it from your browsing history. In fact, you probably should delete it from your browsing history.* Like a guilty soul searching for porn, Lola typed in http://www.tothepowerofzero.org/ and waited. Password? She typed exactly as instructed and she began to read.

"Welcome to the homepage of x^0. Now please relax. As this is your first time here we invite you to explore and learn more about us. Click here to continue."

The only option was to click the small dark red button in the corner. Okay. Lola clicked and read on. After her conversation with Maurice, she was not so surprised by the description of what telepathy was, but the next part caught her attention.

Telepathy is not mindreading because telepathy generally works at a sub-verbal level. The transmitter can attempt to send words, but it is the feeling behind the words that actually goes. If words are received, they are supplied by the receiving brain attempting to make sense of the emotion and are not necessarily the words being verbalized in the transmitter's head. They may be similar, or there may be significant differences. However, the tone and intent will transmit.

Telepathy is also not hallucinatory. Transmitted sounds or images are received "in ones head" in a fashion similar to thoughts, daydreams and dreams, and no normal healthy human would confuse them with real sights or sounds. Physical sensations such as vertigo or heat, if strong enough, may be more confusing.

She clicked to go on to the "FAQ's
Q: Who transmits information telepathically?

A: We all do. Everyone transmits, although most people merely emit an ongoing low-level signal on a day-to-day basis. Sometimes the more emotionally reticent are particularly poor at transmitting their feelings, and occasionally those with secrets to hide become unconsciously adept at transmitting no or false information. Anyone, even those completely lacking telepathic skill, can transmit more effectively with sufficient motivation. Thus an effective cry for help can be made by those with no particular telepathic skill. Also, adept telepaths generally can and do learn to transmit better when they wish to do so.

Lola was particularly eager to read the next answer.
Q: Who receives information telepathically?

A: Far fewer people. Being a receiver is the real gift. About one percent of the population has at least a poorly developed ability to receive information telepathically. This ability appears to be evenly distributed by gender, ancestry, ethnicity, location, and socio-economic status with the exception that over the last few decades there has been a noticeable increase in the number of receivers among younger people.

Yes, Maurice mentioned something about this.

Q: Isn't being a receiver an awful nuisance?

A: It can be, but receivers learn and choose, consciously or not, to shut out most of the input that they receive. This filtering ability is more akin to earplugs than to shutting one's eyes in that it does not keep out all input but reduces it. On the other hand, many receivers use their gift to live a fuller life, even if they do not realize that they are doing so. Receivers typically excel in sales, politics, teaching, litigating, or any profession in which feeling the driving emotions of others is an asset. They make great negotiators, can make highly effective healers, and many are described as being the kind of person who could "sell ice to Eskimos."

Lola paused. So did this explain all her debate trophies in high school? How about the presentations that almost always went so well?

Q: Can a receiver choose to improve his or her abilities?

A: Absolutely, up to a point. Like playing the piano or running a mile, the gift can be practiced and improved to develop it up to a person's maximum potential. However, just as in playing music or running fast, each human will have their own natural limits. A person who has chosen, consciously or not, to develop and use their abilities as a receiver to their fullest is known as an adept receiver. It is estimated that about ten percent of all human receivers have learned to be adept, whether they realize it or not. This is not an insignificant phenomenon, as it currently amounts to almost seven million humans.

Lola paused to sip her glass of wine. So she was, probably, an adept receiver?

Somadina was confused. What she did and felt seemed to be something well beyond what was being described here. She read on.

Q: Is being a receiver the same as being a telepath?

A; No. Only about one in one thousand adept receivers will find that their abilities progress into the range of true telepathy. The delineation between the two categories has no clear boundary, but based on our research we estimate that there are seven thousand or so true telepaths alive today.

Okay. That made more sense, Somadina thought. *I am a telepath. I have always been one.*

Q: How does a receiver become a telepath?

A: Telepaths seem to all be born as receivers, and many of them develop into telepaths spontaneously as children or as teenagers. Less often the ability develops spontaneously in later life, even, surprisingly often, in old age. Just as often, however, receivers are catapulted into being telepaths by a strong experience such as a life-threatening event or danger to a loved one, in which telepathy aids them even though they may not be aware of it at the time. In other cases, the catalyst is close association with someone who already is a strong telepath. Whatever the cause, once the transition to full telepathy is made, there is no going back. And if another telepath has been involved, then the mental bridge that has been built between the two minds appears to be permanent.

Lola started to feel a cold chill. So this is where it was going to get weird. She thought of her imaginary friend, the distraught Nigerian older sister, her panic under the water that had turned to calm as she had asked the right questions, which had saved her life. The diffuse yet very real link she seemed to now share with some woman she had never met. She wasn't crazy. This stuff happened. She wasn't crazy. It was okay. She wasn't crazy. This was good. She read on.

x^0

Somadina was concerned. Being a telepath seemed like a powerful thing. A scary thing. Was she hurting people without even knowing it? She read the next part with relief.

Q: Doesn't this mean that we have the ability to go around placing ideas in other people's heads?

A: No. Remember that the vast majority of people transmit but do not receive. If one tries to place a thought or feeling in the minds of ninety-nine percent of the general population, the recipient will have no idea about it whatsoever. If a thought is placed instead in the mind of a receiver, it will generally result in a vague, fleeting sensation that will likely be ignored.

Unless the person doing the placing is damn persistent about it, Lola thought to herself, thinking over the events of past spring. *So now what? Was she totally vulnerable to whatever this lady sent her way?*

Q: But couldn't someone place ideas in the mind of another telepath?

A; Yes. That is one of the many reasons this organization, x^0, exists. One of our missions is to locate all people who can fully feel another's emotions, and to inform, teach, and even warn them for their own well-being.

Okay. This explained Jumoke's brother's urgency that she meet Maurice. Shit. She wasn't crazy. A minor case of post-traumatic syndrome was the least of her problems. She'd get over that. Maybe had already. No, the real issue here was that Jumoke had been worried about her, had sensed that she was, what, a receiver with issues? He didn't know what those issues were. Hell, he even suspected they might be an abusive husband. But the fact was she was perhaps turning from being a pretty good receiver into a full-fledged telepath, and now she knew that the turning was likely being done by some desperate woman who had no idea what she was doing.

And this group here was trying to educate, warn, and help her. Shit. As if she wasn't weird enough already. But if it was going to happen, why wasn't she, like, turning into one? Picking up more information from people? Did the process take awhile?

Q: Can an unwitting telepath be made to do something they do not wish to do?

Now that's a good question, a guilty and worried Somadina thought.

A: Fortunately, no. As far as we know, no telepath has the ability to force another to do something against their will. At most a suggestion can be transmitted, one as simple as "call me so we can talk," which can then be ignored or acted upon as the recipient chooses.

That's a comforting answer, Somadina thought.
Q: This still seems like it could be a dangerous skill in the hands of the wrong person. Shouldn't we be worried?

Lola winced.
A: It appears that telepathy is a high-level skill when it manifests itself in humans, and to date a certain degree of moral advancement appears to go hand-in-hand with its possession. So far at least there has been no need for policing, as kindness and empathy appear to be a natural outgrowth of being able to feel the emotions of others, and being aware of a potential victim's pain or discomfort is apparently sufficient stimulus to alter any potentially problematic behavior.

That is real good to know, thought Lola. Thought Somadina.

Then the back door started to open and Lola jumped in her seat. "Mom," Ariel smiled as she came in. "You okay?"

"Fine dear. You just startled me. I'm headed off to bed myself actually." Lola clicked her browser shut as casually as she could manage and glanced at the clock. It was already way after midnight.

"Did you have fun?"

"A bunch of us went to see a movie. It was okay. Kind of a dumb plot. A really long car chase which I thought was pretty pointless, but the guys all seemed to love it." She laughed easily and started to head upstairs. "Get some rest Mom. That stuff on the internet will keep." She winked.

As she turned away Lola thought, *Damn. I bet she thinks I was looking at porn.*

The overhead lights flickered and went dim, and then the whir of the computer ceased. The internet users muttered curses and complaints one by one as the screens went dark, but the clerk in charge just shrugged his shoulders and laughed. The generator had gone out. What could one say? It happened. "Come back later and I'll give you the rest of your time," he offered. "It will probably take awhile to fix it."

Somadina sat on her stool sadly. She had not gotten to finish the FAQs, she had not even started on the list of in-laws names Ikenna had given her to search for, and she had not even had the chance to check her brother Udo's email account like he had told her she could, to look for messages from Olumiji, who had still not gotten back to her via her father's cell phone.

Those who only knew the fact that Lola was a scientist might have found her ready acceptance of x^0 and its theories contradictory. But to those who understood what kind of scientist she was, it would have made perfect sense, if she had shared it with anyone. Driving across West Texas with her father, Lola had absorbed his love of wide-open spaces, and the related desire to fly. Her dad had gotten his private pilot's license as a young man, in hopes of ultimately using a small plane instead a car for his business, but had given up the potentially expensive hobby when both the dangers and cost caused his young wife ongoing concern.

Lola, as a young girl, had morphed her dad's dream into that of being an astronaut someday, and meanwhile consoled herself with all the science history and science fiction she could find for young adults. While her friends read romance or mystery, preteen Lola devoured Isaac Asimov, Kate Wilhelm, Ursula Le Guin, and Frederik Pohl. Her idols were Albert Einstein, the failed eighth grader working at a patent office while he speculated about the nature of light, and Marie Curie, a Polish girl in France struggling to understand a behavior which appeared magic but would one day be understood as radioactivity. Lola believed in her heart that the real world remained full of mystery and surprise, and that for all of humanity's continuing proud belief that "most" of the mysteries have been unraveled, she believed that the truth remained far more exciting and complex.

So while Lola shied away from obvious hocus-pocus and scams, she was considerably more open to odd ideas than a casual observer might have guessed. Furthermore, 2009 had brought a series of events she was eager to explain and understand, and x^0 had theories. She was all ears.

She was, however, more than ready to stop taking the worthless little blue pills every morning, and she called Dr. Walker for an appointment to discuss a medication exit strategy. He had had a cancellation, so the next day she found herself in his office explaining that she still had had no effect whatsoever from the pills but felt she was now coping fine with whatever minor PTSD she had experienced, and she wanted to stop taking the medication.

"Lola, Lola," Dr. Walker shook his head and smiled. "You don't understand. The very reason you are feeling better is because you are taking the medication. Trust me, I have seen this so often. The patient does not even realize that they are being helped. However, because I do understand that you may be expecting a bit more of an uplift from the medication than what you think you are getting, I do have two alternatives to propose to you. One is that we up the dosage to one hundred milligrams, which is not at all a high or unusual dosage. It is perfectly safe, and I am perfectly happy to do that. But what I think might work better in your particular case is to add instead just a very low dosage of an additional drug proven very effective in combination with what you are taking. Please don't let the words 'atypical antipsychotic' scare you."

Lola had a strange flash of panic that Alex or Ariel had checked out her web surfing and somehow had found the x^0 website and decided she was delusional and contacted Dr. Walker. Breathe, she told herself sternly. Dr. Walker went on.

"This has nothing at all to do with your being psychotic," he chuckled. "These drugs have a well-established history of off-label use as a supplement to standard selective serotonin reuptake inhibitors. Based on your history, I think you will respond well and be grateful for the uplift and elevation of your mood and energy level."

What history, Lola wondered. "Can I think about it?" Now she was confused. She had come in here to get off the things because she thought the pills were a silly waste of time and money, but what if in fact they were now what was helping her function? Great.

"Sure," he said. "Of course. I will call Dr. Hayes and have him write you the prescription and send it to your pharmacy. Go home, discuss it with your husband. Then fill it if you wish. If you decide that you'd rather not be on two medications, then give my office a call and we can talk to Dr. Hayes about upping your dosage instead."

"What if I just want to quit the medication?"

"Abrupt discontinuation is a very bad idea Lola, and I highly discourage you from getting off of medication now when you are just starting to see positive results. You need to work with me and with the medicine, Lola." He smiled. "You are an important part of this process too. Let's be positive and focus on getting you well."

I am well, she thought miserably as she walked out of the door.

Somadina came back from the trip to town frustrated and irritable. The road had been hot and dusty, as Azuka's father's car lacked air conditioning. He had been in a hurry to get home and unwilling to take her to a café further away or to wait for the generators to be fixed. She felt like she had wasted a whole day and gotten nothing done. As she approached the house little Kwemto ran to her eagerly from the front door on his chubby legs, and she took comfort in his giggly hug and clean smell. Azuka must have bathed him. That at least was nice.

She looked up to see Azuka smiling down at her. She needed little mind-reading skills to feel the intense joy which he was barely holding in.

"Somadina," he said as solemnly as he could manage. "I need to ask you a question." She winced. She knew this meant good news, very good news, in a medical sense. But it also meant she had a difficult decision to now make and with all else that was going on in her life, she felt frustrated and angry with herself that she had failed to give this one thing, this one very important thing in fact, the time and attention which it warranted.

She now knew that she could care for herself. She did not need a husband. And in fact she could probably get another husband if she wanted, but why would she want that? Azuka was about as good as they came, in her opinion. The question to Somadina really was why would she want a husband at all? Did she love Azuka? Did she simply like him well enough to continue the current arrangement? Until she got Nwanyi back safely, it was going to be terribly hard to know her own mind about much of anything else. She swallowed and tried to frame a patient answer.

But, as he often did, Azuka got there first. "Although I wish to ask you a question," he smiled, "I do not wish for you to answer it today. In fact, I do not wish you to answer it until you are quite ready. Quite sure. Either way. But please, let me ask."

"Very well."

"I am happy to inform you that I am not one of the four percent of Nigerians who carry the HIV virus."

"Azuka, that is truly wonderful news." She meant it.

"Therefore, as a man who may now in good conscience choose to take a wife, and father more children, I hereby ask you, Somadina, to choose me as the man you would wish to marry and for whom you would choose to bear more children."

She started to say something but he put up his hand to silence her.

"Say nothing. Think on it. Do not bring it up at all. Not until you have a one word answer for me." And he smiled and walked away, and she felt his happiness grow as he thought to himself that he had handled the situation perfectly.

Chapter 10. August 2009

Lola had long since thrown out any idea of discussing anything of importance with Dr. Walker. She'd been vague about her appointments with him to Alex, mostly because she did not want Alex to worry, and partly because she was embarrassed by her whole overreaction to the canoe accident. She knew that Summer shared her West Texas disdain for all problems psychological, so she hadn't even considered bringing this issue up there. Oddly, she might once have told Teddie, just because Teddie had always seemed so much older than she should have, but obviously this was no time to enter such an odd variable into their struggling mother/daughter relationship. Talking to Ariel made more sense, but Lola was certain that Ariel would have no patience with either Dr. Walker or with Lola's being on medication. So reluctantly, she took the phone out to the porch and called the remaining family member, her resident expert on neuroscience.

"Hey Mom. What's up?" It was late but Lola was sure Zane stayed up on weeknights far later than she did.

"Job still grunt work but a new kind?" she asked.

"Yeah … " It was said in such a way as to imply that glamour had pretty much disappeared from the whole world.

"What do you know about prescribing atypical antipsychotics to enhance the effect of selective serotonin reuptake inhibitors?" She thought she might as well get right to the point.

"Sheeshh," he said. "I think that is a pretty drastic measure. Surely no one is recommending that for you, are they?"

"Actually yes. My psychologist thinks I'll get an 'uplift' over my current meds, but I'm not even sure I needed to be on these things in the first place, much less uplifted. If I'd given the whole thing a little more time I think I'd have been just fine." Lola tried to keep her tone light, not wanting to give Zane cause for worry.

"Well, you were trying to take care of yourself, and he is trying to also. Let me poke around and see what I can learn. Can you stall a bit?"

"'Easily," she laughed. "If I am not paying him for an office visit at that particular moment then I am not a priority," she said.

"Well, he sees a lot of patients, mom. He can't be thinking about all of you every second."

"I know," Lola felt bad for her flippancy. Zane, of course, identified with these folks, hoped to work with them and make his living researching ways for them to be more effective.

"Get back to me when you can sweetheart," she said. "I won't take more or less of anything until I hear from you. I promise. And thanks a million." She really was grateful for his help.

"Hey, no problem. It will actually be good to a have a reason to ask a few questions at work and poke around into something interesting for a change." She felt his cloud of boredom lift just a little.

That's nice, she thought as she hung up. Maybe she had managed to help him out a bit as well.

Djimon and Mairo had sex less often after Nwanyi arrived. There was simply less time spent together, especially on weekends, and they were preoccupied with their own issues. Mairo was focused on her ill mother, whose health continued to decline, and on isolating the children and servants from Nwanyi and Djimon as best she could. She also sensed Djimon's growing preoccupation with his role, and it made her pull back emotionally and physically.

Djimon, a practical man, had never had a problem with providing himself with sexual release when needed, considering it a sensible alternative to more dangerous or inconvenient choices. So he took longer and more enjoyable showers, but as he did he became concerned about the change in the sorts of mental images which took over in the last few seconds before the final release. To his frustration, those images were the one part of his brain over which he seemed to be able to exercise absolutely no control.

Every so often, Djimon believed, a man needed more than he himself could provide, and so he contrived to see that he and Mairo were both in bed earlier than normal, with the rest of the house tucked in for the night.

Lovemaking began as it used to, but as Djimon's passion grew he found himself behaving differently. First he held down

Mairo's leg with his knee. She wriggled it free. Then he bent one arm behind her head, twisting it into a mildly uncomfortable angle. "What the hell are you doing?" she hissed. He let go.

It was a good question however. What the hell was he doing?

Djimon had a degree in psychology, one he had gotten most specifically for the purpose of finding and training a human weapon to carry out the plan he and his group had begun to devise years ago. He knew quite a bit about human nature and so knew that he was not a sexual sadist in the clinical sense. He did not have, and never had had, a desire to kill anything. No torturing of small animals, or of his younger sisters, in his youth. Furthermore, he had no desire to maim or inflict permanent damage on anyone. No mental images of slicing or burning flesh drifted into his fantasies. But during the last few months he seemed to have developed a taste for, what? Dominating his sexual partner, making her physically uncomfortable until he chose to stop doing so? Maybe even a taste for making her fear him and obey him? Was this not just considered deviant sex? Even acceptable in some circles?

Now he was faced with the uncomfortable question of whether that desire had always been there, tucked away deeply as inappropriate in his world, or whether it was more like a massively addictive drug—cocaine or heroine—which he never would have found himself craving if he had not tried it to begin with.

Mairo appeared to have no corresponding desires, at least that she acknowledged, which would allow him to indulge his newly discovered urges. True, he could encourage a little voluntary exploration on her part, or force it, but Djimon understood quite clearly that while Mairo was, by both culture and law, his to do with as he pleased, in reality women had their own ways of fighting back when pushed. And right now the plan was much too important for him to introduce such an unpredictable variable as a resentful wife.

So Djimon muttered apologies into the clearly miffed Mairo's ear, adding a bit of uncharacteristically flowery profession of his love for her. While it didn't work totally, Mairo went back to being cooperative, if not passionate, and Djimon vowed inwardly to behave towards her with physical gentleness in the future. Cause no problems for the greater plan, he reminded himself sternly.

Besides, luckily enough there were plenty of women out there who could be paid to do what they voluntarily would not. He would seek out such, he consoled himself, just as soon as his schedule permitted. Then he had to wonder if it would be as much fun, paying a woman to tolerate what Nwanyi had no choice but to accept. He decided that it might be, if the woman clearly hated every minute of it.

Ikenna had not been over to see Somadina for a week, and he was never home when she came by. Somadina was anxious to know if Olumiji had tried to contact her with her father's cell phone and was sensing with certainty that she was being avoided. To her, that justified overriding the courtesy of not seeking out her father's feelings without his knowledge. Since her abilities had begun to return earlier in the year, she had found that if she let her mind wander to her father naturally, she would begin to pick up information.

She felt him in his back yard, working in his garden. She thought about running over to catch him in person, but it seemed that his emotions were strong right now and not good. Guilt? Remorse? Worry? Worry about Nwanyi, yes. Worry about what Somadina would think? Yes, and not good. Helplessness. What else could he have done? He was doing the best he could. Somadina could feel the strong sense of rationalization all humans feel within themselves when they have made a questionable decision. I had no choice. No choice was a good one. I am doing the best I can. And so on.

Somadina took another approach. She left her thoughts to wander to one of her father's wives instead. They were both people she seldom bothered with one way or another, but Ikenna's frame of mind gave her the distinct feeling that the answer to what was going on might lie there.

She found exuberant happiness. A sense of planning for the future. She saw Obialo (oh bee AH low), the oldest of her half-brothers, dressed smartly in, what, a uniform? A school uniform from a very fine secondary school. One that would almost certainly guarantee the boy a promising future. His mother was so proud.

Somadina was happy for Obialo. He was not a bad kid, even if not overly bright. Although she had not had the opportunity to attend secondary school herself, she recognized that more schooling was a good path. Thinking she knew the answer, she let her mind drift to her father's other wife.

Indeed, the woman was also caught up in planning for the future. Half-brother Udo had gotten into the same school? It looked like it. But the school must be in another part of Nigeria, for Udo's mom was filled less with pride and more with sadness that her boy would not be around. She wanted him to have the bright future and felt guilty about not wanting him to leave. She knew it was probably the very best possible use of the bride price which Ikenna had been holding on to in the foolish hope that he might find Nwanyi and undo the deal he had done. That certainly did not look like it was going to happen. Best to just let Nwanyi go, poor soul that she was.

It appeared that Ikenna had been convinced by his wives that a private detective would only take his money, waste it, and produce no results. If one combined the bride price with the private detective money saved so far then Ikenna could have not one but two sons attending a fine school, and maybe someday they would be doctors or government officials or something important. There was no better, no smarter investment in the future.

Whew. Somadina shook her head with the overload. Thanks to this wife, who transmitted well with a clarity Somadina seldom encountered, she had a pretty clear picture of the situation. Yes, her father was avoiding her. Yes, he had good reason to do so. Yes, he was going to once again be as useless in solving this situation with Nwanyi as he had always been. Somadina felt sadness as, once and for all, she wrote off her father and his assistance. It looked like he could not help being who he was, a man as obsessed with his male lineage as his own father had been.

Which made Somadina happy that her two half-brothers were being sent away at fourteen years old. They seemed like decent enough kids now, and maybe, living away from home like this, they would have the opportunity to develop ideas and opinions which were more modern. So at least the money was being used for something good.

Furthermore, the wives did have a point. Somadina would have spent the money saved so far and more on a private detective who produced results. However, the chances of being cheated, or even of just a well-meaning detective finding nothing, were quite high. And the odds of negotiating a refund of the bride price in exchange for Nwanyi's return were, Somadina suspected, almost nil. It was going to take something considerably more unusual to locate Nwanyi. Fortunately, it looked like considerably more unusual resources were the only kind that Somadina was going to have at her disposal.

Djimon was nothing if not a careful planner, but he prided himself on being able to occasionally improvise with Nwanyi. He was tired and likely coming down with a head cold one Thursday night when he saw her cringe at the sight of a spider. She hated spiders? Perfect. He sent a baffled Ibrahim out the next day to get him a jar with several live, healthy ones. This weekend he would be able to use his wits more than his tired body.

After giving it some careful thought he decided to force her to sit motionless while he let out the spiders slowly, one by one, onto her bare breasts. If she flinched or made a sound then more time would be added. This sort of mental discipline would be good for her. This was, after all, training. She managed a shaky, clammy obedience until one of the delightful little creatures had the sense of humor to place her right nipple right between its tiny legs. Djimon had to laugh aloud. He'd never know whether it was the spider's touch or the laughter which was too much for her, because at that point she brushed them off shrieking at him and began crying and babbling about how she could not take it any more.

He did not have the energy to deal with her that night, so he just locked the door behind him and went to bed, leaving her sitting on the floor crying with the spiders still crawling around her room. He fell asleep easily, happy in his knowledge that tomorrow she'd have to damn well take anything he wanted her to take.

Three weeks later, Lola still had not picked up the prescription for the atypical antipsychotic medication which was to be used in an off-label fashion to supplement her current antidepressant medication, which was supposed to be helping her cope with the post-traumatic anxiety which she was no longer experiencing. So the pharmacy called and left an automated reminder for her to pick up her medication. She hung up halfway through it and on a whim opted for the green 25 mg tablet that morning instead of the blue 50 mg tablet she had dutifully been taking. She had saved the lower dose tablets in an admittedly childish rebellion against being specifically told by Dr. Walker not to do so. Now she decided she would begin her own personal program of tapering off of the medication. Tuesday and Wednesday she went with the lower dosage again, and Thursday morning she decided to declare herself medication free. The main risks, according to a quick google search, were a return of the original symptoms which she figured at the very worst was no big deal, or a sudden onset of the same side effects she might have experienced when first going on the medication, which she figured she could just plain get through.

Thursday at work Lola was restless and had trouble concentrating. She was also starting to feel like she had gone over everything in her data multiple times and was hitting diminishing returns. When was her company going to secure a damn drilling rig already? She decided to take an extended lunch break to research more about Nigeria on the internet. By the time she got home she was wound up more tightly than she realized and she ambushed Alex in the kitchen with the results of her lunchtime information hunt.

"How many barrels of oil do you think was spilled by the Exxon Valdez in 1989?" she demanded.

"Lola dear, I have no idea. A lot. Too many." He was chopping garlic carefully into tiny pieces. But Lola would not be brushed off.

"Somewhere over two hundred and fifty thousand barrels of

oil."

"And that's horrible," he agreed. "Wish I could have stopped it."

"That's not my point. Don't patronize me, Alex. Do you know that there were at least three spills in the Niger Delta before that were all larger? How many of them did you hear about? Three major spills. And another incident that killed more than a thousand people. And in fact did you know that between 1975 and 1995 over two billion barrels of oil were spilled in the Niger Delta, ten times what was spilled by the Valdez? Ten times. And that for over three quarters of it, there was no recovery or cleanup efforts made whatsoever? Where was everybody? Fish died and crops were ruined and nobody did a <u>damn thing</u>."

"I get it, Lola. The plight of Africa doesn't get half the attention here that problems from other parts of the world get. It sucks."

"Damn right it sucks. Do you understand that Nigeria is the eighth largest country in the world? How come over two million people were starved to death in Biafra and most people never really heard about it?"

"Lola, calm down. It's not that you aren't right dear. You are. It's just that yelling at me isn't going to do a thing to make it better."

She started a harsh retort, and then stopped. What was the matter with her? Alex was on her side. She took a deep breath and just let him hold her for a minute.

Then when she went to change out of her work clothes, he shook his head. She was a strange one, his wife. Oddly idealistic, fiery in her opinions, and where others tended to put up walls to protect themselves from what was different, she had the unusual tendency to link herself to other people's traits and troubles. Go figure. He knew that the phrase was probably outdated and politically incorrect, but it still described the situation. After eight months of working for an African company, his Lola had managed to "go native" while sitting at a desk in Houston.

By Friday morning, Lola had gone from feeling restless to

feeling physically disoriented, and by Saturday she could not help but notice that she was downright dizzy. Sort of like an inner ear infection. Saturday night she passed on the wine when she and Alex went out to dinner and passed on the cappuccino and the dessert as well. "Your body is a temple?" Alex had kidded her.

"No," she laughed. Then she had the distinct, strong impression that he really hoped she was not dieting again because when she did it always made him feel guilty about eating, and he hated that he could not enjoy a meal as much.

She looked at him. "I didn't know you hated it when I went on a diet."

He looked at her. "I didn't say I did."

They stared at each other for a long moment before the waiter brought the check.

Lola was glad that she and Alex had made love before they went out to dinner. It meant that once they got home he would head off to bed alone with no expectations, and, with Ariel now back at school and Teddie spending the night at a girlfriend's, she could get back on the computer and go to the x^0 website where she had left off weeks ago.

She wondered why she had been so reluctant to return to it up until now. Granted, the time before school started was always a busy one at their house. And maybe she was scared someone in the family would discover her. She hated doing anything she felt she had to hide, and admittedly the proposed prescription for an antipsychotic had given her pause for a moment. Maybe the whole thing was just too weird, and it didn't seem real. The net result was that weeks had flown by while she pretended that part of her life was not happening. She probably needed to contact Maurice again.

She logged on nervously, and was greeted with a soft "welcome back" message that made her feel glad she had returned. Maybe tonight the website would have some answers for her.

> Q: What kind of information gets communicated telepathically?

A: Telepathy does not work well to communicate complex ideas or complicated information. You cannot feel a math equation or a telephone number, or even feel a red circle versus a blue square, which is why most early ESP experiments were doomed to fail.

Q: So what is easy to communicate?

A: Besides raw emotions such as fear, anger, and joy, telepathy communicates well with imagery, humor, and puns, much as the subconscious does with dreams. For example, a receiver may get an image of a man walking his dog, holding a bag overflowing with dog poop. The transmitter understands the man pictured is lying about something, or, in other words, that the man is full of shit. This particular type of telepathic communication is helped if the two subjects involved share common idiomatic expressions. It can require skill to interpret the images received.

Q: Do telepaths receive information equally well from all people?

A: No. Just as you find it easier to catch some people's words, and maybe more importantly, some people's intended meaning, so do individual telepaths find that some people transmit to them more clearly. We call this being on a common wavelength. Also, if a telepath is emotionally close to another and has a long history with them, such as a spouse or sibling, it is safe to assume that thoughts may be read much more clearly.

Q: Don't telepaths get overwhelmed by input?

A: Yes, they usually do at first. The onset of true telepathy requires acclimation on the part of the telepath, who has to learn to filter incoming information appropriately. In general, being a telepath is very much like learning to walk on a ship at sea. At first it can be difficult and even disorientating, but one usually adjusts and learns to tap into information only as needed and wanted.

Like walking on a ship at sea. Lola realized that seasick was a very good description for how she felt at the moment. And the thing with Alex about dieting had been weird. Was she having a physical reaction to getting off of the medication? Or, by chance, was she turning into a full-fledged telepath like Jumoke had thought she would? She decided to read one more entry, then put her woozy head to sleep. She would find a way to finish reading the website in small doses over the next few days so she could absorb the material calmly and easily.

Q: Can a telepath read an animal's mind?

Maybe not the pertinent subject she had hoped for, but …

A: All animals with enough brain function transmit information, but, unlike humans, it appears that all animals are also receivers. Because telepathy is such a non-verbal activity, some think that our development of advanced speech stunted telepathic reception in humans while it remained as a skill in the rest of the animal kingdom. This means that yes, your dog or cat or horse really does know how you are feeling. However, how well your pet understands the meaning of your emotions depends on the intelligence of the species and the specific animal involved, and how much your pet cares about your emotions depends on its particular personality. One of the more interesting facts to us is that almost every pet owner agrees that pets know how their people feel, and no one seems to find this at all surprising.

At this point Lola paused to give a long, hard look at the

x^0

sleeping cat. The cat opened his eyes slowly, and looked back at her in a bored sort of way, as though to marvel at the oddities that caused humans to be excited.

Sunday morning Somadina sat drinking tea in her tiny kitchen, thinking about how she had to find a way to get into town and get back on the internet to learn more about x^0 and to check for messages from Olumiji. She heard Azuka playing with their son Kwemto in the next room, and in a comfortable, diffuse way she could feel the happy emotions emanating from both of them. It had been almost three weeks, she realized, since Azuka had asked her for a simple answer. Not a maybe. Not a kind of. Not a list of qualifications or exceptions or explanations. If she had to just say yes or no, no was certainly easier.

Somadina had often heard the African proverb "If you want to travel fast, travel alone. If you want to travel far, travel with others." She had always preferred to travel fast, she guessed, knowing that life was simpler and she was happier on her own. She had viewed the obligatory husband as a nuisance her culture would force her to tolerate, and she had always resigned herself to putting up with the inevitable without ever embracing it.

For just a moment, Somadina let herself consider that maybe it was a better idea in the long term to be able to travel far. To choose of her own accord to travel with another. For just a moment, she tried on the idea of saying a simple "yes". And meaning it.

The second time Nwanyi decided to run away it was mostly the spiders that caused it. And the fact that Friday generally meant that both Djimon and Mairo would be at the mosque for weekly prayers at noon, with only the less concerned servants left to watch her. Friday also meant that later in the day Mairo would leave with the children, after sending the servants home for the weekend, and Nwanyi just absolutely could not imagine that she could face another weekend with Djimon, who had actually walked away from her, locking her in the room with the spiders.

So on Friday morning, August 20, when the family seemed

particularly caught up in going to the mosque for some reason, and even bringing the children as well, Nwanyi formulated a quick plan for escape. The new cook almost never left her kitchen, and Nwanyi had long since noticed that when the cook was not there the kitchen door was now kept bolted shut with a key that the cook kept around her neck. The housekeeper stayed towards the back of the house as well, but today was unusual because both the cook and the housekeeper had been given permission to attend Friday services at the mosque too.

So the first part of Nwanyi's plan became to simply wait for a quiet moment after they all left and then to just walk out the front door herself. Because she was never allowed anywhere in the front of the house, she suspected that Djimon and Mairo had not gone to the trouble of keeping it bolted with a key, as that would have been so inconvenient for them. So with her heart pounding in her chest, she walked softly and quickly through the front of the house, and tried the knob. It opened. She stepped out, closed the door behind her. Her heart was racing. She exhaled.

The street was much as she remembered it from months ago, flowering and well kept with modern nice, homes that should have been filled, one would think, with modern, nice people. But one never knew.

The next part of Nwanyi's plan, though simple, was at least a little better thought-out than last time, when she had absolutely no idea what to do. This time she would walk calmly but quickly to a corner, get on another street where she could not be seen from the house, and then run as fast as she could as far as she could. She knew from overheard conversation that this neighborhood was largely filled with Hausa and Fulani families and that in their culture women seldom left their homes. Children and servants were both unlikely to speak to or help a stranger. She would be noticed from windows and remarked upon by those not at the mosque, but likely left alone. When she had gotten as far as she felt she could go, she would go to a front door, bang on it and ask for help. Unless she could get to a part of town with shops, which would be even better because then she could beg for help from a storekeeper or from several of them until she found a soul kind enough to help.

She had started to walk fast towards the intersection of the nearest small street, when, with despair, she heard heavy foot steps behind her. She started to run without taking the time to turn around. The foot steps got louder and closer and she had not made it quite to the corner before a set of large arms circled her from behind, and she tripped forward with Ibrahim, the gardener, tripping on top of her. He pulled himself off but held fast to one of her wrists.

"Please." She looked directly at him. "Please. What's it to you? Just let me go."

The man looked genuinely sad. "I wish I could. I do. But I have been told very clearly that part of my job is to watch the front of the house, and to make sure you do not ever do this. If they come home and you are gone, I will be fired. Or probably worse. I have eight children. I am so sorry."

He was a foot taller, and almost twice her weight. He twisted her arm firmly behind her back and walked her back to the house. Nwanyi thought that never in her life had she been so sad.

Ibrahim remembered what had happened to the first cook all too well. And even though the cook had not understood the mistake she had made, he did. So once he was back at the house, he sadly used gardening twine to tie Nwanyi's hands behind her back, taking care not to make the ropes too tight. He then ordered her into a simple wooden chair in the room and, allowing her to sit in a comfortable position, he tied her bound wrists to the chair as well. But no tea. No sympathy. He would keep his job, thank you. As he walked out of the room, he prayed silently to be forgiven, and promised to look harder for safe ways to help this unfortunate child.

Nwanyi waited far longer for the family to return home than she expected. Finally she heard Ibrahim and Djimon talking as they walked towards her room. "I did not know what else to do with her sir but to tie her up. I hope I did not overstep my bounds." Djimon looked in at her.

"No, no you did just fine. Just perfect." And to think he had been concerned about Ibrahim's loyalty. He made a mental note to instruct the cook to send a large piece of meat home with the gardener for him and his eight children to enjoy once the sun was down and this first day of fasting was over.

After the gardener left, Djimon came back in and looked at her. "Well, well. My second wife has decided to become rebellious, has she? And to think that because this is the first day of Ramadan I was considering leaving you alone tonight and reading the Qur'an instead. Then you go and do this, which cannot be left unpunished. My spiritual growth will just have to wait now, won't it?"

Nwanyi thought to herself that Djimon looked very pleased about the turn of events.

Lola often went to the grocery store on Monday evenings on the way home from work, particularly during football season when she could count on a good many of her fellow Texans of both genders to be glued to their television sets. But even though she was not coming home from work this particular Monday, having spent most of yesterday and today in bed with what she described to her family and employer as flu symptoms, she was anxious to get out of the house now that she was starting to feel a little stronger. Better yet, the Minnesota Vikings were playing the Houston Texans in a pre-season game, which meant that the vast majority of her potential fellow shoppers would be glued to ESPN come eight o'clock.

Once she got to the store, her sense of disorientation began to give way to something else. At first, as she made her way through produce, it felt like a stronger nausea, and she considered heading back home. But by the time she had made it to the bottled drinks aisle, it wasn't really queasiness but more of a driving sensation, a pulse inside of her. In canned goods, it felt like a strength growing into a strange sort of clarity.

She paused at the dairy case to consider. It was the people around her. She was getting information from them as surely as if they were each speaking to her. Which none of them were. And with each little piece of input that she allowed herself to receive, the vertigo was dissipating. Her feet felt more solid and her head was becoming clear. She just relaxed and let the feelings flow into her.

By the time she had made it to frozen foods, every person in the store had a song to sing. A story to tell. The vague and sometimes annoying feelings she had picked up from folks in the past were gone, and Lola felt like a person with horrible vision who had just been given a pair of good glasses or a person with very poor hearing who suddenly was wearing the best of hearing aids.

It was true that most of what was coming at her was boring. His feet hurt. She was annoyed with her child. He was annoyed he had to work today. Right. He was missing the football game. Lola laughed. People were preoccupied, tired, worried, looking forward to some later event, thinking about sex, and one guy in aisle seven was thinking seriously about beating the shit out of someone at work tomorrow. Lola, knowing that most thoughts don't result in actions, decided that without more evidence of intent she should just leave people be. And she did. She could. She practiced. Tone up the intensity. Tone down the intensity. That worked. She could do it.

Not all the thoughts were admirable, but amid the petty and the complaining Lola had to admit that there was an underlying hum of just wanting to love and be loved. To be left in peace. To have a little fun. To have worries solved and some joy at the end of the day. She figured she shared the grocery store that day with forty or so other souls, and she could honestly wish each one well and move on. It was all going to be okay.

She smiled instinctively at the checkout clerk as she finished, and felt the girl's blip of joy at the smile. That was surprising. Lola's smile, an unconscious reflex she often found annoying because it was so habitual, apparently sometimes brought other folks a bit of happiness. Interesting.

And then, just as she was leaving, some lady in produce started singing to herself. Wouldn't you know it, Lola laughed. She had lost twenty dollars once betting that there was a Pink Floyd song called the "*Dark Side of the Moon.*" There isn't, of course, just a 1973 album with that name, and a perfectly wonderful song called "<u>Brain Damage</u>" which talks about a lunatic inside the singer's head and mentions the dark side of moon.

As Lola listened to the eerie <u>lyrics</u>, they were, she decided , a little too on the mark. Probably time to get home and take a break.

As she headed out of the store, she couldn't help singing along.

Driving home, she gave some thought to her next obvious problem. It looked like Jumoke had been right. Thanks to some combination of the Igbo woman and the canoe incident, she had become a telepath. Why had it taken so long? Maybe for the last couple of months the PTSD, or maybe the medication, or maybe both, had suppressed her symptoms. *No, abilities,* she told herself. *This is not a disease. You have abilities, not symptoms.*

At any rate, if this was now the way she was, should she tell Alex? Her children? Her sister? In one sense it seemed only fair, but in another she doubted she'd be believed, no matter how much they loved and trusted her. That was until she demonstrated the truth of what she was saying, which now that she thought about it could be harder than she thought. She could not do card tricks. Tell me what I'm thinking. What she could do was pick up the real driving emotion they were feeling at the time and if she was lucky it looked like she could pick up a few facts related to that emotion as well. Which meant that she would probably just pick up disbelief. And worry. And maybe a little fear because whether she was telepathic or not, the fact that she thought she was meant there was something to be concerned about one way or another. Pointing out the presence of these emotions was hardly going to constitute compelling evidence to any of the fine folks in her immediate circle.

So what was the hurry? First, she should probably learn more about this and how it affected her and her life. The lyrics to Brain Damage kept playing in her head. It was true. Having people think that one is crazy seldom ends well.

Thanks Pink Floyd, Lola thought. At some point, the right point, she would at the very least let Alex know what was going on.

Ikenna knocked harshly in Somadina's door. It had been over three weeks since he spoke with his daughter. He stood with the gruff defensiveness of a man who knows that he is in the wrong. He held the cell phone in his hand like it was a dead rodent, a problem to be disposed of.

"Yes. Come in father," Somadina called from inside.

"How'd you know ... never mind." He walked in muttering. "You have a message from that Yoruba man that came to visit you weeks ago. Olumiji."

"Oh, I had been wondering when he'd contact me," Somadina said pleasantly. "What does he have to say?" Because Ikenna did not read terribly well, he just handed the phone to her.

"Please tell your daughter Somadina that I am sorry I did not revert to her sooner, but I have been unable to find any information which could be helpful. I have been trying to be of help and will keep doing so. Please ask her to call me at this number or text back if she needs anything else and let her know that I will be in touch again. Sooner this time I promise."

"Is he trying to find Nwanyi?" her father asked.

"Yes," Somadina merely said.

"You know about my sons going to school, don't you?" her father asked.

"Yes," Somadina said again.

Her father sighed. "How? You used to do that as a little girl. It scared people sometimes. I was so thankful that you seemed to outgrow it."

"Well it came back," Somadina said. "Maybe because I needed it. Clearly I have serious work to do to find my sister, and I will not be having a private detective or even a computer-adept brother to help me, now will I?" She paused, knowing that if she kept talking she would say words inappropriate for any daughter to say to a father. So she sat in silence.

"It was a hard choice," Ikenna finally said.

"Was it?" She could not suppress the tone of sarcasm quickly enough, and when he heard the sting behind the words she saw a bit of anger grow in her father's eyes as well. He would not be addressed this way no matter how wrong he was.

"Somadina. These are two very fine young men. They will both do well, have a future beyond what I, what their mothers, what this village could ever give them. Or of course I could instead try to rescue a daughter who has never cared much for me, just to appease another daughter who seems to care even less. For what? For the one to come back to this village and hate me even more? And that is the best possible outcome, because it is even more likely that I will waste all my money and then I do not have the daughter back, I do not have the affection of the other daughter, and I still do not have a way to provide a better future for my sons. Be as angry as you like. I am tired of your anger, I am casting my lot with my future and doing what makes the most sense for my sons. Someday they will help provide, not just for me and their mothers, but maybe even for you and your children. Do not question my wisdom so. It is not your place."

And with that an angry Ikenna stood to leave.

"I truly do wish my brothers well," Somadina managed to say. "I have told their mothers I wish to help prepare the farewell feast before they leave this week. I bear them no ill will."

"No. Just me," Ikenna muttered as he walked out of the front door.

x^0

Chapter 11. September 2009

Lola managed work on Tuesday mostly by avoiding being near people. She hoped that the "I still feel pretty queasy" excuse would get her through the week without too much human interaction. As long as she sat in her office by herself and focused on the computer screen, she was fine. No such technique worked at home of course, but she was more comfortable with Alex's wildly open but fairly unsurprising thoughts, and she didn't find it much more difficult than it had been to not be offended by Teddie's fiercely closed and defensive emotional stance towards her.

Wednesday evening she found herself thinking about Summer, and then she found herself thinking with Summer. Oh dear. Summer was looking at Gregg, feeling glad that she had chosen to forgive him. Feeling like he was making a real effort to let her know how she was the one that he loved. Feeling glad that she had kept his infidelity to herself, so that their relationship would not be marred in anyone else's eyes. In Lola's eyes. This was not good. Lola was embarrassed to be present, and left as quickly as she could turn her mind elsewhere. But, she thought sadly, it did explain a lot. Her sister deserved more credit than she had given her, for indeed if Lola had known and had provided Summer with support and a kindly ear, Gregg's bad behavior would always be on the table between them. Lola tried to focus on the cat, and to keep herself out of everyone else's head for the rest of the night.

Thursday night, September 3, Lola picked Zane up at the airport after work. He had not lived at home with them for five years now, and she found that she sometimes had trouble remembering exactly what his face looked like, and for some reason she was always a little surprised when she saw him. At the start of the summer he had looked shorter and paler, and to be honest somewhat less handsome than she remembered. Tonight he looked stronger, and considerably better than the mental picture that she had in her head.

This time around, she had other input to deal with as well. Zane was both open and closed, anxious to talk to her, but reticent and fearful about a thing or two as well. She greeted her son warmly, and did her best to turn her mental volume control way down and to trust that a mutual conversation would come in good time.

She and Alex both had to work on Friday, and while at the office Lola made a concerted effort to shut out the waves of guilt feelings she kept getting from Zane because he was lounging around at home playing his old video games when he had promised his mom that he would use the day to go through some of the clutter still left in his room. *Do not call the house and tell him to get to work*, she told herself sternly. *Do not.*

Lola's Saturdays always began with a leisurely cup of coffee on the front porch. "Mind if I join you?" Zane had an unlit morning cigarette in one hand. Lola winced but said nothing. She felt Zane's response to her wince, which apparently was not nearly as unnoticeable as Lola had always believed it was. *Okay, I guess I don't have as fine a poker face as I thought,* she mused. *Good to know.*

"Sure dear. Go ahead," she gestured to the hated cigarette and watched Zane light it carefully.

"Tell me about this atypical antipsychotic drug stuff," she offered, thinking that was a safe topic. No, apparently not. A rush of fear and worry followed her question.

"This new assignment is interesting, mom," Zane's exterior composure remained far calmer than the turmoil of emotions inside would lead one to expect. "I do understand that the pharmaceutical industry provides a tremendous amount of relief and hope to the sick people of this world."

"Yes. I certainly have no quarrel with that."

"But you know what the problem is with sick people?" Zane asked.

"They're sick?" Lola ventured.

"No," Zane smiled. "There just aren't enough of them." He took a long drag on the cigarette. "Seriously. Not enough of them to fund the new research. To grow profits. To meet the expectations of Wall Street. You can only charge so much for medicine, unless of course it is absolutely the only thing which can save a life, then I suppose you can charge anything. But most medications are not the only way to treat a disease, and they often yield mixed results. So there is a practical ceiling for what you can get away with charging before reasonable people, doctors, insurance companies will all turn to another approach. So then if you have to raise profits, you either have to cut costs, which is not so much an option when you are making medicine, or you have to find more customers."

"Right," Lola agreed. "Only it's not like you're selling video games and need to convince more people to start playing them." *Damn*, Lola chided herself as she both saw and felt Zane's startled look. *Not a good example.*

But he decided to ignore her and charged ahead. "Exactly. You either need to have more sick people, or to convince more people that they actually are sick."

"And making more people sick is clearly bad for PR," Lola laughed. "Thus the marvelous commercials we see to convince us that our acid reflux is causing more damage than we think or that we are more depressed than we realize."

"Right. And thus the concerted marketing push from pharmaceutical companies to physicians to use newer and more expensive drugs, and to use drugs for purposes for which they were not approved. Called 'off-label' by the way. And finally, the growing trend, especially in the psychiatric field, to find exactly the perfect 'cocktail' of drugs for each patient - which generally involves a fair amount of expensive experimenting and often seems to end up with at least one high-cost drug involved."

"So what is so bad about the atypical antipsychotic approach?"

"Well for starters it significantly ups one's chances for other nasty problems like hyperglycemia and diabetes, and its ability to benefit the severely depressed is still largely debated, but the main problem here in my opinion is that under no circumstances should it have been prescribed for someone with mild to moderate anxiety like what you described you have, mom. You have a, I don't know, wrist watch that needed a little repairing and these folks wanted to come at it with a sledgehammer. My guess is that whoever you were seeing is getting some serious pressure from some sales rep to at least try out this drug in a mix and you happened to be the most likely candidate he had available."

"I'm not going back to that psychologist," Lola said.

"You don't have to go that far," Zane was surprised. "Just tell him you want to stick to the oldest and safest medications available and that's that. If you are firm I am sure he will listen."

"No, you don't understand. I don't think I need medication at all and the last time I saw him, he tried to pressure me into staying on it. He even sent this last prescription to the pharmacy when I told him I just wanted to think about it, and now they've called me twice to come pick it up which I am not going to do."

"So are you going to ask him about tapering off the meds and seeing how it goes?"

"I already stopped taking them."

"Mom, its really not a good idea to do that on your own. This is serious stuff."

"I know. And I gave it some serious thought. I took a half dose for a few days before I stopped last week. And I'm fine."

Zane shook his head. "A few days at half a dose doesn't really constitute tapering, mom. But, luckily for you, I have to admit you do seem fine. Actually, compared to last June, you seem much better. Guess you didn't really need it to start with, huh?" And Lola could tell that Zane was relieved that the medication issue was out of Lola's life.

"So what is bothering you?" she tried gently. And felt the door in his mind open slightly wider.

"I'm not stupid," he started.

Lola thought of his perfect score on the math SAT, achieved for the first time when Zane was only thirteen. "Whatever you are dear, it certainly is not stupid."

"I mean, emotionally. I know how hard you and dad worked to make this college thing happen for me. It wasn't exactly in your savings plan for me to go somewhere that cost forty thousand dollars a year, and I know you make too much to qualify for aid and not enough to afford that kind of tuition. But you found a way. And now …"

She felt Zane's sadness. Embarrassment? He was a failure?

x^0

How could a twenty-three year old be a failure?

"Mom, I'm not particularly fond of the field I'm in. No, more accurately I'm not sure I can find anything in this field that I want to do. Am willing to do. To be honest, I never was particularly excited about the idea of the years it would take me to get a Ph.D., even though it's what you and dad always thought I would do. But just because a person is smart doesn't mean they want to spend years more in school. You know? Now, unfortunately, in a field like neuroscience it turns out that if I don't, that even with a master's degree I am going to be relegated to either basically tending other people's lab experiments for the rest of my life or to working in some related branch of the pharmaceutical industry, probably marketing, and I'm starting to have some ethical issues with that.

"On the other hand, if I completely change fields now, I pretty much piss away everything you guys have invested in me, and we are talking about something like a hundred and sixty thousand dollars here, which is not exactly trivial. So either I start over at another much cheaper school or I take out massive loans and start over, but either way I've screwed up a great opportunity."

Yikes. So that was the problem. Time to be the best mom she could be.

"Okay, dear. First of all, you're not a screw up. You're a twenty-three-year-old trying to figure out what he wants to do. We're proud of you."

"Thanks mom." She could feel the eye roll.

"No, I'm serious. And there are a lot of solutions. I get that you don't want to wash test tubes for the rest of your life. And just because you have the brains for years of scholarly research doesn't mean you have the temperament or interest. So looking at your realistic options, I think that you need to remember that no part of any industry is entirely bad. You've obviously encountered a few folks this summer who left you less than enamored with the business side of the pharmaceutical industry. But that doesn't mean there aren't worthwhile people, and a worthwhile career there."

He started to object but she cut him off.

"And if you just plain don't want to do that, period, that is perfectly fine. There are related industries. Maybe related degrees that might not take the kind of years you are fearing they would. And okay, if you have decided you really truly want to go back and be a history major now, there are still alternatives. Yes, cheaper schools. Yes, loans. The point is that your dad and I did not make these sacrifices so you could be trapped in a miserable life you hated. Okay? We happen to love you. Which means we happen to want you to be happy, productive, fulfilled. Not miserable. Not living a dream you think we have for you. What the hell kind of love would that be?"

She paused. Zane didn't say anything but she felt his emotional hug engulf her with love and gratitude. Which was a nice thing because the emotion hardly even registered on her son's face. "I appreciate that mom," he said softly but sincerely. "I really do."

So she went ahead and gave him the hug. And she could feel his appreciation as she saw his soft hint of a smile in return.

Ikenna did not believe in calling his sons often at school even though both he and they had phones. It seemed indulgent to him, like it might lead somehow to his sons being spoiled or whiny or otherwise not strong. Nonetheless, he broke with his habit and called Udo a couple of weeks after he and Somadina argued.

The more Ikenna thought about it the more right he believed that he was. Education gave a child a future. He wanted a future, the best of futures, for all of his children but certainly for his two oldest sons. He understood that Nwanyi was Somadina's only full sibling and therefore Somadina was understandably and even rightfully protective of her sister, but that did not excuse Somadina's criticism of her own father.

However, much to Ikenna's growing consternation, his dear first wife Amaka had been showing up in his dreams with greater and greater frequency since Nwanyi's marriage, and in increasingly disturbing ways. Ever since he and Somadina spoke the last time it seemed that Amaka was there every night, now often covered in blood from the birth. Her face still looked beautiful as she reminded Ikenna that Somadina's concerns and worries remained well founded. But every night he had to look away from the mess on her body as he assured her that he truly understood. That a good father did not ignore such reasonable concerns. He was trying to do what he could.

So after Udo had reassured his father that he was studying hard and doing well, Ikenna made a request of his son. "You must help your sister Somadina in any way you can."

"I have," he eagerly volunteered. "I have been teaching her to use different websites where you can search for people and I've set her up with an email account. She could do better if she could read and type faster, but she is improving at both as she spends more time online looking for ways to locate Nwanyi."

"In that case you must also help be her eyes and fingers. Do some of the searching for her, and try to find new ways to help her with your knowledge. I know it is hard with your studies, but stay in close contact with her and see what you can do and don't give up. This is important Udo."

"Yes father."

"Very good Udo. Work hard now. Make your family proud. And there is no need to mention this conversation."

"Yes father."

Udo was not as strong as many of the other boys, and perhaps not as assertive. But he was very smart, and Ikenna knew that he could be trusted to use well whatever helpful methods the modern world had to offer. If anyone could find Nwanyi, he could, and then perhaps all of Ikenna's children could prosper and get along. Then perhaps Ikenna could get an undisturbed night's sleep and Amaka's soul would go back to being at peace.

Once the gardener returned Nwanyi and she got through the horrible weekend which followed, and the equally horrible one which followed after that, Nwanyi recognized how completely and effectively she was imprisoned. This gave her a change in perspective. She was not a bad second wife who—for reasons she could not understand—kept displeasing her husband and had to try to do better. She was not a woman who needed to learn to accept her situation. No. She was being held against her will and needed to focus on surviving and escaping. She could now see how the seriousness of her situation had crept up gradually, making her more compliant and easy to control because, up to now, there had never really been a point at which she had been absolutely sure. For Djimon, and Mairo too, had never quite crossed the line into making her feel like a captive. Until now.

It was also clear now that merely running was unlikely to work, and the consequences were unpleasant to say the least. There were still other avenues, of course. She could try to beseech a rare delivery person for help, or try to send a message through one of the small children maybe. She suspected that her captors, and yes they were truly her captors in spite of the bride price they had paid, had propagated the story that she was unstable, a poor woman who had probably never been right and now had been pushed over the edge by this marriage. Poor Djimon and Mairo, stuck with this flawed woman in their household. Too kind to return her to her father and thus bring shame upon the father's family. Trying to do the right thing. And the woman says the craziest things.

But Nwanyi also knew that sometimes people hear the truth through the lies. And she could help with that. Her unkempt appearance and fearful eyes were not helping. She needed to keep herself cleaner. And better groomed. And calm. And sane. She could not afford many more failed attempts, or even the few avenues left open to her would be closed. So Nwanyi, who had for all her life embraced life's small miseries to get attention, found herself now actively seeking out small joys.

One day it was a moth which had gotten into her room and which Nwanyi spent over an hour watching. As it took flight and alighted on walls and furniture, she imagined herself flying with it, queen of the moths. Another time, she was allowed to work in the kitchen to help the cook prepare a particularly involved feast for after sundown when the daily Ramadan fast would be broken. A bit of sunlight entered the room and Nwanyi followed the sunbeam with her chair, not caring how it made the room hotter, but delighting in its sparkly light. The cook looked at her oddly, but said nothing.

Nwanyi's most dependable joy was often found in the morning just as she awoke, when she sometimes felt like Somadina was at her bedside whispering words of encouragement. She didn't know where such a crazy idea came from, but she swore she could sometimes hear, *Hold on little sister. I will l find you. I will help you,* in her head so clearly that when she opened her eyes she almost expected to see Somadina standing there. Which of course she never did. And even though Nwanyi recognized it as irrational, she tried to respond in kind, to tell Somadina that she had heard and appreciated it. That she was waiting for help. But she had no idea how to answer back.

Her only other dependable comfort was her impression that, based on her treatment so far, she would not be killed, or injured to the point where she could not function. There seemed to be a certain amount of care being given to keeping her alive. Minimum food each day, unappetizing but adequate. A bit of fresh air once weekly in the courtyard. Also a weekly chance to bathe. It was routine and predictable, almost like someone was using a manual of some sort to determine the basic necessities but no more. In fact, disinfectant had been gruffly provided by Djimon on the rare occasions when a weekend session had left cuts which could become infected. So she was fairly certain that she was more than just an expensive toy for Djimon and Mairo to each abuse in their own way for their own entertainment. There had to be a purpose to this whole thing. But for the life of her, Nwanyi could not imagine what purpose she could possibly serve.

The gardener Ibrahim watched five of his younger children playing in the dirt in front of the house. They had little, but amused themselves with games made up with sticks and rocks. *We need so little to really get by*, he thought to himself. *Does a larger amount of food, a bit more comfort, really justify aiding, condoning, supporting the abject misery of another human being? Even a young woman, even a non-believer?* Ibrahim knew the answer and as he watched his own children play, he felt ashamed.

The next day, Nwanyi found a small piece of fruit in her room. It was just a section of orange placed on her hard cot where she was sure to find it but it would not be easily noticed by another. Her first thought was that the gift was some sort of test, and that she would be in trouble if she actually ate the fruit. But her hunger overcame her fear, and after she savored the wonderful sweetness in her mouth she decided that she would gladly eat any such thing that she found again.

And every day after that, there was another small thing to be found. Sometimes it was a bit of mango, other times a banana or a piece of melon, but always somehow by the end of the day something was there. Nwanyi thought perhaps the gardener was doing this to ease his guilt, but the source of her treats did not matter. Her body welcomed the nourishment, and her heart added this bit of joy to the various ways she was using to get by.

Starting in the 1990s, various political movements emerged in Nigeria in response to the oil spills in the Niger Delta and to the lack of oil revenue going back into the region. Ken Saro-Wiwa, a poet, environmental journalist, and former university teacher who became a political activist speaking out on behalf of the people of the Niger Delta, was executed by the Nigerian government in 1995 for murders he could not possibly have committed. The charges were so blatantly false that Nelson Mandela, then president of South Africa, called it a "heinous act" and Bill Clinton, then president of the United States, said it flouted "even the most basic international norms and universal standards of human rights." The government's desire to silence Saro-Wiwa's peaceful opposition to oil interests in Nigeria resulted in massive condemnation from the international community and Nigeria's suspension from the Commonwealth of Nations for over three years.

Not surprisingly, the next generation of activists embraced a more intimidating approach, and in 2006 the Movement for the Emancipation of the Niger Delta, MEND, was formed in hopes of establishing local control over Nigeria's oil industry and gaining reparations from the government for the pollution.

x⁰

Lola was reading with interest the article in *The Economist* which Ariel had sent her. By now she had heard of MEND, but knew very little about it. The article described MEND as an organization that "portrays itself as a political organization that wants a greater share of Nigeria's oil revenues to go to the impoverished region that sits atop the oil. In fact, it is more of an umbrella organization for several armed groups, which it sometimes pays in cash or guns to launch attacks."

The Economist went on to point out that Nigerian officials were often suspected and accused of working with MEND and taking a cut of the revenue from stolen oil and from MEND's other criminal activities including gun-running.

Yikes. Lola headed back to the internet. Quick surfing confirmed that MEND enjoyed widespread support among the region's twenty million people. Yet another article, this one by the BBC, described MEND as "a loose web of armed groups in Nigeria's oil-producing Niger Delta region." It went on to say that for years these loosely affiliated gangs had kidnapped oil workers and attacked oil fields, demanding that more of the oil wealth be invested in local roads, schools, hospitals, and public utilities. But, the BBC article added, MEND's gangs also ran criminal rackets and kidnapped civilians for ransom. Lola sighed.

Djimon's entire family left the Thursday evening before the end of Ramadan to spend the holiday weekend with Djimon's mother's family up north. As the servants obviously wanted the weekend off as well to pray and to celebrate with their own kin, there was serious talk about needing to bring Nwanyi along. Nwanyi did her best to hide her eagerness, feigning an ignorant disinterest in all the activities of the house as best she could. Nwanyi overheard Mairo suggest that she be heavily drugged for the duration, while Djimon felt that the medications might pose some mild risks of damage or death if given in high enough doses for several days straight . He thought that she could just be threatened into good behavior.

In the end, however, they elected not to bring her. Rather

they invested in a heavy dead bolt for her door, which Mairo felt they should have installed long ago and "let people think what they will." They provided her with a chamber pot, six glasses of water, three large pieces of bread, and double chained her ankle to her bed, which Djimon had already had the gardener bolt to the wall. Apparently a friend whose family was local would check on her once or twice, "And you do not even want to know what we will do to you if he finds any evidence that you have tried to escape." Her leg alone was secured well beyond anything from which she could possible hope to get free, so Nwanyi mentally prepared herself to be totally alone for the next four nights.

    Saturday morning the bolt turned and a stranger looked in. Nwanyi's first thought was embarrassment at the contents of the chamber pot. Indeed the man wrinkled his nose, no doubt smelling the stench. Still he gave her an almost friendly nod. "So you are the young woman Djimon has persuaded us all to invest so very much time and money in?"

    She must have looked baffled.

    "Come now. You must have known you did not come cheaply. But Djimon assures us you are perfect. Are you perfect?" He eyed her up and down, and for a brief minute Nwanyi was worried she might be in danger of being raped. But the man's attention moved on. "You better be, dear. This country, this world, needs us, and we need you. Glad to see you are well secured. I'll be back tomorrow."

    But with tomorrow being Eid al-Fitr, a holiday of great feasting and joy, the man understandably got caught up in activities with his family and did not get the chance to return. So Nwanyi spent the rest of her time trying to imagine what the man had meant.

    The following Tuesday the house returned to its pre-Ramadan normalcy, and that evening Djimon and Mairo were apparently hosting a gathering of some sort. Men and women began arriving in ones and twos and filling the living room. Nwanyi, once again behind a bolted door but at least cleaned, fed, and not chained, listened to the tone of the conversation even if she could not make out the words. There was argument. Djimon seemed to be trying to calm, to placate, to intercede for waiting. Other voices were impatient. "The Christmas season is most definitely the time," she heard one woman shriek in response to someone else. "How can she suddenly not be progressing as well as you expected?" a very deep voice resonated through the walls." More argument followed. A man yelled, "There is absolutely no way we let you start this over with someone else. You said she was perfect. So she is." More argument. Finally the deep voice cut through again. "Bring her out here where we all can see her. Let us judge as a group whether she is ready or not."

Into the silence that followed, Djimon's voice began, "That sort of experience for her could ruin everything! You don't understand. This is a very difficult process. She—" He stopped speaking at a look or gesture from someone which Nwanyi could not see. Then, "Very well, my dear brother-in law. I will get her." Nwanyi recognized the cold fury in Djimon's tone in those last words even if the deep-voiced brother-in-law to whom he was speaking did not.

It was Mairo who came into her room. Nwanyi for her part was desperately trying to decide if it was in her best interest to be "ready," whatever that meant, and if so how she could best appear to be so. Ready had to mean some kind of a change, she thought, and from her point of view any change was good. Furthermore, Djimon had worked hard to make her feel worthless. So ready must mean feeling very worthless. Nwanyi entered the living area head bowed, looking as miserable and beaten down as she could possibly manage. A man she took to be Mairo's brother, the man with the very deep voice, spoke.

"Look up child. Let us see your eyes." Nwanyi raised eyes that were filled with complete hopelessness. Even Djimon lifted a slightly surprised eyebrow.

"It appears to me that you have done excellent work Djimon," deep voice said. "Prepare her with your next phase. This year, the Nigerian people will have a Christmas present."

Of course the whole village knew about the two half-brothers heading off to the very important boarding school, and of course most, if not all, of the village had a pretty good idea of where the bulk of the money had come from. Ikenna was moderately well-off for the town he lived in, but all had seen Djimon's very fancy clothes and very fine car, and in spite of predications that after Nwanyi's wedding Ikenna's two wives would soon be much better dressed and each making substantial improvements to her small house, that had not come to pass.

 Over the last few years Somadina had made efforts to be courteous and even warm to both of Azuka's parents, and although both were courteous back and clearly loved their grandson, neither one was terribly affectionate to her, and she had not developed a close relationship with either. Now that she found herself more receptive to the feelings around her, she was surprised to discover that both dad and mom, in their own ways, had sensed the reticence in her affections for their son, and both, in their own way, had rather resented it. Well, that did make a little sense.

 So Somadina was surprised when Azuka's mother suggested that Azuka take the car and a day off from the repair shop and take her to the internet café in town. It had to do with sisters, Somadina could tell. His mama had an unfortunate experience of her own involving a sister and an unconcerned father, and as humans often nobly did, she wished to make better for another what had gone so badly for her. Somadina hugged the woman with sincere thanks and was granted a sincerely warm hug in return.

 Hours later, at the internet café in the city, she logged on and discovered that Udo had indeed set her up with the email account just as he promised, and she checked that first. There was a happy note from Udo who apparently loved school and gave her several concrete suggestions for how to search for people. Good for Udo. And there was a brief note from Olumiji confirming that he now had this new address and alluding to his ongoing but still unsuccessful efforts to find Nwanyi. Okay. At least he was still trying.

 This time Somadina spent about an hour trying to locate anyone in the list of names her father had given her, using more tools which Udo had described to her. No luck. Then she allowed

x^0

herself to go to the x^0 site in hopes that she might find some helpful morsel or some clue to her mystery lady. As she logged on, Azuka came up behind her.

"What's this?" he asked. Oh what the hell, Somadina thought. Either I trust him or I don't. "I'm a telepath, Azuka."

"I figured you were something like that. They really have a website for telepaths?"

She laughed. "I wouldn't have thought so either. But do you remember the man that came to visit about a month ago?"

"Of course. You must have talked to him for three hours. I was starving for dinner and finally my mother took pity on me and fed me." He was smiling, not angry at the memory.

"Well, he came on behalf of this organization. He told me about the website. I've been dying to get back here and learn more."

"Then learn away, " Azuka said. He kissed her on the cheek. "I'll be back in an hour or so. Okay?" As he walked away Somadina felt clearly that Azuka was only mildly surprised and not really at all bothered. In fact, he thought it was kind of cool that she was a telepath. The mild surprise was mostly about the fact that she had told him. And he thought that was pretty cool too.

Somadina read as quickly as she could manage through the pages and pages of FAQ's looking for something helpful to her. Finally she found:

> Q: Can being a telepath provide any useful function to society?

> A: Often no, but we stand ready to provide subtle assistance in times of emergency. For example, in a panic situation a telepath can sometimes project a sense of calm which can be picked up by one or more receivers at the scene. These receivers may in turn choose to model rational and helpful behavior which others may imitate. Also, in cases of natural disasters we frequently dispatch telepaths located nearby to act as volunteers to seek out those trapped in any type of wreckage, as our gift works particularly well for that need.

Q: Can you locate missing people or wanted criminals?

A: Unfortunately telepathy does not often work well for this. The person being sought must be alive and wish to be found which eliminates many of the former and almost all of the latter. Even a victim seeking aid must be transmitting clearly, and not be drugged, or too disoriented. The situation is compounded by the fact that there is a tremendous amount of ambient emotional information out there, including that which is transmitted from folks who do not have an emergency but are seeking every possible type of assistance, as well as angry, greedy, or lustful people conniving to do harm but who will never actually carry out their plans. Telepaths learn early on that they cannot possibly reach out to every call for help, or send out an alarm for every creepy sensation. However, telepaths do occasionally locate people in true need of immediate help or on the real verge of creating mayhem. When this happens x^0 works with the individual telepaths to manage any resulting publicity.

Somadina sighed. This was not terribly hopeful for finding Nwanyi. She read on.

Q: Do telepaths regularly communicate with each other using telepathy?

A: Yes. When we are together we use it to enhance our verbal communication and occasionally can use it to replace spoken words altogether for simple things like a greeting or an apology. When …

With her own abilities becoming a little more comfortable every day, Lola found that she often went to the x^0 website now to browse and re-read the extensive list of FAQs about telepathy. As Lola skimmed through looking for any new section she had not yet seen, she felt a slight, almost electric shiver grab her attention.

x^0

Q: Do telepaths regularly communicate with each other using telepathy?

A: Yes. When we are together we use it to enhance our verbal communication and occasionally can use it to replace spoken words altogether for simple things like a greeting or an apology. When apart we certainly use it to enhance our electronic communication of all types, we often use it to ask each other to call or write, and for those of us who are friends we use it to just maintain a sense of closeness at a distance.

And Lola knew Somadina was reading the same words. And Somadina knew Lola was reading the same words. And neither woman would ever be certain which one of them started the next thought. *You're here. On this website. So you know someone in x^0 and I know someone in x^0 and these two people know each other. Or they can find each other. And then they can find us. And then we can find us.*
  Lola and Somadina each looked at their screen in amazement. Of course.
  Somadina sent the thought *I'm going to find you,* by thinking of a cartoon picture of a girl looking for something. And she went back to her email to compose a second message to Olumiji.
  Lola playfully sent back the thought *I'm going to find you first,* with a picture of two girls racing and laughing. She picked up the phone to call Maurice.
  And they both understood.

Olumiji read the email with interest. Somadina was clearly one of the strongest telepaths his group had encountered in a while, and there was no question that if she latched on to another telepath, or even a strong receiver, she could forge a powerful connection. But who was this other woman?
  Olumiji remembered talking with his brother Jumoke a few weeks before meeting Somadina and hearing about an American woman engineer or something like that who had come to Nigeria on business and whom Jumoke had met. He had some notion about the

American being beat up by her husband, or maybe it was her sister who was being beat up, but there was some family issue Jumoke had been sure involving somebody beating up somebody. Jumoke conceded that maybe the woman would make the jump into telepathy as an act of desperation or survival.

Although Jumoke denied his own abilities and usually derided Olumiji's involvement with x^0 as mystical mumbo jumbo, Olumiji knew that his brother felt protective toward this particular woman, with whom he had felt a strong common wavelength. Jumoke had, just this once, actually pushed Olumiji to have someone contact her. So the timing on this appeared to fit well with Somadina's story.

But she was not Nigerian. Not even African. It was hard to imagine the circumstances under which she and Somadina could have "found" each other. In fact, she lived in Texas. He had asked Maurice to meet with her, to check out the situation. And Maurice had elected to give her access to x^0, somewhat in violation of guidelines, because at the time the woman's status had been deemed as transitional, a strong receiver likely on a trajectory to become a telepath soon, for reasons Maurice had not known. Members had the freedom to make judgment calls like that, of course, and Olumiji had not voiced his discomfort at the rule bending to Maurice, although he was quite certain Maurice had felt it.

But Maurice might have been more than right in his decision, if this oil business lady was the one Somadina sought. He forwarded Somadina's email on to Maurice with a note saying, "Please get a hold of me soon, as we may have a more complicated situation here than you realized," and then sent Maurice a direct message of concern and urgency, but not panic, which would refine the email in ways the mere addition of more words could not.

Djimon understood that he had risked the wrath of the entire group by claiming that Nwanyi was not ready, and he was trying to figure out why he felt so certain that was the case. Indeed she appeared totally dejected and obedient. But on rare occasion there would be a look in her eyes, or something in her posture, that implied she still felt some sort of hope. Which she was not supposed to feel at this point.

Djimon had based his plan for her on much study, from techniques used by elite military groups, weekend encounter sessions, interrogators, and petty kidnappers alike. He was to completely erode Nwanyi's sense of self and self-worth, and then replace it with the sense of purpose and hope which he would provide. A messy business to be sure, but necessary to achieve a fine and noble end.

So Djimon had to wonder what could have gone wrong. Perhaps he had picked his subject a little too well? A woman who had led an easier life, received more love and affection, and was used to more comforts might have found his attempts to deprive her more impressive and broken down more easily. Clearly he had picked a subject who had very low expectations from life. Frankly, it had sometimes seemed difficult to come in even lower.

Of course he could continue to beat himself up for making the mistake of feeling a certain amount of lust for her, which honestly would probably just have repulsed a woman more used to male attention, but in Nwanyi's case it did seem to have given her an odd boost of self esteem quite contrary to what he was trying to achieve. His mistake, certainly.

Maybe it had been a poor idea to keep her at the house at all. The group had discussed finding a safe, empty building in which she could have been kept more isolated, and considerably more uncomfortable, on a day-to-day basis. There was only so much one could do after all to mistreat someone with one's own children underfoot! But the group had started to balk at the piling up of expenses. And, Djimon had to face it, he had not fought hard for this other alternative because he was so busy planning for the aftermath to Nwanyi's part, that he had appreciated the convenience of having her right at the house.

Well, what was done was done. She was as broken down as he was going to get her, and now it was time to work the magic of convincing her that she had a very important, no, pivotal, role to play in the future of her country. She was going to be the most worthwhile woman ever, if and only if she did exactly what he told her to do.

Maurice was surprised to get a phone call from Lola, but more surprised to feel the strong wave of emotion that came with her voice. There was a breathlessness there, a sense that she was racing with someone. For fun. Which was odd because his email binged just after the phone rang, and he could feel his friend Olumiji anxious to speak with him too. Good grief, he hadn't this much excitement in awhile.

"Hello young lady," he greeted Lola with affection, which was at least in part fueled by his happy recognition that he had been more than right about her. She was indeed a telepath now, and, face it, it always felt good to make a judgment call correctly. "What can I do for my favorite geophysicist?"

She laughed and he felt her happiness. "I seem to have made a new friend, Maurice. It's, well, a friendship which makes no sense whatsoever without the website you gave me access to, and I'm not even sure it makes sense with it. But I do know that she also got access recently and she and I need to talk. Really talk. Can you help me out here?"

Maurice, who was living proof that an eighty-four-year-old can multi-task just fine, was already reading his email while he listened to Lola. "I think I not only can help you, dear, but I should. It may or may not surprise you to know that there is a twenty-one-year-old Igbo woman living northeast of Abakaliki in the Ebonyi State of Southeastern Nigeria who has been trying to desperately find her younger sister and somewhere along the way decided you could help. Her name is Somadina. And a friend of mine right now is looking into ways we can put you two ladies in touch with each other."

Maurice let himself enjoy the sensations of relief and excitement which came from Lola as she passed along the facts and events leading up to her current state. She had already, probably, figured out how to turn down the volume on incoming information, but he was going to have to give her a little instruction on how to tone down her own output, he chuckled to himself. He said goodbye, promising to get back to her as soon as he had more specific information.

As soon as Lola hung up the phone with Maurice, she immediately began looking for information on her friend's homeland, Ebonyi . According to an official Nigerian website it is located in Southeastern Nigeria, is ninety percent Igbo, and its capital is Abakaliki. It has an estimated population of more than two million people, most of whom farm nuts, yams, cassava, bananas, and beans. The state also produces marble, lead, and zinc, and is referred to as the "the salt of the nation" because of its salt deposits. Lola looked through the photographs of the smaller towns in Ebonyi, thinking with fascination that one of them might be where Somadina lived.

It took a day for Maurice to get back to her with a real live phone number, as apparently the Nigerian woman had only gotten her own cell phone just days ago. Maurice assured Lola that this Somadina had been practicing with it, anxious for Lola's contact.

Lola googled, "How do I text Nigeria?" only to get links to multiple companies trying to sell her cell phones, cell phone plans, and so forth. Try again. "How do I text internationally?" That query provided a few sites that could actually be helpful. She picked the one that looked most likely. Of course, you use a country code. Nigeria's code? 234. Use a plus sign. Leave out the zeroes. Would her phone do this? She had texted the US from other countries before with no problem. Just try it.

She fumbled in anticipation. After all of the vague sensations of friendship and needing and giving help, she was a little nervous about making real actual contact with this woman, whom she felt she knew so well and had so very much in common. And so very little in common.

"Hi," she typed. No, that seemed stupid. But after some thought it actually sounded less stupid than any of the alternatives she could come up with, so she pressed send. Seconds passed. "Hi to you," came back with a sensation of warmth, nervousness, awkwardness.

"I am very glad to know who you are." She concentrated on sending reassurance and openness back. Many seconds passed. "Me too." Gratitude came with it. And curiosity.

It seemed to Lola that at this point the situation called for something that was more like an essay question. "Tell me about your sister." It was many minutes before the long, poorly typed response found its way to Texas, and to a baffled Lola.

What? Their dad had sold the sister for money to be somebody's second wife?? Lola was horrified. "No wonder you are upset. I don't know when I have heard a story of something so horrible!" She sent feelings of outrage and sympathy as she hit send.

It was several seconds before she felt Somadina's confusion and embarrassment. Why was the American woman so upset? Somadina had not yet gotten to the upsetting part of the story.

"You can't be serious? This is normal?" Lola typed it back in disbelief. She thought maybe she had not gotten the facts right. But apparently she had, because this time Lola felt Somadina backing off from her.

"You don't understand. You seemed like you were such an open and caring person." The disappointment came through as both text and as feeling, and it felt defensive and angry as well as sad. "This is how we do things here. Is that a problem for you?"

"Yes. It is a problem." Lola hit the tiny keys with sharp staccato taps. Now she was defensive and angry herself. "I cannot accept a dad giving his sixteen-year-old daughter to an already married man for a lot of money," she typed. That was ridiculous.

"Clearly you think that your ways are so much better. I see no point in talking to you. I am sorry I ever bothered you." And this time it was Lola's turn to feel the door click shut completely. For the rest of the day there were no more messages of any kind. So much for using telepathy to achieve world peace.

Lola slept poorly that night, the way she did when she fought with Alex, or when one of the children was out partying and she knew it and she could only wait and hope that all would be well. The next day at work she was irritable as she prepared displays for one more excruciatingly detailed review of the well proposal. It looked like a rig had finally been secured for late November, and to her surprise she would be expected to be in the Lagos office while the drill bit made its way through the objective interval. While she normally loved to travel, today this news annoyed her even more. She found herself annoyed with all the Nigerian protocol and paperwork, annoyed with her Nigerian coworkers, annoyed with the conversations in the office. She picked up a few strong feelings of "What's the matter with her?" to which she silently replied with crude remarks, safe in the knowledge that she could not be heard. Lola knew that she was at her worst, but some days one just is that way.

Finally, in her irritated haste, she brushed against a stack of papers on Okocha's work table and the papers tumbled in haphazard order onto the floor. To her surprise, there was no flash of irritation back from him. Rather, just a sense of sympathy. "Bad day Lola?" he asked amiably while picking up the papers, and Lola realized how quickly just a bit of understanding can sooth a foul mood.

"Okocha? Can I ask a direct question?" He said nothing, which she knew meant "I am not going to try to stop you."

"What do you think of Americans? American customs? American ways?"

"Oh I like you all very much. I like it here very much."

Of course. He answered it like he had said the words a hundred times before, and he probably had. She could tell that he meant it to a large degree. He had more comforts here and certainly more ways to amuse himself. But she also realized that he would have politely made such a response to her regardless of how he felt. She tried again.

"What I mean is, are there things we do, things we take as normal which strike you as odd. Maybe even, I don't know, barbaric?"

"Barbaric?" he laughed. " I don't think so. You're not very barbaric."

"Okay. That was the wrong word. What I mean is that I know this seems like an odd question but I have a friend who comes from a very different culture, and I am trying to be less judgmental about her. It would help me if you could tell me some thing about my world that, well, is hard for you to understand. Just to help me out."

"Okay." He hesitated. It was truly not his way to offend. And it occurred to Lola that the American love of bluntness and your feelings be damned might be one thing which seemed barbaric to him.

"You tend to care less about your families, especially your extended families, and your older relatives, than I am used to. It seems harsh. If you listen to the TV ads it seems like all older Americans need to save desperately for their retirement and worse yet to buy themselves "long-term care insurance" to cover the high cost of a very dismal slow death in a rest home. I guess to a Nigerian that is a bit barbaric. Where I come from it is considered a privilege to be granted a long life and to grow old. When one is granted such a gift, we take care of this person and wonder why you don't do the same. Does that help?"

"Yes. I think it does. Thank you." It was enough to give her something to think about, anyway.

"Good. And most of your fruits and vegetables taste like cardboard." He smiled. "But I do love all the ice cream flavors."

That night, Lola tried to make amends. You are transmitting emotional reactions about somebody else's culture to them, she told herself sternly. You personally get to like or not like what you want, but this woman does not need you judging her family and her ways through the harsh light of your own idea of what is normal anymore than you would need her harsh judgment of you if, say, you had put your mother in a rest home as you came to her for help.

"I'm sorry." She typed it and she felt it. "Things happen differently here. I will try to see this situation through your eyes. Seeing it through mine does not help." And she sent an image of a bunch of red Texas roses, with a cardinal like the ones in her yard fluttering nearby. There was a big bowl of strawberry ice cream and red gingham fabric under it all. In her mind she saw the door open a little, and a hand reach out for the bowl of ice cream. And she heard

Somadina giggle. The text message came a minute later.

"Okay. Let's start over."

"Please. You tell me what the real problem is. I will listen."

Somadina typed and transmitted and typed. It took awhile for the whole story to be told, but this time Lola really did listen.

Human beings, when thrown into a new situation which they know little about, naturally turn to a mentor, a kindly expert who can show them the ropes, if they are lucky enough to find such.

Maurice had lived seventy-nine years as a capable receiver, picking up random bits of thoughts, feelings, images, and sounds from those around him in a way which was diffuse enough for him to never question it as abnormal. He would realize later that he had used his skill without knowing it as he survived the booms and busts of working in the Texas oil patch, but he never considered himself odd in any way, and after he finally retired at a healthy seventy, he was happy with his life and strong in his faith in his Creator. He had expected to enjoy some much-deserved leisure time and then to leave this world for a heaven he fully believed in, with his wife of fifty-plus years at his side holding his hand as he died. But instead, nine years after he retired, she had run a stop sign, been hit broadside by a truck, and died before he could even get to her side to say goodbye.

Afterwards, he did not speak for days. It just wasn't supposed to have gone this way. She was younger and healthier and she was supposed to outlive him. The neighbors and friends and his kids all came and went, but he only grunted, nodded, and shook his head. He had become a seventy-nine-year-old mute.

And then, after about a month of silence, something changed. The longer he was quiet, the louder and more clearly he began to hear fragments of others' thoughts in his own head. Finally, his head felt like it was going to split in half. He was planning on, reluctantly, seeing a doctor, when a trade journal mentioning the Offshore Technology Conference in Houston caught his eye. He had always enjoyed the professional conferences and conventions of his business, and he was secretly pretty sure they were going to lock him up once he told someone what was going on. So he decided on one last outing for old times' sake. He gassed up the remaining car, got behind the wheel with some trepidation, and headed for the George R. Brown Convention Center in downtown Houston.

Which is where he became so totally overwhelmed with the thoughts and feelings that came at him relentlessly that he sat down on a bench outside of the men's room and cried like a small child. And the tallest blackest man he had ever seen in his life sat down next to him. He felt his normal spike of fear at any contact with a young black male, but the man merely said, "Let me help you," and then he realized that the man's mouth had not moved a bit. "My name is Olumiji," the man had added aloud. And newly formed telepath Maurice, a seventy-nine-year-old with all the biases and preconceptions of a man of his generation from his homeland, had found himself a thirty-seven-year-old Nigerian for a mentor and, eventually, for one of his truest friends.

Olumiji saved his sanity and maybe his life, showing him techniques for toning down reception and transmission, for filtering, for establishing and strengthening links he wanted to keep, and not establishing those which would cause problems. Olumiji gave him coping techniques for the headaches that came sometimes with the territory, and linked him up with a rather strange organization of telepaths that had taken him years to get used to. Maurice found that the group had its own philosophies, and few of those ideas jelled well with his strong fundamentalist Christian beliefs. But they were a tolerant group, and Maurice was a genuinely loving Christian, so eventually mutual respect prevailed, and in the end x^0 became a large part of his life as well.

Which is why, as he sat sipping his morning cup of decaf, he thought that maybe he had not done quite right by Lola. She seemed so independent and self-sufficient, so he had merely reached out by giving her the link to x^0, and then by putting her in touch with Somadina. But let's face it, he told himself, she was going to need training, guidance, support. He knew from experience that she was going to find her own biases and issues starkly exposed as she fumbled her way in a world in which secrets were harder to keep and self-honesty was the first step to survival.

Like many a receiver, Maurice was basically a loner. People, with the exception of his dear late wife, had mostly worn him out all his life, and he had always preferred being alone to being with acquaintances or in crowds. So calling Lola did not come easily to him. But thinking of all the ways his own mentor had helped him, Maurice knew that it was time to repay the favor. It was high time he called Lola to see if she would like to have dinner.

Lola had been delighted for Zane when he had called a couple of weeks ago and mentioned gleefully to his folks that he was going to get to travel on business at the end of the month. More incredibly, he was being sent on some sort of jaunt to Samoa to preview a conference venue. All dislike of pharmaceutical marketing seemed to have been tabled for the time being.

A text very late Monday night had let his parents know of his safe arrival, but all afternoon Tuesday Lola kept getting the oddest sensations about Zane. Finally she searched out Samoa in the news and read of the 8.1 earthquake that had hit between the two islands about noon Texas time. She was frightened, but not surprised. She forced herself to sit calmly at her desk and think of her son. She felt certain that she would know it if Zane were injured, or worse.

Breathe slowly, she told herself, forcing relaxation and concentration. *There. You can tell. He's not dead. Keep breathing. It doesn't feel like he's even hurt. See? He is working hard. Trying to help others. But he is fine. Keep breathing.*

As Lola calmed down, she reached out to other members of her family. Alex tended to listen to the news on his radio on the way home from school. He must have heard of the earthquake too, for Lola could feel his concern as he drove. Ariel, on her computer most of the day, must have read of the earthquake as well for Zane was strongly in Ariel's thoughts even though she seemed less bothered than Alex. Odd. For all that Ariel was basically a kind girl, no one would have ever have described her as empathetic and Lola was positive her daughter was no telepath. Why was she so confident that Zane was okay? Lola filed that question away for another day.

The reassurances that Lola's new gift provided for her in such a time of worry emphasized the practical value of this new ability, and left Lola wishing that she knew how to use her talents better to get more information when it was truly needed. Which is probably why when Maurice called the next morning and invited her for dinner, she didn't immediately make up an excuse and say no . Honestly she preferred her own company, and under normal circumstances she would have weaseled out of a random dinner with someone she barely knew. But she picked up and appreciated Maurice's concern and desire to help her, and even his own slight guilt that he had not made more of an effort sooner. And it was true. She really could use some training here. Dinner next week would be great.

Chapter 12. October 2009

On October 1, 2009, Nigeria celebrated forty-nine years of independence from Great Britain. His Excellency, President Umaru Musa Yar'Adua, addressed the nation, reminding his fellow Nigerians of the dream of becoming one of the world's twenty largest economies by the year 2020. He discussed how the Niger Delta has, over the years, posed major developmental and environmental challenges, which now required a "holistic resolution." He added, "With a view to engendering lasting peace in the area, we proclaimed a general amnesty and granted unconditional pardons to all those who had taken up arms as a way of drawing attention to the plight of the people of the Niger Delta. Some remarkable progress has been made and it is our hope that all militants would avail themselves of this amnesty."

The president continued, "As the world begins to recover from the global recession, we are increasingly encouraged by the emerging signs of recovery in our national economy. Our real GDP growth is projected at five percent in 2009 and non-oil GDP growth is expected to remain robust at six and three-tenths percent." He concluded, "May God continue to bless Nigeria."

Phase one had been named "locate". That of course referred to finding and procuring Nwanyi, and Djimon knew that he had spent more time and money on the first portion than this group of fellow rebuilders would have liked. Using the perfect young Igbo woman had been his idea, as the others would have gladly settled for a more readily available young prostitute. But it was Djimon who had contrived the means to keep Nwanyi's story in the news for weeks after the incident, as her shocked and grieving family, and his own followers, would argue about her motivation in what would be the eager eyes of the press. Nwany's status as a legitimate young wife would buy Djimon and his ideas the sort of ample public exposure which he could not begin to otherwise gain.

He had referred to phase two as "isolate". It had mostly involved waiting, which he had no problem with, but others did. There was waiting for the passport, so that he would have no need for contact with her family once the real training began. Others would gladly have opted for a forged document, but again Djimon had convinced them it was important that she be traveling as herself under her own name. Not only was it better that the new nation be forged on a foundation of truth, but there must be no doubt about who the perpetrator was, and frankly her remains would be hard to identify.

Phase two had required that Djimon cover his tracks well in Igboland, and to that end he had invented a convincing extended family and life which could in no way be traced by Nwanyi's kin. His only concession to his own convenience had been using his real first name, but Djimon was common enough.

Phase two had also required time during which Nwanyi could be allowed to make calls home and to reassure everyone she was okay so that she could be truly isolated in a slow manner, with no one panicking and involving authorities. Because Djimon knew that even if he was fairly certain that neither he nor Nwanyi could be found, it was even safer if no one was looking for them in the first place.

Phases three and four involved the gradual removal of self-esteem, first by less and then by more drastic acts of cruelty. Of course that process came directly from his studies at the university, which he had convinced Mairo, her family, and the group to fund. It was imperative that Nwanyi lose all sense of self-worth. She was to be totally reliant on him. She was to be completely broken down, like a car completely disassembled. This part had turned out to be a bit more unpredictable than expected, in spite of all his careful planning. But the group, and most importantly Mairo's brother, had decided that phase four was over, and so it was. Even if he was not completely sure he had totally succeeded, he accepted the decision.

So phase five would begin—provide new purpose, train and strengthen. Nwanyi would learn how she was to become the mother of a new and glorious Nigeria, a rebuilt nation which would become focused on solving its own problems and re-establishing its own ways. Nwanyi was to now learn how she would help with a dramatic gesture that would symbolize the closing of the borders.

Djimon knew well the strong Igbo prohibition against suicide. He was counting on the fact that an Igbo woman's willingness to die for his cause at her own hand would send a message more resounding than any other he could have crafted.

    The final purpose of phase five was, of course, convincing her to do just that—to gain respect and worth and honor by blowing up herself and hundreds of others so that the nation could be rebuilt.

    The yams were being harvested and being carefully washed, carried home, and stored in the yam houses. Food, the best of food, would once again be plentiful for months for those who ate and preferred the traditional fare. Azuka woke up hungry, hoping that Somadina might have heated up a little breakfast for him before he headed off to his parents' repair shop and before her first customer of the day arrived. Instead he found her at the little kitchen table typing frantically into her precious new cell phone. She was intent on her task, so he sighed and quietly found a mango to eat while he walked.

    "Everything okay?" he asked before he headed out into the early morning.

    "Yes." He could hear the excitement in her voice. "The woman has written me back. She is sorry for her harsh thoughts to me. I am telling her all about Nwanyi now." Somadina never took her eyes off of the phone.

    "Well good luck Somadina," Azuka said as he left a little sadly. He supposed that he was glad she and this woman were finally in touch and now getting along, but he could not imagine what someone so far away and uninformed could possibly do to help. But perhaps Somadina would at least just feel better now that this particular mystery had been solved. Perhaps she could stop focusing, for just a bit, on this sister of hers. Perhaps, she could give just a few minutes of time instead to considering her own future, and whether it would be with or without Azuka.

    For although Azuka had been determined to give Somadina all the time she needed to make her decision, the length of time she was taking was frankly discouraging. Keeping up an outward appearance of confidence and patience would have been difficult for a man in a normal situation. But he had a woman whom he knew very well could read his every feeling and often his direct thoughts, even if out of respect for him she did not go out of her way to do so. But she could. And he knew she could.

So Azuka had worked hard at making patience and confidence his true state of mind, day-in and day-out. But as Somadina's focus wandered from Nwanyi to the phone to her father to the mystery lady and back to Nwanyi, maintaining this whole "take your time" thing was getting almost too difficult. As Azuka walked he decided that for his own sake he needed to set some sort of limit as to how long this could drag on. One more month, he told himself. He would not mention anything for one more month. If by then she had not at least brought up the issue, even if it was to do the courtesy of asking him for more time, then he himself would set Somadina free and go find a woman who wanted him. Even if, sadly, he would never particularly return the woman's feelings. It would still be a better way to live.

Lola had always been good at teaching herself, but she had to admit that she was out of practice when it came to learning how to do new things. She had learned both mothering techniques and geophysical software years ago, and had long since perfected her gardening and mastered her favorite games. Sure, she occasionally tried something new, but she pretty much knew how to do the things she truly cared about.

Until this. The idea of reading minds sounds in theory like a very cool idea, until one considers the problems. For starters, what you get is what the person is thinking about at the time. Only what they are thinking about at the time. You don't get to go mining for facts or memories or interesting tidbits.

So Lola would wake up wanting to know how Alex was doing. Just a peek to make sure all was well. And she would find that Alex was filled with intensity. Puzzlement. Then joy. Interesting. Why? Because Alex was standing at his dresser trying to find a pair of socks that matched. Surely there was one. Where did all the unmatched pairs go? Ah yes. Here was the other sock. Lola had never considered how much energy a human spends on such things.

And if a person was thinking about a past event, Lola discovered that she was not privy to what had really happened, but rather to what the person thought had happened. She had unwillingly listened to a fight between Teddie and Alex from each of their frustrated mental replays, and it had amazed her just how different the two versions of the disagreement were. Particularly because she had been sitting in the next room when the real discussion had actually occurred, and what she had heard then had been fairly different from either Alex or Teddie's later versions in their own minds.

And then of course there was the human version of physics' famed Heisenberg Uncertainty Principal. Physicists have explained for years that the very act of observing something affects what one can know. The better one measures a subatomic particle's exact location, the less one can determine where the particle is going and how quickly it is going to get there. One has interfered by watching.

Ditto with people. Lola desperately wanted to know what her increasingly sullen and distant fourteen-year-old daughter was thinking and feeling. Most frequent thought? *I wish mom would stop looking at me like that. It is creeping me out.*

That night when Azuka came home, Somadina could feel the difference. *He is getting tired of waiting for me,* she thought. *Of course. What man wouldn't?* She watched him pick up their son as he came in the door, playfully tossing him in the air as he so often did. The little boy giggled.

Do I want a husband? Somadina asked the question of herself. *No. Not particularly.* Something deep in her soul resented the privileges accorded the man and the accommodations expected of the woman. It was true that an Igbo woman by custom largely handled much of her own household and her own day-to-day affairs, and that she typically managed her money from her own business ventures. There even had been a time when a very successful Igbo woman might actually take wives of her own, to add to her status and to perform her household chores. Somadina had heard of how different things were for women born as Hausa, as Yoruba, as Fulani, and thought once again how very happy she was to be Igbo.

But no matter how much freedom and autonomy she had, there was no getting around the fact that fathers and male offspring and male lineage were the very basis of the structure of her society. A daughter could never mean as much, or matter as much, to her father as a son did, because only a son could produce the heirs that mattered.

Somadina's frustration with the system lead straight into her frustration with having to marry. She liked being a mother, but she hated that in producing her beautiful baby boy she was also producing one more man, to make happy one more man, who had made another man happy just by being born.

And her gifts made a life alone in many ways easier.

So did she wish to divorce Azuka? No man could have made the option easier for her. Aside from the fact that Azuka clearly loved her, he also clearly liked her. He was her friend. He had no desire to keep her in a relationship that she wanted to end, which alone was admirable.

She thought to herself that in his own quiet way he was a very strong man, strong enough to wait for an answer, strong enough to move on if she said no to him. And given his warm disposition and handy mechanical talents, plenty of girls would happily replace her. In fact, he could probably manage a couple of wives if he really wanted, and that would make Azuka's father proud and happy. Why not leave him to that future?

But, when she thought of him softly stroking another woman's hair, or worse yet, another woman's belly, she felt a tightening in her own stomach, which made no sense. If she did not want him, then certainly another should be welcome to him.

So she did want him. That was the problem. She realized it with a quick burst of certainty. She did not want to be his wife. She did not want to be anyone's wife. But she wanted Azuka and frankly did not want anyone else to have him, which in her culture just did not leave a lot of options.

She greeted him warmly, glad that she had already started preparing something nice for his dinner. She would need to get the man an answer soon. For the first time, Somadina started to think that the answer might be yes.

The annual making of the family calendar was one ritual Lola had not tired of for over twenty years. It had begun when Zane was two years old, with a single incredibly cute photograph of him, and grown into an artsy-craftsy project created with sophisticated software and using dozens of photographs.

The software package she had bought for making the 2010 calendar included dates in history which could be automatically "checked" to appear, a feature which Lola had been looking forward to using. However, the options were disappointing. They were all either birthdays for recent celebrities from current TV, sports, and reality show notoriety, or dates in history which involved mostly battles from World Wars, dates individual states joined the Union, and, most surprisingly, every single date a state had seceded from the Union.

As Alex joined her on the living room couch to take a sneak peak at this year's "winning photos" he agreed that, of all things of historical significance, that seemed an odd category to include.

"But you know, at my high school we've still got plenty of folks who obsess over the Civil War," he mused. "And plenty of kids whose parents I think are still genuinely angry about the way it ended."

"Are these folks all making calendars?" Lola wondered aloud.

Alex laughed. "So many fine things to commemorate. The day we landed on the moon. The day the Berlin Wall fell. When was penicillin invented? When was the first performance of "The Nutcracker Suite"?

Indeed. Lola snuggled against him and, as they sat in silence for a minute, she let herself enjoy the simple sensation of feeling warm and safe, knowing that she loved him, and that he loved her. In fact, she could feel the same sort of feelings emanating from him with more or less the same sense of contentment. He was feeling that it was nice to share life with someone who mostly held the same values and beliefs that he did.

Not the least of which was, of course, honesty and openness. A small pang of guilt worked its way into Lola's contentment. Truth was especially important between two people who had chosen to share a life together.

"Alex. Could I talk to you about something kind, of well, odd?"

"You can talk to me about anything dear. Odd or not. What is it? You want to start attending Civil War re-enactments? You secretly want to be General Grant?"

Lola smiled. "Abe Lincoln, if anybody. No, this isn't about the civil war. It's—"

"Are we totally out of frozen cheese pizzas? Mom??"

Teddie was in the doorway, looking annoyed.

"Maybe dear. There are pepperoni and sausage ones. Help yourself."

"Do you two have any idea what sort of disgusting stuff is in sausage and pepperoni? I mean, seriously? I do not understand how anyone could possibly eat either."

Alex spoke up. "Teddie, pick the pepperoni off."

"Are you crazy dad? The grease from all that disgusting stuff will have already dripped all over the pizza. Ick. Can one of you please show me how to make those little pizza things on English muffins? Please?"

Alex was happy for the distraction. Lola had that "I'm going to bring up something emotional and difficult to talk about because talking about things like that actually makes me feel better" look on her face. Great. Just when sitting there together had felt so simple and so nice … Alex loved Lola dearly, but frankly he could have done with a little less emotional intensity and a lot less analytical interpersonal conversation. He usually tried to use humor to deflect the discussion, which would inevitably turn out to involve the dissection of some obscure aspect of their relationship. But the humor often didn't work because Lola was just so damn serious. So this time he had been saved by a child, so to speak.

Alex got up, murmuring to Lola, "It's okay, I got this one. Finish your calendar."

Lola was going to object, but as Alex got up she got the distinct feeling that he was relieved to go make little pizzas.

For months now, Azuka had let Somadina and their son share the small bed in the single bedroom while he slept in the living area on a cot that doubled as a bench to sit on. He was tired as he began arranging the bench for the night, planning on retiring early. Somadina had gone to some lengths to prepare him a very nice dinner, which, given his general irritability today, had been particularly appreciated. And tonight she was keeping herself and the boy out of his way, knowing he was tired. Azuka smiled to himself. There were certain advantages to sharing a small house with a woman who could read his mind and who wished to see him happy.

Azuka knew that whatever else Somadina did or did not feel for him, she at least wished him well and thought kindly of him. That was something. If only she also felt love. He looked up to see her watching him oddly.

"Azuka?" Somadina was smiling at him in a way that was unusually welcoming. "I was thinking that maybe tonight—"

She stopped. He could tell she was sensing something, something elsewhere, and it was causing her distress. "Oh no," she murmured and shook her head sadly.

A second or two later three older men could be seen approaching the front door with a pompous business-like air about them. Azuka recognized them as two of the older Dibia from the village and one of the village's more well-known and sought-after herbalists. While younger people more often would travel to receive conventional medical care, the medicine men known as Dibia and the variety of part-time local herbalists were still much used by the older people in the village, and they still commanded a good deal of respect from all.

The message they came to deliver to Somadina was brief and

not entirely unexpected. She listened respectfully while they told her that because her father was well-thought of locally, they had granted her a good bit of latitude in her fortune-telling business. They had agreed among themselves that it seemed harmless. However recently it had become apparent to them that with the all-important yearly harvest of yams underway, the yam goddess Aha Njoku was uncomfortable with the unauthorized and unsanctified fortune-telling being performed by one of the women in the village. They were sorry, but it would have to cease, lest it threaten the success of the harvest.

Azuka wanted to snort in disgust. The older people were more than entitled to their ways, but surely no one believed in this nonsense so fully that Somadina had to actually stop an activity which as far as he could tell was pretty much benefitting everyone. But indeed, the men were insistent, and the truth was that no one of any age or set of beliefs was going the risk harming the harvest by coming to Somadina after this.

Azuka watched her sadly agree to comply, and as the men left he put his arm around her in comfort. She stood still in his embrace for a full minute or two, then she thanked him for his kindness, but he could see that the look of eagerness was gone. Instead she picked up their child with a discouraged sigh and headed for bed.

Lola tossed and turned in bed that night, thinking of the possible outcomes of her announcing to Alex that she could sort of read his mind. Right. What had she been thinking? There had to be better way to have that conversation. Nonetheless, she was driven to clear the air between them, and the quicker the better. She promised herself that she would seek out that better way and find it soon.

Somadina woke early and began her morning ritual of tossing and turning. She tried to be careful not to wake her son as she fretted over Azuka. She had almost invited him into her bed last night. What had she been thinking? The man loved her. She had no right to play with his heart. If she said yes to him, it needed by all rights to be a real "yes," one that she was prepared to live with for the rest of her life and not for just a few enjoyable hours. The permanence of that decision gave her pause. Somadina promised herself that she would come to terms with the consequences of a decision, one way or the other, and would do so soon.

As she made the promise, she felt a similar promise being made. Lola? Lola. Making a promise of her own about the man she loved. As they had before, the two women found each other within the commonness of their situations. In the very early morning light, Somadina let herself just enjoy the feeling of having a friend, a real girlfriend who understood her and who was going through something so like she was at that moment.

Lola savored the feeling of Somadina's friendship. She'd had so few women friends over her adult life. She'd been too busy with work, with Alex, with the kids. Too often there had been so little in common. And here was a woman, for heavens sake barely older than Lola's own daughter and a world away in every sense of the word. Yet in her hearty self-sufficiency, in her attachment to her child, her loyalty to her sister, and in her good fortune in attracting the affection of a genuinely good man, they had more in common than Lola had with most women she knew.

Lola reached back with a mental equivalent of a hug.

We are both strong telepaths, she thought, knowing that Somadina would pick up the feeling and fill in words which were close enough to the meaning to get the point. *We know that Nwanyi is at least a weak receiver herself after all of her association with you. At least Olumiji thinks so. Let's try to send her a message together. Sort of doubling the transmitting power, if you will.* Lola felt Somadina's confusion over the last phrase. She tried again. *Let's push together.* An image of two women pushing a large rock. Somadina got it.

Music, Somadina suggested. *Nwanyi and I both like music. American music.*

Okay. Let's pick a song to encourage her. Lola thought for minute, and tried singing something in her head. Out came Frank Sinatra's hit "<u>High Hopes</u>" about a over-achieving ant trying to move a houseplant.

What is that? Somadina asked. *Don't you know any rock and roll?*

Yikes. She didn't think she knew any that would be particularly encouraging about someone surviving. Wait. Maybe she did. Gloria Gaynor's heart-wrenching disco anthem for every woman ever wronged popped into her head. She began singing a bad mental karaoke version of "*I Will Survive*" and Somadina laughed.

Perfect. I know that song. Let's sing it together as hard as we can and maybe together we will get through.

Nwanyi awoke to music so real she thought that the radio must have been moved for some odd reason to the back of the house. It was playing "*I Will Survive*", an old American pop song she had heard often, but as she became more awake she realized that it was accompanied in her head with the oddest of visions. Somadina was singly loudly, belting out the song with all her heart, as though her life depended on her singing. Standing next to her, with their arms around each other's shoulders, was a crazy looking white woman, with this long, wild, dark auburn hair, dressed in some sort of armor, with metal over her breasts and an odd helmet adorned with the horns of some beast. The white woman was giggling self-consciously while she sang, like she was embarrassed to find herself on stage but determined to stick it out with her friend. How had Somadina even found such a friend?

Nwanyi realized that they were looking hard directly at her while they sang. They were repeating the chorus over and over, but now the words seemed to have morphed and they were telling Nwany that she would survive. The sound and image faded as Nwanyi came fully awake, but the memory of the spontaneous karaoke performance in her head stayed with her all day. It made her smile, something she almost never did.

Then at one point she caught Mairo looking at her oddly and decided she best keep her joys to herself, for the more miserable she appeared to be, the more she was left alone. Nwanyi pursed her lips and lowered her eyes. Yes. Miserable.

Nwanyi found herself filled with anticipation when Djimon told her a few days later that they would meet that night, but that things were now going to be very different between them. He explained that he had treated her so poorly only because he had been training her in the way a coach might train an athlete. In due time she would understand. Now they were going to begin an entirely different phase of her preparation, one that she would probably find much more pleasant. She felt sure she had been right to appear so very defeated in front of all of his friends.

That evening, although she was still fed in her room, the food was better, even perhaps what the rest of the family was eating. She savored each flavorful bite, and after she had time to eat, Djimon knocked on her door respectfully. He offered her a small sweet pastry as he entered.

Does this mean that we are going to finally have sex, she wondered? But judging from the serious way he began to talk to her, she guessed not.

He was obviously very passionate about his subject matter. Something about the Fulani and the Hausa and the history of Nigeria. Nwanyi had never actually gotten to go to school, although Somadina had taught her to read and write, and she knew almost nothing about the rest of her country except for what she picked up in conversation. She knew that these people were Muslim of course, and originally from the north, and that, like many Nigerians, they considered themselves first and foremost members of their own original tribes and only secondly members of their country.

But Djimon's feelings appeared to go well beyond that. He thought his particular group of people should rule the country. Well, that was not so uncommon either.

She could see the beginnings of his distress that he was failing to reach her, to persuade her, and so she tried, really tried to appear more interested and concerned. The fact was that she could care less who ran her country, but the last many months had taught her well that she did care whether Djimon was happy with her or not.

He finally made his way to the one subject she did care about.

Her own fate.

"And you, my beautiful Igbo princess, are the woman who has been selected and trained to make this very thing happen. You, singlehandedly, will bring the eyes and ears of the whole country to my cause. You are going to write a letter to your family. We are going to make tapes of you. You will beseech your fellow countrymen to listen to me and to follow me, to close our borders to all manner of foreign influences, to shut out the uneducated thugs from the north who besmirch the very name of Allah with their insane wild mob behavior that defies the intellect and greatness of my religion. You will implore your fellow countrymen to shut out the greedy Westerners, the Chinese, and the Indians who would milk us dry, taking our resources for their own and leaving as little in return as possible. You will explain that we must cease letting countries steal our smartest young people, luring them away from building this nation with promises of more ease and comfort than they can resist. The pleas you will make for me will be fodder for newscasts around the world for weeks, as I release them one by one according to my carefully planned timetable.

"In their hearts, as they hear the message grow in truth and complexity, the people of Nigeria will know that I am right. Those who do not know already will learn well how the Fulani, and the Fulani alone, successfully built and ruled an enlightened nation in the not so very distant past and how we could easily, willingly, do it once again if asked. More will join our cause. They will ask for our rule. And the history of this great nation will be substantially different because you, Nwanyi, got and held their initial attention from that first great day."

Nwanyi nodded obediently and even enthusiastically. Djimon was satisfied that she had agreed to do her part, until she asked the next question.

"What happens to me after I do this great deed?"

"Well, you will be honored and revered."

"But will I get to hold an office? Have a position in the new government?"

Oh dear. Had the woman not understood she would be

setting off a bomb that she was wearing?

"Nwanyi. When the bomb goes off you will probably be … badly hurt."

"I would think so. But of course you will make me protective gear. You know, so I will survive. Then when I heal I can be in charge of, I don't know. Something."

Djimon had to remind himself how uneducated Nwanyi was. How young. She had been subjected to fantasy entertainment all her life but never had a science class. She apparently actually believed she could set off a bomb attached to her person and live through it. Maybe she had seen something like it in a movie once, or on a television. In a cartoon?

Djimon had been concerned that the most difficult taboo he would have to overcome would be the strong Igbo prohibition against suicide. It hadn't occurred to him that maybe he could get around that obstacle by giving Nwanyi hope that she would live. It frankly had not occurred to him that she might be dumb enough to believe that such was possible. But a little improvisation once in awhile could be a good thing.

"Nwanyi," he smiled. "We are going to specially design your clothing for you so that you have absolutely the best chance of survival possible. Our top engineer is working on it. I cannot lie to you. You will probably be hurt somewhat. But we will get you the very best medical care in the world afterward, I promise. If you do exactly as I say, exactly when I say to do it, it will maximize your chances of getting hurt as little as possible. Are you willing to do this thing, exactly as I tell you to?"

Nwanyi thought to herself that after all she had been through, this was probably the best sort of deal she could hope for.

"Of course, my husband," and she smiled as demurely as she could. "Because I know that I will survive."

That night, Djimon told Mairo of the strange turn of events, and even Mairo had to laugh. In their shared amusement at Nwanyi's innocent stupidity, they felt a camaraderie that had been sadly absent for the past few months. Once the lights were out,

Mairo reached for him and Djimon felt a satisfaction that his partner, his helpmate, his original inspiration (well, the woman who had inspired him most after his mother) was back in his camp and wanted to be close to him. He pulled her nearer and began expressing his affection with his hands, with his mouth. But the shared affinity, the caressing, did not have the effect that they used to have. His mind still wanted Mairo. His heart certainly still wanted her. But his body wanted something else.

He gave up and turned away sadly. Mairo said nothing. It happened at times of course, with all men. But it had never happened before with him and her, and the timing could not have been worse. He read hurt in the way she turned away from him. Worse than that, he heard just a hint of contempt in her voice when she wished him a good night's sleep. This was not good. Djimon knew very well that Mairo was the sort of woman from whom even just a little contempt was a bad thing.

Maurice had given Lola a second website with a new password and suggested that she give it a look before their dinner. He explained that it would give background information about the organization itself, as opposed to information about telepathy, and would save him a good bit of explanation. Lola was becoming less skittish these days about having someone catch her on an internet site concerning telepathy, mostly because she had taken the time to prepare several half-true and reasonable-sounding explanations. Yet she waited until her family was in bed, and began.

This x^0 website had simple text, with no effort made at adornment, and contained only a short FAQ section.

Q: When was x^0 founded?

A: The organization's original roots are in South and Southeast Asia, where it began many centuries ago, and tenants of the organization still reflect these origins. When a surge of interest in telepathy emerged in the U.S. and Western Europe in the late 1880s, a group of telepaths became frustrated with the typical telepathy experiments, and scams, which were prevalent at the time. This group discovered the original x^0 group and found common ground on which to build, expanding the original sect well past its founders' size and scope into an international organization which includes telepaths of all beliefs and backgrounds.

Q: Where does the name x^0 come from?

A: It is a modern, Western, and mathematical rendition of an earlier name which cannot be easily translated or explained. This difficult-to-translate name once echoed the founders of x^0's recognition that the human race was growing in size with each generation, and therefore it was not feasible for the past generations to furnish enough souls for the reincarnations of future generations. Logically this meant that reincarnation was not bound by the rules of time. Thus a soul which lived a life in the future could be reincarnated into the past. In fact, x^0 originally concluded that each soul was destined to take an individual path, weaving its way through time and space, living a series of lives which followed a sequence of its own need and making and which jumped back and forth through time as the individual soul required. This was in stark contrast to the prevalent belief of that time which held that each soul was mandated to lead a series of successive lives which occurred in the same order as the passage of time was experienced by humanity at large. The group x^0 was considered radical when it was founded.

Q: What does this have to do with telepathy?

A: Nothing yet. But because x^0 attracted a group of followers willing to question accepted beliefs, eventually the question had to be addressed of whether a soul could happen to be alive in two different bodies at the same time. That is, could a soul be leading two lives simultaneously, maybe existing as an old man in one village and yet already needing to be a newborn in a different town. A large number of the elders said absolutely not. The universe would not permit such an abomination. However, the small group which would break away and become the x^0 of today said, "Why not?"

Q: What does this have to do with telepathy?

A: More than is readily apparent. After awhile it became common belief among the followers of x^0 that any given soul was quite likely to be having several lives at any given time on earth. And while full knowledge of one's past lives was believed to be mostly hidden from view and only fully available to the soul in between lives, it was believed that the various reincarnations of the soul felt a deep bond for each other, and thus could communicate telepathically if and when they happened to meet. This was the beginning of the modern x^0 organization.

Q: So do today's members of x^0 believe in reincarnation?

A: Some do. Many others reconcile their abilities with the tenets of Christian, Jewish, Muslim, or other faiths, and still others have no particular religious affiliation or in some cases are agnostic or atheist. Over the years, the leaders of x^0 have developed their own additional theories about reincarnation which are well-removed from the mainstream of most traditional religions, and most of the actual leaders of x^0 subscribe fully or in part to these unique beliefs.

Q: So there is some kind of cult at the center of this group?

A: Not at all. There is a group of people who have chosen to accept one view of humanity's role in the universe. However, the membership remains highly diverse, and all of its members are entirely free to practice the faith they find in their own heart. No one in our organization has any desire to convert anyone.

Q: Are these core beliefs secret?

A: Not secret, but more privately held. If one is curious to know more, our leaders ask that the discussion be held in person rather than having this information conveyed over a website.

Okay, Lola thought. *So besides having dinner and learning how to be a better telepath, I guess Maurice wants to tell me more about x^0. And it sounds to me like knowing more is probably a good idea.*

Maurice was once again waiting for Lola at the restaurant, and once again he stood up to pull out her chair. Lola again said nothing but found it as annoying as she had the first time. But this time she felt his exasperated wish that she would let him act in ways that made him comfortable.

But it makes me uncomfortable, she thought. *I'm not an invalid. I'm not even a physically weak person.*

"Well at least this time around we understand each other," he said aloud. And they both had to laugh.

"There are no easy answers to conflicting preferences other than just understanding each other, are there?" she replied.

"Well ideally we each are willing to do what it takes to make the other feel more at ease," he responded. "But of course that can turn into the kind of nonsense where two folks sit at stop signs for five minutes motioning to each other to go ahead. No, I don't know the answer either. ... I just know that a little mutual understanding helps."

"Maurice, how did this happen to me?" Lola got to the point, her point, of the visit.

"You are a complicated one. Olumiji is one of our better experts on the subject. He thinks the fact that you established a link with Somadina in the first place is evidence that you were on the path to becoming a telepath already early this year. Stress can often work as a trigger, we think because in the process of fighting for survival the mind tries all the tools it can find, and for some minds a push into telepathy is one of those tools."

"But I wasn't under a lot of stress."

"A new job at your age after decades with the same employer?"

"Yeah, but I seemed to be handling things fine. And the things Somadina and I found in common involved a bond worrying about our younger sisters. That seems to me to be what got the whole thing going."

"Well, maybe your sudden immersion in such a very different culture at your new job was part of what kicked things off with her. It's not like you were terribly familiar with or even interested in Nigeria before all this, right?"

She had to agree. *Maybe.*

Maurice went on. "At any rate, managing to have a near-death experience is often enough to jump start another person into becoming a full-fledged telepath all by itself. Almost drowning while somehow interacting with Somadina during that experience must have been part of what forged this ability inside of you."

"But then it didn't show up for a couple of months."

"Well some delay is normal. We haven't had much occasion to study the effect of any kind of drugs on a telepath's ability, but your particular experience would certainly lead one to conclude that at least some sorts of medication can suppress it. Which in some cases could be useful."

"What got you started, Maurice? Have you really lived this way for decades?"

She was sorry as soon as she asked, for the flood of sorrow from Maurice almost brought tears to her own eyes. "Oh. A thoughtless question. Forgive me."

"It's okay." He both said it and sent her the feeling. "I still miss her every day. But the shock of her death left me mute for weeks, and when I recovered just enough to be aware, this nonsense began." He smiled ruefully. "Honestly, I was quite a bit older and quite a bit less receptive to the new and the unusual than you are Lola, and if Olumiji had not literally found me I'm sure that I'd be heavily medicated in a rest home somewhere right now. It is not particularly easy to have this gift, and it's even less easy to get it in your old age."

Lola nodded in sympathy.

"The point is that he taught me how to survive being this way."

And, Lola felt clearly, *now you want to return the favor and teach me*. She felt his agreement.

"You've already taught yourself a good deal, and that is wonderful, but please let me help."

She opened the doors she had learned from Somadina to imagine, while she smiled inwardly at the idea of being an "open-minded person". For the next hour or so, Maurice used words and thoughts, mental images and raw emotions to communicate total information to her as best he could.

Modulate what you transmit. Like this. Even a weak receiver will appreciate the courtesy. Privacy is possible. See? But secrecy will wear you out. Remember that those within sight are the strongest. Learn to filter. Umm, no, Try doing it like this. That's it. Most ongoing feelings are just noise. Don't panic at the unpleasant ones. You can't save everyone who is unhappy or sooth everyone who is upset.

He took her by the hand, mentally, and walked the two of them outside of the restaurant with their minds.

Remember that you can get information from those at a distance and sometimes it will happen without your even trying. But if you do try to do it, it's kind of like reading really small print. Don't try it for very long. For those with whom you already have some kind of connection, this won't apply because a link that transcends spatial separation will happen, sort of the same way their phone number is stored in your cell phone. You can find the link the same way that you try to feel your kneecaps or wiggle your ears. It's there.

You will link with some people very easily. Yes, like you and Jumoke. Others only with difficulty. Yes, one should try to give one's loved ones privacy. It's all about respect. Use what you know lovingly, for good, or not at all. This is a little like getting the keys to the car. It demands maturity. Or it makes a mess of your own life even faster than it makes a mess of the lives of others. x^0 has more than a few members who have had to learn that the hard way.

"What do you think about my telling Alex about this?" Lola asked it aloud, wanting to be clear.

"I think you will sooner or later." Maurice chose to answer in words as well. "In other cultures where skepticism is considered less of a virtue, it is less of an issue. But here in the U.S. of A., you'll want to make sure Alex can and will believe you, so the timing and the way you approach it both matter. I'd say choose them wisely."

"You mention x^0 and its members. The second website to which you sent me was a little cryptic. How many of us are there?"

"Members? About five thousand. Just using statistical analysis we think there are about another thousand telepaths, or near-telepaths, whom we haven't yet found. It's a gradational thing, not so easy to classify folks. Some are very adept and some barely. We are thinking that it's the barely folks that we mostly haven't found. But then along comes someone like Somadina, who's so powerful she is almost off the charts. I gather that if she hadn't shut her own powers down as a child because of some deal with her sister, she'd have been found long ago. And then there are the new folks, like you, who keep coming in."

"But didn't your website say that this whole group grew out of a belief in reincarnation? Which, by the way, I don't particularly believe in at all."

"Yes, that is true, and no I don't either. In your case I think your scientific skepticism extends into the realm of the religious and the supernatural, yes?"

"It does," Lola agreed. "I can go with 'anything's possible' but there seems to be a lot of logical obstacles to reincarnation."

"And in my case it violates some of my most basic beliefs. But x^0 also has its devout Christian members, and we sort of have our own take on the situation. Experiencing the feelings of others promotes charity and good works and helps us to live a more Christ-like existence."

"And what do the more traditional members of x^0 think of your variation?"

x^0

"Well, some agree very much in principle. There is the feeling that as the human race has become more adept at killing, and harming its own environment, we are not developing the maturity fast enough to keep pace with the damage we are able to do. Many of these folks agree that Christ's purpose was to tip that balance and increase the human race's capacity for empathy."

Unsuccessfully, unfortunately, Lola noted.

"I disagree," Maurice said. "Do you really think we'd be here talking if weapons of mass destruction had been commonly available in, say, the year 500 BC?"

Maybe not, she thought. Maurice thanked her for conceding the point.

"But there are others who also believe in divine intervention, by the way, who think Christ's coming had a simpler and more functional purpose."

"Seriously?"

"Quite a few of the x^0 folks actually think that a thousand years of dark ages in the West was just the purpose. They contend that generating a slowly growing religious "fanaticism," in their opinion, which would squelch human curiosity and advancement in the regions it touched was exactly what the human race needed."

"You mean they believe that Christ was sent to gum up the works?"

"Well, to give us time to grow up a little anyway. Getting most of the Western world in churches chanting in Latin for a millennium or two did buy us some time, they think. This particular bunch says that when I claim Christ was sent to save us, I am speaking the literal, not spiritual truth. Anyway, my point is that the group ends up having a lot of lively discussions about a lot of topics—everybody's religion, everybody's politics, racism, sexism, biases, taboos and cherished beliefs. When you can feel each other's emotions and sense each other's thoughts, you just plain don't tend to spend a lot of time discussing trivial matters. It's a fairly intense group of people, Lola. If you're going to get involved, and I hope you will, you'll have to leave your cherished pet beliefs behind and enter with a literal open mind. I know that I had to learn to do so."

231

"And your faith?"

"Lola, what I used to believe with one hundred percent certainty, I now believe with ninety-eight percent certainty." Responding to Lola's un-verbalized, *Don't you think God might be mad at you for that?* he smiled. "My faith might be a little more flexible now than my minister would like, but strangely enough, I think God is pretty happy with the curiosity and tolerance I've managed to grow in my old age."

"You know Maurice," Lola paused trying to find the words. Maurice laughed.

"Yes, I know dear. Elderly devout Christian men who insist on holding out your chair for you are not exactly your favorite demographic. If you were going to choose a mentor to help you deal with your new talents, I'd be at the back of the line." He chuckled, mostly to and at himself. "That seems to be the way this deal works. One of your least favorite stereotypes comes along to show you the way."

Her next thought was barely formed before Maurice added, "Thanks. Indeed I've thought of making a T-shirt that says, "You know, we're not all assholes and idiots," distributing one to every one of my born-again brethren, and asking them to pick a day and we'll all wear it."

"How about instead," Lola offered, "we distribute one to every man, woman and child on the face of the earth? And pick a day and all wear it."

Touché, Maurice thought. *You are going to fit in just fine.*

Lola's coworkers did not discuss Nigerian politics with her much in the office unless Lola specifically brought something up, so it wasn't until late in October when Lola was doing a lunchtime internet browse that she came across a BBC article from early October titled "Will amnesty bring peace to Niger Delta?"

Amnesty? That sounded hopeful. As she started to read, Bob walked by, singing in his head one of the many great oldies he had managed to amass on his iPod. *Where did the man find so many good old songs?*

x^0

"_What's Up?_" had been the 4 Non Blondes' 1993 hit, coming out the year that Ariel was four. Lola loved it, and the two of them had sung, actually, screamed it together whenever it came on the radio when Lola was driving little Ariel to preschool. Now, the frustrated lyrics demanding an explanation for the absurdities of the world echoed in her head as she read the BBC article.

Ms. Duffield, the reporter, described talking to taxi drivers, shopkeepers, and hotel clerks in the Niger Delta region who were all hoping for peace as they watched militants hold disarmament ceremonies which involved relinquishing guns, rocket-propelled grenades, explosives, ammunition, and gunboats. _Gunboats??_

The BBC article added that while no one appeared to have given up their entire arsenal, the quantity of weapons released, presumably for cash, was significant. Concerns had been raised that no independent monitors were tracking what was being done with the weapons, and this caused particular concern because in the past, corrupt officials had sold confiscated guns, which had then made their way back into the hands of a wide variety of criminals.

The article noted that another major obstacle to peace was that there were now thousands of young men in the region effectively unemployed, given that their previous full-time profession had been guerilla fighter, with resumes that included kidnapping, blowing up oil pipelines, and stealing massive amounts of crude oil.

The government plan, according to the article, was to retrain these young men in new skills. It noted that they were already being processed at centers where they were being asked about their other career interests. _Other career interests??_

The BBC said that retraining would be a daunting prospect, and that in the case of failure, the young men would likely return to their previous activities.

She looked at the photo of the giant pile of automatic weapons. Seriously, right now in Nigeria there were actually thousands of angry young men filling out employment questionnaires??

Chapter 13. November 2009

Somadina had agreed to help an older woman in the village the next morning, one who suspected her husband of all sorts of misconduct. It was the very sort of session Somadina hated most, with no good outcome for anyone, and she was relieved and not at all surprised when the woman failed to show. Word would have spread quickly about her possible association with harvest problems, and even those most skeptical of the old ways would not wish to risk the censure and even the wrath of their elders should the harvest encounter any misfortune whatsoever. Her business was effectively closed.

Azuka had left early for the repair shop, and Kwemto was smashing an over-ripe mango into his mouth. So far his face held more fruit than his stomach, and she had to laugh at the orange pulp covering his chubby cheeks. As she started to clean him, she thought, *perhaps I am not being creative enough about my situation*. True, the Dibia had their rules and procedures, and it was true that the rules of the older ones often irritated those who were younger like herself. But the Dibia, like all Igbo she knew, were essentially businessmen. They could be, well, flexible when it was in their best interest.

Perhaps she had not paid enough respect to the older ways when she started in with the fortune-telling. Perhaps some spirits could be appeased if she requested most humbly that it be done, and even if she didn't personally happen to think anything needed appeasing, she could keep those thoughts to herself. That was just being smart. Perhaps the Dibia would even perform a sacrifice on her account if she asked or if her father asked? Perhaps a small offering on her part would be appropriate, perhaps even a percentage of the fortune-telling take point forward would compensate the Dibia for their ongoing intervention with the spirit world on her behalf? Somadina did not find the idea of paying the Dibia for their help distasteful or unethical. It was simply how business was done. You help me. I help you. She had clearly failed to help the elder spiritual leaders, and now that needed to be corrected, as they had understandably pointed out to her.

As she placed Kwemto, who was now scrubbed shiny clean,

on her hip and headed out the door, she had another idea. Everyone, even the elders, were always trying to raise up the reputation of the village. Perhaps if allowed to continue with her practice, both at her house and in the marketplace, she could use some of the proceeds to better educate herself. She would not have to travel far to train to be a nurse's assistant. There was a school a few towns over. She could do it part-time. Girls and women did this, and she had in fact thought about it before Azuka's parents had approached her father with the possibility of marriage.

She could read and write well enough, and she could pay for it herself. Then she could also offer to assist the Dibia and perhaps help merge their two worlds, lending some new skills and respect to their own practice. Maybe in return, although she was a woman, they would train her a little in their ways, enough for her to assist them. Then she could better treat the older folks who had a fear of modern medicine, and better treat the young who were starting to insist on some formal outside training for their medical needs. She could be an asset to the village, as it currently had no one with any formal modern medical training at all, and she could be a bridge between the old and new. And provide the Dibia with a little additional income. So they would win.

And meanwhile she would also provide herself and her family with a little extra income and some additional prestige. So she would win too.

Azuka would be proud to have her do this. She was sure of it. He would help get her over to school and would see to it that Kwemto was cared for while she studied. Azuka. She realized then that he was so embedded in her long-term planning that she couldn't imagine doing something like this without him.

Okay, she told herself. *If you like a man and want that man and you can't imagine tackling the future without his help, you probably ought to go ahead and marry the man. That is, if he actually still wants to marry you. Don't you think?*

Perhaps because Lola's telepathic abilities had begun with a link to a woman far away, she remained fascinated by the idea of telepathy over large distances. She had now learned that a link spontaneously formed between two people physically far apart was rare, and it almost always required people with strong, well-developed abilities and a common bond of some sort. The situation of someone like Somadina finding someone like her was almost unheard of.

Maybe her fascination with telepathy at a distance also had to do with the physicist in her. She had, over the last few months, reluctantly accepted that the remote sensing that she could no longer deny as real must somehow work according to physical principles she simply did not understand. It was odd, but possible.

However, the idea of links that worked over large distances, the mental equivalent of science-fiction wormholes in the vastness of space, she supposed, was too bizarre for her to quite get her head around it. Which was why it remained a pebble in her shoe, the one thing that irritated her and drew her back to it.

Maurice had said that once a link was formed with another mind that was nearby, the link would hold over vast distances as long as it was occasionally used. That sounded more like biology than physics. If left unused it would atrophy or dissipate, depending on one's choice of analogies. A link barely forged with just a brief touch would dissipate quickly. But one years in the making would take years to disappear. The link could be two way—between two telepaths such as her and Maurice. It could be lopsided—like strong Somadina's link to the barely receptive Nwanyi. Or it could be entirely one-way—like Lola's link to her two distant children.

In fact, Lola discovered that one of the upsides of her new skill was the connection that she now felt with her two older kids. Although they were far away, she could reach out for quick reassurance that all was well. Granted, all she usually got was a sense of looking in the refrigerator for milk, or beer, or irritation at a noisy neighbor upstairs.

Ariel gave off a general sense of purpose with her studies and a sense of confidence with her life. She laughed often, at herself, not at others, and she spent a reasonable chunk of time noticing guys and thinking about them. All basically healthy as far as Lola was concerned.

    Zane, however, caused Lola more worry. He seemed to have formed some work-related friendships, but there was one man in the office whom he had been advised to avoid and even fear. It had the feel of corporate politics about it, where pleasing one person above you ignites the suspicion of another boss. While Lola worked to give both children privacy, she was glad her gift had given her a heads up on Zane's situation because only a week or two later the problem also became her own.

    The office manager of her little company called her in to let her know that they had received several calls from someone seeking information about her. By chance did she have problems with unpaid debts? IRS obligations? Custody issues? Lola denied all of the above and was baffled until the next day. Leaving for lunch she noticed a man watching her in the parking garage. It wasn't hard to tell that he was studying her, and making notes about her. What ever for?

    So Lola pretended to search in her purse for items while she willed this new found skill of hers to be please, just for once, be of a bit of real use. And it was. Lola felt the mans desire to learn about her, more specifically to learn something damaging or hurtful about her. She could sense that it involved Zane, and involved Zane's company.

    Some corporate yo-yo is seriously trying to hurt my son by trying to find dirt on his family? Lola was incredulous. Yet, the more she let herself relax and feel the man's thoughts the more she was sure of it.

    Okay. Two could play at that game. Lola allowed herself to remain still long enough for the snooper's thoughts to wander. To what he had for dinner last night at the hotel. To what he was going to order tonight. To how he was padding his expenses. A little but not too much. This company had plenty of money. But he had to be careful because last time he had done a job for this guy he had faked enough receipts to put down a decent down payment on a car. And the time before he had made up a few facts just because he had been in such a hurry to get the job done because an old girlfriend was back in town. Now that had been a great night and the wife had never suspected. And the silly exec never knew either.

But he, Harold, was going to play it smart this time because you had to be careful and not try to get away with that sort of shit all the time, you know. That's how people got caught. They got greedy. So for this job he was only going to pad a little and really try to find some truly juicy tidbit on these folks that his client and benefactor could use to make some young upstart employee go away. He'd been assured that the kid was a real asshole.

And Lola thought to herself, *buddy you have picked the wrong mama to use to hurt her children.* She picked up her purse and walked straight up to the man's car and knocked on the windshield. He rolled down the window in surprise.

"Harold? It is Harold, right?"

Harold looked startled. " Harold. We're going to have a little talk. I need to explain to you why you are going back to Chicago this evening, and exactly why you will be letting your client know that you have never met nicer, less blameless people than the Zeitman family." Lola smiled, and then she started talking. And for the first time it occurred to her that maybe she could learn to like having this gift.

Mairo and Djimon had little to say to each other the next morning, and indeed for many days thereafter. He was preoccupied with his role in the upcoming rebuilding of the nation, as he thought of it, and she was increasingly involved with reaching out to women's groups which, while largely non-political now, she hoped would step in and support the effort once its obvious appeal to the women of the north became apparent. It was easy to avoid each other's eyes.

But Djimon could feel the difference in the way she spoke to him, in the way she stood in his presence. It angered him on so many levels. First of all, he was angry with Mairo, who should be mature enough to understand that he was a tired and busy man with heavy responsibilities, not a teenage boy. He was also a little angry with himself. Why was he making such a big deal of this? Why not surprise Mairo and wipe that look off of her face? Because he was afraid the surprise would be a disappointment, and her look afterwards would be twice as intense?

That fearfulness inside him made him angry most of all with the true source of his problems, the stupid ugly woman whom he now dare not touch in any way. For phase five required that Nwanyi feel secure and trusting in her role, and that for as long as she was obedient to his cause she be encouraged and cared for. No harsh words, no harsh actions, unless she deserved them. Now the ignorant, docile cow was doing nothing but acquiescing and agreeing, too meek to argue and too stupid to realize she was certainly going to die.

Djimon hated the girl more than he had ever hated anyone in his life. Her death could not come soon enough. Maybe once she was no more than a cloud of fragments of flesh and bone then maybe his heart, soul, mind, and libido could once again merge in lust and love for a truly worthy woman. Maybe it wouldn't even be Mairo, now that he thought about it. As the leader and mastermind behind his cause, he should certainly have his pick of feisty bright women who would share his ideology and melt at his very touch.

He passed Nwanyi in the hallway leading toward the kitchen, and the sight of her looking at him expectantly for more flattery and praise pushed him to mutter something he knew he shouldn't have. "Leave me be right now. You have cost me so very much more than you realize." And he moved on.

Nwanyi froze. Djimon could not know that no other single phrase, no other possible set of words, could have upset her more. For with every rejection from her father, with every unwarranted punishment, with every denied bit of love, her father had uttered the very phrase "You have cost me so very much more than you realize," until she had come to hate those words.

She moved silently to her room. Yes, she thought angrily, she would do this thing he wanted of her. But not for Djimon, the worthless, unappreciative two-faced piece of shit. Not for his stupid cause which meant nothing to her. No, she now knew clearly that she would do it for herself. If she survived his crazy scheme it gave her the very best chance of a life of freedom and even power, if his scheme worked, and hopefully freedom and sympathy if his plans did not. For if he was successful she would be a follower of his cause, and if his plans failed she would be a terrified woman forced into compliance. Nwanyi was not terribly astute, but she realized that she was in a fine position to play whatever role was the most advantageous to her. If she lived.

And if she died? She was not stupid. She did know that was possible. But if she died then there was the satisfaction of knowing that she would be a source of great shame in the Igbo world, the shame of a relative who had taken her own gift of life. And that shame would go most directly, most thoroughly, to her father and her father's family. He, her father, would finally feel the burn of remorse, as he realized that thanks to his disdain for her, his lack of love shown to her, she had finally gotten even by costing him one thing more that he had not counted on. She might have "cost him so very much" in ways she had never been able to help, but thanks to his behavior she would now, by her own choice, cost him at least a piece of his good reputation as well. There was a very real satisfaction to be had in knowing that.

Nwanyi, who had always been reticent to speak, who moved softly so as not to provoke, lay down on her small cot then and began to cry. In a very short amount of time she was sobbing more loudly than she ever had in a life filled with sorrow. With the great giant gulps of air she had to take to keep from choking as she cried so hard, her mind finally found its voice. Her pain and her misery, long held mute inside her head, came spilling out in a soundless scream of frustration at the things in her life she had never been able to help. The scream said, *It's not fair*, and it said, *It's not my fault*, and it said, *I didn't kill my mother*, and it said, *Don't blame me*, and she sobbed it over and over and over until she was hoarse with exhaustion both inside and out.

Lola, sitting at her computer at work, was startled by a sudden intense flood of wailing self-pity, with tears of indignity at injustice, with frustration at the unfairness of it all. She calmed her mind the way Maurice had shown her, and listened. Someone was screaming emotion, and if she was picking it up like this, there was a reason. It was someone nearby or someone familiar. Nearby was unlikely. Of course. Lola was suddenly sure of it. Nwanyi, who up until now could barely transmit at all, had for some reason just found her mind's voice.

    Azuka was working late and not home yet. Kwemto had been fed and was lying on the bed, sucking his thumb and comforting himself to sleep when Somadina was overwhelmed with a feeling both familiar and strange. Familiar because it felt like Nwanyi, like Nwanyi's mind, like Nwanyi's feelings. Strange because her always quiet, meek sister was yelling and screaming emotions of rage, sorrow, self-pity, and frustration. To be honest, those were things Nwanyi generally felt at some low level most of the time, but something had given her the courage to shout them, to shout in her own head. *It is not my fault I cost you so very much. Not my fault! Do you hear me? Not my fault!*
    Somadina thought to herself, *This is good. This is very good.* Working her way gently, carefully to Nwanyi's mind she fought for the slight connection she could sometimes manage with her barely receptive sister. *Keep talking Nwanyi. Keep shouting. Shout all you can to me. Shout me information. Shout me where you are. Shout to me about how I can help you. Don't go silent, dear sister. Keep screaming to me until I find you.* And in between the indignant sobs she was sure that Nwanyi heard her.

    Maurice had suggested to Lola that they meet for dinner every couple of weeks so he could continue to help her acclimate to her growing talents, and she willingly accepted the idea. Maurice was fun and comforting in an odd sort of way, and his very existence, along with that of the odd x^0 website, kept her grounded and made her feel less crazy. Except for Alex, Lola lacked people with whom she felt like she could talk to about, well, philosophy and the meaning of life, the things that had always fascinated her. Most of the folks she encountered socially, and in her profession save for her new Nigerian coworkers, seemed to share a fairly rigid viewpoint that frustrated Lola with its circular reasoning. We have a book that gives us all the answers. We know it does because it says it does. Therefore it does. So other answers cannot exist because it says so. It made Lola want to scream.

In fairness, Maurice shared the same philosophy, yet he managed to do it with an open, questioning mind. Lola supposed it was hard to stay closed-minded and be a telepath, and she was enjoying having her preconceived notions about an entire segment of the population challenged by one feisty elderly gentleman's existence. For his part, he seemed to feel the same joy in finding common ground with a "pretty, young liberated woman" (she knew that was how he thought of her), who shared few of his core beliefs. As Maurice himself put it, "Welcome to the world of actually understanding how another human being feels."

After eating dinner while doing some practice exercises and going over a couple of new approaches which he showed her to filter input, Maurice asked her if she had gone to the origin of x^0 website. She picked up a bit of nervousness from him. He smiled wanly. *It's true I am a little uncomfortable with this part*, he said, sending the thought to her wordlessly.

Why? Puzzlement was an easy emotion to send. The answer was not, however, so Maurice switched to the spoken word.

"I do like to think that I am open-minded - thank you for your compliments - and in fact I happen to believe that is how Christ himself behaved and how he would want me to behave. Yes, yes I know it makes you uncomfortable when I mention Christ, and trust me I'm not going to do it often with you. What a shame that years of living in the Bible Belt and feeling pushed have left you doing a mental cringe every time someone says His name. But that's another matter. This group of folks, x^0, is a wonderful group. They do a lot of behind-the-scenes charitable works for all sorts of people, both telepaths and those in general need who can be helped by our special skills. They work to train and inform and heaven knows that they probably saved my sanity. But at heart their philosophy is based on the idea of reincarnation which I just don't share."

"They think telepaths are old souls?"

"No. Well, yes kind of, I guess. Let's just say for the sake of argument that you have been reincarnated multiple times. How many lives do you think you have lived?"

Interesting question. Lola started doing the math. Human race in its more or less present form for say fifty thousand years. One lifetime every hundred years just to keep the math easy. Okay. "Five hundred lives, of which all but the last few dozen were likely short and horribly uncomfortable."

"But, like the website said, why couldn't the lives overlap? No reason." Maurice said.

"Okay. Let's say I lived ten lives every hundred years. So I've had five thousand lives. I can't imagine why it matters since I can't even remember half the time why I got up and walked into the kitchen, much less anything about any past life."

Maurice chuckled in sympathy. *At least you remember why half the time.* "Suppose your soul remembers better than your physical brain, and in-between lives you have no trouble remembering every detail of each life. Then five thousand lives would be different than five hundred right?"

I suppose.

"And if each of us, say, had lived five thousand lives, how many of us do you think there actually are?"

"Well I guess that depends on how many humans have ever lived. I have no idea."

"It's a difficult number to estimate, actually, starting with the question of at what point in our collective history were there creatures who constituted a human? Given it seems to have been a gradational process, and yes, I am not going to go with Adam and Eve and four thousand years here—I'm a paleontologist, remember, and a person who can recognize an allegory when I hear one. Anyway, one reasonable source puts the estimate at about <u>a hundred billion humans</u>, total, almost seven billion of which, of course, live right now. To make the math easier can we say you've had ten thousand lives?"

Sure.

"Well assuming you are an average sort in this regard, that means there are only really about a million humans who keep doing life over and over. Not unreasonable, right?"

"I get it." Lola squirmed in her chair like an eager schoolchild who has figured out the answer to the questions the teacher just asked. "And there is only one real telepath, so everyone who is a true one in a million telepath is just one of the reincarnations of this single person??"

Interesting theory, Maurice thought. *But no.*

"Wait. That means you and I would actually be the same person, and me and Jumoke and Somadina and Olumiji and frankly that's a little creepy. I'd rather not be people I actually know. "

"I agree." *And no offense taken*, he added.

"But why stop there?" he continued aloud. "I think you could manage two hundred lives every century if you could have them simultaneously, in different places, because time as we know it just isn't a constraint in reincarnation, and then there are only a hundred thousand real humans."

Lola could follow a train of thought. "So exactly how many humans does x^0 think actually exist? Just two—back to your Adam and Eve?"

"Mathematically, what does x^0 equal?"

"One." She said it as she thought it.

And that is exactly how many humans they believe exist.

"Okay, so aren't we just back to some kind of collective unconscious? You know, we're all linked, ask not for whom the bell tolls, all that junk?"

"Except that these folks don't believe there is one human linked metaphorically, or cosmically, or whatever. They really believe that there is actually just one person, and that he/she/it lives a life, fully experiences that life, dies, and then regains touch with every previous life. The memory comes back. The soul fully feels every feeling, fully has every memory. This is no vague sensation of 'we are all one' blending back into a giant collective. This is a person. And they believe that furthermore, she/he/it, upon death, reviews that most recent life carefully, feeling the giving and the receiving of every single kindness, experiencing the pain and the suffering of every single moment of indifference, or worse yet, cruelty. They believe that this person, both of us, by the way, feels, evaluates, tries to grow, and then comes back to try another life, to try to do it better.

"So, like I could be attempt number ninety-eight billion six hundred forty-three million two hundred thirty-seven thousand five hundred and ninety-nine, and you could be—"

"Ninety-eight billion six hundred forty-three million two hundred thirty-seven thousand six hundred," Maurice chortled. *Got you beat!*

"Actually," Maurice corrected himself, " the x^0 folks don't think the progression forward is quite so linear. They argue that folks can be advanced in some ways and not in others, so they don't think we all actually have a number."

"Yet there is some kind of progression?"

"Oh, definitely. I've been told it's a little like spinning."

"On a bicycle in a gym?"

"No," Maurice had to laugh. "Like spinning silk, or cotton, or wool, into thread. We're all a tiny piece of silk. We get spun into a long thread, and yes, some of us are further along the thread than others. Many of us are touching each other. And the threads are woven together to make a yarn. And the yarns are woven together to make a braid. And the braids are twined together to make a rope. And the rope reaches upwards, growing as we strain to achieve some height we do not understand, with some lives further along than others, but we—I, you, he, it—has to do every single life to get to the end.

And what's at the end?

"I have absolutely no idea. And neither, really, does anyone else. I've heard speculation that maybe we decide to go be a species somewhere else and see if we can do better as Alpha Centauri Boogaklies than we did as human beings? …"

"But my point is that this group genuinely believes that telepathy is related to this intertwining. One has an affinity for some people, those in one's own thread so to speak, while others who one may admire or like but just don't understand as well, are lives in a whole other part of the braid—lives that have been done, will be done, but are further removed somehow from one's current life."

"So these folks think I'm going to remember this conversation two ways. As me. And as you? That's weird."

"Exactly. You will experience everything you do, everyone you touch in any way from both perspectives. Every single thing. And in between your lives, you will know it."

"Wow. That sure would tend to make one, say, drive a little more courteously."

"Even the possibility has me being nicer to folks in the checkout line at the grocery store. …" Maurice admitted.

So do you believe this at all?

Olumiji believes it, Maurice thought, *and he is the kindest man I know*. Aloud, he answered, "On one level I reconcile it with my own beliefs by saying its just 'What you do for the least of my brethren you do unto me,' but with the idea kind of on steroids, you know?"

Do unto others as you would have them do unto you, Lola thought, and in her head she saw the famous Norman Rockwell painting at the United Nations with all the faces of humanity standing together with that saying written across the bottom.

Indeed, Maurice thought, *that is this philosophy at its best.* Then he continued aloud. "On the other hand I find the idea of being, say, Lady Gaga in my next life, rather repulsive. Although in fairness to the theory, the belief is that I/you/he changes rather slowly, and that in the next life, I will have a very similar personality and a lot in common with my present self. So probably not Lady Gaga."

Lola smiled. "So if you do meet yourself, or yourself just a life or two removed that is, it will be one of those folks that when you meet them you feel like you've always known them?"

"Exactly. That really does happen, and it's always odd when it does, and that's how x^0 explains the connection."

"And Somadina and I?"

"Right. Given how you two found each other over such a great distance, the whole organization is just sure this is one of those rare occurrences of two consecutive lives occurring at once on earth. You two are separated, in their minds, by only one death. They believe that that is highly unusual, that the soul is inclined to jump around through time, perhaps to avoid that kind of intimacy. But, they also recognize that had you two not been in a telepathic portion of our evolution, you never would have found each other. But because the telepathy was there, they believe that it was inevitable that you two would find the link. They also think that one is seldom privileged to meet our joint soul occupying two bodies separated by only one death, and as such, it makes you two very special in their eyes. You're like, I don't know, a little like twin sisters in a culture that idolizes twins."

"That's interesting. And weird. Do they have any theory about which of us died first?"

"Lola," Maurice sighed, "x^0 does not consider this a competitive sport."

Lola smiled. *Neither do I.* "I don't know what I consider it actually. I don't think I believe it, but ... well ... it is interesting."

"Drive safely going home," Maurice stood up preparing to head out. "And courteously. I don't want any inter-life memories of you cutting me off to make a left-hand turn young lady." They hugged a slightly awkward hug, each wondering if by some very strange chance x^0 was correct, what the hug would feel like when they were the other person.

In the days after Nwanyi's outburst, she found herself calmer. It was easier to be less emotional and more focused on her own well-being. Several times each day she spent time with Djimon's two engineers, practicing the assembly of the various components she would be expected to know and deal with. Djimon had assured her that her chances for survival increased dramatically if everything went off exactly as designed and that it would take practice. She needed to be able to put it all together in her sleep, he told her.

He explained that because the bomb would be on her person, with the explosive material largely hidden in her elaborate headgear, it was by necessity a very small device. Its sole purpose was to just put a hole into the plane itself, creating a dramatic inability for the aircraft to complete take off, and therefore keeping, symbolically and literally, Nigeria's precious resources and people here. And of course grabbing the attention of a news hungry world.

He comforted her by taking pains to point out how there were no small pieces intended to be turned into tiny projectiles designed to hurt her or others. In fact, if she did her job exactly right, the force would blast directly away from her, leaving her and her fellow passengers to deal basically with only the aftermath of a high-speed collision of the plane with the ground and surrounding landscape. There would be injuries with that, of course, but Djimon assured her that his greatest hope was that not a single life would be lost. He seemed totally sincere when he said it.

Nwanyi still wasn't sure she trusted him, but her best odds seemed to involve appearing cooperative now, and maybe even being cooperative later. She was encouraged with her sister's ongoing attempts to reach her, and now felt like she was growing strong enough to reach back. Each night before she fell asleep she tried to let Somadina know that she was okay, that she was getting stronger, that she was going to keep surviving just like the song said. Every once in awhile, very faintly, she caught the sensation of Somadina smiling back.

In mid-November Lola's company received word that the rig they had contracted to drill the well was nearing the end of its previous commitment and it would likely begin moving to her company's location in several days. Lola was not pleased. The process of moving would take a few days and the process of rigging up would take a few days more, as would driving pipe through the soft mud, setting surface casing, and drilling through the very shallow sands which could not contain oil. Lola did the math. That meant that if all went without major problems, sometime in mid-December they would be drilling into the shallowest zones they cared about. Damn. Lola would need to be in the Lagos office for the couple of weeks that the drill bit would take to make its way into the increasingly deeper potential reservoirs, and right now that was looking like mid- to late December. Lola had really been hoping that this would not happen until after the first of the year, when the kids were all back in school and the holidays were over. Damn.

Her office mates were quick to joke with her, recommending

local foods, and laughing about coworkers they knew there, and kidding her that one drilling problem or another would surely keep her there through Christmas. Oh heavens, she hoped not. They were a kindly group, and more than one offered to put her in touch with their own relatives if that were the case, assuring her how very welcome she would be at their own families' celebrations. Which was very sweet, but frankly not what she wanted.

Lola did have to wonder if there might be some way for Somadina and her to meet while she was there. She tried to send Somadina a feeling of excitement that she was coming back, but it seemed to come out more as apprehension and frustration. Which now that she thought about it, it kind of was. So she opted for a more direct and yet less informative text message. "Coming to your country on business in middle of December. Can we maybe meet? Can I be of more help to you if I am in Lagos?"

Lola hit send, and then she had second thoughts. It wasn't like she was going to have a lot of free time on her hands or an ability to travel around. And she certainly couldn't just go looking for this missing sister. "I will be very busy with work but because I will be closer maybe we can think of some way this can be good." It sounded pretty weak but, well … Lola tried to keep her lack of enthusiasm in check, thinking of Maurice's admonitions about privacy versus secrecy and not wanting to offend Somadina.

The message came back quickly. "So glad you told me." But the feelings Lola received in her mind said, *Let's not rush. I know you have responsibilities. I am really your friend now. I will think if I can get to Lagos to see you or make this work, but it is okay. I do not want what you cannot give. Friends, right?*

Lola felt relief and warmth as she sent back her own emotions. *Yes, friends. Let's see how things go. Thanks.*

Sitting at her desk, still fretting about the timing, Lola was surprised to get a mid-day call from Ariel. "Is everything okay, dear?"

"Oh not just okay, it's great mom. I signed up for a tennis league here at school and I just played my first match and I kicked butt. Seriously kicked butt. I haven't hardly played since high school, so I was really surprised. Just sharing the joy."

"Your dad is going to be so proud," Lola laughed. Alex had served as informal tennis coach to all three of his kids, all three of whom had objected at various times and in various ways to his sometimes overly enthusiastic coaching. But Ariel at least still enjoyed playing the sport, and Lola was just glad to hear her happy. With a little prompting she shared her travel timing worries. "Mom. It's going to be fine. You will be home for Christmas. I promise."

"That's nice sweetie, but it's not like there is anyway to know at this point."

"Trust me, you will be. You'll be here in time to make the seven layer dip."

"Which only has four layers because you kids all hated the vegetables." They both laughed and Lola felt better. Sure. She would go, do her job, come back. And try to be more like Ariel who seemed to seldom worry about anything.

Azuka walked home more slowly than usual. The last few days had been particularly hectic for Somadina. The oldest Dibia had met and discussed her request to receive some training from them appropriate to her gender and age in return for working to please the local spirits with her fortune-telling. They were still considering the specifics involving the request, but it looked like there might be a positive outcome.

Nwanyi had surprised her with some sort of mind contact that Somadina had not thought her sister was capable of, and Somadina had been so happy about that. She felt certain that more specific and useful information about Nwanyi's whereabouts would certainly be forthcoming soon. Meanwhile, late last night she had found out that the American woman was apparently coming back to Lagos and although neither woman appeared to have much of a plan yet regarding this visit, Somadina was hopeful that this would somehow be good news as well. Woven through all this joy was normally sweet and playful Kwemto, who was now cutting a new tooth and clung to his mother constantly in his discomfort and irritability.

x^0

So of course Somadina had no time to think. A month had flown by. Azuka promised himself that tonight he would tell her he was leaving her. Because, frankly, if it took this long for her to decide that she wanted him, she could not want him very badly. Enough. He was not a beggar. He could make a life with another.

Somadina looked out and saw Azuka coming down the road and realized how tired and discouraged he looked as he made his way so very slowly to their small house. The truth was that she had made up her mind days ago to marry him, again and by her own choice. Then so many odd things had happened, and Kwemto would not give her a moment's peace, and so the right time just had not yet presented itself for her to tell him. This did not, after all, seem like the sort of proclamation one just made out of nowhere. Please pass the pounded yam, and oh yes, I will indeed happily be your wife.

But Somadina sensed that the time had come to speak up. She allowed herself to reach out to Azuka's mind, gently, and was surprised to find frustration and even anger at her for taking so long to answer him. Anger? Azuka, loving Azuka was never angry with her. But she had waited too long. His eagerness had started to turn sour with time, and today was some sort of deadline he had set without telling her. Oh dear. He was now feeling resentful and toyed with and resolved to end his wait. Where did this come from?

She felt a little angry in response. What was this about a deadline? He had told her to take her time. He had made it clear she could have all the time that she needed. This was not fair. He had changed the rules on her, and then he hadn't even told her. She was going to lose the man she loved all because he had decided to complicate the situation without even letting her know.

As her anger rose, she heard Lola. Her own mind put words to Lola's thoughts. *Calm down. I can hear you screaming in frustration all the way in Texas, dear.*

Somadina sent back a rush of panic and irritation. Lola replied. *No. Absolutely do not get mad at him. Don't be an idiot. Yes, especially if he is being one. Yes, I am very sure about this. If you are lucky, for the rest of your life the two of you will take turns occasionally acting like idiots. Today it is his turn. You love him. You tell him. Trust me. It ends way happier that way.*

But even though she understood that Lola was right, Somadina did not trust herself to speak. She was afraid her irritation with Azuka and his secret deadline would bubble out of her mouth instead of the words she really wanted to say. She looked around frantically for a pencil. Why could a person never find a pencil when they needed one? So she found a nail instead and looked around the front yard. There had to be something she could at least scratch on. She found a flat rock about the size of a hand and grabbed it for lack of anything better. On it she scratched out the word "ehe," because she wanted to say yes to him in Igbo. And then she ran out the door to give him the rock.

Azuka saw Somadina running towards him holding something, and her eagerness alone lifted his mood and halted the harsh words that were forming on his tongue. It was true that in spite of everything she had managed to cook for him in an unusually fine fashion for the last few days. But then again, maybe she had been merely trying to soften the blow of telling him no.

"I have one word for you," Somadina said as she offered him a flat rock about the size of his hand. Azuka had seen her scratching on the rock like a child might do, so he reached for it, but then he was almost afraid to look. His eye caught the letter e, saw none of the dreaded "mba," for no, and he burst into a grin. She was grinning back at him. "Yes. The word I have for you is 'yes.' I would be honored to be your wife."

Once inside the house, Azuka lost no time in carrying the sleeping Kwemto over to his parents, and Azuka left the boy in his own mother's arms. She patted her grandchild's head with affection and asked no questions. For once, Azuka did not stay even for a moment to visit with his parents.

Lola expected that neither Alex nor Teddie would be pleased at the news that she was leaving town again, but both of them took it in stride better than she expected. Alex was clearly distracted with a group of students and some problems at the school. Unlike Lola, he didn't particularly like discussing his work, and had explained to her more than once that while venting about job-related problems seemed to help her cope, and he was happy to listen to her, the truth was that during his time off he would just as soon not spend time even thinking about his job.

    Lola continued to try to give Alex his privacy, but she couldn't shut him out completely. What she did pick up from him supported what he said. He hadn't lied to her, he didn't secretly want to talk about work at all. He liked to think about sports. He liked to think about how his car was running. He thought fondly about her and the kids and his house and his couch and his refrigerator in which he liked to have plenty of good materials for making a sandwich. Not that he was shallow. He also thought about the news, about politics, about world problems. He was curious, alert, and compassionate. But he really, truly did not like analyzing situations the way she did.

    As for her travel, this time around he seemed more resigned than anything. He had known for months that the well would get drilled, that she would have to go. The timing didn't bother him the way it did her. To Lola's surprise it pleased him a little. Really? Indeed, he was hoping this meant she wouldn't make such an elaborate deal about Christmas this year. Maybe spend less money. Decorate less. Get less hassled and wound up about it. Okay. That was interesting.

    Teddie, on the other hand, was having a better time at school this year. The transition to high school seemed to have improved things, and she was making a few new friends and getting involved in more varied activities. She'd stopped playing volleyball, which Lola thought never was a good fit for her anyway, and instead she was writing for the school paper, a first in a family that up until now had been mostly about sports and science. While both Zane and Ariel had only reluctantly attended the high school where Alex taught, Teddie seemed to actually like the idea of having her dad around. Alex reported that Teddie had surprised him by actually dropping by his room often and even spending time in his class room.

Lola could tell that Teddie did that because it made her feel safe. Safe? Yes, apparently having a dad nearby all day had changed something for Teddie, and she now felt more protected. It was showing in her disposition. Lola now occasionally got a cheery look or thought, even a considerate question or two. While Teddie wasn't glad about having her mother gone for a couple of weeks, she was okay with it because the important thing to her right now was that her dad wasn't going anywhere. Okay, that was interesting as well.

Lola mused that too much information could be a difficult thing to handle. Years of being so receptive to others' emotions had helped prepare her for the fact that not all truths are what one wants to hear. But of course there had always been doubt about whether she was reading her family and her friends and her coworkers correctly. Thanks to the dramatic increase in her abilities, however, there was no more doubt. She pretty much knew, for example, exactly who at worked liked her, who disliked her, and maybe most surprising of all, how many people didn't really think much about her one way or the other at all.

That had to be one of the more difficult parts of being a telepath, she laughed to herself. Here one is, the absolute center of the universe from the day they are born. And then one day, they develop this ability which enables them to begin to find out that most of the world doesn't particularly notice that they exist, and worse yet, if they do notice they don't particularly care. Most of the world is absorbed in their own problems, their own joys, their own fight for survival, and sometimes their own petty squabbles. Lola thought to herself that being a telepath was in some ways an unexpectedly humbling experience.

Then there were the rarer times when one did learn something that involved themselves. Yikes. Thinking you knew what people thought of you was one thing. Knowing what someone thought of you called for all the maturity one could muster.

Djimon watched closely as Nwanyi played with the small parts and pieces he had given her. She continued to practice obediently. He continued to respond with modest praise and small ongoing privileges and comforts. For example, she was now allowed access to both water and toilet facilities as she wished, though Mairo generally walked her to and from the bathroom, lest she wander off through the house. He had even considered briefly letting her call home, as that had once been her most cherished opportunity, but because she had not asked to do so for so long, he decided to let that issue alone. Plus, contact with family would be likely to provide at least a certain amount of confusion of priorities. Best to keep her focused and sure of her mission.

But was she sure of her mission? Djimon wondered. For while he seemed to have successfully attained her compliance, he did not see the sort of zeal he had hoped for in a true convert. Perhaps, he told himself, Nwanyi was just not a person capable of a great deal of zeal for any cause. That could be a personality issue, not a belief issue. If in her core he had convinced her that what she was going to do must be done, then she would act as expected. As instructed.

But what if he hadn't convinced her? What if her agreement to all of his political lectures was just lip service born of fear and a lack of other alternatives? Then she was going along, telling him what he wanted to hear, in hopes of some sort of last-minute escape. Surely she did not have a plan, at least not a real one of any kind. With no contact whatsoever with the outside world for so long, he could not imagine any plan more sophisticated than her just plain running like she had before, and he certainly had the good sense to see that no opportunity to do that would present itself at any point before she was on the plane.

As to her getting on the plane and then choosing not to act? Well, Djimon was not a stupid man. He had considered that possibility and admitted that there was a small but not insignificant chance that at the crucial moment his latest convert would lack the zeal, or maybe just lack the courage, to do his bidding. Which was why Nwanyi's device had a simple but adequate backup detonation system which she would not be able to reach herself without completely disrobing.

He had done an excellent job of ensuring that she would not

turn to an airline official or a stranger for help once she had boarded. He had barely needed to exaggerate when he told her stories of the "kill first and investigate later" policy that she was likely to encounter if she even mentioned the word bomb, and the fear in her eyes had been quite genuine. He had made a point of telling her the stories often. That left only the remote possibility of her being helped by an accomplice, and for the life of him he could not imagine how she could have one.

But, Djimon reminded himself, just because he could not imagine something did not make it totally impossible. And he was a man who planned for every possibility. Which was why sending three of his best men to London was worth the expense. He had found three whose histories did not point to association with him or his wife's family and who could obtain a travel visa for Great Britain. They would fly in a day ahead of time. They would remain on alert. If called and told that all had gone well, they would merely come home, to join him in the very busy and exciting nation-rebuilding that Djimon was sure he would ignite once he had the full attention of his countrymen. Their trip would merely have been a minor expense and inconvenience.

But in that worst of worlds, where everything failed for reasons Djimon could not fathom, then his men would be waiting just outside of security at the time when the passengers from Nwanyi's flight would reasonably be expected to clear immigration and enter the airport. Djimon allowed himself the brief pleasure of detailing in his mind some of the treatment Nwanyi would receive directly from him if she had the misfortune to be returned to his care.

Udo knew that he was supposed to be doing his schoolwork, but Udo also knew that he could get the schoolwork done later, in less time than it would take most of his fellow students. Across from him sat Obialo, his half-brother and best friend, working diligently as was his way and his need. Obialo and he might, had their personalities been different, been fiercely competitive with each other. In fact, half-brothers so close in age often ended up more enemies than friends. But Obialo was by nature a content, plodding child who had always been secure and happy in the knowledge that he was his father's first-born son. Paranoia did not come naturally to him. And Udo, who had lost the first-born contest by a full two weeks from the moment he was born, was not inclined to fight for what was not his by right. Instead, Obialo was the older son. Udo was the smart son. Both boys could live with that. Udo helped Obialo, with school and with life. In return, Obialo did not lord his position over Udo, but treated him as almost an equal and certainly as a friend.

  Truth be told, Udo thought that he might actually prefer being the smart son. For while Obialo would in all probability someday be the most important member of the family, Udo would someday leave home and in all probability be an important member of the world. He preferred the latter by far.

  And it was Udo to whom his father had come to for help. Not Obialo. For what could Obialo do? Udo had taken to a computer's connection to the rest of the world from the first moment he had been allowed to touch one. He understood them, in ways he sometimes failed to understand his own family and his people. The computer made sense.

  Determined to uphold his reputation, he had secretly spent hours and hours trying to help free his father from the horrible dreams the man was having regarding his poor first wife who had died before Udo was born. Udo had heard from his mother that it was an awful, bloody death in childbirth involving a midwife's incompetence, and that now visions of the woman soaked in blood were hounding Ikenna as Amaka's spirit urged him to do something to save the child that she had died birthing.

  But the child had to be found before she could be saved. Udo now had every scrap of information the family had been able to gather which could possibly be helpful. And he had his own astute brain.

  The leads of extended family names which the clearly fraudulent husband had provided had led nowhere now several times over. Udo thought back to his own meeting of the man. He had seemed pleasant, sincere. A good actor? Udo remembered asking the man himself a question or two, trying to play well his part as a concerned family member. He remembered his feeling of addressing the man by his first name, as an equal, challenging him to provide information and assurances which would demonstrate his worthiness to marry a member of Udo's family. In fact, he remembered the man turning to him as he said his name, surprised perhaps at the smaller, slighter of the two brothers addressing him so boldly and directly.

    And Udo thought: Djimon is really his name. He turned so naturally when I said it. I don't think one could fake that. He used a different last name, easy enough to do. But he kept his first name. I need to forget all the other information he gave us, which all was apparently no more than smokescreens intended to throw us off. I need to just look for Djimons in Lagos. Djimons of the right age. Let's start with that.

    Udo went happily to work. A second son who saved his father from nightmares and his half-sister from captivity would certainly be a well-respected and well-rewarded second son.

    On November 22, 2009, *Fela!* opened on Broadway, celebrating the life and music of Fela Kuti, a Nigerian composer and musician, and also a political activist and human rights advocate. The show featured the musical genre known as Afrobeat that Fela helped create. Lola read the promotional material, which said that the musician had been "inspired by his mother, a civil rights champion," and that he had "defied a corrupt and oppressive military government and devoted his life and music to the struggle for freedom and human dignity." Wikipedia added information on a variety of ways in which the man had been controversial before he died from AIDs-related complications in 1997.

    Lola went to YouTube and found and played some of Fela's most well known songs. She wasn't so comfortable with the web's allegations of misogyny and in fact, his music wasn't particularly to her taste, but she could appreciate its energy and intensity as well as Fela's struggle for political freedom. But the most interesting thing was that once she found "the sound," she realized that she had been hearing his music for months, simply shutting out that which she did not understand. Now that she knew of it, it was surprisingly easy to recognize his music when she heard it in someone else's head. For indeed, one of her Nigerian coworkers listened to Fela's Afrobeat music and its more recent derivatives for much of the day. Once Lola became aware of it, she heard it more. And the more she heard it, the better she liked it. Finally, she wondered if she could persuade Alex to see the musical with her, if it came to Houston.

      Thanksgiving night, after the dishes were done, the television off, and Teddie and Alex in bed, Lola curled up on the couch with her laptop. With both of the older two kids flying home in just a few weeks for Christmas, the Zeitmans had for years passed on the effort and expense of a family reunion at Thanksgiving as well. So, with other family far away or passed away, it had slowly become less of a holiday for them, with four days off to relax being its chief asset.
    She found a series of new links on the x^0 website, apparently posted by members. One area caught her eye. Crime statistics. Hmm. She followed a link, to the website of an organization called the <u>Geneva Declaration on Armed Violence</u>, and discovered that there now was a group out there devoted, purely and simply, to reducing the amount of times one human being intentionally uses a weapon to kill another. By any means. War, gang warfare, murder, mass murder. Whatever.
    She read that this declaration was first adopted by forty-two nations in June 2006 and saw that it was now endorsed by more than a hundred countries, but the good old U.S.A. did not appear to be one of them. Why not?
    According to the website, an estimated seven hundred and forty thousand men, women, and children are shot and killed each year worldwide. She had to wonder how many of those humans would not have died if the person pulling the trigger had been able to read the mind of the life which they were about to snuff out. Would telepathy have prevented every single such death? Most of them?
    She doubted it. What about those who were under orders to

kill? Those whose fellow warriors faced death or whom faced death themselves if they failed to shoot? Solving that mess required more empathic ability on the parts of those actually giving the orders, she thought, and probably more creative options than shooting for those in the midst of armed conflicts as well.

Lola let herself try to imagine a world in which that problem had been creatively addressed. She saw in her mind's eye imaginary news footage showing hoards of foot soldiers, armed with tasers instead of guns. Occasionally a bomb would fall from the sky, spewing pepper spray. The fight for territory, for whatever reason it was happening, was harsh and brutal, but it was being done by soldiers on both sides who were taking unusual pains to spare every life. Why? Because in the war Lola was imagining, the soldiers operated in a world where murder was so abhorrent, so disgusting, that its commission, even in war, would certainly lose either side the hearts and minds of those they were sworn to protect.

Seven hundred and forty thousand people a year. Could humans change enough to change the very rules of warfare if society demanded it of them? We'd walked away en masse from cannibalism, incest, slavery, and human sacrifice, she thought. We were capable of declaring some actions not worthy. Why then not the action of taking another human life?

How about those cases where a person was acting of their own volition? Were there circumstances in which the uncoerced telepath would choose to shoot? Lola could think of two. The first seemed a contradiction in terms because it required a telepath who could sense the feelings of others and simply not care. He feels the other persons fear, anguish, possible remorse, hope for life, and then he shoots anyway. But to feel and not to feel was an oxymoron, or at least she hoped so. So she counted that one out.

The second possibility made her shudder as well. In this case the armed, yet caring, telepath sensed the potential victim's thoughts and feelings, but instead of finding compassion, he or she would find those feelings so reprehensible, and so dangerous, that the telepath would make the painful and yet the fully informed and enlightened choice to pull the trigger. To shoot anyway. Lola wondered what kind of victim it would take for a caring and moral telepath to make that choice.

Chapter 14. December 2009

Lola left Sunday evening December 6. Her dread of the trip had hung in the air throughout the Thanksgiving weekend and through the week that followed. Once she arrived and was settled into the comfort and safety of her now-familiar Lagos Sheraton hotel room, she ordered room service early and sadly thought of Alex celebrating his birthday without her. She opened her laptop on the scratched and worn desk and was happy to find that the internet connection was working well today. Too bad she had not gotten one of the refurbished rooms this time around. She sent a short arrived-just-fine email to all before getting her things ready for the morning.

This time she had no presentation to make, but rather would be escorted daily to her company's office to work with the operations geologist as the well began to drill through the more shallow of the targeted intervals. Nature always managed to surprise, especially in an exploration well like the one which was being drilled. Lola knew from experience that the main pay zones would at best come in differently than predicted, that oil would in all probability be lacking in one or more zones where it had been hoped for, and that an unexpected sand might well materialize and contain the bulk of the reserves which this well would ultimately produce. For all the phenomenal tools, data, and software at her disposal, and all the certainty continually espoused by her industry regarding reserves in the ground, Lola knew all too well that in the end an exploration well remained somewhat of a crapshoot. Which was why folks either loved or hated being in this business. And why they had wanted her there while drilling.

After a lifetime of effectively compartmentalizing pieces of her life, Lola was quite adept at it. Home was handled with the email. No, wait. Sometimes she forgot that she could now do better. She took a moment and felt around for Alex, for Teddie, for the older kids. All were busy with their mornings, but otherwise they all were well. Good. Now it had been really handled.

Work was then taken care of with the clothes laid out for tomorrow and a briefcase full of data ready to go. Lola herself would be cared for shortly with a long, hot shower and the predictably slow arrival of a perfectly reasonable room-service steak, no salad, no ice, but a big glass of perfectly adequate red wine.

Now for Somadina. Lola had to wonder if worrying about and checking in with Somadina almost daily had conveniently replaced that niche in her life which used to be filled with worrying about and checking in every day with her aging mother. She sat in the lounge chair and closed her eyes. She found that if it had been awhile since they had been in contact, it helped to focus by having her mind locate something else that was easy. Tonight she used the small toe on her left foot. Find it. Feel it. Wiggle it. Very good. Find Somadina. Indeed, the link was there, grown almost as strong as the link to a seldom used appendage like a toe. Lola focused on being in Nigeria, ready to help. An email would be sent to Udo with her contact information. Somadina should call the hotel when she could, any evening. Lola would probably eat out by the pool after work most days, so call later. Picture of her dining outside at sunset. *I will be here for many days. Please call often.*

Nwanyi felt like a mute woman who had learned to formulate sounds. She was certain she was responding to Somadina now. Certain that Somadina could now somehow hear her. The problem was that she had pathetically little useful to say. After the first rush of information—*I am alive, I need help*—there was almost nothing to add.

Her sister kept sending her images of Somadina standing on a hillside, hands shading her eyes as she looked into the distance searching. Nwanyi understood. *I am looking for you. Where are you?*

But Nwanyi could not answer the question. *I am in a house. I am on a nice street.* How can you possibly tell someone where you are when you do not know yourself? Nwanyi sent back pictures of herself shrugging. Shaking her head.

Frustrated, Somadina had sent back images of Nwanyi looking at mail. Standing outside looking at a house number. But Somadina did not understand. Nwanyi was not allowed out front at all, and she could find no mail. She was barely allowed outside of her room these days, as Djimon seemed increasingly nervous. She saw the courtyard and occasionally the kitchen, in which her eyes scanned desperately for bags or receipts or anything which would leave Somadina less exasperated with her. But someone was always there to keep her from snooping, and nothing of use ever seemed to be lying around.

Plus Somadina did not understand that Nwanyi could no longer afford to look like she wanted to escape. Her safety, her very life now depended on being a woman who had thoroughly embraced the role Djimon had designed for her. Nwanyi was concerned that Djimon feared that she still wanted to run away. She worried that on some deep level he suspected that only part of her wanted to do anything to please him, while another part of her still despised him. And she knew that it was not in her best interest to give him cause for further concern.

In fact, when he and his friends escorted her to the airport, she would go most willingly, and she would do what she could to assure him that she was going to act in the ways he had trained her. She had accepted that setting off the bomb and surviving was her best hope.

Wait. They were going to take her to the airport. The airport. What was wrong with her? Everyone could find the airport. Nwanyi's soft expressions of *I don't know any more to tell you* escalated into a scream of mental energy to Somadina. She sent her sister pictures of planes. Sounds of the roar of jet engines. The feel of sweaty, noisy crowds greeting, meeting, and saying goodbye. *Yes. The airport. One day soon, I am going to be at the <u>Lagos airport</u>.*

Lola had started to get used to the sound of Somadina's accented pidgin English when she spoke aloud, but she still had to rely heavily on the accompanying telepathic transmissions to understand the meaning of much of what Somadina said. They had talked by phone several times over the past two weeks while Lola's stay in Nigeria dragged on. Otherwise, Lola had entertained herself by playing endless word games online, sadly imagining the Christmas parties and decorations she was missing at home, and trying every dish on the hotel menu. The well had been making its

x^0

way deeper into the earth with painful slowness, fortunately finding enough oil in the shallower zones to already barely be an economic discovery. But the shallow pay had been cause for taking small rock samples called cores and running additional wire line logs, both of which had slowed down the drilling of the well. And of course it had not found nearly as much oil as everyone had hoped it would. Yet.

Now they were paused in the drilling process, just finishing setting pipe in the ground which would protect the lower-pressured shallow oil reservoirs they had found from being damaged by the heavier drilling fluids which they were going to have to start using point forward in order to keep both water and oil in the deeper, more highly pressured rocks from spewing out while they drilled.

With this Sunday afternoon's phone call she luckily clearly understood Somadina's words spoken into the phone, which was good because Somadina was so happy that no other information but happiness was coming through anyway. "Yes. Lola! I have good news. Very good news. She is going to the airport. The Lagos airport. And she is going sometime very soon."

"That is great news! Somadina. Listen. Surely we can get the police to intercept her? We can have everybody in authority looking for her there. This could not be better."

Lola felt Nwanyi, and in particular Nwanyi's sharp spike of fear in the background, behind Somadina's joy.

No police! No authorities! To Lola's surprise, Nwanyi's feelings came through as clearly as if her words had been spoken directly into the phone line.

She let Somadina respond. "You are guilty of nothing dear sister." Soothing thoughts. "The police can bring you home. Do not worry about the bride price. We will settle with Djimon's family. This marriage can and will be ended. You need not be afraid." Lola felt Nwanyi's frustrated *You don't understand* in response. Then Lola started to pay closer attention.

Nwanyi was managing to send clear picture and in fact she was sending it rather well. In it, she was standing at the airport in some ridiculously fancy dress, scared, holding a giant cartoon image of a ticking bomb.

"I think we have a more complicated problem," Somadina said softly over the phone line to Lola. "If he is making her carry a bomb, our authorities will not care why she is doing it. At least not at first. In the very best case she will end up in jail for awhile until things are sorted out. It is possible that in the end she cannot prove her innocence and spends her life in jail.

"That hardly solves your problem, does it?" Lola sent sympathy.

"Hardly," Somadina agreed. "And in the most likely case, they will kill her there at the airport and then deal with the bomb." Nwanyi added her agreement.

"Okay," Lola gulped. "Then we need a better plan."

Jumoke had been happy enough to see Lola again in person at the office, and the two had maintained a friendly interaction and a careful mental distance for almost two weeks as the well drilled. The subject of telepathy never came up. Lola found it was easier if she avoided looking him in the eye, which she had.

Unfortunately, this particular Sunday, Lola had to call Jumoke to ask a favor of him.

"I know how much you do not like your brother's affairs to mingle with your work," she began.

"I think you don't," he replied, and for just a second she felt the waves of embarrassment and discomfort which mentioning Olumiji evoked. "Okay, now you do." He smiled slightly. She nodded with understanding.

So Lola cut the soft sell and the preamble and described how her relationship with Somadina had evolved ever since he had helped put them in touch through x^0. Even though she had been desperate to get home by Christmas, she now needed to make sure she would not be sent home too soon, if by chance the well hit its final total depth before Nwanyi had made her journey to the airport. On the other hand, her absence would need to be somehow explained if she disappeared suddenly before the well finished drilling.

"I don't understand. Are you telling me that you are seriously going to try to intercept a stranger at the Lagos airport who is armed with a bomb? And do what? Forgive, me but this is beyond stupid. This lady needs to come get her own sister. Or you need to send my brother. Lola. This is the Lagos airport. Do I need to remind you that you are a white woman who has 'foreigner with money' written all over her?"

Lola felt his fear for her. He felt her stubbornness.

"This lady," she responded, " is a twenty-one-year-old girl with a baby, no car, and little money, who has no practical way to get here quickly or to camp out at the Lagos airport once she does. Furthermore, she is worried that the sister's husband knows her on sight, and she feels certain he would not hesitate to kill her or anyone else for that matter whom he thought might interfere with his plan, whatever it is. And I have the unique advantage of looking like someone who could not possibly know Nwanyi or want to help her." It was embarrassing but they both knew it was true. A well-dressed American business woman would not cause a blip on Djimon's radar as someone who was concerned or involved.

"And my brother is in Tokyo at some get-together with his fellow crazies." Jumoke mumbled what Lola took to be an Igbo cuss word of some sort.

"I have already asked him to call me," she offered. "This all only came together last night. I'm not foolish. Somadina and I are going to be working together to do this, and she will be with me every step of the way. She was able to get a surprising amount of information. Nwanyi knows she is going to have a ticket to London—she is sure that it is London—and that she is traveling in a wedding dress, which strikes me as a little odd, but apparently it is lavish and will hide the various components of this small but rather clever little bomb. Her husband's group is very proud of this design. Some engineer in the group came up with it."

Jumoke winced. "Great. One more success for Nigerian engineering," he muttered.

Lola went on. "The story they are using is that she is being sent to meet her future husband, an Igbo man in England, and her family wants him to first set eyes on her in all her glory. Something like that. Somadina understood that part. Anyway, she is getting help from some woman in the group who has secured work as a lady janitor, who will meet her in the restroom inside security, provide the rest of the pieces, and help with the assembly. I guess that the individual parts are all things one can get through security separately, at least in Lagos, which is why they are so proud of it. They have been making her practice putting this thing together over and over for weeks now. She is supposed to board the plane first class, look and act like a princess, and then do whatever it is she is supposed to do. But the odd thing is that she seems to think she is going to live through it, so I'm not exactly sure what it is."

"And just how do you propose to know what plane she is on?"

Lola smiled. "There are only two direct flights to London a day. One morning and one night. She gets word to get suited up, I get on the phone and change my reservation, which, not surprisingly, went through London to begin with, and then I hightail it to the airport and I board the same plane."

Jumoke shook his head. This actually did make a little sense. Lola added "She should be easy enough to spot."

"Don't you think he'll have men on the plane? And as soon as they see you interfering they will stop you?"

"Nwanyi seems to think the group is small and very focused on some particular cause or grievance. It's not like they have, well, spare fanatics to sacrifice. With any luck it is going to be just her and me, and with Somadina giving me instructions I can simply convince Nwanyi that she does not have to do this."

"I'm doubling the guards going with you to the airport." It was her turn to feel Jumoke's stubbornness. "I know that it won't necessarily help anything, but I am doing it anyway. And I'm coming over and staying at the hotel with you until this thing is over. And yes, I'll handle management and any irregularities of your departure if needed. That part will be easy. One more thing. I'm getting my damn brother on the phone now. If he and his fellow flakes want to play at this shit, they damn well better get you some help."

x⁰

  Lola realized that Jumoke's anger came from the fact that he genuinely liked her. He would like to see to it that she did not get killed in his country. And she could not help thinking that this was rather a nice trait in a friend.

  The night before she was to leave for the airport, Djimon had Nwanyi put on the entire dress, the shoes, and the very important and elegant headdress and brought her out to present her to the group. He was proud. True, it had not all gone exactly as he had planned, and he hated that, but in the end there she was looking very Igbo, very bride-like, and very committed to the rebuilding of a flourishing nation. The symbolism of the young woman dying in a wedding dress was all he could hope for. The modified bullet-proof vest she wore underneath was probably hot and uncomfortable, but it made her look slightly less scrawny, which was good, and it seemed to be making her feel invincible, which was even better.

  First Djimon had Nwanyi read aloud and copy in her own hand the brief but heart-wrenching letters he had composed on her behalf, begging the nation to listen to Djimon's words, taking full blame for the bombing scheme as her own attempt to help her beloved husband and his cause, absolving Djimon of all part in it.

  Nwanyi wrote slowly but obediently, without comment or question, and although the group grew a little impatient with her deliberate printing, several muttered their approval as she read aloud. Djimon filled the pauses caused by Nwanyi's slow penmanship with his own explanations of how he planned to release one of the three letters each time the explosion itself began to fade out of the news, trusting the media to then bring the story back to feature each new development.

  Of course, he explained, he was also trusting Nwanyi's outraged family to refute the authenticity of each letter as it was released, after which, each time, a carefully selected follower of his would come forth with a story of a conversation he or she had held with a highly committed Nwanyi that would lend credence to Djimon's side. When the media had tired of that back and forth, out would come the video tapes in which a poised Nwanyi would declare Djimon's innocence and plead his political cause. Djimon had calculated that he would have a full three to four weeks of fame that would run through the Christmas season and well into the New Year, in which he could make his case from the safety of a very carefully chosen hideout. By the end of that time, he hoped to have achieved the status of Nigerian cult hero, and the rest would be history.

Djimon did not fail to see Mairo's brother eyeing him thoughtfully. "Of course, I will only be a figurehead for all of you, for our cause," he added hastily. "My role will always be to take orders from the actual wise leaders inside our group." His brother-in-law smiled slightly at this last minute but very important addition.

Djimon had arranged for a member of his group to be the photographer that evening, and before taping the two short videos, he first announced with great flourish that he wished to have Nwanyi's formal portrait taken. "You may be healing for awhile afterwards, and yet so many places will want to hang your portrait right away," he explained to her quietly.

With those words, Nwanyi obediently seated herself elegantly on the beautiful chair that Mairo produced, and while the group discussed the particulars of the portrait, she found herself fantasizing, once again, about her favorite of all the possible scenarios. It was the one in which she set the bomb off perfectly. The one in which she was hurt badly, but not too badly. The one in which the nation actually rose in acceptance of Djimon and his theories and she was then hailed as a true heroine of the new Nigeria, just like Djimon said she would be. People, important, well dressed beautiful people were surrounding her bedside. They brought her flowers, they brought her gifts. And as they looked into her eyes as she lay in her hospital bed, they held her hands and they all said the same thing. "Live Nwanyi. Please live. We want you to live. We need you to live."

"I will," Nwanyi muttered back graciously to each one. "Because you all want me to very much." And all the beautiful, important, well-dressed people were so happy to hear those words from her, in the scene as she imagined it.

And then in real life, she smiled softly while the bulb flashed and the small group cheered. She liked the cheering. It made her feel happier than she had since, well, since the ritual bath on the morning of her wedding day.

Jumoke insisted on coming over to the hotel, and arranging for a car, driver, and two armed guards to be on call that night. The well had resumed drilling and in a matter of hours would be crossing a large fault and entering a high-pressure zone. It was unlikely that anything would be encountered by the drill bit which would require that Lola be escorted into the office in the middle of the night, but the remote possibility of needing quick geophysical interpretation gave Jumoke a pretense for his actions so he took it.

They opted for another Indian dinner just for old time's sake, and partway into the meal Olumiji called Jumoke's cell phone, sending a direct message of greeting to them both as he did so. He was clearly in a fine mood. It was nearly three in the morning in Tokyo, and Olumiji's somewhat inebriated hello bespoke of a night of partying, which unfortunately started the conversation off poorly. Jumoke, who had remained somewhat more of a devout Muslim, seldom drank alcohol. Tonight his brother's alternate choices irritated him more than usual. Jumoke's greeting, Lola thought, was unnecessarily curt. She could sense and sympathize with Olumiji's baffled hurt.

"No, clearly putting Lola or anyone else in danger is not part of my world mission." Lola could hear the conversation.

Jumoke switched almost immediately to speaking aloud in Yoruban, which offended Lola a little at first until she realized that the cause was embarrassment, not an attempt at secrecy. Jumoke was embarrassed at his brother's mild drunkenness and embarrassed to be seen fighting with a family member. He was embarrassed that Nigeria was sometimes such a dangerous place. He felt Lola was far more naive than she thought she was, that she had no idea how quickly she could end up dead. Jumoke was embarrassed at even having to explain that fact. Olumiji, on the other hand, had gone from jovial to worried. He was trying to reach out to Jumoke, assuring him he would be on a plane home tomorrow.

Geez, I'm getting good at this, Lola thought. *It doesn't hardly matter what language someone speaks.*

Which is what I expected. She heard it, in actual English words, loud and clear from Jumoke. She looked at him startled. *You do know most telepaths are not nearly this good, don't you?* He asked her the question with both his eyes and his mind. *That they never exchange actual conversation in words like we are right now? Most telepaths can't really do words like this.*

Six thousand telepaths. The number popped into her head. Like six thousand people who can see infrared light.

And sixty highly functional telepaths maybe in the whole world, she heard back. *Who can see perhaps dangerously deep into the infrared spectrum. Olumiji does not tell people about them. But even they are only this good, this directly conversational, when they are right next to each other looking right at each other. And, for this to happen they have to have spent a lot of time together recently, usually for the past several days, sort of tuning into each other, if you will. It can't be counted on which is one of the reasons they tell you it doesn't happen at all. Yes, it's eerie when it does. And it's yet another reason I don't spend much time around my brother. We go to this place in less than a day. I prefer to keep my telepathic exchanges vague, thank you.*

I don't blame you. She found that answering him was as easy as hearing him. *This is even weirder than all the picture/music/emotional stuff. And poor you—now you have a coworker who does the same damn thing as your brother. What are the odds?*

She felt his laugh. And a friendly affection behind it.

Yeah. And said coworker has a new best friend who probably leaves the rest of us in the dust at doing this and who is about to send her into serious danger. Come on. Let's get you upstairs and to sleep. Trust me, this kind of exchange will wear you out way faster than anything you know. Between stopping bombers and drilling oil wells you need your rest.

Jumoke walked her upstairs and then opted to go back to the lounge for awhile. She understood the move. He took her key, letting her know that she would find him eventually on the small couch in her room and to just yell, one way or another, if she needed anything before then. She was glad to see him leave. Short of actually having sex, she had never experienced anything in her life quite as intimate with another human being as the exchange of words that she had shared with him. In fact, it might in some ways have been even more intimate than sex.

That thought made her a little sad, as she thought of Alex half a world away, missing her as he started his winter break. Planning to take Teddie out Christmas shopping later today. Planning to pick up Zane, who was arriving tonight from Chicago. Planning to call daughter Ariel, who for heaven's sake was turning twenty-two years old today, planning on getting drinks with her friends before she started packing for her trip home. All of which Lola would miss. She tossed restlessly.

She must have finally dozed because she did not hear Jumoke come in, but woke instead to a shrill, insistent voice in her head which made her think of getting a dress on. That it was morning. That she was going to the airport. Getting dressed. She saw an elaborate lavender dress, folds of material with the hard-to-disguise wires carefully sewn in here and there, each of which had been memorized, and she clearly felt both panic and excitement. Right. She needed to get a ticket modified quickly. What time was it?

Jumoke's cell phone rang as she was getting out of bed. She knew just from his tone of voice that it was the office. But why? Ouch. As she stood she realized that she had a killer headache. Once when she was a child, she had eaten a lot of frosting that had been left over. It had been so sweet and wonderful and she must have consumed at least a cup of it straight up. For weeks after that she had felt nauseous if she even smelled or saw frosting, and she hadn't been able to eat the stuff for years. Come to think of it, she still didn't particularly like it.

She looked at Jumoke. The idea of entering his mind and finding out what was going on with the well felt like eating frosting had the next day. Too rich, too intense. She went for a couple of ibuprofen tablets instead and waited for him to just tell her what was happening.

He smiled at her sympathetically as he hung up. "I told you it would wear you out. Like a migraine, huh?"

And it was. *What's happening with the well?* She let herself just think it.

Jumoke responded courteously with spoken words. "Your fault came in one hundred feet shallower than you predicted. They crossed it about an hour ago. Pressure shot up. They had some minor well-control issues but they were prepared for them. They are upping the mud weight now and going to drill ahead. They should be back to drilling in a couple of hours."

"Great. And I am flying to London this lovely Monday morning on a ten a.m. flight. I think. I hope."

Jumoke rolled his eyes. "Of course it would happen this way. Okay. Let's get you booked on the flight at least. My driver and two guys can get you to the airport and watch you go through security. Maybe you can do whatever it is you think you are going to do and still manage not to actually fly to London when you are done doing it. That would be really preferable, because otherwise we are going to have to cook up one hell of story to explain your departure.

"And while I really wish I could go to the airport with you, I'm going to have to head into the office now because there is no way I can not be there. As far as I am concerned I've been told that you have just been hit with a nasty bit of food poisoning which will improve quickly if you can get this solved and get yourself into the office before anyone gets suspicious. Please."

Djimon sat uncomfortably close to her in the back seat on the way to the airport, while a definitely awkward Mairo hugged the door on her other side. In the early morning light, Nwanyi recognized both the man in the front seat and the driver from the meetings at the house. She just wanted peace, time to gather her strength, to enjoy the sight of the morning sky and the feel of freedom. But Djimon talked to her the whole way, muttering instructions she had long since memorized, reminding her how once the country finally listened to his message, others would rise up, other deeds would be done, but always her wonderful deed would remain the most glorious.

He went over the safety precautions he swore would save her life. He extolled her to be strong, that she would have the very best medical care in Nigeria, and that whatever damage she endured would heal. He reminded her that there was no timer, no back-up device. It was so important that she, a young Igbo woman, detonate this revolution by her own hand and her own choice. And this need for her action was also in part a favor to her, so her role as hero and mother to the new nation would be without dispute.

But mixed in with Djimon's instructions and adulation for her bravery, there were other messages. The woman in the restroom would be waiting. Do not let fear keep you from going to her promptly, or she will seek you out. She has been instructed to provide you with a mild sedative if it appears to her that you need one. One that will wear off enough before you need to board.

"Upper class will board early," he reminded her. "Once on the plane, you will have more freedom and space in the upper-class cabin, which is why we have put you there. Be calm and friendly, but do not converse with anyone. Arouse no suspicion. We have booked the seat next to you as well for a fictitious passenger, so you will have more space in which to fully prepare yourself. You have the window seat. After all passengers are on board, begin to ready yourself, but do not act too early. Remember, this must not happen here, on Nigerian soil but rather exactly at the second that the plane attempts to leave the country. The symbolism is very important. Just at the second in which you feel the liftoff, you will feel a light feeling in your stomach as the plane takes to flight. It must happen right then."

Nwanyi nodded. How many times had she been told this already.

He looked deep into her eyes. "Do not hesitate at the critical moment, my dearest Nwanyi." Mairo cringed visibly. "But if you do hesitate for just a second, as even true heroes sometimes do, then you must act a second later. Do you understand me? Or even two seconds later. Or even three. But you must act."

His voice changed slightly. "The longer you wait the higher

the plane will be in the air, and the more injuries you will sustain. So act quickly and boldly like the hero you are."

She nodded. He continued.

"Nwanyi, I am so sure I do not need to tell you this, but even a true hero can be tempted. So trust me. You do not want to deboard this plane at Heathrow Airport. Three of my fellow rebuilders will be there to intercept you in the very highly unlikely event that the bomb does not go off. If that happens, Nwanyi, there better have been some clearly provable mechanical malfunction which you can explain and could not possibly have caused or corrected. Or your life up to this point is going to look like a year spent at a fancy resort compared to what it will be like point forward."

Her eyes widened slightly.

"It would break my heart dear Nwanyi, but I would be forced to treat you like a coward. I'd have to see how long you could stay alive in a sealed metal trash can out in the sun all day. Every day. Until you do die. I think you might live for several weeks inside that stinking, steaming can, don't you? So if you hesitate, I want you to picture that metal can glistening in the sunshine with you sobbing and dying inside of it. So much better to be a hero, don't you think? Beloved. Cared for. Even the remote chance of death is better than that, don't you think?"

Nwanyi swallowed hard. *Yes, it was.*

x^0

Chapter 15. Late December 2009

Lola had finally made her way to the front of the horribly long, slow line, only to find that, just as they had told her over the phone, the plane was completely full with the increased holiday traffic. Her stories of a sudden family emergency had no more effect than the warmest, most pleading smile she could manage. Finally, she just stood there, looking dejected but unwilling to give up her hard-fought for place at the counter. Almost a minute passed while neither she nor the woman behind the counter spoke, and people in line began to noticeably fidget.

"Maybe. I might have something which could work," the lady at the counter finally offered reluctantly. "It is now exactly two hours before flight time. And I have one upper class passenger who has failed to check-in in any way. If your emergency is such that you are willing to pay the fare difference of about fifteen hundred dollars, I could offer you his seat on a conditional basis and let you proceed to the gate. But be advised that if he arrives soon the airlines will likely bump you back to tomorrow's flight, or try to get you on a connecting flight to London later in the day."

"That would be fine. Would be great." She pulled out her credit card and figured she could worry about the money later. Hell, this would get her into the boarding area, which might be all she needed, and if she was really lucky maybe she'd get bumped back off again. "Thank you very, very much."

The woman flashed her a look of being totally unimpressed by her show of thanks.

But the line at security took forever, and by the time Lola got to the gate the plane was well into the boarding process. The missing passenger had yet to show up, and her conditional boarding pass had been fully approved. She felt Somadina trying to see through her eyes, and right now her friend's very effort was making her headache worse. She clearly needed more painkillers and at least a few hours of sleep. It was six p.m. in Tokyo. She had a fuzzy image of Olumiji boarding a flight as well. Must have been the earliest he could manage. Jumoke was at the office. She felt his worry about both her and the resumption of the drilling. Oh yes, the well at a crucial point. That was something else to worry about later.

As she made her way to the front of the line, she scanned the remaining passengers waiting to board and got a consistent and emphatic "No" from Somadina as she looked at every possible young woman. Pulling her roller bag briskly behind her, she entered the upper-class cabin, maneuvered around the attendants serving free drinks, and saw the only empty seat. Amazing. It was next to an incredibly skinny woman wearing a ridiculously bouffant lavender dress and an even more lavish matching piece of lavender headgear. *Yes yes yes!* she heard Somadina screaming, but she would have known anyway. The woman looked up briefly to acknowledge her.

"Hello Nwanyi," Lola said softly. "I'm the crazy white woman you heard singing Karaoke in your dreams. I'm a friend of your sister Somadina."

Lola wasn't sure what sort of reception she expected from Nwanyi, but it certainly involved a certain measure of relief and gratitude. Maybe even a hug and some tears. Instead Nwanyi seemed confused and angry as she hissed at Lola to get off the plane. "I don't want you hurt. You don't have protective gear. If you are really a friend, get out of here."

Protective gear?? What was this about?

"Nwanyi, no one is going to get hurt. That's why I'm here. What is this about protective gear?"

The two women talked in whispers, and Lola finally understood that Nwanyi had been convinced she might actually survive setting off a bomb attached to her person. "It's a special design. Djimon promised."

Oh good grief. That was ridiculous.

More hushed whispers. Thank heavens for the engine noise. "There is no such type of design Nwanyi. None at all. I promise. You've been sent to die." Lola sent Nwanyi all the calm convincing thoughts she could, even though she knew that Nwanyi was barely a weak receiver. Anything to help.

"Is there a timer? Something that will make this go off by itself if you don't?"

"I … I don't think so. Djimon said no, that it was very

important that it be done by my own hand. But he could have lied."

You think?

"Okay. Then at least his plan A is that you will set it off. And I am going to bet that he rightly believes that he has enough of your loyalty that you—all by yourself—were not going to sit here and try to sabotage him during the boarding process. So he has not protected against that. When are you supposed to set this thing off?"

Lola could feel Nwanyi's confusion and irritation lifting as it sunk in that she now had help. That now she maybe had a choice. Lola pushed her own rising sense of panic back into the corner from whence it was coming. Not now, she told herself. Please not now. Think clearly.

"We put the final pieces of it together in the bathroom before I boarded. And now I am going to set it off right as the plane lifts into the air. To the very second if possible that it tries to leave Nigerian soil."

"Okay. That is helpful. Except that you are not going to do that."

"Maybe not," Nwanyi agreed, like she was seriously considering the change in plans. "I do know how to undo some of what I did, and I don't think it goes off early if I do that."

"Okay, that is even more helpful. I'm going to guess then that Djimon has some sort of back-up, because he sounds like the kind of guy who would. Maybe there is something that will sense the acceleration of the plane and act if you don't? No, that could make it go off while still on the runway. Maybe there is some sort of pressure sensitive device which, if you fail to do what he told you to, is going to set it off at a certain altitude?"

Nwanyi gave her a very blank look.

"Umm, what I mean is that once the cabin doors are closed the air is held in tight, just like we are on the ground. At some point as we go up, the airplane makes the air thinner, more like we are up on top of a mountain. Djimon could have put something in that would sense the thinner air and make the bomb go off, because if it is sensing thinner air that means you didn't do what you were supposed to do. Is that something he might have done?"

"Maybe."

"Okay. Then you are going to have to tell me absolutely everything you know about this bomb so we can pretend to be fooling with your dress while we quickly and quietly disable everything we can before they change the pressure in the cabin after take off."

Nwanyi looked at her blankly. "Why don't you just get off the plane now instead?"

Lola bit her lip and actually considered, for a second, doing just that. Then she considered the idea of hearing nearly five hundred people die in her head while she went on to live, maybe for decades, remembering every day that she could likely have saved them all. Could she maybe get Nwanyi to get off of the plane with her? She doubted it. So although she thought of a dozen responses to Nwanyi's question, in the end the only one which came out was "My leaving isn't an option. So start talking to me." And she pulled out the little toenail clippers that always went through security with her.

There was a wire which ran along the inside of Nwanyi's left armpit and up her back into the head dress which clearly needed to be cut or disconnected. Cutting was going to be a lot more discrete, if only the little clippers could handle the job. Lola took Nwanyi's arm into her lap as she prepared to go to work on the lovely lavender clothing. A helpful cabin attendant had to be brushed away with assurances that Lola was only helping with a minor dress issue. Then Lola snipped open the seam of the sleeve and proceeded to squeeze the clippers as hard as she could around the wire, over and over. As she worked the clippers, it wore its way through the plastic coating and finally through the wire. Good. Their odds of surviving had just increased dramatically.

At that point the cabin doors were closed and the crew took their own seats for takeoff. Lola felt like she now had a little more freedom to maneuver without being questioned, so she asked Nwanyi to describe one more time what she had put on and what she had been told to do when. Between what Nwanyi had been forced to memorize and Lola's above-average understanding of mechanical devices born of helping her dad string wires and a career that relied on instrumentation, they managed to identify three more parts of the device which could benefit from being isolated. Lola felt Nwanyi wince as she had to reach up the girl's thigh to rip apart one connection, and she felt the girl shudder as she reached her clippers down into the back of her shirt and roughly started to squeeze them as hard as she could to cut another. What a shame she didn't have the time and privacy to make this easier. But she didn't. In the end Lola managed to tear or snip apart three more parts of the device before the plane, sitting at the end of a runway, was cleared for take off.

Lola hoped that they were crucial parts. It seemed like they were. She didn't actually know much about bombs, but this was a simple device and she did not believe it would still work after what she had done. But she was admittedly nervous and discovered that unfocused fear did nothing to help her telepathic abilities.

When she had boarded the plane, she had hoped by this point to be getting direct advice from someone who knew more about bombs, but the best she could muster now was feeling a vague sense of Maurice's concern from far away, and an even vaguer sense of worry from Olumiji. Jumoke was totally preoccupied with something else.

Somadina felt more clear, but she was busy looking out for Lola and Nwanyi by doing a mental search for Djimon, seeking out his odd soft-metal-in-your-mouth feel. Lola followed Somadina's thoughts and reasoning and agreed that Djimon was likely still at the airport, as he would want to stay to watch. Soon she too found his mind and felt it brimming with hope and plans and an astounding sense of self-importance. Lola had to shut it back out. She was sure that anger would be no better than fear at helping her focus better on the problems at hand.

She felt the plane turn onto the larger runway designated for takeoff and listened to the increased roar of the engines as the plane picked up speed and headed for flight. Instinctively, she reached over and held Nwanyi's hand, partially in shared fear that they had failed, partially out of some remaining glimmer of fear that the girl might still be able to set it off somehow, and might still be strangely compelled to do so. Their hands locked as the giant piece of metal lifted into the air, three-quarters of a million pounds soaring in apparent defiance of gravity, and in real and astounding proof of vector geometry and the concept of lift.

The plane rose, rose higher, rose higher still. Lola listened carefully for the sound of the air pressurization equipment, a trick she had learned so many years ago flying with three different babies, each of whom had hated the feel of cabin pressure changes in sensitive little ears. That sound, both during takeoff and landing, had meant time for wiggling a toy, time for a jiggle on the lap, and worst case, time for a teat in the mouth. Now the noise meant time to hold one's breath, time to hope that Alex would realize how damn much she loved him, time to hope her kids would lead fine lives. Time to hope she'd be able to tell them all that once again in person.

The engines droned on uneventfully, and, finally, Lola exhaled.

Nwanyi stared straight ahead and said nothing for a long time, and Lola used the time to try to calm herself down and think about what to do next. Her head was still killing her, and now that the adrenaline rush had passed she could feel the exhaustion from almost no sleep setting in as well. She tried to focus. The fact was that she had used both company funds and a lot of her own money to book a ridiculous flight and that she had, from her employer's point of view, clearly left where she needed to be before she was needed most. She was having trouble even imagining a story that could adequately explain such behavior. The truth didn't seem like much of an option.

"What are you going to do about the three men who are meeting us?" Nwanyi finally spoke.

"Three men?"

"I thought you knew."

Lola checked her watch. They would be landing in fewer than four hours. Great. This possibility had not even occurred to her, but it made sense that Djimon would have let Nwanyi know before leaving, in one more way, that defying him was not safe. The question was if he had been bluffing, or if the man really had the resources to have thugs standing by at the aircraft's destination in the unlikely event they needed to intercept a surprisingly defiant and clever Nwanyi. Lola decided that having thugs in place would make Djimon feel more in control and more important. If he could afford, it he would do it.

"Where did this guy get his money for all this, do you know?"

Nwanyi thought. "He and Mairo—that's his real wife—used to argue about money, and in the last couple of weeks they argued about it a lot. I think most wives would not be so bold. Not with him anyway. So I guessed that the money must have come from her family."

Okay, Lola thought. *I've financed a lot of this plan and it is costing way more than expected, and now my husband wants to send three people to London to ensure that my probably hated co-wife dies like she is supposed to. Do I spring for three plane tickets ahead of time? You know,* Lola thought, *I'm going to go with "yes."*

"What are you doing?" Nwanyi asked.

Lola was holding her head in her hands.

"Thinking," Lola said. In fact she was trying to concentrate, trying to search for help, but right now it was like trying to wiggle a half-frozen toe that she could not feel. She wished to hell that she wasn't so tired and that she had a better sense of what she was doing. And more practice doing it. Damn it. She tried to calm down and focus, but it was getting harder as this ordeal wore on.

Somadina! Olumiji! Anyone else! Listen to me, I've got a serious problem. I need some assistance here. She felt pretty certain that her words were all lost in the projection and that thanks to her frazzled and frantic state of mind the best she could hope for was a totally inelegant scream for help. But that might work too.

Somadina almost completely lost her sense of Lola as the plane headed into the clouds, but she hardly noticed as she allowed herself to savor Djimon's anger and frustration as he waited and waited for the long-anticipated flash of light. At one point the anger grew into sheer fury, as apparently he accepted that some back-up plan had failed as well. Somadina had the clear impression of him contacting another at that point, setting in motion a final fail-safe. She saw in his mind's eye Nwanyi exiting the plane into the arms of those who would make her pay dearly and Djimon's sad acceptance that that would be the best he could get.

    Somadina's head snapped up. She reached for the new cell phone and searched for someone to call. Damn Olumiji was still on the plane. Who else did she know who could help. She could text America. She had a number for Lola's phone but that was no use. Wait, she also had a number for Lola's x^0 contact, Maurice. How did one do another country again? *Wake up, wake up, and check your phone,* she thought to this Maurice as she fumbled several times with the typing and the numbers. This was too complicated to send by telepathy. Finally the message was legible enough and went through. Maurice almost instantaneously sent back an answer straight from his mind. He was awake. He had heard a cry for help from Lola. It had been vague and muffled, but he would get help. Maurice signed off by adding, *Everybody, just calm down.*

    It was just after five a.m. the first Monday morning of winter break, and Alex's alarm had just woken him up a few minutes ago. A teacher's day starts early, and he had forgotten to shut off the alarm now that school was out for two weeks. He was surprised to hear the phone ring, and picked up hoping that it might be Lola, indulging them both with a phone call to share good news about her well and maybe the even better news that she had a date and flight to come home. Instead it was an elderly male voice who described himself as a friend of Lola and her family. Lola was fine as far as he knew, but he had been contacted with an odd question from someone in her company, sort of, to which he really needed a quick and good answer.

    "Okay," Alex was groggy and cautious.

    "If an absolute stranger were to meet Lola coming off of an airplane, and he needed to be wearing, holding, doing, and/or saying something which would not only get her attention, but would let her know in a split second that he was on her side and there to help her, what would he need to do?"

"I do not want to know why you are asking such an absurd question, do I?"

"No," Maurice said softly, "you don't, young man. Just give me your best answer. A song? A costume? A lot of things will be competing for her attention and he needs her trust almost instantaneously."

Alex thought for a long minute. "I think I know what would work. Would your greeter be able to get to a sporting goods store?"

Lola convinced Nwanyi that the three-men problem had been handled. "How?"

"Your sister has some unusual abilities," Lola began reluctantly.

"Oh, that. She reads minds. Used to be really good at it as a little girl, my aunts said. Everybody blamed me for making it go away. I never meant to. But she can still do it some. And maybe she got better at it again after I left, because she sure kept talking to me in my head at Djimon's like she never did when we were little."

Right. Not as big a deal here. Okay.

"Well I do a little of that too. And Somadina and I have been in touch, and she is getting us help. I don't know how exactly, but I do trust her. And I trust these other people helping her. Now, why don't we get you out of this dress and into some clothes in which you can get some sleep."

Nwanyi crossed her hands and held on to the top of the bodice of the dress protectively.

"I'd rather keep it on."

"Good grief, why?"

She looked hurt. "It's pretty. It's the wedding dress I really wanted when I got married and he wouldn't let me have it. Then he finally told me, when he was done doing all the horrible things he had to do to me to get me to understand, that the only reason he would not let me have a lilac dress when we were married was so that I could have one instead for this very important occasion. He wanted me to have the most beautiful dress in the world for it. And isn't it?" She straightened up a little into a primping pose recognized the world over. Lola sighed. It was worth remembering that this was still a highly damaged, highly vulnerable teenage girl.

"The dress is absolutely gorgeous. Way too gorgeous to risk ruining in case we have to run away from these guys. Let me get you into some good running clothes, and we will put the very beautiful dress very safely into my big bag. It will be better for the dress, Nwanyi. You want to take care of it." And with that she risked the attention and irritation of those seated around her to get her bag out of the overhead compartment and produce a t-shirt which would be huge on Nwanyi and sweatpants with the best drawstring she had. Socks. Spare tennis shoes. Nwanyi got only a few odd looks as she returned from the restroom looking like a homeless person who had picked clothes out of a dumpster, with the giant hat and dress now bundled in her arms.

"Good. Give me the little pouch with your passport and stuff, and I need the beautiful hat as well. And the shoes. Very good." Lola secured Nwanyi's documents with her own, then took a few more things out of her own bag to make room as she crammed all the lilac material inside it and with a big friendly smile on her face headed with her bag to the restroom. Geez, the dress was heavy.

There, with the door firmly locked, she grabbed enough tissues to keep from leaving fingerprints, she hoped, and then she used the nail clippers to rip out every blessed suspicious wire and little plastic component which she could find. Much of the weight of the dress came from a thin bullet-deterrent vest that seemed to have been filled with sand, which she supposed was part of Nwanyi's "special protection."

She started next on the huge scarf-draped headdress which was where the actual explosives had been. She shook her head as she worked her way down to the pathetic thin plastic helmet which formed the basis of the hat. Another piece of "protection?" Finally, every odd and suspicious thing was crammed into the trash can. Lola would happily have added the dress itself, but there was no way it was going to fit, and besides, the whole upper-class cabin could link the dress to Nwanyi.

x⁰

When Lola got back to her seat she figured she had just over two hours now before they landed. She could not remember when her brain had last felt so fuzzy and so useless. She would let herself sleep for an hour or so, and wake up hopefully with enough strength to get the two of them to safety.

Lola awoke groggily at the unmistakable lurch of wheels hitting the runway. Damn. How had she slept for so long? She and Nwanyi were about to exit a plane and clear immigration and customs, she supposed. Surely Nwanyi's paperwork was all in order, or they would not have let her on board.

As they exited the plane, Lola saw the waiting bus. Damn again. This was Europe, and she had forgotten that one didn't always exit into the terminal. She kept a hand firmly on the dazed girl as the lurching bus crammed full of people took forever, then herded her through the terminal doors, up the escalators, and followed the purple signs. Non-EU. She pushed Nwanyi into the correct line, smiling protectively as she kept her arm around her. Traveling together. Sister-in-law by marriage? Complicated multi-national family. At least that was the story she was formulating as they made it easily past a customs' clerk who could not have been less inquisitive.

After successfully entering the U.K., they wound their way into the baggage claim area. Had she checked luggage as part of her subterfuge? Maybe, but come on, Lola, you aren't going to bother to claim her luggage.

She steered Nwanyi straight towards the nothing to declare exit, and found herself finally at the end of the secured area. Think, Lola told herself. When you walk through those doors you have got to be able to go straight to whomever is here to help you, if anyone. And you have got to avoid whomever Djimon has sent, and they may or may not look Nigerian. You're a telepath Lola. You can do this. Focus. Think like a telepath.

But as she stepped through the doors and saw the holiday mass of people packed behind the usually unoccupied silver rail, her aching head was bombarded by the intense emotions of longing, irritation, love, joy, fear—the surge of human feelings which occur when people see other people whom they have not seen for awhile and for whom they have strong feelings. Lola realized that the greeting area of a busy major airport was a nightmare place for a beginner telepath like herself. She froze in the doorway.

And then she saw him. A tall, faintly Scottish-looking man in maybe his fifties or sixties, holding a white canoe paddle with a yellow top. Just like hers. And as she took the final step through the doors he hissed loudly, "Grab the paddle." She shoved Nwanyi under the silver rail straight into his arms and followed, and they exchanged a second of mental understanding as he engulfed both her and Nwanyi in a convincing welcome home hug.

"Keep an arm around me tight, keep your gaze down, and keep moving with me and do so very quickly," he said softly as he gently pushed them through the arrivals crowd and toward the departure area of the ground floor of the terminal building, all while nodding and smiling like a dad listening to his happy family's stories. The man moved fast.

"What are you doing with us?" Lola asked.

"Getting you on your next flight," he said, waggling two boarding passes in one of his hands. "At Heathrow, if you don't have luggage then you can check in online, which you've done, and just show your passport at the gate. Keep moving."

And with that Lola finally saw the three men. Two looked Nigerian, the older third one looked more like he was North African, and all three were eyeing them suspiciously from clear across the ground floor of the terminal. "They just made us," her new fake husband chuckled as he herded them onto the escalator up to the first floor. "We got a nice head start. Good job ladies. Let's walk as we ride. That's it. Keep moving."

The men had made their decision and were now running towards the escalator themselves. "Faster." Somehow Nwanyi had ended up holding the paddle as the man had produced the boarding passes, and now she held on to it tightly.

"Where are we going?"

"To security. Your flight leaves in just over an hour. Another friend worked this all out, including her visa which, trust me, was no small feat, but fortunately my friend has very good contacts, and Nwanyi had a visa for Great Britain already and that helped. You see, you two have had a family emergency and everyone has been so extremely helpful."

"Wait. You are talking about Nwanyi's visa? We're not going back to Nigeria?"

"Are you nuts?" he said. "People there are trying to kill you. We're just trying to figure out a way here to keep you two safe until somebody who knows more about what is going on gets a better plan. Let's be honest. I'm not equipped to protect you guys, and frankly I couldn't think of a safer place to put you than on a twenty-three hour flight."

"Twenty-three hours?"

"That's right. All the way to New Zealand. It's a lovely, long flight. By way of Singapore. And be sure and spend your entire layover in Singapore in the very secure first class lounge. You'll be fine. Oh, also stop on the other side of security here and get a copy of *The Daily Telegraph* at the first stand on your left. Take the purse the lady says you left behind. It will have some items to help you." He never stopped talking as he hurried them towards the security line. "We are just damn lucky these clowns behind us were looking for an elegant woman in full wedding attire, and not a couple of older white folks with their adopted daughter in sweat clothes, huh?

"Nwanyi, I've just stuck your visa in your passport. And Lola, when you finally do get home thank your husband for his fine suggestion about the canoe paddle. Made it all so much easier. And here you two go." He virtually pushed them into the podium of the lady checking paperwork for the security line as the three men came up behind them.

"Goodbye honey. Have a good trip, pumpkin."

Lola and Nwanyi rounded the paperwork-checking woman's podium just as the men got there. Lola winced when the lady waved them on with a loud "Have a nice time in New Zealand."

"We need to talk to those two women," the smaller and older of the three men declared brusquely to the woman checking paperwork. Lola could feel his determination, fueled largely by his own fear of the consequences of failing to carry out Djimon's orders.

"No sir," she put her arm out to stop them. "No one passes this point without a valid boarding pass." Then she hesitated. "Madam? Do you need to talk to these guys?" she yelled to Lola, who was now quickly pushing Nwanyi down the cordoned pathway towards the x-ray machines.

"Good grief, no," Lola yelled back truthfully over her shoulder as she kept walking. "I've never seen them before in my life."

When one of the men started to push by the security lady impatiently, she blocked his path by stepping out from her podium. Taser in hand she declared in a surprisingly loud voice, "Need backup. Now." Immediately, four assorted armed security personnel began moving quickly toward the podium from four different directions, and the men backed off quickly with apologies. Lola just kept moving, pushing Nwanyi ahead, thinking of all the many times she had cursed airport security. Go figure. It turned out that if one was running from someone nasty, there was probably no safer place to be in the world than clearing the security line at a major international airport.

"Love you girls. Call me when you get there!" The helpful man's voice boomed across the distance towards them.

Nice touch, Lola thought. *Thank you dear.* She felt his amused appreciation in her head.

But it was dazed and confused Nwanyi who had the presence of mind to turn around and yell back, "Thanks dad. We love you too!"

Lola absolutely did not want to go to New Zealand. But even more than that she did not want to miss her plane and then have to leave the secured part of the airport and try to figure out what else to do instead. So she did as instructed, and grabbed a quick copy of *The Daily Telegraph* at the newsstand on the left and was a little startled when the sales clerk actually did call to her as she turned to go.

"I, I think you left this miss." The girl offered a small brown ladies handbag out to her.

"Thanks, yes." She slipped her own purse onto Nwanyi's shoulder and took the new bag. "Thanks so very much."

She allowed herself to slow down enough to look inside while they walked. There was a wallet containing quite a few New Zealand twenty-dollar bills. Wow. She had been considering just staying put in Singapore, but decided against that option completely when she also found the little disposable cell phone bearing the logo of Vodaphone New Zealand. These folks were really looking out for her.

She dug further into the purse. More ibuprofen and lots of aspirin. Headaches must be a well-known part of this gig, she thought. And then at the bottom of the purse was the item that made her heart stop. Oh my. She knew this one. A little Beretta Bobcat. Her gun collecting and gun-loving father had bought her one for protection years ago, and the two of them had spent hours getting her familiar with the gun. As a girl she had shot rocks and tin cans with whatever her father gave her, like most kids did who grew up where she had, but this particular model had been his gift to her as a young woman, and he had wanted her to know it thoroughly. She'd kept it locked away for years now as Alex did not share her ease with guns, and he'd had little trouble convincing her that a house with teenagers and their friends was not a good environment for firearms. But still, she knew this gun, and though she had not touched a handgun in years, it was a comfort in her hand. Who was this guy who had met her anyway? Some sort of super-spy?

She felt a chuckle and saw her helper whose name she did not even know working on a pile of tax returns. He was a tax accountant? She felt a surge of gratitude for her unknown benefactor, and in return she felt a soft feeling of *You're welcome*, and *Be safe*. She had a reassuring image of him heading over to say hello to an old friend who worked in airport security, and Lola had the distinct impression that his visit with his friend would last at least until the man was very sure that he could leave Heathrow safely himself. As a final gift, she heard him softly singing the words to her favorite Bob Marley song ever, "*Three little Birds*".

Nwanyi, who had been walking quietly, stopped and gave Lola a funny look. Lola realized with surprise that she had been so grateful to hear those lyrics assuring her that everything would be well that she hadn't noticed that tears had started to run down her own cheeks.

The boarding of their flight was called almost right after they entered the secured area of shops and restaurants, so Lola herded Nwanyi on toward the gate. They were producing their paper work once again when Lola turned around and saw that Djimon's three men were coming in through the security area, once again with the smaller, older man in the lead.

She wondered with a surge of panic if were these guys now on the flight to Auckland with them. Wait. There were no direct flights. Even though the men unfortunately knew her final destination, they couldn't have known by which route. Maybe they were going home to Lagos? Already? No, Lola decided that it was more likely that they had just bought any old ticket to get through security. That made more sense. Well, at least by choosing to stick together, none of three would be bothering the man who had helped her and Nwanyi.

It took the men a moment to locate her, and Lola could feel clearly now how that was all that they were after. Of course. They just wanted to see what particular flight Nwanyi was on. She saw one man pick up a cell phone and start dialing, and had to wonder if Djimon could possibly get new helpers of his to somewhere as far away as either the Singapore or the Auckland airport.

Djimon forced his fury inward as he disconnected the call from his fellow rebuilders in London. This was a time for thinking clearly. The girl had boarded a plane for Singapore, but his men had definitely heard a final New Zealand destination from one of the airport people. So what security force from New Zealand had sent this mystery woman after Nwanyi, and why? How the hell were the Kiwis involved with internal Nigerian affairs anyway? And who was the man who had met them in London? Nwanyi's entire escape smacked of a plan more carefully thought-out and practiced than his own. How was that even possible?

Djimon went directly to an internet kiosk and began to search for ways to get from Lagos to Auckland. If you wanted something done right you absolutely had to do it yourself. Yes, there was in fact a flight that left Lagos in about an hour and a half. He could possibly still get on it. He would layover briefly in Dubai. That was good, he had some contacts in Dubai. If all went well he would arrive in Auckland thirty-five minutes ahead of the one flight arriving that morning from Singapore.

Of course, Djimon himself could not obtain permission to leave Nigeria. But years ago Djimon had come by an altered British passport with his own photo, and it had still not expired. That morning, he had taken it out of his top drawer and put it with his wallet the way another might have added extra money tucked away for an emergency. Admittedly, the fake document might no longer pass deep scrutiny, but it would at least get him on-board an aircraft. He just might not be able to come back. Which at the moment didn't matter so much to him, as he did not particularly have much to come back to. On the other hand, he could not wait to see Nwanyi's face as she walked off of the plane in Auckland and saw him waiting for her in person.

Lola had been surprised to find herself and Nwanyi booked not in business class, but in the even more ridiculous first class section. She had to admit that it made the idea of the two very long flights more palatable, and the friendliness with which the cabin steward gently took the canoe paddle from Nwanyi, promising to keep it safe and return it as soon as the plane landed, made her realize that the quieter surroundings and more courteous and lenient treatment might have been more necessary for Nwanyi than Lola had realized. Lola passed on the alcoholic beverage but sipped on some juice. This first leg was just short of thirteen hours. She really should try to get some more sleep. Nwanyi had her eyes closed already.

Lola couldn't help cringing a little the very second the plane lifted off the ground, remembering the tenseness of her last takeoff.

Then she curled up in her seat to rest and looked over at Nwanyi. My goodness. She was still more child than woman. Sixteen years old, uneducated and naive. What sort of chance had she ever had in this situation? Lola could hear her whimpering softly.

As Lola started to doze off herself, a link between them began to form in that involuntary way that it tended to do. As the link became stronger, Lola began to see and to feel the memories which Nwanyi herself was reliving as she lay curled up falling asleep.

Lola got flashes of the beatings, the fear, the insults, and the intimidation. She felt the complete lack of freedom and self-respect. She tasted bad food, breathed bad air, strained in bad light, knew a world in which no kind word was allowed. She felt being naked. Being hurt. Being taunted with treats she could not have. Being forced to say things she did not mean. Being forced into sexual poses, embarrassing and without affection. Being forced to declare her own lack of self-worth over and over in order to lessen physical punishment. The creativity and the cruelty were amazing in their depth and breadth.

Lola could see Djimon consulting a notebook in which he had apparently designed and outlined his techniques. Occasionally he would make her select a random number and then inflict the indignities described on the particular page she had picked, taunting her that she had asked for that treatment herself. One day she was forced to clean between his toes with her tongue. On yet another he made her crawl and fetch sticks in her mouth for him to beat her with, as though she were a dog. And all of this was designed, in his mind, to break her will so that she would become his devoted disciple.

During the first thirteen-hour flight, Lola thought she must have relived most of Nwanyi's ten months or so in captivity as Nwanyi lay with her eyes closed and relived them herself. Lola certainly didn't sleep on the flight, and she felt like throwing up for much of it. In the end she understood in a way she never could have before. She understood the horribly damaging man who honestly believed that his cause was so righteous that it justified every deed he had done. She understood how this man, in the end, had come to enjoy and even crave the role he had selected. And she felt the pain of the horribly damaged girl who had managed to hang on to a shred of herself in spite of it all.

It was only near the last part of it that she realized Somadina was involved in the link as well. The overwhelmed big sister had also seen, heard, and felt all the horrors Nwanyi had been unable to show her when they were actually occurring. Lola was so sorry. She tried to send sympathy, but a sad Somadina just brushed her away with a feeling that it was better that she knew. And that she needed to be alone for awhile please.

Mercifully, Nwanyi finally fell asleep a few hours before landing, and as the link dissolved, Lola swallowed two of the thoughtfully provided aspirin. She reached out for her own family and for any information from Maurice or Olumiji or Jumoke, but felt nothing at all from anyone. She realized she was much too tired to function, and sank into an utterly exhausted fitful sleep herself.

Thanks to having to divert around a series of thunderstorms near Singapore, they landed much later than scheduled and had no time to visit Singapore's opulent first class lounge. Lola was disappointed. She had wanted to stretch her legs and to experience the luxury, but more importantly she had been hoping that the lounge might be holding a friendly message for her from anyone in x^0, and might provide her with a chance to contact her own family in Texas. But there was simply no time for any of that. So she reluctantly boarded the second flight and ate, dozed, and watched bad television reruns until they arrived in Auckland Wednesday morning, only a few minutes late.

As they exited the second aircraft, yet another thoughtful steward placed the canoe paddle back in Nwanyi's hands. She tightened her grasp on it immediately.

"You're okay," Lola whispered, almost amused. "He is a continent away and he cannot hurt you. We have good people helping us. There is no danger. We are going to be fine."

Her fingers went to the little Beretta in her purse. She had checked it while in the bathroom, and yes, it had a fully loaded eight round magazine of .25 caliber cartridges. She did not know what to expect once they got out of security, but she was truly hoping to be met by friends. If, however, she was only met by foes then the little Beretta would be ready. And in the less dramatic but far more likely event that neither friend nor foe were there, then she'd use the cash instead to get to a safe hotel and start making calls on the phone. But first, of course, she had to get them through immigration.

She guided Nwanyi off of the plane, but as they approached the end of the walkway leading into the airport itself, Nwanyi suddenly stopped walking and froze. Lola could clearly feel the girl's sudden spike of fear, feel her revulsion and her sheer disbelief. A baffled Lola was ready to physically push Nwanyi forward into the gate area when she felt the metal in her mouth. Lola looked beyond Nwanyi and experienced a second of absolute panic. A slightly built but well-muscled, very dark-skinned, thirty-something man was there waiting, smiling an odd smile of victory and walking toward them. Lola could not imagine how the man had managed it, but she was certain he was Djimon.

"After I got off of my plane, I decided to wait for my dearest wife before clearing immigration. Welcome to New Zealand, Nwanyi."

Then to Lola, with no trace of a smile at all, "And who the hell are you?"

She answered without thinking. "A woman who has a gun pointed right at you through this very flimsy purse. Step away from us."

"I don't think so. You see Nwanyi and I are both committed to rebuilding our nation, which is none of your concern. She has lost her way a bit. That can be fixed. I however, am quite sure about the path I am on, and that path oddly enough includes the gun in my pocket acquired in Dubai and pointed at you. I am very sure I can fire it if I see your hand move. Therefore, you will let Nwanyi and I leave together. Now."

Lola willed her mind to work. Indeed. This asshole had a Glock 21and she could feel his joy at possessing it. People in his network apparently had contacts too. Now what? She looked straight into his eyes.

    Lola had killed a lot of fish. Thousands of insects. A few pheasants. She had never taken a human life or even had to seriously consider doing so. She recognized that others had done so for her, indirectly at least, as soldiers and police who had kept her safe from the likes of the man she was facing. Yet she also recognized that the taking of another life was often an unnecessary extreme, born of fear, born of conflicts fought for politics and money, or born simply out of a lack of information about the true nature and intentions of the person who was being killed. It was seldom necessary, and almost never heroic. The circumstances under which she would choose to look a person in the eye standing three feet away from her, and willfully and with full knowledge end his or her life, almost did not exist. Almost.

    Lola realized she was now in exactly that position. This scumbag would not hesitate to kill her, kill Nwanyi, kill numerous strangers, wreak havoc on the world, and be cruel while doing so if it would advance a cause he fully believed in. Thanks to the way her mind worked and the events of the last twenty hours, she knew exactly what sorts of awful things he was capable of. In fact, thanks to the way her mind worked, she felt certain that she would have known if hidden beneath the bravado and certainty there was doubt, hesitation, or more importantly any form of human decency trying to emerge. She looked hard for it now, so there would be no misunderstanding. She found nothing, and found no other reasonable choice.

    He could and would take Nwanyi and kill her horribly. Meanwhile, he was prepared to put a bullet in her own heart. Lola gently adjusted her grip on her Beretta, and, with her eyes locked on the man's, considered exactly where to aim on his body. Could she manage to incapacitate thoroughly but not kill? Should she take that chance?

    And why hadn't he just fired at her already? Of course. Passengers were still filing off of the plane behind them, preoccupied with their own travels, but surely they would have security all over them as soon as a shot was fired. And Djimon's main goal was to get out of the airport safely with Nwanyi in tow. He was fixated on getting his revenge from her, not Lola. So Lola aimed low into his stomach, with full intent to end this standoff and deal with the consequences.

So concentrated was she on her decision, and he on maintaining his bluff that he could shoot before she did, that neither saw Nwanyi take a step back and quietly move her hands down to the canoe paddle's base. Lola held her fire, for she felt Nwanyi's intent, and that knowledge was enough to cause her to pause. In that second, Nwanyi twisted back and swung the paddle like a baseball bat at the side of Djimon's face, with all the force she could muster. Lola felt the anger which powered Nwanyi's coiled energy and could hear the crack of cartilage, maybe bone, as he crumpled forward. Nwanyi swung a second time across the back of his head, and he fell completely to the ground.

"No, you bastard." It came out of Nwanyi's mouth in a harsh whisper. "You have no idea how very much YOU have cost ME!" And she spat on the side of his face as he lay crumpled on the floor. Lola wondered if he was dead.

As Lola had guessed, it took only seconds for Auckland International Airport's finest to be at the scene. Lola was quick to point out that Djimon had attacked first. Had a gun in his hand, please look for yourselves. They were just trying to defend themselves. She was relieved for her and Nwanyi's sake when medics determined that he was unconscious but alive.

Lola identified herself as part of a rescue organization—that wasn't too far from the truth—one that rescued abused women worldwide. She was improvising a little. It was based on an internet site. That part was kind of true, but the airport security people looked a little more dubious.

"So you find battered women on the internet and bring them to New Zealand?"

Lola decided to try a different tact and pointed out that she had to pee very badly. That fact was totally true. This horrible man had met them coming right off the plane. Please? A younger lady security officer with her thick, dark hair pulled back into a tight ponytail and a name badge which identified her as Mary Turner shrugged and walked Lola to the nearest ladies room, which she entered with dramatic relief. She could feel the young woman's slight suspicion and was afraid that she might have been guilty of a bit of overacting.

In the stall by herself, she carefully wiped the tiny gun for prints. Now what? It certainly wouldn't flush down the toilet. Lola wrapped it thoroughly in toilet paper so it would resemble in size and appearance, if not in weight, the object it was now supposed to be. Then, covering her own hands in toilet paper as best she could, she placed it at the very bottom of the receptacle for used sanitary pads.

Leaving the restroom the woman shook her head as Lola thanked her, and they rejoined the group which by now was moving to an office for further questioning. Lola and Nwanyi were searched. Their bags were searched. Their passports were checked. All was right. Djimon, however, had a fake passport, two illegal weapons, including a knife, in his bag, and he had regained consciousness cursing and threatening to kill Nwanyi. Which had been helpful.

Security apparently had planned on bringing Nwanyi to the police to be booked for assault, but something about her thin, sad face and angry, fearful eyes must have rung true with the story, so they hesitated. What had the women's plans been exactly once they got there, the security folks wanted to know. Lola had seen that her benefactors had left her with two open-ended tickets back to Lagos, so she volunteered that the women had been hoping to just stay safely for a week or so while authorities back in Nigeria handled the violent husband and his, uh, violent network of friends. This got a raised eyebrow.

"But now that we have him, there is no reason for you to stay here?" Mary asked hopefully.

Lola nodded.

"In that case, instead of all the complications for everyone, how about we just put you on the very next plane back to Lagos?" one of the men offered. "This man will be booked on charges involving his passport and weapons so that way you will not be needed for testifying, and we will consider the little incident between you two a personal matter, as I am sure he can be persuaded not to press charges."

They were going to spend twenty-three more hours in the air now?? Lola felt a little nauseous at the thought. But it clearly seemed like their best alternative. "You won't even have to pay New Zealand's twenty-five dollar departure charge that way," Mary said brightly. "You'll be back home in a day and fifty dollars richer." Oh boy.

So they were back in yet another boarding area about to get on the plane. Lola used the little disposable phone which worked only in New Zealand to quick text Teddie and asked her to please tell her dad that mom was okay and it was a long story and she would call soon. She was so sorry she had not been able to contact them earlier. She was just finishing the text when Mary walked up.

"I just wanted to let you know that I did find a small weapon with no prints on it in the ladies room. In the feminine hygiene receptacle in the stall you used. You wouldn't know anything about that would you?"

"Absolutely not," Lola said. "I wouldn't dream of putting my hand into one of those in a public restroom."

"That's what I thought you'd say," Mary said. "Be smart point forward, okay?"

"Absolutely," Lola agreed. "You have no idea how smart and careful I intend to be once I get back home." The lady smiled and Lola could feel her clear relief at Lola and Nwanyi's departure.

Nwanyi had said almost nothing since she had smacked Djimon. Lola felt Nwanyi holding her feelings in tightly. It wasn't until they were walking on the plane that she asked, "Am I really going home?"

"You are. You are absolutely going home."

She was quiet. Then, after they took their seats, "Hitting him like that did not begin to make up for all the things that he did to me."

"No," Lola replied thoughtfully, "I do not suppose that it would."

Then she felt just a hint of a smile, even though it did not show on Nwanyi's face, as the girl added, "But it helped."

With that Nwanyi put her head on Lola's shoulder, and as the plane took off, Nwanyi drifted asleep. Lola felt Somadina sigh in relief. *Thank you. Thank you, friend. Thank you so much.* She felt Somadina's joy and gratitude.

Lola brushed away the solicitous flight attendant determined to give her a beverage, and closed her own eyes. She slept more soundly for the next nine hours than she felt like she had slept in almost a year.

Lola and Nwanyi were met at the Lagos airport by a friendly foursome. Jumoke looked just plain relieved to see them alive. A man almost identical to Jumoke in appearance, but with a very different feel to his mind, hugged her warmly. Lola felt the clear message of welcome from him, and realized that she was being welcomed into more than Nigeria. In the background was another, younger Nigerian man with a warm, friendly feel to him as well, but he felt out of place in his village clothes, and he was just trying to stay out of the way. Azuka.

At the front of the group was a tall, stunningly beautiful young woman with high cheekbones in a heart shaped face with large clear eyes and a sense of inner strength. Lola could feel the woman's power as she engulfed Nwanyi in a hug. The two held each other, and laughed, and finally cried.

Awkward with all the emotion, Jumoke turned to Lola. "You have a nice little discovery to map in detail when you get back to your workstation in Houston." She felt his pride and happiness at the news. "That deep sand came in about forty feet thick, eighty feet high to your prognosis, and filled with oil. It's not going to be huge, but it's a nice addition to the portfolio. The folks back in Houston are very happy."

At that point, Somadina turned her attention to Lola. She did not have to say a word. Lola knew what she felt. Somadina knew Lola knew. The two women simply hugged, and they both understood.

"I am proud and happy to call you my friend," Somadina finally said aloud.

"And I, you."

"And we have Olumiji and his group to be very thankful to," Somadina added.

Lola turned to Jumoke's near look-alike. "I don't have any idea how you managed all you did. What was with the canoe paddle?"

Olumiji chuckled. "Maurice got a little helpful information from your husband. You probably will have a few questions to answer when you get home."

Oh, yes. She would have quite a few.

"How am I going to pay you guys back for plane tickets? The gun? This mess has cost a fortune."

Olumiji shook his head. "We are lucky enough to have some means put aside for the emergencies in which we occasionally find ourselves. Tom did a great job at Heathrow, didn't he?"

Tom. So that was the man's name. Lola caught a faint whiff of Tom's acknowledgement. "Indeed he did."

"And," Olumiji continued, "my reluctant but wonderful brother here played no small part in this as well." Olumiji gave Jumoke a long look. "He knows how very grateful I am."

"Thanks Jumoke. I don't know what you told the folks in the office, but I really really appreciate however you handled it. Have I been fired?"

Jumoke laughed. "Not yet. You've had the worst little bout of flu I've seen in awhile for the last three days. Could not leave your hotel room, poor dear. I've been bringing you medicine and fluids, but for the last twenty-four hours the company has been insisting I get you to a doctor, and I began to think that if I didn't comply they were going to fire me."

"So I am going to a doctor now?"

"No," and she could feel sadness and reluctance from Somadina, Olumiji, and Jumoke. "I've convinced them to send you home instead, where you can get to your own doctor and recuperate in comfort. It was my only choice Lola. You leave in just over an hour." Jumoke handed her the travel bag and her computer that she had left in her hotel room days ago.

"What? I am absolutely not getting on another plane." But she could tell by looking at all three of them that she was.

The goodbyes were mostly filled with promises to keep in touch. From Somadina came the promise to text often, with emotions attached. "I've so much more to tell you, and there is so much about you that I want to know."

"We'll always be in contact," Lola said, knowing that it was true.

From Olumiji came concern, appreciation, and hope. "You have so much to learn, and this whole incident has catapulted you into an almost dangerous level of ability. It doesn't go away once you have it. We will be there to help in any way we can, in any way you want us to. Maurice is planning on getting together with you as soon as you're rested and ready. Maybe right after the holidays?"

"That would be good," Lola said and felt a touch of warm agreement from Maurice. "I'll call him on the phone when I feel ready."

"Oh, and Lola?" This was from a smiling Jumoke. "Merry Christmas. You might have understandably lost track of time the last few days, but this happens to be Christmas Eve here in Nigeria." Lola looked around in surprise, her eye catching the shiny red balls hanging on a fake tree. She noticed for the first time how the airport was less frantic and full, and remembered how driven she had been just a week ago to get home. Oh my. "You'll be in London Christmas morning, and thanks to gaining six hours, you'll be in Houston early afternoon, in time for a nice holiday meal with your family."

As she turned to walk back through airport security one more time, the emotions from them all overwhelmed her to the point of dizziness and nausea. Too much frosting. She felt herself put up a fuzzy, semi-permeable sort of wall in response, made up of some kind of hippie beads. Shiny glass red ones that she liked. She felt Olumiji's approval. *There you go. That's the way. You're going to figure this out.*

She walked onto the plane seeing the glistening red beads in her mind and thought, *Yes. I am.*

After
Chapter 16. January 2010

    Christmas afternoon, Lola's family had met her at the airport with hugs and Santa hats, and Ariel had placed all the ingredients for Lola's four layer dip on the kitchen counter waiting for her. Lola was so happy to just spend the next several days surrounded by the people in the world who brought her the most joy of all. The kids had been told she had been delayed by a serious bout with the flu, but Alex looked at her quizzically knowing there was more to the story. Fortunately he was a patient man, willing to let the traditional festivities unfold while he waited for a better time to get his answers.

    The holidays made for an unexpectedly nice buffer in the office as well. Many folks were out for numerous days, trying to use up their vacation time before the end of the year. By January, when everyone was actually back, no one was really sure where she'd been or when. But they all knew that the well had been good, and luckily that became the focus of everyone's interest point forward.

    Zane was home for only a few days, but he managed to reassure his parents in person that his September earthquake experience had left him better off, with new friends and certain amount of satisfaction that he had been able to help with the rescue efforts. And now that he was assigned to the group that was planning this conference in the South Pacific, he would get to attend the conference himself at the end of January. Alex had laughed that an opportunity like that would lift any worker's morale. Lola was just glad to see her son with a temporary sense of purpose, even if for now that purpose was just putting up with his job so that he could go on a great boondoggle.

    Ariel got to be home for another week before she headed back to college, and she and Lola just took the time to have some fun together while Teddie and Alex got back into their school routine. Finally, after Ariel left too, Lola faced her situation.

    She began to use late nights to research, to practice, and to learn more about her peculiar new skill. It was time she had generally spent tossing and turning anyway. But now, instead of worrying, she grew. Her seismic interpretation software, designed to deal with masses of data, some of which was significant to solving a particular problem and most of which was not, gave the capacity to the user to design and apply a lot of filters. Lola found that the concept worked equally well for telepathy.

She also found that her new network of friends could be helpful and supportive, but not intrusive. Maurice had been right when he told her that while most telepaths appeared outwardly to be social and were generally well-liked, in fact most were loners at heart who highly valued their privacy and craved time alone. She was sure it was a reaction to the bombardment of information they had all received from others before each had learned to control and filter the input.

She realized that she had been secretly afraid that her touch with Maurice, Somadina, and even Jumoke and Olumiji would prove to be exhausting and ultimately leave her longing for relief, like the sound of a waterfall one could not shut off even once one has grown tired of it. Instead she was delighted to discover that both Maurice and Olumiji had a deft, gentle way of not being there except by mutual consent. Somadina, fortunately, was quickly learning the same skill. Even Jumoke was letting Olumiji teach him, just a little, how to control his abilities, and he was doing it partially out of respect and affection for Lola, now that the two of them had forged such a strong bond. Lola appreciated the pride that had cost him.

Over the next few weeks, others introduced themselves, slowly and unobtrusively, only as she was available and interested. She came to learn that it was a high-end telepath who could find and communicate with a perfect stranger, even when a mutual friend had provided guideposts so that she could be found. Those who came gently knocking on the door to her mind were respectful and curious, and represented the most powerful and evolved that x^0 had to offer.

Lola slowly allowed herself to make some new acquaintances. Using the website, she was able to find them in "real life," so to speak, and to communicate the sort of concrete information like an email address which eluded even the most adept at telepathy. Thus the technology aided the telepathy, making communication work in a way it never could have in the past. Once the technology was used to communicate, feeling flowed with the emotionless words on the screen, making the technology far more effective than it ever could be alone. Lola was starting to come down firmly on the side of those who believed that these two tools were meant to work hand in hand.

And using both, she learned. For indeed x^0 was an organization of philosophers as well as telepaths, many of whom loved nothing more than a heated friendly discussion and dissection of beliefs, the nature of which Lola had never experienced. In Lola's life, people had gotten so incredibly offended and defensive when their own beliefs, or lack of beliefs, had been scrutinized. But here, the faithful of every religion Lola had ever heard of, and many she had not, were all represented in the many ongoing spirited chats. Lola shared ideas and feelings with the agnostic, and with the rather large group of telepaths who were devotedly atheist, a group that included Tom, her helper from Heathrow Airport,

Of course there were many who found themselves still searching as they dealt with their current apathy about organized religion, and Lola supposed she belonged to that latter group. But in all the lively exchanges, she found kindred spirits of all sorts. These were open-minded, loving people who were genuinely curious about each other, how the universe worked, and how the human mind and spirit functioned within it. All were aware of x^0's belief in a single human, and there were enough kindly jokes related to it to let Lola know that x^0's core philosophy was also no sacred cow. But all of the participants clearly considered the possibility of someday being each other in their minds. It guided their actions. Lola could not help but think that was part of the reason that no one ever pushed or proselytized or even insisted they were right. Curiosity and respect. Lola knew that she had a found a home.

Lola was also able to get some specific information on the aftermath of Djimon's arrest. The New Zealand authorities had booked him but had been unable to determine his real identity until a Nigerian boy named Udo had managed to locate a Lagos man named Djimon in an extensive search involving his first name, his approximate age, his make and model of car, and his Fulani heritage. The boy had come forth with information that the man had kidnapped his half-sister and that another half-sister believed that he had fled with his captive to New Zealand. Nigerian authorities were looking into the kidnapping matter, but, meanwhile, had established that this was the man already being held in New Zealand, and that the captive woman herself had escaped him and returned home. Nigeria was just fine with Djimon being held elsewhere.

 Somadina speculated somewhat sadly that the kidnapping charges would not be able to be pursued, as Nwanyi had been legally a wife. Therefore Djimon had been within his rights to confine her to his home as he saw fit. Lola suggested prosecution for assault instead, but had to be told that in Nigeria a man could legally beat his wife all he wished as long as there was no permanent physical damage. Lola swallowed hard, feeling Somadina's white hot anger that everything Djimon had done to Nwanyi was perfectly legal. Morally reprehensible to reasonable people of any nation, but still legal.

 Meanwhile a gardener in Lagos named Ibrahim had become concerned when his employer and his employer's possibly ill second wife disappeared from the household a few days before Christmas, causing great distress to both the first wife and to their circle of friends. Ibrahim claimed to have been suddenly dismissed by the confused and tearful first wife, who then left for Northern Nigeria, along with her children.

 This man Ibrahim was concerned enough about some of the things he had witnessed, he said, to have quietly kept his key and returned a few days after Christmas, at which point he had found all sorts of incriminating items and writings in his boss's private study. He had dutifully contacted authorities. After the holidays settled down it was determined that the missing man was the same Djimon who had already been charged with kidnapping and who oddly enough also was being held in New Zealand on charges involving weapons and a forged passport. Authorities were working to sort out the details when Djimon's house burnt to the ground.

 Somadina felt that the dismissed gardener's testimony alone

would never be enough for any sort of charges to be made, and after the fire she feared for the man's safety. He must have feared for his own safety as well, for the last report was that he and his family had left Lagos and returned to his father's house somewhere in Northern Nigeria. Olumiji was monitoring the situation, he said, and stood ready to provide aid to Ibrahim if needed. He promised to keep those in x^0 who had an interest in the outcome fully informed.

Nwanyi was unreachable to Lola, and Somadina explained in their frequent contact that her sister was having a difficult time. A lot of damage had been done to one already not strong, and on any given day Nwanyi went from anger to fear to hostility to occasional hope. But instead of feeling the gratitude Lola might have expected, Somadina was embarrassed to tell Lola that Nwanyi sometimes held Lola to blame for robbing her of her chance for greatness. Not sensible, Somadina was quick to point out, but Nwanyi had a ways to go before she could be considered stable and sensible. Somadina was hoping Nwanyi would get there someday.

Somadina, on the other hand, was doing great. Yes, she occasionally got annoyed with Azuka and with the concept that she herself had chosen to be his, to be anyone's, wife. And then she'd remember that she loved him. And he loved her. And the wife thing was just a nuisance she had to put up with. And then she felt better.

The upside was that his parents seemed to be warming to her. Also, she and Azuka were hoping for a second child soon. A little girl would be nice. Lola got the giggled impression that Somadina was quite enjoying the process of trying to make this daughter. Sexual pleasure seemed to be a new thing in the relationship.

Yes, of course it is normal for the woman to enjoy it, Lola assured her. *Yes, even that much.* Lola agreed that it was odd that women weren't usually more forthcoming with each other about how much enjoyment was involved in good sex. Yes, it was true that it would have been nice if someone had told Somadina it could feel so incredibly wonderful. Lola had to giggle a little herself.

Udo was doing exceedingly well in school, even though his half-brother Obialo was not, and therefore might be returning to the village school instead next year. Ikenna had been very proud of his second son's role in finding Djimon, and in his own mind that had justified his choices to anyone who might question them. Thus Ikenna and Somadina were speaking, and though the relationship remained strained, Somadina was working to improve it. Nwanyi, however, avoided her father, and he had yet to make much of an effort to spend time with her. Maybe, over years, this would improve.

    Somadina's other piece of good news was that the Dibia had indeed chosen to take her under their wing, and, adjusting to new times and changing beliefs (they said), they were willing to modernize somewhat and provide her with some of their training. In return, of course, they expected to receive both monetary benefits from her fortune-telling business, which they would fully support, and also to receive occasional assistance from the unique set of gifts with which the spirits had blessed her. Which was to say that they expected her to sometimes read minds for them.

    Somadina was a bit uneasy with this latter requirement, but she was also hopeful that she could control the situation. After all, only she knew what she could really do, and the Dibia had no way of knowing when she was holding back. While it might sometimes be tricky to finesse it so that her skills brought no harm, Somadina hoped that she was up to the challenge.

    Then once she had enough money saved, she was hoping to finish her high school education and train also to be a nurse's aid. She still had the goal of ultimately combining more modern skills with her own people's ancient wisdom and with her own special talents, in order to help the health and well-being of her fellow Igbo in ways she believed that no one type of skill alone could.

    Lola joked with her. *So will you be painting up your face like a medicine man?*

    Somadina chuckled. *I'm no medicine man, white woman. I'm Igbo. You get to call me witch doctor.*

    Lola laughed harder. *I love it. Every good American scientist needs a witch doctor for a best friend.*

    It was the feeling of a hug that came back. *And every good*

African witch doctor needs a friendly geophysicist to confide in too.

Through the joy of their shared laughter and affection, Lola had a horrible, embarrassing memory. It bubbled out before she could control it, like that little bit of pee that makes its way onto your panties when you are laughing so hard. She froze, with a very similar sense of humiliation.

It's okay. The words coming from Somadina were kind. *We all have memories like that, times where we didn't stand up for what we believed, times when we embarrassed ourselves by going along with a crowd.*

No, Lola thought. *I should have said something much more furious. Much more effective. I was a wimp.*

Lola, your answer wasn't so very bad. Everyone in the room knew just how you felt.

Why in the world did I have to remember that horrible joke at just this moment? Lola's frustration was aimed at herself, not at Somadina. But Somadina answered.

Face painting? Your thought of the Dibia's traditional face painting and your sequence of thoughts makes sense. Pen pals. Internet scrabble buddies. Foreign exchange students. National Youth Corps. Listening to the dreams of ... twittering for ... traveling for ... sharing telepathy for ... hell, just sharing tea for... none of it solves everything of course. ...

Lola smiled. Of course. That is why she had remembered the awful joke about the busload of drowned children in Lake Ponchartrain from decades ago. She finished the thought for her friend.

None of it, individually, will bring about world peace. But all of it put together? It's a really good start.

Throughout the holidays Alex had clearly tried to give Lola the space to deal with whatever it was that he suspected she was trying to handle. Yet she felt, all too well, both his confusion and his growing concern for her. And so shortly after Ariel returned to college, Lola began searching for that right moment to talk to Alex about what she could do. And ran right into one more reason to delay.

January 26, 2010, Lola would turn fifty years old. She wasn't sure why the day affected her so much. She had breezed through thirty and forty. But somewhere in her mind fifty was a half-way point. The crossover place between the younger half of her life and the older half. Not a bad thing. But a big thing. And Alex knew it.

So even though Tuesday night was not a usual night for going out for the Zeitmans, he had persuaded her well in advance to plan on meeting him at a very nice restaurant after work. The problem was that he was determined to make the evening even more special. Although Lola tried to give him privacy, she had not been able to ignore his glee at locating Maurice's number off of the call log, and convincing the old family friend to surprise her by joining them that night for dinner. Maurice was able to hide the surprise, of course, but that turned out not to really matter.

Then in a moment of exuberance Alex had invited Ken and Sara to join them as well, which had been followed by doubt as to whether that had been a wise move, since Lola really did not like crowds and did not like surprises. So Alex had tried to "fix" it by persuading Ariel, who did not have a Tuesday class, to fly in Tuesday afternoon, attend the dinner, and fly back to school on Wednesday. A goofy waste of money, but Alex knew how happy it would make Lola.

Of course he then invited Zane, who obviously could not get away as he was leaving for his company's big conference, and then he decided to invite Summer and Gregg as well. Gregg could not come, but Summer would not only be there, she cheerfully put herself in charge of the cake and decorations.

Maurice had then suggested that the two coworkers from Lola's office whom she was closest to be invited also, and they had been such happy additions that for days they had thought about the dinner every time they saw Lola.

And through the entire process Lola could feel Alex's growing joy at pulling off this surprise. It might have been silly, but somehow it just didn't seem right to tell the man that she was a telepath and had been following the growing guest list all along. So the conversation with Alex was postponed until the day after her birthday. Not a day later, Lola promised herself, no matter what.

As Lola entered the restaurant she did her best to appear graciously surprised. Only Maurice knew how thoroughly she was faking it as she gave the first hug to Ariel in apparent disbelief, and he hid his smile well as she gave hugs all around.

At the end of the meal, Summer produced an elaborately decorated dessert which went well beyond the obligatory cake, and presented it with her characteristic flourish. There were a few small gifts, very thoughtful, but of them all, the one which grabbed Lola's heart the most was Maurice's beautifully framed eleven-by-fourteen-inch print of the Norman Rockwell painting of a cross-section of humanity with the "do unto others" words woven into it. *In memory of a task well done*, she heard both Maurice and Olumiji say as she studied it.

Lola thought to herself, *This is it. This is the neat, tidy wonderful moment when a person realizes that they are incredibly lucky and that their life is incredibly good. It's the blissful moment when the movie ends. The heroine smiles. The picture starts to get kind of dim and fuzzy as it freezes in time, and the audience understands that all is well now and it always will be. It's the way every story should end.*

So Lola did her part and smiled. As she blew out fifty flaming candles she let herself savor and fully enjoy the nicest of happily-ever-after endings.

Chapter 17. The End: March 2064

Who was making that noise? It was gurgling ... loud ... annoying ... Oh yes, the medical equipment she was hooked up to. It never stopped. It drove her crazy. She tried to force the fog and the pain from her brain. Random thoughts seemed to come and go these days so quickly. The harder she tried to hold on to one the faster it flew away.

She saw little Teddie—geez it had to be at least fifty years ago, proudly giving her a present—to cheer her up? She couldn't remember why she had needed cheering. But her day-to-day troubles back then had always loomed so large. How funny.

Teddie had been so proud if it. It was something that had said, "Everything is okay in the end. If it's not okay, then it's not the end." That's right. It had been a small magnet to keep near her desk at work. Teddie, she'd been Lola's little cheerleader, back before life had forced her so rudely into adulthood. Lola remembered smiling as she read the words and thinking that it was wisdom from a wise thirteen-year-old. But even middle-aged Lola had known how very false those words were.

In the end, she smiled at her own pun—there was just one end. One real end. The very cost of life itself was that your own personal story did not ever truly reach its conclusion until the one exact moment when, by definition, everything was not okay. You could be trapped under a canoe at forty-nine, in a cancer ward at fifty-nine, or lying on your own lawn paralyzed at seventy-two. But at some indisputable point everything was not okay. And that is when one's own story finally concluded.

Lola knew that she had reached the end, the real end, of her story. She'd been approaching it now for months, accepting comfort but refusing any further life-prolonging intervention. Her children and grandchildren and come and gone as often as they were able. Wasn't there a great grandbaby who had been presented with much pride at some point, with grandma Ariel's face beaming under her rust and silver hair as she held the tiny child? Lola thought it had happened, but she couldn't be sure she had not dreamt it instead. Ariel had looked so happy, and no wonder, after all she had been through. Lola hoped that the memory was real.

And Alex. Where the hell was he now that she needed him so badly? She needed to tell him how glad she was that she had gone ahead and decided to marry him. She almost hadn't, you know. Good thing she did. He really should be told. Where the hell was he?

Then she remembered. Oh, right. Why did she keep forgetting that? Unless you got killed together in a car crash or something, one of you simply had to go first. Was it the lucky one who lived on? Lola thought so. She'd always considered being alive to be a lucky thing. ... Even if it meant you were the one who had to experience the worst pain of your life.

Speaking of pain, what the hell was the matter with this shit that was supposed to be keeping her comfortable? Comfortable my ass.

"Mom? Do you need me to ask the PA to up your pain medication?" It was Zane. He'd been sitting there holding her hand all along. Oh Zane. Her first-born baby, the child she'd stared at in wonder while she nursed him. The boy she always had a sort of link with, ever since she had read his tiny baby thoughts while he was still in her womb. No, it had turned out that he was no telepath, of course, and thank heavens for that. He'd struggled enough with his own strange gift and the many talents that nature had bestowed on him instead.

Still, the experts at x^0 had always told her that she and her son shared the distinction of being separated by only a very few lives, which they considered to be a rare occurrence for direct blood relatives. It wasn't as close a connection as the one she had shared with lifelong friend Somadina, of course. And then Lola felt a pang remembering Somadina's death as well. Ahhhh maybe it was good after all that she kept forgetting who in her life had died already.

In fact, those experts at x^0 had told her a lot of things over the years. Some, in her opinion, had the ring of truth to them, other things less so. Still other ideas she had out and out ignored. Now, she had to wonder how much truth there was to it all.

"Zane?"

He jumped in surprise, and Lola had the distinct feeling that she had not spoken in a long while.

"Have you had a good life?" The words were hoarse, but intelligible.

Oh damn. Zane thought she was looking for reassurance that she had been a good mom. That's not what she meant. Funny how the telepathy now came and went for her, pretty much just like everything else. For the moment, her abilities were working just fine. But she didn't have the physical strength to correct his wrong impression.

"Yes mom. Actually I have had a very, very good life." And Lola knew that while he thought he was saying it to reassure her of her motherly success, in fact he truly believed that his life had been a fine one.

The folks at x^0, like always, had refused to speculate on whether Lola was a more evolved Zane, or Zane was a more evolved Lola. But Lola had watched Zane all his life, and she was sure in her heart that if they shared a common soul, it was Zane who was slightly more evolved. She didn't think it was just a mother's pride.

That meant of course, that if by some chance the wisdom of x^0 was in fact close to describing how the human spirit worked, she had Zane's life still ahead of her, and in her very near future at that. There would be countless other lives too of course if that really were the case. But Zane's experiences, at the very least, were something very specific to look forward to. Lola found herself oddly excited about the prospect.

And what of all the other metaphysical theories she had debated and discussed with such relish for the past fifty years? Well, she was about to find out which one, if any, was the right answer. And she was about to find out by doing the one and only thing which produced the actual answer. The one thing every single human being does sooner or later.

"Mom?" It was Zane. He was still there and still holding her hand. She thought he'd left. "Try to hang on Mom, please. I just called Teddie and she's on her way, she'll be here in just a few minutes. Please mom. You know Teddie. She'll be so upset if she doesn't make it in time."

x^0

Lola smiled to herself. Of course. Even though she and Teddie had said their goodbyes, more than once already she was pretty sure, Teddie would still be upset. Oh well. It was okay. She'd get over it.

"Ariel is trying too Mom, but it's going to take her longer to get here. Hang on, okay? At least a little longer."

Lola tried to nod, but she didn't think that she succeeded. It was okay. She'd said goodbye to Ariel too, and there was nothing more to say, not to any of them. They would all understand that.

Her remaining emotions? Not regret, that was for sure. Not even really sadness. This had been a full life and a fine one. There was love. There was gratitude. And yes. There it was. The one feeling that was getting her through this. Curiosity. Through all the pain, all of the fatigue, Lola realized that she was ready for some answers. In her heart she believed that she fully accepted that no answer at all was a very real possibility, and she even accepted that she would not be around to process that particular piece of information. Too bad, because it would have been very interesting information to know. Either way, she thought, it was high time to find out.

She was tired. So very very tired. So she closed her eyes and this time, it really was the end. Maybe.

More

If you enjoyed reading about Lola's adventures, please look for y[1], a second novel about the Zeitman family, and watch for z[2] available in early 2013.

Thanks

To the family members and friends who served as such capable editors and proofreaders for me -- thank you. You are wonderful.

A special and specific thank you goes to my husband, to each of my three children and to my sister, for also acting as contributors, cheerleaders, and coaches as needed. I am a very lucky woman to have each one of you in my life.

Additional Information

Although this book is work of fiction, where news items, statistics, cultural information, and scientific facts are included, it was my intent to be as accurate as I could. Therefore I would like to express my thanks to the following printed and internet sources for general information and background material used in this book. Any misrepresentations of information from these sources is unintentional and regretted. The author can be contacted at lola.zeitman@gmail.com.

Printed Materials:

The Economist Pocket World in Figures, 2011 Edition. Published by Profile Books Ltd.

The Igbo of Southeast Nigeria by Victor C. Uchendu from Case Studies in Cultural Anthropology published by Harcourt Brace Jonanovich College Publishers, 1965

The Nigerian legal system by Charles Mwalimu published by Peter Lang Pub Inc (August 30, 2010)

Introduction to Igbo Medicine and Culture in Nigeria by Dr. Patrick E. Iroegbu published by Lulu.com publishing, 2010

Half a Yellow Sun A Novel by Chimamanda Ngozi Adichie published by Anchor Books, 2006

The Bottled Leopard by Chukwuemeka Ike published by University Press, reprinted 2001

(author's note: these last two are works of fiction by Igbo authors and were used to provid general background on Igbo history and culture. They are highly recommended for those wishing to read truly authentic fiction about Nigeria)

Websites by Chapter in order presented

Chapter 1.
http://wnew.radio.com/2010/06/29/rock-101-the-beach-boys-vs-james-watt/

Chapter 2.
http://lib.lbcc.edu/ukwu/chiamaka/igbonamess.htm
http://www.motherlandnigeria.com/names.html#Igbo
http://www.who.int/mediacentre/factsheets/fs348/en/ World Health Organization on maternal mortality

Chapter 3.
http://www.afrikaworld.net/afrel/igbo-marriage.htm MARRIAGE AMONG THE IGBO OF NIGERIA by Celestine A: Obi (Taken from unpublished doctoral thesis submitted to Pontifical Urban University, Rome (1970) by Celestine Obi)
http://www.everyculture.com/Ma-Ni/Nigeria.html
http://www.afbis.com/analysis/slave.htm Slave trade: a root of contemporary African Crisis By Tunde Obadina (Director of Africa Business Information Services)
http://www.nytimes.com/2009/01/27/business/economy/27jobcuts.html
http://uk.reuters.com/article/2009/01/26/us-iceland-factbox-idUKTRE50P3YZ20090126

Chapter 4.
http://www.youtube.com/watch?v=2PqhOrgk11A
http://www.amazon.com/Time-After/dp/B00136LQQ2/ref=sr_1_1?ie=UTF8&s=dmusic&qid=1328202556&sr=1-1
http://www.oraifite.com/culture-and-traditions/igbo-wedding-pictures.php
http://oilandgasbrief.com/knowledge-base/history-oil-exploration-production-nigeria/351/ for "History of Oil Exploration and Production in Nigeria"
http://www.doctorswithoutborders.org/aboutus/?ref=home-sidebar-left

Chapter 5.
http://www.avert.org/aids-nigeria.htm
http://www.starwoodhotels.com/sheraton/property/overview/index.html?propertyID=445
http://www.globalpost.com/photo/5653257/lagos-traffic-taxi-2011-6-23

Chapter 6.
http://www.lonelyplanet.com/nigeria
http://www.whenweruled.com/articles.php?lng=en&pg=28
http://www.wisemuslimwomen.org/muslimwomen/bio/nana_asmauhttp://www.nigeriavillagesquare.com/articles/nvs/colonel-sada-abubakar-is-new-

sultan-of-sokoto-14.html
http://www.americancanoe.org/resource/resmgr/sei-educational_resources/brochure_paddler_s_safety_ch.pdf
Chapter 7.
http://www.nigeriavillagesquare.com/articles/wayo-guy/wayoguy-in-naija-part-2-homes-sweet-homes-in-owerri.html
http://news.nationalgeographic.com/news/2004/12/1206_041206_global_warming.html
http://www.themystica.com/mystica/articles/t/telepathy.html
http://www.straightdope.com/columns/read/1865/whats-the-story-on-ganzfeld-experiments
http://www.gallup.com/poll/16915/three-four-americans-believe-paranormal.aspx
Chapter 8.
http://www.ebonyionline.com/zzz-photos-abakaliki-streets.html
http://www.youtube.com/watch?v=xy1gp3F5NhY
http://www.amazon.com/We-Are-The-World/dp/B001FXOL4W/ref=sr_1_1?ie=UTF8&s=dmusic&qid=1329799926&sr=1-1
Chapter 9.
http://eosweb.larc.nasa.gov/EDDOCS/Wavelengths_for_Colors.html
http://www.youtube.com/watch?v=f5M_Ttstbgs
http://www.amazon.com/For-What-Its-Worth/dp/B0011Z76UA/ref=sr_1_1?ie=UTF8&s=dmusic&qid=1328835150&sr=1-1
http://news.bbc.co.uk/2/hi/africa/8126353.stm   BBC "Shell should end Nigeria 'abuse" Tuesday, 30 June 2009
Chapter 10.
http://www.nytimes.com/2010/06/17/world/africa/17nigeria.html
http://www.youtube.com/watch?v=PwNYqHRHUOQ
http://www.amazon.com/Brain-Damage-2011-Remaster/dp/B005NNUNUQ/ref=sr_1_1?ie=UTF8&s=dmusic&qid=1328993143&sr=1-1
http://www.pinkfloydlyrics.com/Brain-Damage-Lyrics.html
Chapter 11.
http://www.goldmanprize.org/node/160
http://www.economist.com/node/12267373?story_id=12267373 for "Risky toughness: The army's tough approach to Delta militants could end up uniting them" from the Sep 18th 2008 | *Lagos* | print edition of The Economist

http://www.bbc.co.uk/news/world-africa-11467394 for "Who are Nigeria's Mend oil militants?" By Caroline Duffield BBC News, Lagos BBC News Africa Mobil Edition October 4 2010

http://www.ebonyionline.com/zzz-photos-okposi.html

Chapter 12.

http://www.godchecker.com/pantheon/african-mythology.php?deity=AHA-NJOKU

http://www.youtube.com/watch?v=cJVewWbeBiY

http://www.amazon.com/High-Hopes/dp/B000TE0Q0Q/ref=sr_1_1?ie=UTF8&s=dmusic&qid=1329079417&sr=1-1

http://www.youtube.com/watch?v=ZBR2G-iI3-I

http://www.amazon.com/I-Will-Survive/dp/B001NZVSVG/ref=sr_1_3?ie=UTF8&s=dmusic&qid=1329079730&sr=1-3

http://news.bbc.co.uk/2/hi/africa/8291336.stm for Will amnesty bring peace to Niger Delta? By Caroline Duffield BBC News, Niger Delta Monday, 5 October 2009

http://www.amazon.com/Whats-Up/dp/B000WLOKKS/ref=sr_1_1?ie=UTF8&s=dmusic&qid=1329087176&sr=1-1

Chapter 13.

http://www.prb.org/Articles/2002/HowManyPeopleHaveEverLivedonEarth.aspx for "How Many People Have Ever Lived on Earth" *by Carl Haub,* chair of Population Information at the Population Reference Bureau.

http://gardenofpraise.com/art12.htm

http://www.youtube.com/watch?v=5XOP7M-PMzM&ob=av2n

http://www.amazon.com/O-D-O-O-Overtake-Don/dp/B002TA15O4/ref=dm_att_trk5

http://www.thetalkingdrum.com/fela.html

http://www.genevadeclaration.org/the-geneva-declaration/what-is-the-declaration.html

Chapter 14.

http://www.time.com/time/world/article/0,8599,1950695,00.html

Chapter 15.

http://www.youtube.com/watch?v=CY6A5arNCQQ

http://www.amazon.com/Three-Little-Birds/dp/B000ZM7DXK/ref=sr_1_1?ie=UTF8&s=dmusic&qid=1329436862&sr=1-1

About the author

Sherrie Roth grew up in Western Kansas thinking that there was no place in the universe more fascinating than outer space. After her mother vetoed astronaut as a career ambition, she went on to study journalism and physics in hopes of becoming a science writer. She published her first short story in Isaac Asimov's Science Fiction Magazine, but when the next story idea came to her it declared that it had to be a whole book, nothing less. One night, while digesting this disturbing piece of news, she drank way too many shots of ouzo with her boyfriend. She woke up thirty-one years later demanding to know what was going on.

The boyfriend, who she had apparently long since married, explained calmly that in a fit of practicality she had gotten a degree in geophysics and had spent the last 28 years interpreting seismic data in the oil industry. The good news was that she had found it at least mildly entertaining and ridiculously well paying. The bad news was that the two of them had still managed to spend almost all of the money.

Apparently, she was now Mrs. Cronin, and they had produced three wonderful children whom they loved dearly, even though that is where a lot of the money had gone. Mr. Cronin turned out to be a warm-hearted sort who was happy to see her awake and ready to write. Sherrie Cronin discovered that over the ensuing decades Sally Ride had managed to become the first woman in space and apparently had done a fine job of it. No one, however, had written the book that had been in Sherrie's head for decades. The only problem was, the book informed her sternly that it had now grown into a six book series. Sherrie decided that she better start writing it before it got any longer. She has been wide awake ever since, and writing away.